DECEIVED
with
Greed

DECEIVED
with
Greed

Rich Kazlausky

3rd Edition

ISBN: 978-0-9863224-1-9 - Paperback
ISBN: 978-0-9863224-2-6 - Hardcover
ISBN: 978-0-9863224-3-3 - eBook

Printed in the United States of America   1 2 0 3 2 0

∞ This paper meets the requirements of ANSI/NISO Z39.48-1992 (Permanence of Paper)

Dedication

Every writer hopes his or her work reaches out to millions of readers, sharing their dreams with them. The gratification comes knowing they have written an interesting story and the readers acknowledge that. There are four people very dear to me that will never have the capability of reading my book. They are gone from my life only in their presence, but never forgotten in my memory. The least I can do for them is dedicate the book to them.

Lillian….my mother who passed away in February of 2015 at the age of 99. There are not enough adjectives in our vocabulary to describe what a person she was. So caring, lovable and I'm so proud she was my mother. She loved to read and every Christmas I would buy her books to read. I'll always miss her, love you, Mom. I'll bring my book to heaven when I see you.

Sandra Kruger…. My twin sister, a sudden shock to our family, one day smiling and jovial, the next, a memory. She was a friend's best friend, always willing to help and never seen an angry moment with her. Although, we lived miles apart, we talked constantly as if she lived next door. For me, no words can describe how much I miss her. RIP, Sis.

Pamela Hastings….my youngest sister, a little blonde bombshell, smiling and laughing all the time. After battling breast cancer, she left our world in April of 2012, 54 years young. So sad. She was a great mother, three super children and a wonderful husband. To bad he was a Cub fan. Just kidding, Mike.

Lisa Drabek….my niece, the butterfly as we called her. Soaring with joy and very carefree lifestyle. She also died from cancer at a very young age. The sad part about living, never take anything for granted, live the best you can every day and that's the way she looked at life. We all miss her.

These four people left an absence in our hearts. Their memories are cemented in our lives and never will they be forgotten.

Chapter 1

Ready... Set... Go!

They call it the Windy City, Chicago, Illinois. It was Wednesday, March 11th, a brisk, windy, overcast morning when three gentlemen strolled into the Loop offices of Priority Investments, Inc. The three visitors were of German descent, dressed in tweed suits, vests with the customary gold chains, and all wearing fedoras adorned with a colorful pheasant tail feather.

"Good morning. We'd like to speak to Mr. Fossett, if he's available?" the oldest of the three asked Alice, in a heavy German accent.

"Yes, he is. May I ask who is calling?"

"Adolph Kaiser."

"One moment, sir. Please be seated while I inform Mr. Fossett." Alice rose from her chair and walked down the hall to William's office. She leaned against the oak door framing and spoke, "William, a gentleman by the name of Adolph Kaiser is in the lobby asking for you."

There was William, swallowed in his massive green leather throne, surrounded by the mammoth oak desk, peeking over his large black-rimmed glasses barely hanging on to the edge of his nose. The name, Adolph Kaiser caught his full attention.

"Adolph Kaiser is here, in our office? The Adolph Kaiser? For heaven sakes Alice, show them to my office."

She returned to the lobby and escorted the three guests back to William's office.

"Adolph Kaiser, what an honor to meet you. I've read so much about you and your Kaiser Foundation and its world-renowned success. What brings you here?"

"Well, thank you, Mr. Fossett. With the overwhelming success of our foundation, we are deeply interested in expanding our assets. That alone has given us the opportunity to invest. Mind you, our board of directors has researched our options and accumulated positive feedback regarding your firm. So positive, that we have traveled from New York to meet with you in person and discuss our options. Your firm's reputation has caught our full attention."

William knew he had struck gold. Nearly every periodical in publication had documented the success and the wealth of the man sitting in his office. Signing Kaiser and his Foundation to a contract would be monumental for his firm and tremendous financial gains. It was true about the success of Priority Investments, Inc. Just viewing the wall behind William's desk would substantiate their accomplishments, plaque after plaque and expensive oak framed awards proving his company's worthiness. As they continued their talk, the time swiftly sped by just as fast as the whirling winds gusting outside William's office window.

"How long will you be in Chicago?" William asked.

"Well, our flight is scheduled to return to New York this evening. We have a busy schedule to maintain, therefore, time is of the essence."

"I perfectly understand, Mr. Kaiser. Well then, I'll have my agents propagate some interesting proposals for you to look over."

"Excellent. Again, thank you for your time." Adolph Kaiser and his group rose, then William escorted them back to the lobby, adjacent to Alice's desk. While William and Mr. Kaiser concluded their business, an associate from Mr. Kaiser's group handed Alice a business card, explaining that all the information and proposals should be sent to the address on the card. They all shook hands, said their goodbyes, then William and Alice watch them disappear into the hall elevator.

"Holy shit! Can you believe what just happened? Adolph Kaiser in Chicago, in our office?" William grasped his head with both hands, "Let me think." William leaned against Alice's desk, his forefinger resting on his chin. There were countless days when William sat behind his desk, anticipating that pot of gold to drop in his lap. *Today was his day.*

"Charles will be the one to handle this, Alice. He's our best advisory and he works hard to research things. Send Charles to my office."

"Charles isn't here. He's in Switzerland and won't be back till Friday."

***

A few days have passed since the meeting with Adolph Kaiser. Friday morning at the office began like any other morning for Charles. He entered his office, set his briefcase on his desk, and headed to the coffee machine. *You would think that after eighteen years working at Priority, the coffee would taste better, it didn't.* He dropped two quarters down the throat of the steel box and waited till the plastic cup filled. No matter what they called it or how it tasted, Charles would drink it.

On his way back to his office, he stopped at Alice's desk to collect his mail and phone messages.

"Oh Charles, William would like to see you in his office."

"I'm on my way, thanks, Alice."

He drifted toward William's office, sipping on his coffee. "You want to see me, William?"

"Yes, Charles. Come in and sit down." He rose from his chair, head down, reading the information in his grasp.

"This is the file I put together regarding Adolph Kaiser and his Foundation. Mind you, this account is extremely promising with very high profile people involved. Your work has been impeccable during your time here. Therefore, I've decided you are the right person to handle it."

"Adolph Kaiser was here? William, I don't know what to say. I'm speechless. I've read numerous articles about Mr. Kaiser and his foundation. You know I'll do my best to make this account successful. Adolph Kaiser, wow. I wish I was here to meet him."

Charles knew full well that if he inked Kaiser to a contract with Priority, his own fame would skyrocket to the top of the Investor's list of Who's Who.

"Never a doubt in my mind, Charles." William patted Charles on the back. "Since you're here, two more things. I'm going to raise your commission to six per cent, and with good luck, in a few weeks you'll be flying to New York. There, you'll meet Adolph Kaiser and the people from his foundation. So, you better get moving and formulate the perfect investments for Kaiser."

"Of course. In the meantime, I'll begin researching their portfolio, therefore, I can put together a list of promising investments that will make them very happy. Oh, of course, I'll want you to review what I've selected to be absolutely certain this is the best for the Kaiser Foundation."

"Excellent. Yes, I would like to see what you've put together. Oh, Charles, I forgot. One more thing. I'm about to hire another employee to act as your liaison. His name is Dennis Reading, a graduate of Lewis University, worked at TransUniverse Securities. He has an interesting résumé and comes highly recommended. You'll meet him later today."

"Very well, sounds great."

***

Later that afternoon, William brought Dennis to Charles's office to introduce him. Dennis wore a white shirt, no tie, no socks, a black sport coat and denim jeans. Charles noticed his attire along with the fact that his new understudy looked more like a pro athlete than an ordinary office employee. He had curly brown hair, an athletic frame that definitely, a threat to the women in the office.

"Charles, when you're finished with Dennis, send him back to my office, okay?"

"No problem." Charles scanned his résumé. "Your résumé is pretty impressive. Citizens Bank, then TransUniverse. I've heard good things about Trans. In fact, I have dealt with agents from there and everything went extremely well. One thing puzzles me, though. You've been at Trans only two years. What was your reason to quit there and work here?"

"Yes, the two companies are similar, but at Trans, I was really at the bottom of the ladder. It would take me years to get where I wanted to be. Then, I heard about the opening here, applied, and now I'm sitting in your office."

Charles studied the report and looked closely at Dennis. He was never aware of a job opening at Priority. If there was, why didn't William inform him?

"Yes, well, most of your duties here will be similar to what you've done at Trans. Are you married?"

"No."

"Okay, good. Let me explain a few details about what to expect while you're working here. We have numerous oversea accounts, meaning you'll be traveling to those countries whenever the occasion needs. Getting contracts signed, discussing proposals, setting up bank accounts, things of that nature." Charles walked to his file cabinet and withdrew several folders.

"Here are a few portfolios I want you to become familiar with. Read through them. If you come across any possibilities for improving their accounts, bring it to my attention. Any questions?"

"No. I'll review them right away and let you know."

"Well, Dennis, it was nice meeting you, that's all I have for now. You can go back to William's office."

Charles began to evaluate the Kaiser folder. Without any doubt, it would be Priority's biggest account. After a cursory look at the data submitted, Charles knew that he would be spending his majority time working this account, meaning, he'd assign his smaller accounts to his new understudy. He also estimated that more capital would be invested through the Kaiser than probably all of his other accounts combined.

Fossett was right. Charles was the best agent to handle the Kaiser account. If everything worked as planned, Charles could make a substantial commission from only this account. It would be the biggest test for Charles since he began working at Priority. He must succeed; he must prove to William that he was the right man to handle this account.

"Congratulations!"

Charles looked up to see Alice and a group of women standing in his doorway with a tray of cupcakes. They began to applaud.

"Hey, I see the news travels fast in this office."

"We all heard about the new account and knew that William would give it to you."

"Thank you. I sure hope I don't disappoint any of you."

"Enjoy the cupcakes, a little token for your achievement."

"Thanks, again."

Chapter 2

Infatuation?

As soon as Jack reached his locker that morning, he glanced at the clock on the wall above him...8:37. That left him three minutes to get to Algebra III, a class he actually enjoyed. He walked into the classroom and before he sat down, he spotted an unfamiliar face. Wow, a new student. Jack couldn't take his eyes off the very cute new classmate. She had light brown hair, shoulder length, wore little make-up, but it was her eyes that magnetized Jack to her. By the end of his classes that day, the charming beauty was in three of his remaining classes. Now, Jack realized coming to school every day was something to look forward to.

The loud, throbbing of the bell in the hall signified that classes that day had concluded. Jack fought his way through the crowded halls and when he closed in on his locker, he noticed Aaron, Terri and, of all people, the newbie gathered there.

"Hey, what's going down?" Jack inquired.

"Hey, Dipshit. I want to introduce you to April, April Logan. Her first day here, moved in from Chicago and...needs a ride home today. She doesn't know what bus to catch and I've got practice. So, you've volunteered to give April a ride home, okay."

"I did?" Jack answered. *Yeah you did, idiot. Here's your chance to get to know this beauty.* "Yeah, no problem. Where do you live, April?"

"Do you know where Stone Brook Estates is located?" April replied softly.

"Hey. I gotta get my butt to practice. Nice meeting you, April. And, Jack, I'll call you tonight."

Jack nodded and held his right arm up, his fist closed but his thumb stuck out... "Got ya, buddy".

"Yeah, I know where you live. Let me grab my books and keys."

Jack escorted April to the student parking lot and while they walked together, they approached his flashy new red Jeep Wrangler.

"Wow. Is this your car? You must be rich to afford a new Jeep when you're still in high school."

"Emily."

"Who?"

"Emily. Emily is my mother. She bought it for my birthday this past summer. My birthday was in June."

Jack unlocked the passenger door and helped April into the passenger seat. Once inside, the engine roared and away they went. "So, April. I've noticed that you're in three of my other classes."

"I am? I didn't realize that. I've been so busy my first day, trying to find all the right rooms. It's been crazy."

"What was the reason you moved to Manford?"

"My father works for the government, actually for the Post Office. When the Postmaster position opened here, he was nominated for it and he took it."

"Cool. I think you'll like it here. It's quiet and the people are really friendly."

"Well. I'm sure glad I met you, Aaron, and Terri today. You've sure made my day a lot easier." The dashboard radio broke into their conversation. Local station WMAN was playing, "I Want To Make It With You," by Bread. *How appropriate. He glanced over at April, hoping she's was thinking the same thing.*

"What's your favorite kind of music, April?"

"Hmmmm. I like almost everything out there. This is a cool station. Is this all they play, the oldies?"

"Yep. I listen to this station all the time. I've always wondered what it would be like to live back in those days. So many awesome songs, so many great singers—The Beatles, Buddy Holly, Elvis, Righteous Brothers…"

"Oh, you can turn left on Stone Bridge. My house is the fourth house on the right." Jack guided the Jeep into April's driveway, exited his Jeep and opened April's door.

"Well, thanks for the ride. I suppose I'll see you tomorrow."

"You bet. I'll be looking forward to it."

As April walked slowly away from the Jeep, she made sure Jack got a full view of her sexy, petite body. Jack's eyes were like a pair of zoom binoculars. *How do women get a pair of Jeans to fit so perfectly tight?*

***

Once Jack got home, he entered through the back door of the house that led into the kitchen. Immediately, he noticed that all the dirty dishes from the previous night and that morning were still unwashed, piled in the sink for him to wash. Was his mother's social life so busy that she couldn't find time to at least wash the dishes in the morning? *Damn it!*

He emptied the dirty dishes out of the sink, then filled it with clean, soapy water. After he finished, he dried his hands and…

Droid…Droid…Droid. A call on his cell phone.

He picked up his cell from the kitchen table and opened the cover. "Yes, Emily?"

"Hi sweetie. Sorry for not getting the dishes done, but I had to leave in a hurry."

LIE.

"That's okay. They're done."

"Also, because I was in such a hurry, I forgot to take something out of the freezer for dinner."

LIE.

"What would you say if I treated you for dinner at Simoni's tonight?"

"Ummm…I'll see. We can talk about it when you get home."

"All right. I'll be home around five."

"Bye."

Jack stuffed his cell in his back pocket and climbed the stairs to his hideout, his man cave. He plopped his body down on his bed, turned on the radio and settled back to try to catch a quick wink. Radio station WMAN was playing another great oldie by the Everly Brothers. "Dream."

"April, this is a great movie we're going to watch. Have you ever seen any of the Jason Bourne movies?"

"I don't think so. I really don't have much free time to watch movies."

"Matt Damon plays Jason Bourne. He's a government-trained hit man. There are three movies, *The Bourne Identity*, *The Bourne Supremacy*, and *The Bourne Ultimatum*.

"Wait. I think I've heard of him. Wasn't he in *Good Will Hunting*? That was really an awesome movie."

April found a place on the sofa and curled her legs underneath her so she was comfortable. Following her, Jack brought two Cokes and a bowl of freshly popped popcorn, and removed the disc from the packet, inserting it into the Sony Blue-Ray DVD player.

He settled back on the sofa, and put his arm around April. The lovebirds were set for a good movie and an enjoyable time together. His hands stroked her long, silky hair. Their lips met in a kiss full of passion, long and intense, but soft and intimate. April responded, eager for his touch. He began to unbutton her blouse—slowly, taking his time, not to rush the moment he'd been waiting for so long. With all her buttons undone, her full breast was in his hand, he caressed it softly, rubbing the tip of her nipple. The thrill and excitement were beyond what he could describe.

April moaned, wanting more from him. Piece by piece, clothing was discarded, as if melting from their hot bodies. Soon, they lay completely naked on the sofa, their lips locked, tasting each other. No need to talk, just letting their desires go wild.

"Love me, Jack. I want you so badly."

He was ready. He'd been ready for sixteen years. *Show her how much you love her, Jack.*

April's legs started to separate, allowing Jack to begin a night he'd never forget.

"Oh, Jack…"

Droid…Droid…Droid.

Jack's eyes popped open. Really? The god damn phone.

The sound of his cell awakened him from his steamy dream. He opened the phone to hear Aaron's voice.

"Hey, Romeo. So, what do you think of the new girl, April?"

"She's cool. Seems to be very friendly, likes the school. We just talked about her move here, what kind of music she likes. By that time, we reached her house, so I dropped her off and told her I would see her in class tomorrow."

"Right! I think she'll fit in nicely with us. You gonna ask her out?"

"Hey. I gotta go. Emily's home and taking me out for Italian dinner."

"Cool. I'll see you at your locker in the morning, dude."

Jack had little energy to get out of bed, especially after the dream he had about April. Why, all of a sudden, was he so infatuated with her? Was it fate? Was this meant to be? Whatever. But he couldn't wait to see her at school. Up on his feet, he bounced down the stairs and into the kitchen.

"Well, what do you think, Jack?"

"About what?"

"Do you want to go to Simoni's for pasta?"

"Hey. How can a guy pass up a free meal, huh?"

"Good, because I'm starving too. And Italian pasta is just what my stomach is aching for. But, you drive."

"Deal."

Chapter 3

Jack Needs Answers

In 1968, Louis Simoni opened a small Italian restaurant in downtown Manford. Here it was over 50 years later, his restaurant has become a landmark within the community. The delicious menu and the grateful hospitality that Louis provided created the flocks of customers eager to fill their appetites. People as far away as Chicago have driven that distance to experience the reputation of Simoni's Italian Restaurant.

It was a short drive from the Collier house, about two miles, and familiar to both Jack and Emily, because the restaurant sat one block south of Manford High School. On the weekends, you could bank on the restaurant being packed and reservations were in demand. That was a given. But tonight, Tuesday, the lot was half empty, no valet parking and the Colliers did not need a reservation. Inside, the always smiling Tony Simoni, Louis's son and now owner, greeted them.

"Good evening, Emily. How nice of you to join us this evening. Hello, young man."

Tony, the perfect host, helped Emily get seated, then handed each of them a dinner menu. Maurice approached their table, set a glass of Emily's favorite wine in front of her. Then, pencil and pad in hand, he was ready to take their order.

"I think I'll try the Tortellini Alla Panna. How about you, Jack?"

"Pizza for me, thin crust, cheese, sausage, green pepper and pineapple."

"Very well. I'll bring your salads."

Once Maurice departed, Emily reached for her glass of wine,

took a slow, enjoyable sip. "How are your classes at school been going lately?"

Jack didn't want to answer her question. He stalled for time, thinking her question would fade away and it did, for the time being. Then, Jack noticed Tony escorting three more customers into the dining room, seating them at a table not far from theirs.

Holy shit. That's April and her parents, I think. He took a long sip from his Coke and stared in their direction. *Yes, it's her.*

"Did you hear me?" Emily repeated.

"Huh? Oh, yeah…you know me, nothing exciting ever happens in my life. I'm just the same, ole' boring Jack Collier."

Jack looked up again and turned toward the Logan's' table. April's eyes connected to his. She smiled and waved to him. Bingo! It hit him like a tsunami.

Emily noticed, "See? That's just what I was talking about, Jack. That young girl over there. I'd say she likes you. Strictly female intuition, mind you, but something is connecting. Right?"

"No, no, Emily. Her name is April Logan and she just started at Columbia today."

"Only her first day, and with that wave and cute smile, I'd definitely say she's kind of liking you."

"Well, if you must know, her locker is next to Aaron's and she needed a ride home from school today. Since Aaron had practice, I volunteered. So, I gave her a ride home. Simple as that."

Emily finished her salad just as Maurice glided up to their table with their entrees. Throughout dinner, Jack peeked toward the Logan's table. They were still there, and April looked fantastic.

As soon as they finished their dinners, Jack beckoned, "Let's go, Emily. Okay?"

Without saying a word, Emily removed two bills from her wallet and placed them inside the check holder, leaving Maurice a generous tip. On their way out, the unexpected happened. Emily stopped and began a conversation with April and her parents. After introductions and a short conversation, a bit awkward for

Jack and April, they exchanged goodbyes and Jack and Emily left Simoni's for home.

Once home and inside the house, Emily turned and looked Jack in the eyes, "Jack, I had a very pleasant evening with you. These times are precious for me. You're the only person I have left to be with. Can't we share more time together as mother and son?" Emily put her arms around him and with no response, she turned and walked with her head down toward her bedroom.

Lies. Damn it. I never wanted it this way, but she started all of this. Her and that Sergio.

Uncomfortable with what just transpired between him and his mother, Jack stormed upstairs. His thoughts were tossed between his mother, his father and even April. Where are all the answers I need? Where is my Dad when I need him the most? Why is Emily acting like this? Why did they have to split up? Why, why?

***

He'll never forget that day, sitting on the living room sofa and listening to his father explain his reasons for the sudden move. Why he needed to leave the family and work hundreds of miles away. It was a shock to Jack, but Charles said it wasn't a permanent situation. After awhile, things would be back to normal, back to being father and son. Soon after his relocation, Charles would call and talk to him at least once a week. Then it became once a month. Now, nothing from his Dad. Could something terrible have happened to him?

Every day that passed by, Jack worried about his safety and whenever he probed Emily, she played dumb and said she didn't have any answers, and didn't have a clue on how to reach Charles. This left Jack believing Emily couldn't care less about his father, now, enter Sergio. The stoppage from hearing from his Dad has broken Jack's heart. He knew deep down that something was wrong. Was he still alive? *I need to know....but how?*

Every day Jack reflected on the predicament and the more his ire began to rise, the sudden and wild exploits between him and Emily and the mysterious presence of Emily's new roommate, Sergio, left so many unanswered questions. Something strange and eerie was going on. So many things weren't making any sense and not adding up. How could this happen? Somebody out there had the answers, but how could he find out?

Chapter 4

Meet Charles Collier

Charles Collier was born in Chicago and lived his entire childhood in the northwest corner of Cook County, namely Kilborn Park. He was the only child to Elsie and Herb Collier, above average middle-class parents. Herb and Elsie bent over backwards to raise Charles as they had been raised: Be respectful, courteous, well mannered, work hard and like any normal parents, they wanted the best for their only child.

Charles excelled throughout his school years, and received numerous awards for his achievements, either from his teachers or his classmates. He was president of his class, president of the student council and a four-year member of the National Honor Society. Those around Charles had their perception that someday, Charles would become President of the United States. Why? It was his positive outlook on life, his beaming personality, his talent for communicating with other people, and his ability to problem solve. Unfortunately, Charles had other plans.

During his senior year in high school, college recruiters visited his school from all over the United States, trying to recruit students to enroll in their college. Charles had his mind settled between three colleges, all within close proximity of his home: they were Northwestern, DePaul, or Roosevelt University. It was his class ranking, his SAT scores and a good word from his school teachers that all three colleges provided lucrative scholarships to Charles.

After considerable discussions with his father, and long talks with the college recruiters, Charles chose DePaul. Charles would become a DePaul Blue Demon.

His years at DePaul moved rapidly. Although his studies were a high priority, Charles discovered another side of college life, the social side. A few of his classmates were members of a fraternity and eventually seduced Charles into joining Tau Epsilon Delta, the TEDs. The fraternity gave Charles a sweet taste of a second life in college. He was in high gear on the social ladder. Almost every weekend there was a social gathering at the TED house or at some other fraternity or sorority. The beer flowed, the talk flowed, and everyone knew the way to make millions of dollars after graduation.

On a Saturday evening in late March, there was a lot of excitement around the DePaul campus. The Blue Demons basketball team had advanced to the final four in the NCAA basketball tournament. You would've thought the game was being played in the fraternity's living room. Full kegs, empty kegs, fanatic fans, drunk fans, and sober fans, yelling and jumping all over the place. It was unheard of that such a small college from Chicago would be competing for the NCAA championship, but it was happening. The city of Chicago was electric, the college was going crazy, classes closed, and Final Four T-shirts were selling out faster than they could be printed.

At the frat house that night, if you wanted a beer, you had to wrestle your way to the kitchen and stand in line until your time came. As Charles waited patiently, he was hit by a stroke of lightning from Heaven.

There she was! The most beautiful girl he'd ever seen. *What now, Charles? You better grab her before someone else does. Hurry.*

"I'm glad you're here."

"What?"

"I've never seen you here before. Are you attending DePaul?"

"No. I go to the Circle Campus. I just stopped here with some crazy friends. Because of the basketball game, the word got out that we had to attend the party at the TED house."

"Cool. I'm Charles. Charles Collier. I'm a TED, and welcome to our tavern."

She laughed out loud. "I'm Emily Dearborn."

"C'mon, follow me. I'll get you a beer. Then I'll show you around, okay?"

The frat house was Old English ambiance, all brick two-story frame with climbing ivy vines crawling toward the roof. Inside, a very cozy atmosphere. The house plan was simple, five bedrooms upstairs and downstairs consisted of an easy workable kitchen, a well equipped library and comfortable living area, with a large screen TV, a massive fireplace and several sofas and lounging chairs.

"Great night for a cold beer and a hot fire, huh?"

"Yeah. So, do you live here, Charles?"

"No. I still live at home, Kilborn Park. I commute every day."

"I'm from Manford, about fifty-five miles south of here. Ever hear of it?"

"I think so. Isn't there a state park near there?"

"Yeah. Big Hollow State Park. It's a great place to party, not much security there. So, no one bothers you."

"I take it you like to party?"

"I guess, but after spending all week cramming, a gal needs to get out and away from that."

"Well then, this is the place to be, and it's all free."

As fast as the beer flowed, so did the time. Charles and Emily enjoyed each others company, seeing who could impress each other the most. Later that evening, the word spread throughout the house, the Blue Demons lost to Kentucky, 74 to 68, another reason to drink more beer.

"Emily, lets find a quieter place?"

"You wanna do that?"

He put his arm around her shoulders and began to search the house for a secluded room, anxiously hoping this would be the lucky night he'd been waiting for. But that night, the house was swamped with people celebrating the historic day for DePaul. Room after room was filled with beer-drinking sponges, drinking to forget the devastating loss..

Charles remembered that Freddie had a room in the basement, renovated the past summer for one more frat brother.

"Follow me and stay close, okay?"

"Whatever you say, Charles…"

Emily took a firm grip on Charles's hand and hurried behind him. He opened the basement door and flipped on the light. They descended the fragile, creaky wood stairway until they reached the basement concrete floor.

Emily coughed. "How come all basements smell the same?"

Charles was not familiar with the basement layout. He was down there only once, during daylight hours to help Freddie move in. The farther they moved away from the stairway the darker the basement became. *Damn, I can't find a switch at all.* Waving his hands aimlessly, his left arm abruptly made contact with a string hanging from the ceiling. Grasping it, he pulled down on it.

"And there was light!"

Now to find Freddie's room? Charles saw the only door that had a light shinning from under the door. Charles was assured it must be Freddie's. The large room was set off behind the furnace and laundry area, the perfect place for them to get romantic. Charles prayed that Freddie went home for the weekend and left his door open. He tapped lightly on the door.

"Freddie, you there?" Charles whispered.

The room was silent. It could mean two things, either Freddie was asleep or so drunk he passed out or went home for the weekend. Charles grasped the door handle and began to turn the knob. The door opened and Charles peeked in. There was no sign of Freddie, meaning the room was theirs, even the bed was made. *Thank you, Freddie.*

Within seconds, they lay beside each other, so tight a single sheet of paper couldn't fit between them. Charles definitely was not a natural born lover, in fact, this would be his first time being alone and intimate with a female. Well, there was that time when the frat brothers had an exchange with Omega sorority. One sister got so drunk, she was taking on any guy who could do it. Teased by his brothers, Charles was forced to lose his virginity. Not in the manner explained to him by his father, but either jump on her or become the laughing stock of the entire frat house. He did it. It was quick, and even today he couldn't remember what it was like.

Charles and Emily's kisses became more passionate, their breathing became much faster, and his hands were all over her. They unzipped this and unbuttoned that until... A whisper from the past from the Madonna song, "Like a Virgin." If only he knew, the night was not at all unfamiliar to Emily.

Chapter 5

And... Emily Dearborn

The Dearborn family lived on the other side of the tracks from the Colliers, literally speaking. Emily had an older brother, Johnny and there were the twin boys, Mike and Ike, they were eleven years old. Her parents had a difficult time establishing steady employment, which put a strain on the children and did create occasional family problems. Emily's father, Donald, drank more than he worked and her mother, Martha, worked more then she drank. She held onto several waitress jobs, but her hours were long and tiresome, leaving Donald to watch their four children. For Donald, it was more of a burden, something he couldn't handle, creating communication gaps between the kids and the parents. If either Johnny or Emily had a problem, they had to work it out on their own.

Before the troublesome times, when both parents were sober and steadily employed, they lived in a nice, respectful neighborhood and enjoyed life as any normal family. The house was clean, the lawn mowed, food on the table and the kids were happy and doing well in school. Then the bottom fell out. Donald was fired from his job with the electric company for not obeying safety standards when a fellow worker was seriously injured during Donald's watch.. From that day forward, he drank and drank and continued to drink. Their financial circumstances took a huge hit, and considering that, the family was forced to survive mainly on Martha's minimal earnings. This didn't last, causing the Dearbons to sell their house and look for a cheaper place to live. What they found was disgusting and shameful to the kids. However, they had no other choice, but living in the run-down trailer park would be their new home. It was disgusting to Emily, and embarrassing to her friends, but under the circumstances, what choices did she have? It was like living in a shoe box, there was no privacy, there were only two bedrooms meaning both her and Johnny shared one bedroom and the twins slept on the living room couch.

Emily, a junior in school at the time, was an eye catcher. A very attractive young woman with a very attractive body, slim and all the curves in the right places. Nevertheless, her most astonishing asset was her flaming auburn red hair. It was during this stage in her life that boys took an interest in her and vice-versa. She began dating, but when family troubles took center stage, moving to the trailer park put a damper on her social life. Reason being, embarrassment. Totally ashamed for living there, Emily tried to hide that condition from her friends. When she spent times with them, it was always meeting them at a different location, never having them come to the trailer. It was a tough life for Emily, especially at her age when her social life should be exciting and boys becoming an interesting stage of growing up. If there was any positive benefit from the move, it caused Emily to bond closer to her brother, Johnny.

Johnny's middle name was "Trouble". From his childhood days playing with kids on his block, he never connected closely to any of them. In fact, it was the opposite. He never fit in while growing up, even to this day he didn't attract many friends, an absolute loner. Living that kind of life, troubles became an every day occurrence to him, and that reflected on his relationship with his parents, especially his father. They argued a lot, were at each others throats constantly and simply putting it, with no support from him, Johnny finally dropped out of school. The living conditions in the trailer took its toll on Johnny, ultimately, after a couple of months living there, he packed up and moved out. Johnny bounced around town, staying with friends until he was thrown out or caught stealing from them. His home now was the streets, sleeping wherever he found solitude. His life crumbled, in and out of trouble on a daily basis, fighting, selling drugs, or breaking into people's houses, living that life, one thing finally stopped, his bedroom was the county jail. Emily tried her best to keep a close eye on him. She felt sorry for her older brother because what his life was turning out to be. When ever they talked, she tried desperately to get him to listen and a chance to straighten his life out. However, long she pleaded to him, it didn't work and, oddly enough, the opposite chose Emily. Johnny seduced his gullible sister, telling her things were good, and his life was turning around. She believed him. Emily was so vulnerable to Johnny that her path was beginning to follow Johnny's, not stealing or breaking into houses, but getting sucked into the drug world.

At the onset, it was marijuana, a joint here and there, a cheap high, but after marijuana became stale, Johnny introduced her to more explosive addictions, like crack cocaine and LSD. It was toilsome to fight her struggles, her home life, school, her friends, and on desperate occasions, selling her body. But for some odd reason, Emily focused on her future. She was determined to finish high school and continue her education, a must to save her life. She needed to find stable employment and escape from the nightmare she was living. If she could only succeed, it would free her from her addictions, her shameful existence, and start over.

Her dependence brought the scum of the trailer park to her. It was either acquaintances of Johnny's or complete strangers looking for the same escape as Emily—the wild adventures from the highs. Luckily for Emily, this wasn't an everyday requirement. As each day passed, her mind collided with thoughts that tormented her severely. Which was lesser of the two evils, the prostitution or her weak addiction to the drugs? Or maybe it was her way of trying to save Johnny, she dearly loved him and desperately wanted to save his life.

Emily never wanted to know the names of her tricks. Who cared? It was all about getting laid, paid, and getting the hell out of there. It was the same guilt, trick after trick, regular after regular. The shameful subjugation seemed to never stop. Suddenly, dropping out of the clear blue sky was Richie. Richie was, altogether, a different trick. He definitely did not live in the trailer park, she knew that by the clothes he wore. He was polite, smelled terrific, and always paid Emily with a crisp one-hundred dollar bill. Their sex was always in a motel, never in the back seat of a car or some obscure dark alley. This was a trick that Emily looked forward to, but without any warnings, Richie simply vanished, floating back into the clear blue sky. It saddened Emily, but the realization finally came to light, all good things must come to an end.

It was Saturday, the Fourth of July, just like the previous years on this holiday the family packed a cooler of beer, wine and pop, carrying their folding chairs and headed to Jefferson Park to watch the fireworks the town offered. But not this Saturday, instead of celebrating the holiday, they were planning a funeral. Early that morning, two police officers knocked on the Dearborn's front door. Donald answered the knock and when he saw the officers, he knew exactly what they were there for. For Donald and his family, the news wasn't shocking because they all new the dangerous life Johnny was living. The officers explained to Donald that they found his son dead in an old vacant house on the south side of town, apparently from a drug overdose. In every addict's life, living or dying was based solely on chance. The death of her brother opened the door for Emily to rediscover herself. Within weeks, Emily checked herself into a local rehab center to cleanse her body as well as her soul. It was time to straighten out her life and get on the right track to her future. She promised that to Johnny. The funeral was small and short, but sad for the family. It was there that Emily met a gentleman named Jerry Culpatic, who befriended Johnny when Johnny lived off the streets and employed Johnny on and off at his car dealership. Jerry Culpatic would become Emily's blessing in disguise, taking her under his wing, sort of. He set her up with a job at his place of business, and after high school graduation, he helped her enroll in college.

***

That fall, Emily began her college life at the University of Illinois, Circle Campus. This was the start of her new future, determined to succeed, and also, prove to Johnny she wanted to make something out of her life. College life was a challenge. It didn't come that easy at first, committing every night to studying and reading, cramming for tests, but if she failed, she realized it would only bring her back to the life she never wanted to return to. Just that thought alone, inspired her to achieve that goal.

Her roommate was Cindy Nealy, a young girl from Iowa, who appeared to have a similar background as hers. Although Cindy's family wasn't as bizarre as Emily's, the girls had the same tendencies—getting hooked up with the wrong crowd, using drugs, and going through the pain of rehab. Emily didn't want to tell Cindy about her life as a prostitute, she deeply regretted that. They hung around together on campus, and sometimes spent the weekends in the city, going to plays, a movie, or attending a local bar on Rush Street. Eventually, it became just hitting the bars on Rush, one in particular, the Roust About. Most of it's clientele were college students from the surrounding areas, or young workers from the Loop. It didn't take long for Emily and Cindy to become regular customers on a first-name basis with the bartenders and the bouncers and, best of all, never having to bring any money with them. All their drinks were free, sometimes taken care of by the bartenders, but mostly paid for by guys looking for a cheap thrill. Both girls knew that and were totally aware of the circumstances. That's why they pranced from sucker to sucker. A little curiosity here, a few sexy innuendos there, and they were set for the evening. Neither Emily nor Cindy became serious with any of their acquaintances, they were there for the free drinks and some excitement on Saturday night.

Then enter Clyde Barton, a handsome, classy, extremely well-dressed African-American in his mid-twenties, who always flashed a roll of money. His entourage of friends and bodyguards traveled with him, in case trouble occurred. To Clyde, scoring with white chicks was a prize, a trophy to him, stealing from the white crowd. He always got what he was looking for and he was always looking. He noticed the two young ladies sitting alone in a booth, and the looks on their faces sold Clyde, he strutted toward them.

"What are you waiting for, Clyde? We're here to help you spend all your money and drink you under the table."

That was an invitation Clyde couldn't pass up. The nerve of those two beautiful young ladies to challenge the suave, debonair Clyde Barton. Clyde and his entourage became social steadies to Emily and Cindy. Each Saturday night, the group shared a reserved booth in the rear of the cabaret, a private sanctuary for Clyde to slip a small line of powder in their direction. Cindy sniffed the powder instantly, but Emily backed off. The alcohol would be her means of getting high and not bring back the dreadful past. Week after week, it was the same scene at the Roust About. The drinking, dancing, and heavy flirting bounced from one gullible creep to another. Ultimately, the temptation got the best of Emily, and excitement finally overcame her, she had to be part of it. It was back to her past life and habits, sniffing up a line of white powder.

Emily never dated Clyde, but from time to time, she purchased a small bag of cocaine for her personal use. Clyde always cut her a deal, a deal he hoped would end in an invitation to her bed, but that never happened. His unsuccessful moves on Emily discouraged him enough to direct all his attention to Cindy. If he wanted sex for the entire night, she provided it, including for his entire entourage. She thrived on it.

Fun was fun, but during the day Emily had to work toward her future. She knew both worlds: drug addiction and the gifted chance to redeem herself. If her life was worth living and keeping her solemn promise to Johnny, she must continue to study hard and graduate from college. She was doing well, getting good grades and actually, enjoying herself.

In early spring semester of her junior year, everyone, including Emily, had to be aware of the DePaul Blue Demons, sweeping the city off it's feet, shocking the NCAA basketball world by surviving to the final four. There were only four teams left in the NCAA basketball championship. The smallest college team of the final four, the Blue Demons, would butt heads with UCLA, Kentucky, and Indiana

"Yo, Emily. A bunch of us are going out Saturday night to see if we can catch the DePaul game. You up for that?" Max asked. He was a teacher's aide and a friend to Emily who helped her occasionally with difficult assignments.

"Yeah. Sounds cool to me. Just call and let me know where you're going to be and what time, okay?"

"Got you. Most likely, we'll be at Shorty's."

Shorty's Dugout was a corner sports bar located within a stone's throw of the Circle Campus. Shorty's was the number one hot spot to catch any sporting event, featuring the largest flat screen TV in Chicago, mounted on the wall above the main bar. It was the high-priority attraction, where rabid sport fans came to watch the Chicago sport teams play.

Max and his friends gathered early, allowing them to corner off a section of the bar in front of the large screen. It was like having tickets on the fifty-yard line, or directly behind the home team's dugout. The crowd started filling up the bar and it was getting louder, fans chanting for the Blue Demons. Soon after Max had solidify the corner of the bar, Emily entered. The usual pitchers of beer were lined up in front of them, a variety to choose from: a light beer, a dark beer, a Budweiser, or a Heineken. To Emily, every beer seemed to taste all the same, but beer was the only drink on the menu.

"Max, Max!" Jimmy, another friend of Max's, dashed into the bar, shouting as if the establishment was on fire. "Hey, the word is out that the TEDs are having another one of their incredible parties."

"Really, now. Well then, what the hell are we sitting here for?"

"What's happening, Max? Where's everyone going?" asked Emily.

"Emily, you have to check this out. The TEDs are throwing another party, and I mean P-A-R-T-Y. Words can't describe it, you just have to be there to experience it."

Time to zip your coat Emily, and zip out the door to the famous animal house.

The TED house was an old two-story brick manor house that was swarming with people on the lawn area, all with one or both hands clutching a plastic cup of beer. Inside, she was star struck. She envisioned the house would resemble the frat house in the movie, "Animal House": broken windows, sloppy furniture, and holes in the wall. Wrong. It was the complete opposite: expensive furniture, pastel painted walls with pictures, windows surrounded with stylish curtains, high ceilings, and chandeliers, a study with a fireplace and several sofas circling the fireplace. She continued, creeping through the house, step by step, wondering how a college fraternity could afford…

Then, out of nowhere, an unknown fanatic handed her a beer. So far, awesome. She'd just sip on her beer and continue her tour of this extraordinary residence they called the TED house, watching all the crazies spilling their beers and going wild. She entered, or tried to enter the kitchen area that was heavily crowded, realizing this is where all the beer was poured.

"I'm glad you're here."

Emily turned to see who was talking to her. Little did she know it, but the future of Emily Dearborn had now been etched in stone.

Chapter 6

A Life Begins and Lives End

The puzzle of Charles's life were falling into place perfectly. In less than four months, he has found the love of his life, graduated from DePaul with high honors and mulling over several worthwhile job opportunities. But Charles was a home boy and being close to his family meant a lot to him. He has an offer from Priority Investments located in Chicago's north loop. When Charles and his father met William Fossett, CEO of Priority, they talked in length about his role at Priority, his salary and commission, his pension, health insurance, traveling to other countries, and very important, still living in Chicago. After they finished their conference, Mr. Fossett excused himself so that Charles and his father could talk privately. When he returned, Charles stood and shook Mr. Fossett's hand. He was now an employee of Priority Investments, Inc.

What more could Charles ask for? He had his college degree in business, he had the love of his life in Emily and a new career working in Chicago at Priority Investments. The stage was set for Charles to solve another piece of his puzzle. He asked Emily to share their lives together, she accepted without hesitation and moved to live with Charles. They found a two-bedroom condo not far from the Loop on the corner of Cedar Street and Lake Shore Drive. They lived on the ninth floor, facing Lake Michigan, with views as spectacular as those from Charles's office window. He and Emily would sit for hours viewing the long stretches of beach and watch the sailboats drift up and down the shoreline, the sun bathers, it was awesome.

How could his life be any better? And it did get better. After dinner one night, Charles settled into the sofa and Emily snuggled up to him. She handed him a small instrument resembling a thermometer.

"Do you know what this is?" Emily was so excited.

"It looks like a thermometer."

"No, knucklehead. It's a pregnancy test. Look what it says."

"It says... Positive." Charles, finally realizing what was happening, leaped to his feet. Jumping up and down like a small child on Christmas morning. "We're going to have a baby?"

"Yes. Aren't you happy?"

"This is so wonderful, I can't wait till Jack is born."

"You've given our baby a name already, have you?"

"Yes. It will be a boy and I think Jack Collier will be the perfect name for him. Oh, no. You know what that means now?"

"Your parents?"

"Well, yes, that too, but we'll have to get married soon, don't you think?"

***

Emily and Charles married when Emily was four months into her pregnancy. They had a small ceremony at Herb and Elsie's church and afterward a small party at his parent's house. Donald and Martha met Herb and Elsie for the first time, an unusual experience, but Charles made sure the Dearborns remained sober and in harmony with the celebration. It was a joyous occasion, everyone attending the event wished the best for the newlyweds, not knowing that the sudden marriage was the fault of the pregnancy. It was their little secret. When the reception ended, Emily hugged her mom and Dad and they said their goodbyes. She was tearful, explaining how she wished that her relationship with them could've been stronger and happier.

It wasn't long after the Dearborns left, Herb cornered Charles and asked, "Well, son, she's pregnant, isn't she?"

Charles knew his and Emily's sudden marriage caused suspicion from both families. Their only explanation to them was that they were madly in love with each other and wanted to spend their lives together.

"I knew you would ask me that. We thought it best to get married and get on with our lives. We love each other. And our son, hopefully it's a boy, will be raised as well as you and mom raised me."

"I think so, too. Remember, we are always here if you need us, understand? Any time."

"Thanks, Dad." Charles embraced his Dad and patted him on the back, "I love you both."

In June 1993, Jack was born, a son to Charles and Emily. The young Colliers were enjoying a good life and their future was getting brighter. Although she would stay home and raise Jack, Emily decided to put her education aside, and when Jack got older, maybe she could return and finish her dream. Johnny would be proud of her.

***

Several months passed with the new parents enjoying every second of Jack's life. They took turns changing diapers, feeding the baby, rocking him to sleep… life was good.

Around eleven am on a sunny Sunday in September, Emily heard an unexpected knock on their front door. As she opened the door, she was startled to see two uniformed Chicago police officers.

"Good morning, officers."

"This is the residence of Charles Collier?"

"Yes, it is. Is there anything wrong?"

"Is your husband home?"

"Yes." Emily opened the door letting the officers enter. She called Charles.

"I'm Charles Collier. What is this about?"

"Your parents are Herb and Elsie Collier?"

"They are."

The uniformed officers looked at each other, nervous and uncomfortable about what was going to happen. "We're terribly sorry to inform you, but your parents were killed earlier this morning."

"What...what?" Emily and Charles were stunned. It was only yesterday that they were over, having lunch and playing with Jack.

"We will need you to identify the bodies just as soon as you are able to."

He didn't want to hear that. Emily cradled him and helped him to the chair in the living room.

"We'll...we'll try to do that as early as we can."

"I understand. Thank you. Again, we're very sorry to bring you such heartbreaking news."

"Thank you."

It was later that day that Charles learned the circumstances about how Herb and Elsie died. The police explained that while walking to Sunday Mass at their nearby church, they were run down by a senseless car chase between two rival gangs. The drivers and any of the passengers abandoned the vehicles, and ran away. The police had witnesses, but a positive ID of any of the gang members would be nearly impossible.

Losing his parents was a very difficult pill to swallow for both Emily and Charles. The funeral and burial were even tougher. Mr. Fossett allowed him to take as much time as he needed to deal with his loss. He remembered how his Dad preached to him about loyalty, working hard, following the rules and most important, being honest. At the end of a week, Charles thought that getting back to work would relieve him from his emotional strain. The memories of his parents were cemented into his brain, but life has to go on. This was exactly what his father would tell him. Every life suffers tragedy, but every life has a future.

There was one painful task left for Charles, the selling of Herb and Elsie's house. He and Emily talked about moving there and raising Jack, but too many recent memories haunted Charles. They decided it would be in their best interest to sell the property and use the money for Jack's education. It didn't take long to sell the property. The house was immaculate, a great location and situated in a very upper middle class subdivision. The house sold one month later.

Chapter 7

Along Came Dennis Reading

Dennis Reading was born and raised in Cranston, Illinois, a small farming community where, like every small town, everyone knew everyone's business. At the age of six, his mother died of lung cancer, leaving his father, Alex, to raise him. Alex never remarried, but raising his only child wasn't that difficult at all, he just let Dennis grow up on his own. Dennis idolized his father. And the older he became the more he understood the difficult life his father was living, lonely and timid, reclusive, devoting his life to his son. Alex loved to fish, so as time allowed, they would drive north to the Wisconsin border where there were numerous lakes to fish. They would fish all day long, and at times neither had a single bite, but it didn't matter to Dennis, just being together with his father meant the world to him.

It was known throughout the neighborhood that Dennis was never wrong, alias, a smart-ass. Many of the neighborhood kids avoided Dennis because of that simple fact. It didn't bother Dennis, who needed friends after all. During the summer months, just before entering high school, he befriended an older neighbor down the street named Mr. Treeberg. The Treeberg family owned Citizens Bank in Cranston, the only bank in town and also, lived in the biggest house in town. The property sat on the corner of Main and Lincoln streets, adjacent from the bank and local park. The yard was massive, the manicured lawn, the collection of huge oak trees and a touch of pine trees, which made you feel you like walking in a forest.

***

One day, while Dennis was riding his bike past the Treeberg residence, Mr. Treeberg stopped Dennis and started a conversation. He asked Dennis if he had a job. Of course he didn't, so Mr. Treeberg offered the job to Dennis, maintaining his lawn and garden during the summer and to shoveling the sidewalk and driveway when it snowed. Without hesitation, Dennis accepted and was paid a whopping six dollars an hour. Dennis continued to work for Mr. Treeberg through the summers until he reached his senior year in school. Late one afternoon when Dennis was mowing the lawn, Mr. Treeberg approached him.

"Dennis, if I'm guessing right, you're going into your senior year, aren't you?"

"Yep, one more year and I'll be finished with school."

"In the wink-of-an-eye, you'll be graduating from college, getting married, and raising a family of your own. You are planning on going to college, aren't you?"

"It's my dream, but I'm not sure. If I do, I'll need a better job than mowing lawns."

"Well, as a matter of fact, a young man is leaving our bank to attend to college. You think you may be interested in filling his spot?"

"Gee, Mr. Treeberg, I wouldn't know the first thing about banking."

"Nonsense. He learned the same way you can. I guarantee, you'll be making more money."

"Well, aah...I aah...."

"You think about it, Dennis. Then one day next week, stop by the bank and we can talk about the position. I'll explain everything to you, what you need to know, and what you need to do."

"Okay, I can do that. Thanks, Mr. Treeberg."

***

The next week came. Dennis had given Mr. Treeberg's offer

much consideration and asked his father what he suggested. If anyone knew better, it was Alex.

"Son, now would be a good time to start planning your future. Mr. Treeberg has given you that opportunity. Better to start early than later."

Dennis's ambition was to attend college. If he took the job, he could save enough money to do that. As expected, his meeting with Mr. Treeberg went well. The following week he was the new employee of Citizens Bank and started his training immediately, working after school and a full day on Saturdays. Things were looking up for Dennis Reading and it was all good.

Following the graduation from high school, that fall Dennis enrolled into Lewis University, and four years later graduated with a degree in finance. He continued to work at Citizens Bank for six more years, until Mr. Treeberg became very ill and passed away a few months later. Soon, the bank was sold and when the new owners took over, everything changed, even Dennis's job. He couldn't adjust to the new system and, subsequently, submitted his resignation. Although working at Citizens, it was a far cry from working in downtown Chicago, but an associate from Citizens informed him of the opening at TransUniverse. With his background and a very good recommendation, Dennis landed the position at Trans and quickly moved to Chicago. His job was similar as at Citizen, but instead of making loans, he was learning to invest for his clients through the stock market. It was a challenge to Dennis, but a challenge he relished.

While working at Citizens Bank, Dennis had countless opportunities to meet people from all different walks of life, from the average blue-collar worker to the high-class moguls of the business world. One of those moguls was William Fossett. Dennis and William developed a unique friendship. Of course, there was always two sides to the relationship they had, the business side and the social side. On the business side, Dennis became conversant in what he saw in William, and liked it. They both were greedy, both wanted to get rich fast and both had a way to do it. They devised a clever scheme for certain clients, investing into risque stocks that, eventually failed, but getting marginal profits. Higher profits landed in the hands of the conniving duo, it was them that laughed the loudest. The scam was a classic and it was working.

On the social side, they were inseparable. Traveling to places all over the world, from sunny hot beaches in the Caribbean to the mountains of Europe, especially Switzerland. Whenever Dennis contemplated his future, about being rich and at ease with his life, this was the place where he wanted to finish his dream. The snow covered Alps, the chalets, miles and miles of pine forests and Bavarian beer. How could it get any better than that.

Then William introduced Dennis to the sport of golf. William loved the game of golf and played the game with serious tenacity. He was a four handicap and, when the invitation called upon him, he played in several tournaments around the Chicago area.

By all means, Dennis didn't play the caliber of golf that William expected, but both enjoyed the times being out on the course and playing with well known famous people. On rare occasions, William's sister, Helen was invited to participate, but only when a fourth player was a last place substitute. It was more of an invitation from Dennis that Helen accepted. The relationship between Helen and William was noticeable, obvious to all the people surrounding the group and it wasn't pretty. This was an opportunity for Dennis to get closer to Helen. Who cared about their golf game, they were having fun and enjoyed being together. This didn't sit well with William. They began dating and seeing each other on a regular basis, eventually becoming romantically involved. When William caught wind of their involvement, there were no more golf outings involving Helen and when Dennis inquired to William, William scorned at him and never had a nice word to say about his sister. Helen was well aware of her relationship with William and when she and Dennis spent time together, they kept their distance from him.

Then the bomb fell on Helen. As wicked as William was toward her, for his own personal greed, possibly in spite of what he thought of Dennis dating his sister, he set up Helen on a deal that would assure her millions. She invested everything she had. Months later, the bomb exploded in Helen's face and the investment that was going to bring her millions, vanished. Behind closed doors, William laughed because he knew the outcome even before Helen signed all the papers, the sizable commission would fill only his pockets and not hers. It was a despicable trick. She lost everything and begged William to help her. Not a chance. Dennis did his best to help Helen, but he was caught in the middle of a fire storm. William's greed was his destination.

Helen was so furious with William she wanted to get as far away from evil as she could. She packed her bags and moved to California. Now, Dennis was caught between a rock and a hard place. What would he do? Should he move to California with Helen or stay in Chicago? He did love Helen but it was a very difficult decision to resolve. He had a great job with William and was making a considerable amount of money. Could it be the same if he moved to California? The more he thought about it, the outcome became easier, his greed for money, just like William, swayed his decision. He was the same person as William and greed was the consequence. What couldn't be overlook was what made their friendship unique—it was the cleverness between them to swindle money. It was their uncanny ability to make sizable profits from their little secrets. They cheated and lied, but that didn't matter to them. Pure selfishness prevailed. Still, there was the ever present devil, William himself. Although their friendship was put on the back burner, William and Dennis worked to achieve a long time plan William had up his sleeve. Sure, they were making good money together, but William had another plan that Dennis would never know about. When the time was right, William needed a fall guy.

***

William knew that inking the Kaiser Foundation account to a

contract would mean to him. For years he concocted a plan, a strategy designed to pilfer money from his clients without them knowing. With the Kaiser Foundation in his pocket, the plan would proceed immediately. He needed someone to help him and that was why he made the call to Dennis. Immediately following his short briefing with Charles, Dennis was back in William's office. Enter the fall guy.

"Good, sit down." Before he closed his door, William checked the hall to see if there were any lingering, nosy associates.

"You ever hear of Adolph Kaiser or the Kaiser Foundation?"

"Sure, of course. He's in all the magazines, even on the TV news. Every one associated in investment banking knows about Adolph Kaiser."

"Well, guess who stopped in my office last week?"

"You're kidding. The man himself?"

"I'm handing over the account to Charles. He's a master at closing deals." William was so excited, he couldn't sit down.

"I'll have their foundation under my thumb shortly. Charles is traveling to New York soon to deliver their investment proposal."

"So, what are you suggesting?"

"I've had a plan up my sleeve for years. I've been thinking more about it now that I met Kaiser. I'm talking millions here."

In his excitement, as William leaned on his desk his hand knocked over the intercom box, but he shoved it back into place. He moved closer to Dennis, then whispered,

"Charles Collier has been with me for more than eighteen years. A very intelligent person and a genius in designing profitable portfolios for special clients. If you learn half of his secrets, you alone could conquer the investment world. The reason I assigned this account to Charles is because of his ability to maximize Kaiser's profits. Once I feel the time is right, we'll eliminate Charles, then finish out my plan."

"I'm all ears, William. I love it." Dennis pounded his fist on the desk.

***

Charles arrived at Priority earlier than the rest of the staff. It would be the day that he handed over the Kaiser portfolio to William. He had contributed an excessive amount of time and research to organize a portfolio like no other he'd ever put together. His prize work contained stocks, mutual funds, annuities, options and ETFs, all worthy of the money Adolph Kaiser would invest. Charles expected to become "The Business Man of the Year," heralded by all his peers and master of the "Golden Portfolio." Over and over he scanned his figures, making sure there were no errors, no discrepancies in the figures and no way the Kaiser Foundation could refuse this offer.

He heard some commotion in the lobby as the other agents started to arrive. He picked up his portfolio and headed toward William's office. The door was open and William was standing, looking out the window.

"Excuse me, William. I've finished the Kaiser portfolio. Before I leave for New York tomorrow, you may want to review it and see if you're okay with it."

"Splendid Charles." William reached for the folder and began his review.

"I have some other things I need to attend to in my office. When you're finished, just buzz me."

About an hour later, William entered Charles's office.

"Well done, Charles. This portfolio has everything Kaiser's foundation could want. I'm positive he'll accept it and we'll be on our way to financial riches."

"I sure hope so. I've spent long hours and researched this till I was blue in the face. I can't wait to get there and explain all the benefits to him."

"Very well. Delivering the proposal in person looks very professional. Call me as soon as the ink dries on his contract."

***

That evening when Charles sat down to dinner, he was in such a happy mood, Emily was dumbfounded. "Emily, if I get the

Kaiser Foundation to agree with all I have to offer, we'll be able to buy New York with the money I'll make from my commission."

Emily burst out laughing. "Yeah, right."

***

Charles woke up earlier than usual, minutes before the radio alarm started buzzing at 4:30 am.. Charles showered, dressed, then collected his belongings for the trip. He double-checked the contents of his briefcase to make sure everything was there before locking it. Majority of his business trips lasted one day, but this meeting was so important, the possibility of spending the night was a reality. His flight departed at 8:30 am. from O'Hare and scheduled to land in New York around noon. He'd lose an hour traveling east, so catching the earlier flight would give him some leeway to review his proposal. Their meeting wasn't scheduled until two o'clock that afternoon, so Charles had time to break for lunch and rehearse his presentation speech.

He carried his luggage into the kitchen, being quiet as possible, not to wake up the family. Quickly, he dropped a K-cup into the coffee machine and hit the "brew" button. He stood, waiting, noticing it was still dark outside, and his time in New York would be long-drawn-out. Consequently, after eighteen years, this was a chance of a lifetime. He glanced at his watch, hurried to finish his coffee and donned his coat. Just before leaving the condo, he jotted down a note to Emily.

> Wish me luck. I'm hoping to be back home tonight, but
> if this meeting lasts longer, which I think it will, I'll call
> you and let you know whats going on. Give my love to
> Jack. Love ya.
>
> Hubby

Looking for the first available taxi, he walked to the corner of Michigan and Cedar, looking north and south. The city streets in the Loop were desolate, which made finding a cab at that early hour a whole lot easier. He flagged down the first cab he saw, entered the back seat, "O'Hare, please." Now he was on his way to destiny.

Chapter 8

When the Cat's Away...
the Mice Will Play

Thursday afternoon, Emily started to prepare dinner for her and Jack. Something light and easy was in order—maybe a meatloaf. As soon as she gathered the ingredients, the kitchen phone began ringing.

"Hello."

"Hello, dear."

"I believe this call is telling me you won't be home tonight, correct?"

"You're so smart, and I'm so lucky I married you. Anyway, we just finished our meeting. The group is getting ready to have dinner and Mr. Kaiser insists that I stay. He wants me to visit his foundation tomorrow. So, I can't say no to that."

"How did your meeting go?"

"Perfect. I'm sure Mr. Kaiser is satisfied with what I offered him and the Foundation. It only took his people less than an hour to overlook the proposal. They didn't have any questions and Adolph signed the contract."

"Wow, I'll bet William is popping the cork on the champagne bottle as we speak."

"No doubt. I called him immediately after the signing. He was like a little boy in a candy store."

"Well, about what time shall I expect you tomorrow?"

"Hard to say. I'm hoping to get out of here soon. It depends on what Mr. Kaiser has planned. If I'm running late, I'll call you again."

"All right, be careful. I love you."

"Night. Say hi to Jack."

"Will do. I'll see you tomorrow. Bye."

Before the receiver hit the cradle, Emily was thinking. A free night to party. She'd heard of a new nightclub opening on Rush Street called The Crowd Pleaser. How appropriate. It sure fit her requirements: wild, loud bands, lots of dancing, and an exciting houseful of loose men. She couldn't wait to get there.

When she was a single woman and before she met Charles, every weekend found her partying at a local bar or hitting the big clubs around Chicago. That was her excitement. That was how she learned to survive the boredom within her family life. Once she tasted what the clubs offered, the sex, booze, drugs, she was hooked.

Her marriage to Charles put an end to the bar scene. There were no more parties, no more one-night stands, and no more drugs. There was no way of getting free of Charles. Besides, she was pregnant with Jack, and after the birth she knew it would be a long time before the taste of partying would wet her appetite again. Charles was by no means a kill-joy. He partied when he was in college with Emily, but after graduation his life changed drastically. Although she loved Charles, after the birth of Jack their sex life hit a dry spell. If and when they enjoyed each other, it was over before each of them knew it. Slam, bam, thank you, ma'am…and Charles was fast asleep.

Standing in the kitchen, Emily's mind was in overdrive. She peeked around the corner and saw Jack watching TV, oblivious to her intentions. Slowly, she walked toward him.

"Jack, Carol just called and wants to know if I'll join her for dinner and a movie. Will you be okay here alone tonight?"

"I'm eighteen years old now, very capable of taking care of myself, thank you."

"I know, but I feel guilty leaving you here all by yourself."

"Just go and have fun. Don't worry about me."

Those were the words Emily wanted to hear. That night, the

taxi dropped her off at the entrance of the new nightclub. She expected the new club to be crowded, and it was. People were interested in finding out what a new place had to offer, and how it differed from the other clubs around the area. Emily got what she expected. There were lines of people waiting to get in and lots of men to tease and seduce. Her time was valuable; she knew she had to move fast.

Surprisingly, the line moved quickly and before she knew it, she paid the ten-dollar cover charge and stepped inside looking for a place to sit. She pushed and wiggled her petite frame toward the bar. She spotted two empty stools and rushed to grab one, but felt uneasy sitting at the bar alone. It had been years since her single days, but this was now, a bit nervous, she was ready to enjoy it. The lively band had the crowd chanting and singing. Most of their songs were hits from the 70s and 80s, songs that Emily grew up with and liked to hear.

She finally caught the attention of the bartender to order a drink, but before she could get her order out, a male voice from behind her shouted, "What are you drinking tonight?"

Emily thought he was talking to someone else, but when she looked back, she saw that a young Latino man was talking to her.

"Excuse me, were you talking to me?"

"Why, of course. I saw you come in and I wanted to buy you a drink. My name is Sergio."

It didn't take long for Emily to ask herself if she was ready to start over. It wasn't like years ago when she was single, and knew how to react to those situations. But now, she was a married woman that needed to remove the rust and remember how it was back then. She knew exactly what she was there for. To have a few drinks, dance, meet some young and wild men, snort a line or two, and then leave.

"So, what are you drinking?"

"A beer will be just fine." *Did I order a beer? Yuk, a beer!* Beer was not her favorite drink, but tonight a beer would do. Sergio sat next to her.

"Cheers."

"Cheers." The taste of the beer was better than Emily anticipated, and it was free.

"As I said, my name is Sergio. What's yours?"

"Emily."

"Emily, very nice to meet you."

They carried on the same line of patter, as though everyone
there was hoping to get laid. After another beer, then another,
Sergio whispered into Emily's ear. She smiled and nodded. He
took her hand and they retreated to the rear of the club, to a large
booth occupied by a couple of women and men sipping their
drinks. Sergio introduced them as friends of his. As Emily slid into
the booth, she noticed remains of a white powder scattered over
the glass covering of the table. Emily had cast an eye over this
scene many times before. It brought back memories of her, Cindy,
and Clyde. It sent chills down her arms.

The music was getting louder and the dance floor becoming
overcrowded with couples without a care in the world, at least for
the evening, giving no thought to tomorrow's work. Emily
reveled in the excitement, drinking free drinks, meeting strangers
and feeling back in the groove. Sergio tapped her on the shoulder
and pointed to two thin lines of white powder. The lines were
daring her to annihilate those lost years.

Sergio handed her a tightly rolled dollar bill. She lifted it,
placed her finger on the side of her nose and expertly sniffed the
powder into her body. Within a matter of seconds, she was
heedless to anything that was around her. Colors flashed before
her eyes, her body floated, dancing in the clouds, now numb to
everyone and everything. She closed her eyes to the sounds of the
pounding music—lyrics from Sly and the Family Stone. She sang
to herself … I wanna take you higher… higher. Her longing for
those addicting highs were back.

She felt Sergio's soft, wet lips on her cheek. She responded,
her lips meeting his, now hard and meaningful. His hands
controlled Emily. Every inch of her body awaited his touch,

begging him to please her. Begging him to bring back those memorable lost years. Sergio's hand maneuvered under her mini-skirt, rubbing her inner thighs, slowly but methodically probing his way to her fire. That's what she was there for, right?

She answered, inching her hands onto Sergio's lap, already finding an exposed… Oh, yes. This is exactly why she needed her time to be naughty, her time to tease and to be teased.

When Emily raised her head, Sergio was waiting with a satisfied smile. All of a sudden, who did she see on the dance floor? William Fossett. No, this couldn't be. Was she hallucinating? She shook her head, looked again and there he was, looking her way. He stared, but the dancing crowd absorbed him into the center of the dance floor and disappeared. Emily, quickly grabbed her purse and said to Sergio, "I need to use the powder room, the other powder." As fast as she could, skirted out of the booth and darted to the front entrance. She bounced from one body to the next, fondled by every horny man in her way until she reached the door. The bouncer had the look of a pro-football lineman. His massive arms were folded across his hulking chest. She asked him where she could get a taxi. He noticed the remains of white powder around her nose. He pulled his handkerchief from his back pocket and wiped away the danger signs, then led her outside to a row of waiting taxis.

"You know what time it is?"

The bouncer rolled back his sleeve on his left hand, exposing a gold Rolex. "Ten after twelve."

Ten after twelve? What does that mean? The cocaine hadn't worn off yet and her equilibrium wasn't at its best, making it obscure for her to get home. They approached the taxi and the bouncer opened the door for her.

The Iranian driver spoke in broken English, "Where to go, lady?"

Emily hesitated. *Think, Emily. You've lived at that same address for over fifteen years, surely you must know that.*

"Where to go, lady?"

"Umm, Cedar Street…105." She fell back into the hard leather seat and closed her eyes. Her head felt like a hunk of steel attached to a powerful magnet trying to remove her head from her body. Such an eerie feeling. Then she remembered the face of William. She closed her eyes, desperately trying to erase the demented memories of William and what he had previously done to her. She sensed the taxi coming to a halt. She struggled to sit up, looking out the window trying to recognize the familiar 105 Cedar Street surroundings.

"Eight doughlar."

Emily was still looking out the window, wondering if she was in the right place.

"Lady, eight doughlar, peease."

Emily found her purse, removed a single bill and handed it to the cabbie, not realizing the value of the bill. She opened the back door and exited the cab.

"Tank you, lady."

Emily stood on the sidewalk, the brisk, cool air breezing across her face. She could feel her senses beginning to function, allowing her to recognize the surroundings. This was 105 Cedar Street. The elevator stopped at the ninth floor, the doors opened, and Emily shuffled her way to her condo. She fished through her purse to locate her keys. When she removed them a yellow napkin fell to the floor. Thinking nothing of it, Emily picked it up and unlocked the front door. She tossed her purse on the coffee table and dropped her body into the nearest armchair, totally exhausted, totally messed up.

Was it the drinks or the powder she snuffed up her nose that got her in this condition? Most likely, both. She had used drugs before, but never experienced the sensation she experienced tonight. Was it better or worse? Was William really there? The yellow napkin was still in her grasp. She opened the napkin and noticed the number on it, 312-555-6261, along with Sergio's name. Should she keep it or throw it away? She sat debating the issue—

keep it or burn it? The choice was easy. She stuffed the napkin back into her purse and retired for the night.

***

The offices at Priority were about to close for the weekend. Most agents were gathering their coats, laptops, and briefcases, hustling to leave the building. All except Charles. He remained in his office with his door slightly ajar. The digital clock read 3:50 pm. As he rose from his chair, he opened his door and walked to the reception area. No noise, no sign of lingering agents, the office was all his.

The room located behind Alice's reception desk was her office. Where all the files were stored, where all the mail was sorted, and all the copying took place. It was the hub of Priority Investments. He walked past the reception counter and into her office, straight to the long row of steel file cabinets. Each drawer from each file cabinet was color-coded. Each colored tag identified specific identities in that drawer. Charles was looking for one file in particular. The file of Dennis Reading. He started at the far left of the row of cabinets, until he saw the yellow tag. "Employees."

Shit, the drawers are locked. As he tugged each drawer, he realized they were all locked. *Now what?*

He assumed that the keys were hidden somewhere within Alice's office. He sat behind Alice's desk and opened all the drawers, one at a time, looking for the keys. He opened the bottom drawer on the right, where Alice kept her manuals and books and…

Looky, looky, looky…shame on you, Alice! Charles removed a bottle of Chevis Regal blended Scotch whiskey from her drawer. *Alice, you must have known I was coming.* A smirk escaped Charles's lips, but the Scotch didn't. He twisted off the cap and helped himself to a mighty swig.

Ooh, *that's good stuff.* He set the bottle in the exact position he found it. Bingo! Charles located a small rack of hooks containing numerous keys. He selected a key from the first hook and returned to the cabinet labeled with the yellow tag. The key fit and he opened the drawer for employees, fingering through a series of folders until the Reading folder was at his fingertips. He removed the entire folder and hurriedly copied each piece of paper, front and back, then returned the file to the drawer, locked the drawer and the key back to Alice's desk. Now, he had the life of Dennis Reading packed in his briefcase.

He switched off the lights, closed the door and left the office before some unlikely sole forgot something and returned to the office.

***

Emily cooked spaghetti for dinner. It was the favorite for Jack and Charles, with Italian meatballs, lots of oregano, basil, and especially her delicious homemade tomato sauce. It took Emily hours to prepare her sauce, not from any store-bought bottle but strictly homemade. Jack would tease her about opening her own Italian restaurant, serving only her delicious spaghetti and meatballs. Every time Jack brought it up, Emily laughed at the thought. It was a standing joke among them all.

Jack helped her clear off the table and wash the dishes while Charles was off to his inner sanctum, his little corner of the living room, his second office. Especially tonight, he was eager to read all about his new associate, primarily, his background and why he was hired.

Jack and Emily raced to the sofa to grab the remote, but Jack got there first.

"Mom. You gotta watch this."

He sat on the edge of the sofa while Emily sat close to him with her arm around his neck, listening to him explain the show.

"It's called Double-Dare You, a reality show where competing contestants vie against each other, conquering bizarre contests for large sums of money. It's so cool, Mom. They make them eat exotic insects, jump off tall buildings, do underwater stunts, or extreme physical endeavors."

"Eating those bugs? You must be crazy."

Meanwhile, Charles sat at his desk, opened his briefcase and removed the file of his new assistant. Huh, that's weird. The red colored file contained only two pieces of paper. One, a police report from the Cranston Police Department stating that Mr. Reading was arrested in 2008 for possession of a firearm without a valid registration and sentenced to one year probation. Why did he need a gun? The second piece of paper was blank, only having the name Ed Weldon and a phone number. Charles knew Ed and regarded him as a good friend sharing clients and, at times, they would meet for lunch and discuss client transactions. Ed recommended his clients interested in the stock market to contact Charles. Although no contacts had crossed his desk from Ed for a couple of years, he still respected the dedication Ed showed.

Then Charles remembered his talk with William, the day Reading was hired, that he came highly recommended. Really? By whom, Ed? He slouched back in his chair, both hands clasped behind his head, thinking. Tomorrow would be an excellent day to call Ed and catch up on lost time. A chance for good friends to talk about business over lunch, but on Charles's plate, the menu of Dennis Reading.

Chapter 9

The Smell of Fishy Tuna

On Monday morning, as soon as Charles stepped into his office and before he could take off his coat, he picked up his Rolodex and started thumbing through it hoping to find Mr. Weldon's card. There it was. Charles set the Rolodex down, took off his coat and reached for his phone, dialing the number on the card.

"Ed Weldon here."

"Hello, Ed. Charles Collier here. Its been awhile."

"Well, Charles Collier. I haven't talked to you in years. What an unexpected surprise. What's going on?"

"I ran across your name on my Rolodex and thought it was about time to get together and hash out old times over lunch."

"Oh, boy. That could take us all day."

"How true. Check your appointment book. If you're not busy, what do you say we have lunch today?"

"Hold on a sec. Looks good. No appointments till Wednesday."

"Cool. You know where the 5th Street Deli is?"

"Sure."

"How about 12:30 at the Deli?"

"I'll see you there. Bye."

***

Entering the deli, Charles scanned over the restaurant and didn't notice anyone resembling the looks of Ed. Charles was the first to arrive. It had been awhile since he last saw Ed, but he

should have no problem recognizing him. Ed had a stocky 6'4"
build, long curly brown hair, and a beard that was as long as his
hair. Grizzly Adams, that's how Charles remembered him.

He sat at an empty booth close to the entrance, so that when Ed
arrived he could quickly catch his eye. Sipping on his coffee, there
he was, easing through the deli's revolving doors. He had gained
considerable weight and his hair was shorter and thinning, but
something was missing, his long, curly beard.

"Ed."

They shook hands, Ed removed his coat and squeezed into the
booth opposite Charles.

"Well, if I remember correctly, the last time I saw you, your
beard was as long as your hair."

"I remember that. I wish I could lose weight as easily as I can
lose my hair."

"The older we get, the more inches we gain."

"Are you still working at Priority?"

"Till I die. Going on my nineteenth year. A little slow right
now, but the economists are optimistic."

Their talk was interrupted by their waitress, setting down their
orders and refilling their drinks.

"What about you? Are you still at Citizens Bank?"

"Oh, gosh no. I left there soon after the place fell apart."

"Really. What happened there?"

"Not long after Treeberg's illness, the business was sold and
nothing went right after that. We were losing accounts by the
handful. You could say, the writing was on the wall, so, in my best
interest, I resigned. There was a job opening at Republic Credit
Union. Been there ever since."

"Is that the Republic downtown?"

"Yeah, right. Located on Monroe."

"How are your wife and family doing?"

"Karen is doing great. Mean and ornery as any typical wife.
She's still teaching at Riverdale High, unfortunately, no kids yet."

"You know what? Come to think of it, we recently hired a guy from TransUnion. His name is Dennis Reading and when I read his work history, I believe I saw something about working at Citizens. Was he there when you were there?"

"Oh, yeah. Dennis was Treeberg's right-hand man. Did absolutely nothing after the old man passed. So, he went to TransUnion? And now he works for you? Huh?"

"We have him. He seems to be doing okay."

"That's strange. Dennis and, aah, I forgot your boss's name?"

"Fossett. William Fossett."

"Right. Now I remember. Fossett would stop in and see Dennis quite often. They were pretty close friends, and if I remember, they golfed a lot. Dennis bragged about Fossett a lot, saying that Fossett wanted him to join his firm."

"Honestly? I'm surprised to hear that."

"Yes, I remember while he worked at Citizens, the rumors floated around the water coolers about how Dennis was hot for Fossett's sister. I can't remember her name but we all believed that. We also heard about the troubles they had with each other. Dennis told me it was a real estate investment that went sour, they became bitter enemies, then she split. You know about gossip in a small office, right?"

"So, Dennis and William were buddy-buddy, huh? Did you recommend Dennis to Fossett?"

"Hell no, not me. I don't think I've ever talked to Fossett. Like I said, they traveled, played golf a lot, and spent lots of time with each other. You would think he was part of the family. Not many days went by that Dennis didn't have something to say about Fossett or that woman. Helen, that was her name, Helen, Fossett's sister. Does Reading work under you or...?"

"Sometimes. I see him around the office. Fossett has him traveling a lot. Most of our clients have accounts overseas, so he has the responsibility of maintaining them."

"Charles, you must know what it's like working in the investment business. Rumors end up smelling like dead fish. With Reading, something just didn't click right. Within the blink of an eye, he just packed up, split, and I never saw or heard from him again."

"Oh, well. If you ever want to see him again, come over to Priority."

"Gee, look at the time, Charles. Hey, I've enjoyed our lunch. We must do this again."

"I agree. It was fun to reminisce about the past, even more so about your buddy, the smelly tuna."

"Yeah, my buddy," Ed laughed. "You got him now, my friend. Just keep a close eye on him."

Charles pulled out his debit card and paid the hostess. Outside the deli, they shook hands and promised to have lunch again. While on his walk back to the office, Charles was still bothered about the quick hiring of Reading and his close relationship with William and why Ed mentioned keeping a close eye on him. William never mentioned Dennis Reading before and from what Ed was saying, they've been friends for quite some time. Yes, he would have to keep a close eye on Fossett's smelly tuna.

Chapter 10

Cold As I.C.E.

Five months had passed since Charles secured the contract of the Kaiser Foundation. Their portfolio was showing a steady climb in assets, not breaking records by any means, but considering the state of the economy, they weren't losing any money. Adolph Kaiser and the foundation were satisfied and happy.

The month of December was the dreaded month for all Priority agents. The Christmas holiday, combined with year-end tax compilations, meant Charles would be accumulating data on each account for the year. It was a tedious, time consuming chore getting all the accounts ready for tax time. But this year, he had Dennis helping him with his smaller accounts.

The Kaiser account was the largest and most important client at Priority. Charles would be the only person handling the data in their portfolio and responsible if anything that went wrong. There could not be any mistakes when the reports were submitted because it was Charles's neck hanging in the balance. How would he try explaining the mistakes to Adolph Kaiser.

Two weeks before Christmas, he began the day sitting at his desk with his open laptop in front of him. His screen displayed data from the Kaiser account as he checked and rechecked all the available figures. It was the last day for all agents to finalize their clients' portfolios and drop them in the mail.

Okay, that's good...good...I like that...perfect. Charles was satisfied that everything on his report was correct. To be sure, he wanted to match his figures with the totals from the firm's financial documents. He knew this should've been done weeks ago, but getting past William was another story.

"Alice, would you be so kind to print out Priority's year-end totals for the Kaiser account. I want to be absolutely sure that both totals are showing the same data. This account has to be flawless."

"Charles, I would need William's approval to print out any statements from Priority. It's a new rule with him."

"What new rule? Since when? How come I never hear about these new rules? Look, this is the last day I can check my figures. I know William isn't here, but I'm sure he wouldn't object. This is our largest and most important client. If William were here, he'd probably do this himself. Now, if you want to be personally responsible for any errors on the Kaiser report, then I'll go ahead and send it as is."

"You know William as well as I do, Charles, but since he's not here and this is the last day for tax reports, I'll do it just for you." She opened her computer, typed in her password and instantly had all the information about the Kaiser Foundation. She clicked on the print icon, closed out the Priority home page, then retrieved the pages from the copier.

"Here you are, Charles."

"Thank you. Oh, Alice, do you need these copies back?"

"I would think so. This information is classified. William would shit a brick if it got into the wrong hands. I did it because of the Kaiser account and you. So, don't tell him."

"I understand. My lips are sealed."

Back in his office, Charles scanned the figures on the printed pages, matching those with the figures on his computer screen. Everything looked good, page after page—until the very bottom of the last page he read, Imposed Custom Expense. He read it again, Imposed Custom Expense.

"What the hell is an Imposed Custom Expense, and $200 thousand." Charles was stunned. That fee didn't show on his report. He's sure the Kaiser Foundation was fully aware of the expense, because someone had to put it there and he never received notice from the

Foundation about this tax. In all his years employed by Priority, Charles never ran across an Imposed Custom Expense.

His curiosity got the best of him, so he closed out the Kaiser file and opened the Castle Premium account. Nothing. No such tax appeared. He opened another account, the same result, nothing. Not a single account managed by Charles, according to his data, contained the questionable expense. That questionable fee only appeared on Priority's reports. Charles wanted to find out if any other agent's accounts were showing that expense, but in order to do that, he needed access to Alice's computer. But how?

He hesitated what to do. Should he call Adolph Kaiser and ask him if he knows about it? Should he ask Alice? What about William? Did anyone from Priority inform him of this and, possibly he forgot about it?

He sat in his office chair, hands folded on top of his head, staring at his computer screen. He glanced at his watch: one-forty-two. For once in his life, he did not know what to do. He was baffled and time was against him, plus the reports needed to be mailed at by the end of the work day. He needed answers.

Charles's eyes focused on his Rolodex. He remembered that Dustin Taylor, a TED brother who graduated with him from DePaul, majored in banking law, and worked in his father's law firm.

He grabbed the Rolodex, found Dustin's card, and dialed his number.

"You've reached the desk of Dustin Taylor. Sorry I cannot take your call, but please leave a number and a short message and I'll return your call as soon as I return to my office. Thank you."

"Dustin. Charles Collier here. Hey, call me ASAP. I need an important question answered, 555-1115. Thanks." He sat silent, contemplating the sudden predicament. He jotted down the numbers from the Imposed Custom Expense listed on the Priority statement, gathered the report papers, and headed to Alice's desk.

"Everything check out okay?"

"Yeah. But Alice, did you ever hear of..." Charles thought quickly, "Dicky Marshall. I think the Bulls just traded him." *Cool move, Charles. Don't mention anything to her until you hear from Dustin.*

"Who? Dicky who? Yeah, right."

"I'll be in my office if you need me."

Charles typed Imposed Custom Expense on the Google search box, then hit enter. Nothing appeared on Google's page. His phone rang, startling him.

"Priority Investments. Charles Collier speaking."

"Charles, Dustin here. So, what's the big question?"

"Hey, thanks for returning my call. I've run across something on a contract that I've never heard or seen before. Have you ever heard of an Imposed Custom Expense?"

"Oooh, that's a new one. I've never heard that either. Wait one second." Dustin put his hand over the receiver, but Charles heard him yelling, "Anyone ever hear of an Imposed Custom Expense or I.C.E. on a contract?"

"Sorry, Charles. Everyone here is shaking their heads. It could be new, but I'll check it out. If I find or hear something, I'll call you right away."

"Thanks, Dustin. I've seen it on one report, but I don't know what the hell it is."

After the phone call, he slouched into his desk chair, wondering where to go from here. Should he pursue it, or just let it ride? Could this be something William and Dennis were planning? What did Ed Weldon say about Dennis? The smell of fish!

Charles didn't have much time to think about his predicament. His report had to be mailed to the Kaiser Foundation, so he packed all the papers in the UPS overnight delivery box and handed it to Alice.

"Everything checks out. You can ship it."

It was a long day for Charles, he was exhausted and very hungry. He couldn't wait to get home and see what Emily had in store for dinner.

***

"Mom, the meal was fantastic."

"I'm glad you liked it, Jack. I'll have to remember to make it again." Emily removed her apron and entered the living room, Charles and Jack were sitting on the sofa. "Hey, why don't we all go see a movie tonight?"

"Oh, cool. Dad, can we? Can we go see the new Jackass movie?"

Charles was still sitting finishing the last few sips of his coffee. A movie would get him out and away from thinking about business, thinking about what William and Reading were up to, and a good time to ease his mind.

"That's a splendid idea, son. I think we all need a night out at the movies."

Donning their coats, the family hiked off to see the latest Jackass movie. Charles wondered what in God's name a Jackass movie would be about? He found out two hours later when Jack asked, "That was a cool movie. Did you like it, Dad?

"Yeah. A bit peculiar, but funny as hell. It's surprising to me, with all those crazy stunts, that more of those characters don't get seriously injured."

"There are several Jackass movies. I think three more. Can we rent all of them, Dad."

"We'll look into it. We'll need to get a new DVD player, our old player isn't working at all."

They decided to walk home, rather than calling a cab, and by coincidence walked past the Loop Appliance store. There it was, sitting in the window. "Ultimate Theater and Sound System, the Sony Theater at Home." That's what the sign in the store window read. It was a 46" Sony Plasma HD Flat Screen, Sony Blu-ray HD DVD player and the Sony 1000 Watt 5.1 Home Theater Sound System, on sale for only $1,999.99.

"Will you look at that! All that for a penny under two thousand dollars. Sounds like a fantastic deal," Charles laughed.

"It's huge, Charles. I don't think it would fit in our living room."

"That's awesome. I can see us playing a Jason Bourne or a Harry Potter movie on that system."

***

Days later, Charles was at his desk when his squawk box bellowed, "Charles, Adolph Kaiser is on line two."

Shit, he found it. Charles was certain that the call might create a problem with the fee charge by William. Charles never knew what I.C.E. was and how would he explain that to Adolph. Would Adolph be extremely upset at an unexplained $200 thousand dollar fee charged by Priority, possibly ending their ties with Priority? Charles really didn't want to answer the call.

"Hello, Mr. Kaiser." Charles nervously paced the office, waiting for the shit to hit the fan.

"Good morning, my dear friend Charles."

"Adolph, are you in town?"

"Oh, no. Still here in New York. You remember that idea we discussed awhile back, about changing the parameters of the tax structure?"

"Yes, I have everything on my computer."

"Well, since it's the start of a new year, we've decided to proceed with the framework and benefit from the changes. We think it's in our best interest, don't you think?"

"Absolutely. It's a good solid structure. You won't go wrong by choosing this program."

"Very well. Just send the documents to our office and I'll get my legal staff to look it over. Then I'll sign the documents and get them back to you."

"It'll take about two or three days, Adolph. As soon as I get them ready, I'll have them in the mail."

"Good. Well, enjoy the rest of your day. Goodbye."

"Thank you. You too."

Whew… The good news gave Charles more time to investigate what William was up to. Maybe the fee was legitimate after all.

An anticipated call from Dustin would let Charles know if the fee was valid or illegal. Then, Charles would have his answer.

Charles thought for a second, wondering who else knew about the Imposed Custom Expense.

The recent news from Adolph Kaiser put Charles in a good mood. He wanted to surprise Emily and Jack with something they would enjoy for Christmas. After work, he drove to Loop Appliance. As he walked past the store window, he stopped and visualized how excited Jack would be, sitting in front of their new plasma TV watching a Harry Potter movie.

"Yes, sir. My name is Bill. How may I help you?"

"I saw that home theater system in the window. I'm thinking about purchasing one."

"Excellent choice. Follow me." As Bill and Charles walked to another Sony Home Theater inside the store, Bill explained how it performed, and demonstrated the complete system.

"Great. Exactly what I'm looking for. This will be a great Christmas present for my wife and son."

"You'll love this system. It comes with a two-year warranty on all parts and labor. And during our Christmas sale, we've included free delivery and setup."

"Wow, excellent. When can I schedule that?"

"Any day except Christmas Day. We're closed."

Charles followed Bill to the checkout counter to fill out the invoice.

"Looks like Monday, the twenty-second. Would the morning or afternoon better for you?"

"Any time. My wife doesn't work, so she should be home."

"Could you please fill out the top part of the invoice? Name, address, phone number."

Charles started filling out the information while Bill punched numbers on his calculator.

"Your total comes to two thousand, two-hundred-eleven dollars and eighty-nine cents. Are you paying by credit card or check?"

"Check."

"I'll need a form of identification, a driver's license will do."

Charles handed his check and license to Bill. The entertainment system was now his.

"Okay. We'll be there Monday morning. I'll have the service-man call this number to let your wife know approximately what time he'll be there. Sound good?"

"Yes, very good. Thank you."

By the middle of the next week, Charles and Emily were enjoying the new home entertainment center as much as Jack was. They'd lost count how many times Harry

Potter movies were played, but Charles was able to relax, especially after talking with Adolph Kaiser. Maybe he was making more out of the situation than it actually was. The more he thought about what he uncovered, the more he was convinced that Adolph's Foundation knew about the mysterious $200 thousand expense in favor of Priority Investments.

Monday morning, Charles went to work as if nothing happened. Getting his coffee, stopping at Alice's desk to pick up his messages from the weekend, and going to his desk. He planned to spend most of the morning checking the stock market and which stocks on the Kaiser account were stable, which were rising or losing strength.

Dennis entered Charles's office and leaned on his desk. "I think some changes are needed to some of these portfolios. Some stocks are old and stagnant and I think we should update them and replace the ones that aren't doing so well."

"Good idea. Sorry, I haven't spent much time with you on these, but this Kaiser account is taking up all my time."

"No problem. Just buzz me when you want to sit down and go over them."

"Okay. I'll try to finish up here shortly. When I get this organized, I'll call you."

Dennis picked up his folders and left the office as Alice entered.

"Morning, Charles." She dropped the mail on his desk and exited his office. He picked up the envelopes and scanned through them. Most were junk mail that he tossed into the waste basket, but the last envelope was from the Kaiser Foundation. He opened it to discover that he was invited to the fifth annual Kaiser Foundation Award Dinner in New York on February 13th, 7 pm at the Waldorf Astoria Hotel. He looked to see what day fell on February 13th. A Saturday.

Damn it. Just what I need, another trip to New York. There was no way he could skip out on Adolph Kaiser and his foundation. The gala date was only six weeks away, and

Charles needed to answer the invitation. He leaned forward, rolled his index cards to locate Adolph's number, and began dialing.

"The Kaiser Foundation."

"Adolph Kaiser, please. Charles Collier calling."

"One moment, please."

"This is Adolph Kaiser."

"Adolph, Charles Collier here. I received your invitation this morning."

"Lucky you," Adolph chuckled. "Yes. You'll enjoy this, believe me. The folks at the Astoria are fabulous. Food, the drinks, entertainment, and lots of well-known people will be attending."

"I'm excited that you invited me. I can't wait to get there."

"It's always exciting, so bring your wife with you. You'll need a dance partner."

"That I will, and thank you again. I'll see you in February."

"Goodbye, Charles."

When Charles arrived home from work, he handed the invitation to Emily.

"This will be one hell of a party. It's at the Waldorf Astoria, the most famous hotel in the United States."

Emily read the invitation, but her mind was on another party. Not at the Waldorf Astoria, but a party with Sergio and his dope. Her mind was racing to concoct some sort of wild excuse to get her out of going to New York.

"Charles, what are we going to do with Jack? And February

13th, I think that's the Saturday Carol and I bought tickets for a new play. I can't let her go alone."

"Sure you can. I'm sure she'll understand. It's six weeks away. I would think she could find someone else to take your place, don't you think?"

"You don't know Carol. If I back out on her now, he'll never talk to me again."

"Did I hear you right, you said he'll?"

Suddenly, Emily realized her slip-up. "I never said he'll, your hearing is getting bad. I said she'll. Besides, Carol lives in the far suburbs and will be very pissed off if I stand her up."

Charles left the kitchen shaking his head. He'd change into something more relaxing, then watch a show on his new toy. Emily was still spinning the wheels in her head. *He's not buying it.* She had to think of something better than going out with Carol. Her only choice was Jack. Emily sat down next to Charles on the sofa, cuddling up to him.

"Honey. Jack is only eighteen years old. There's no way we can leave him by himself. And…I don't think it would be wise to take him to New York and let him spend a night cooped up in a hotel room. It's just not fair to him."

"All right, all right. I get your point loud and clear. I'll go alone." The tone of Charles's voice became belligerent.

Jack came into the living room. "Dad, I'll challenge you to a game of Madden football."

"You're on, buddy boy."

Chapter 11

If a Hummingbird Could Talk

It was Saturday morning, February 13th. Charles had his bags packed, ready to leave for the airport. "Hey, Jack. I think there's going to be some very famous people at this party. You want some autographs?"

"You mean like Derek Lawson, Payton Johnson, or Michael Conlon?"

"Well, I'll see. I'll do my best and talk to Mr. Kaiser. He'll make sure I get some good autographs."

Charles hugged Jack and put on his heavy wool topcoat, then walked into the kitchen and hugged Emily. "Enjoy the play and tell Carol I said hello."

Emily tried to hide the guilt. "I will. You enjoy yourself and we'll see you tomorrow, I guess."

When the front door closed, Emily scrambled into her bedroom. She opened the drawer containing her underwear and bras, uncovering the yellow napkin with Sergio's number on it. She hid it there because Charles would never open that drawer. It was personal and private.

She went into the bathroom with the napkin and her cell phone, where there would be less chance of Jack hearing her conversation. She dialed the number from the napkin and after a few rings, Sergio answered.

"Sergio. Emily."

"Miss party girl. Your husband must be out of town."

"Yes. Anything going on for tonight?"

"It's Saturday night, Emily. There are parties all over. Listen, I'll call you back in a little bit."

"Okay. I'll wait for your call." Emily closed her cell and returned to the living room, where Jack was watching a basketball game on ESPN.

"You remember that Carol and I are going to the play tonight, right?"

"Yeah. You've told me about a thousand times already."

"Well. What do you say we go out for breakfast? After we eat, we can shop for some new movies or another game. That sound like fun to you?"

"Really. I'm up for that." Jack hustled to his bedroom to change clothes. In record time, he was standing in front of Emily, waiting to fill his empty stomach.

They walked several blocks to a small mall just off Oak Street. They ate breakfast at a family restaurant and purchased two movies for Jack. She had one more thing to do. She needed to stop at Walgreen's to pick up her birth control prescription, to prepare for that upcoming party.

"Visions of Love" by Mariah Carey played on her Blackberry, letting her know she had an incoming call. She opened her cell, and heard Sergio's voice.

"Emily. Three-four-four Lexington Court in Crayton. Party starts around nine. I'll meet you there."

"Hold on. Let me write down the address. Got it. See you there."

The excitement in her body was pumping up. She wasn't familiar with the Crayton area, but as soon as she got home, she Googled the address. There it was. A map and a printed outline of directions. She printed the page and stuffed it in her purse.

By early afternoon, Charles had checked into the Waldorf Astoria. His room was on the fifth floor, room 517 and when he exited the elevator, inlaid gold plaques mounted on the corridor wall indicated the direction of his room. Once inside, he was amazed at what he saw. The room was large, larger than he expected, embodied a very stylish decor, probably 18th Century. The room contained a seating area with a sofa, wide screen plasma TV, a mini-bar and a working desk. Beyond the seating area, a set of white French doors led to the bedroom. He passed through the doors and saw a queen-size bed, another plasma TV, and off to his right, a spacious marble bathroom. He set his luggage on the bed and began to unpacked his clothes, hanging up his tuxedo, and putting his toiletries in the bathroom. A small clock on the nightstand displayed 3:10 pm, and since the gala event wasn't starting till 7:30 that evening, Charles decided to take a short nap. He has never attended an event with so much prestige and glamour, therefore, getting some rest would benefit him because he assumed the party would last well into the wee hours of the morning.

***

The keys for the Escalade were hanging on the wall next to the refrigerator. Emily put them in her coat pocket and walked to where Jack was watching his new videos.

"I'm going. So, under no circumstances let anyone into the house when both of us are gone. You understand?"

"You tell me that every time you go out and nothing has happened."

"I know. I just love you and don't want anything to happen to you. I won't be late."

The silver Cadillac was heading north on Interstate 94 and trusting the GPS mounted in her dashboard, a woman's voice from the GPS informed her Ravenwood Drive was one mile ahead. She steered as instructed and drove until her next command.

"Turn left on Lexington Court."

Emily located house number 344, turned off the engine, pulled down the visor, and took one last look at her makeup.

Am I that early? Her watch read 9:20 pm. Well, she wasn't early, but noticed only two other cars in the driveway. She rang the lighted doorbell button, moments later, a tall, curly-haired man answered the door.

"And you must be Emily. Am I right?"

"That I am. And you are?"

"Myron. Come in, come in."

***

When was the last time I wore a tux? Charles stood before the mirror, making sure he looked proper and ready for the occasion. This was the only time he could remember he'd ever worn a tuxedo. Didn't need one for his senior prom, or graduation, or even his wedding. Well, there was always that first time. Convinced the mirror reflected his handsome characteristics, Charles made his way to the Grand Ballroom.

The lobby outside the ballroom was packed with celebrities, sports figures, entertainers, and movie stars. Standing among the crowd, Charles felt somewhat subdued. With all these famous people attending, he seemed out of place. What a blessing it was for him that Adolph had invited him to such a prestigious event. He smiled to himself, understanding how important the Kaiser Foundation was to Adolph and how important it was to the city of New York.

A long line of guests formed outside the doors of the ballroom, patiently waiting to greet Mr. Kaiser. If Charles only had Emily with him, maybe the tension would be easier to handle. As the line of celebrities filtered into the ballroom, Charles caught a glimpse of Adolph standing with his wife and welcoming the guests as they entered.

"Charles. We're very happy you made it. Where is your beautiful wife?"

"A last-minute emergency. Our son Jack has come down with the flu, so sorry she couldn't make it and wanted to meet you in the worse way."

"Oh, I'm so sorry to hear that. Well, you go in and enjoy the fun.

Mingle with the guests, maybe you can drum up some business." Adolph shook Charles's hand and patted him on the shoulder as Charles disappeared into the sea of lustrous, gifted celebrities.

***

As soon as Emily entered the house, it's appearance paralyzed her. The house was bare. She noticed no furniture, no pictures on the wall, no curtains on the windows, nothing. She saw only a floor lamp, a folding table with four chairs, and two other people, Sergio and a scantly dressed young woman.

What kind of party is this?

Sergio excused himself from the young woman.

"Emily, you made it. What can I get you to drink?"

"Gosh. Anything."

Sergio seized her hand as they walked into the kitchen area, where she saw numerous bottles of whiskey, rum, vodka, and wine. The first bottle she saw was a bottle of Absolut vodka.

"Vodka would be fine," she responded.

Sergio dropped a few ice cubes into a plastic cup. No need for a shot glass, not at this party. He poured a significant amount of vodka over the ice and finished it off with a splash of Seven-Up and handed it to Emily.

Once she had her drink, Sergio lifted his glass and pronounced, "Let the party begin."

Emily raised her glass in response. She swallowed a long gulp from her cup, a bit strong, but it hit the spot.

"Emily, I want you to meet Isabella. Isabella, this is Emily. Now, everyone knows everyone."

The drinks were flowing and so were the scandalous white lines. All four were talking the same talk, similar to what you would hear at the Crowd Pleaser. By then, Emily was well aware only the four of them would be attending this party.

From drink to drink and line to line, Emily was back where she felt most comfortable. The life of enchanted excitement. The drugs took her soul. Not a care in the world, not any thoughts of Charles or Jack, just partying.

After awhile, Sergio stood and announced, "I think it's time, people."

Isabella and Myron began clapping, hollering, and dancing around the table.

Okay, thought Emily, *time for what?*

Sergio put his hands around Emily's waist and nudged her toward the stairs. The group ascended the stairway till all reached the top. It was a small bedroom, but as she approached the room, it contained a king sized circular bed and nothing else. Above the bed, hung a lighted crystal chandelier with an exposed light bulb. She knew exactly what kind of party laid ahead of her.

***

When guests entered the Grand Ballroom, the hostess handed each a placard directing them to their assigned table, and the names of the guests joining them. Charles was assigned to table number fourteen, joining Ms. Nancy Soothers, Director of Foundation Personnel, Mr. and Mrs. Jordan Cumbers, social advisory to Mr. Kaiser, and Ms. Sonja O'Neal, singer and actress.

Once inside the massive ballroom, his breath escaped him. He felt like he was on the set of a major movie production. The huge ceilings decorated with elaborate woodwork and glowing chandeliers, the colorful drapes that hugged each window, and numerous paintings that lined the ballroom walls. Slowly, he maneuvered to his table and sat down. Immediately, his eyes focused on the vase of flowers and a small, colorful bird sitting among the flowers. It was a mechanical hummingbird, a radiant red and effervescent green bird with its wings flapping and its long beak probing a flower. Everyone seated thought the hummingbird was real and alive. How cool was that? Emily would love having this on her kitchen table.

Soon, everyone had found their seats and waited patiently for the event to start. They all introduced themselves, but the conversation centered around the colorful hummingbird. It was amazing to watch the bird, so lifelike and colorful.

The imported egg white china, pure silver dinnerware, crystal water glasses and wine glasses were stunning. There were two bottles of wine, a red and white, and a carafe of champagne to satisfy anyone's taste. Placed on each dinner plate was a menu of the evening's entrees and a booklet outlining the success of the Kaiser Foundation. The table settings were perfect, as if you were sitting down having dinner with the President of the United States.

"Welcome, welcome." Adolph, wearing a black tuxedo with a vibrant red satin cummerbund, stood behind a long eloquently dressed head table with a microphone in his hand, flanked by his beautiful wife, Ingrid. The crowd applauded.

"Thank you, thank you. Everyone from the Foundation welcomes you to our fifth gala event. This is a very special night for us. It could not be possible without your generous contributions. So, from the bottom of my heart, I personally thank you. Enjoy the wine, the fabulous dinner, and when you are finished, please glance through the booklet about the Foundation. Bon appétit."

As soon as Adolph sat down, the waiters and waitresses began swarming all the tables, filling the water glasses, pouring the wine and champagne. And if guests were ready, taking their dinner order. Charles studied his menu list, which included cured Alaskan Salmon, roasted Duck Magret, Veal Agnolotti, and Filet of Beef au Poivre. Jesus! How fancy he thought.

He was never a person to stick his neck out and attempt something exotic. So, he was a beef lover and the filet is what he'd order along with a Mesclun salad.

"Ms. O'Neal, what an honor to be sitting next to you. I try to follow most of your movies. I loved *"Silent Evidence."*

"Of all my movies, that was my favorite. It was exciting making that movie and I worked with a great cast, too."

"Sorry that I haven't seen more of your movies, but my job doesn't allow me much time."

"Really. What line of work are you involved in?"

"I'm an investment consultant for the Foundation and Mr. Kaiser."

"Oh. I can understand why that takes most of your time, then."

"This is quite a spectacle, isn't it? Is this your first time here?" asked Charles.

"Yes. Adolph always goes overboard with this event. It's a great cause he's doing."

The waiter started to clean their table, leaving just the wine and champagne, and of course the hummingbird.

"This is my first year attending the gala. I hope it's not my last."

"By the way, Charles. Do you have a business card with you? I've been mulling over my finances and thinking about investing a little money for my future."

"I'll make a deal with you. I'll give you my business card in exchange for your autograph."

"You got a deal." Sonja reached for her pen and signed her name to the Kaiser booklet. In return, Charles handed her his business card.

***

You didn't have to draw Emily a picture. Four people, one bed, and plenty of action. She knew exactly what it was time for. As they surrounded the bed, Isabella began to remove her clothing, followed by Sergio and Myron. They were naked, looking at Emily, waiting for her to join them. Isabella had a superb body, a body that made Emily envious. Myron? Well Myron was Myron, nothing to write home about., a hairy chest, signs of a developing sizable beer belly, and below average to what Emily thrived. When Emily's eyes saw Sergio, it was time for her to join the crowd. Sergio had what Emily wanted.

Within seconds, she was naked and squirming up to Sergio. She wanted him all night. The night was non-stop sex. From switching positions to switching partners, Emily was at her best.

The simple, innocent housewife became a ferocious, ungovernable little nymph. The hours passed, the activities slowed down—Emily had passed out.

The bare, single light bulb chandelier hanging from the unpainted ceiling shined in Emily's eyes, awakening her. Her eyes opened wide, her mind open wider. Where was she? Startled, her eyes frantically searched the room. Nothing she saw registered, just a round bed, a bare light bulb, and numerous soiled condoms lying on the floor. No one but her, alone on the bed. She located her clothing next to a glass tray filled with dope. *Fuck!*

Her groin ached as she pried herself from the bed, the tears swelled in her eyes, *What have I gotten myself into? Where's Jack? What time is it?*

In a panic, she realized she had to get home before Jack left for school. If she didn't, how was she going to explain everything to Charles? Agitated, Emily collected her clothes and hurried to get dressed, she dashed out the bedroom door and down the stairs into the kitchen. Lying on the floor, still naked, was Sergio, still passed out. Getting home as soon as she could was the only thing on her mind. She found her purse on the counternext to the booze. But wait! There was a plastic bag beside her purse that was half-full of the white powder. She looked over to where Sergio was lying, motionless. He could be dead for all she knew…then glanced back to the plastic bag, should she or shouldn't she. She did.

She ran out the door to her car and for her, luckily, it was still dark out. The dashboard clock read 4:35, but was it am. or pm.? All she wanted to do was get back to Cedar Street in a hurry, and without getting stopped. Jesus! If the cops stopped her with all she drank and sniffed, and possession of drugs, she might as well kill herself now.

She was convinced she must quit using drugs because sooner or later she would lose everything, a shame to Charles and Jack. She flipped on the lights near the visor and looked into the visor mirror.

God. Is this really me? She turned off the visor lights and concentrated on getting home. She made it without getting stopped. *Thank God. Home at last.* She found the keys to the front door and entered the condo. The condo was very quiet, dark and Jack was still asleep. She rushed to her bathroom, removed her soiled clothes and jumped into the shower. Once she passed the test of being human again, she tiptoed into the kitchen, deposited a pod into the Keurig and waited for her brew. Her body ached and so did her guilt. She began to cry, so guilty.

***

The gala was coming to an end. Adolph spoke to the crowd, thanking them for attending his special night. Charles accumulated several autographs and couldn't wait to get home and show them to Jack. He also confiscated one last souvenir, the mechanical hummingbird for Emily. He had one autograph in particular that he knew Jack would flip over. Derek Lawson, the All-Star shortstop for the Yankees, the photograph signed and addressed to Jack. He'd have to frame it and put it on his dresser. When the crowd thinned out, Charles approached Adolph to thank him personally.

"Adolph. What an incredible night. I can't remember the last time I had so much fun. Meeting famous people, just an unbelievable experience."

"That's what this Foundation Gala is all about, Charles."

"Well, goodnight. I ate so much and drank so much, I'm beat."

Charles drifted to the elevators and joined the rest of the people waiting for the doors to open. They filed in, the doors closed, and a voice rang out, "What floor, please?"

"Five."

Ding…The doors opened to the fifth floor. Charles reached into his pocket and removed the plastic card to his room. Approaching his door, he noticed a blond woman standing in the corridor near his door. As he got closer, he recognized Sonja O'Neal.

"Sonja, are you lost?"

"No, I don't think so."

"Is your room around here?"

"No. I thought I'd like to get to know you better. Maybe talk about some stocks." Her powerful blue eyes were telling Charles that there was no way Sonja wanted to talk about stocks at this time of the night.

Charles inserted the plastic card into the door slot. "Really. I don't think..."

The little green light appeared on the door lock, the door opened and so did Charles's options.

Chapter 12

The I.C.E. Is Melting!

As the weeks passed, Charles wrestled about the mysterious fee William has charged all the oversea accounts. Were any of the clients aware of such a fee? This bothered Charles and he was determined to get to the bottom of it. He decided that the next time Adolph called, he would discreetly ask him if he knew about I.C.E. If Adolph wasn't aware, then William was up to something illegal. With all the legal help and advisers the foundation employed, you would think that someone, by accident, would stumble across the $200 thousand dollar fee. Later that week, Charles got his chance.

"Charles. Adolph Kaiser is on line one."

"Thank you, Alice." Charles pressed the speaker button on his phone, "Adolph, are you having another party?"

"Good morning, Charles. No. Time to recuperate. My staff has informed me that your latest modifications to our portfolio are doing very good. So, I just wanted to let you know how pleased we all are."

"Thank you, Adolph. That's my job. Every day, I study the latest stocks and markets. Speaking of that, our office received a letter from the FTC about a new tax they are proposing. It's called an Imposed Custom Expense..." The bomb had dropped. Adolph's answer would immediately tell Charles about William's intentions.

"Not another tax! Will that damage or improve our investments?"

"Can you check with your advisers and ask them about this Imposed Custom Expense?"

***

"That's a new one on me. Let me write that down. But, I'll ask them. Once you find out what the FTC proposes, please let us know as soon as possible."

"From what I'm reading, and after talks with my colleagues, I think it's highly unlikely that it will ever surface. I spent some time on the Internet gathering the feedback regarding their recommendations. It's not very favorable, so I wouldn't worry too much about it, Adolph."

"Very well. I'll let you get back to your work."

"If I hear anything, I'll call you immediately. Goodbye."

In all the years Charles worked for William, never has he been so disturbed and perplexed. After the hiring of Dennis and the incidents he's heard about him, Charles knew both of them were planning something that was very wrong. Charles relaxed into his leather desk chair. *Okay. William, I'd love to hear your explanation about this.* Charles looked at the amazing shoreline off Lake Michigan through his large office window. The snow and ice left over from the winter began to disappear. Several scenarios sifted through Charles's mind. If it was illegal and he knew it, why is he charging this fee? What is he up to? Is he in financial trouble? Who else knows about I.C.E. and is Alice involved?

Trying to obtain information from either William, Dennis, or Alice would be difficult, especially if they were hiding something. There's $200 thousand that Fossett has confiscated from the Kaiser account alone. Charles had several routes open to him, which was the right one?

First, confront William and tell him you know about I.C.E. Second, inform the FTC about the illegal activities at Priority. Third, ignore the entire situation. Or fourth, strike a deal with

William and walk away with a good chunk of money in his pocket.

***

Charles fought with his conscience. The more he thought about his fourth option, the more he felt just like being William himself. What was the right thing to do? How much money was in that I.C.E account? He remembered talking to Dustin and if there were new laws regarding the investment industry, then he would definitely know. He dialed his number.

"Dustin Taylor."

"Dustin, its Charles. Anything on the Imposed Custom Expense?"

"Nothing, Charles. I looked up every link imaginable. There's nothing regarding that subject matter. I talked to other experienced lawyers in our office. Still a blank. I even talked to an agent at the FTC. So, either someone is pulling your leg or something illegal is going on."

"Very well. Thanks, again, Dustin. Maybe it was a misprint, or maybe I didn't read it right. Anyway, I do appreciate your help. I'll talk to you later. Bye."

"No problem. Anytime, Charles."

***

Over the next couple of weeks, Charles kept an eagle's eye on William, Dennis, and even Alice. He couldn't overlook any mistake that would backfire on him and cause mass hysteria throughout the office. Methodically, he listened and watched all their moves.

He checked and double-checked everything he saw or heard from any of them. He knew he would have William over a barrel, but were the risks worth the consequences? He needed time to think. If it backfired on him, chances are he'd loose his job over it. The possibility of discussing it with Emily was another alternative, but what help would she be? There was one very important clue sitting in Priority's financial documents, he needed to find out how much money was in that I.C.E account. Once he had that figure, then he'd know the consequences.

***

His first move was to probe Dennis, further. He found him in the break room, depositing quarters into the vending machine that produced the imitation of coffee.

"Hey, Dennis. When you're not busy, can you drop by my office?"

"Sure. What's up?"

"Just a follow-up on some stocks I came across. Some might benefit their portfolios. Grab Castle Premium, World Wide Tire, and Osaku International."

"No problem. I'll be there in a few minutes."

Dennis removed his coffee from the machine and snatched a doughnut from a tray of treats. When he reached Charles's office, Charles closed the door and stood near the large office window.

"All right. Let's tackle Castle first. All their stocks seem to be promising, so no readjustment there."

"Check."

"World Wide Tire. We may want to suggest a multiyear equity index strategy to them, so mark that down. As far as their annuity, the S&P 500 is doing fine, so leave that as it is. The Imposed Custom Expense, change the rate from two per cent to three." Charles immediately looked for a reaction on Dennis's face.

"Excuse me, Charles. Imposed…what's that? I don't recall seeing that expense."

"Well, hmm. It's on this report. Check the other two."

Charles studied Dennis's reactions, hoping he'd screw up.

Could he be telling the truth and not know anything about I.C.E.?

***

"Nothing. I've never seen or heard that before. What is it?"

"Well, they're on here. These are your figures, right? You must have put them on here, didn't you?"

"Yeah, but no. I didn't enter them."

"Hmm. It might be a new tax the FTC has imposed this year and it's possible that William entered them without telling us. I'll ask him. Anyway, leave the portfolios here. I'll jump on the Internet and check all this out. I'll call you when I find out, okay. If you hear or read anything about this custom expense, let me know right away."

Dennis left the office. *Well, that didn't work.* Still not sure if Dennis was telling the truth, Charles couldn't deviate from his plan. He sat with his hands clasped, thinking…*I'm sure Dennis will mention this to William? If he does, then I was right. I now know why Dennis was hired. Time would tell.*

***

That night after dinner, Charles couldn't forget about the meeting he had with Dennis from his mind. Unsure whether Dennis was telling the truth bugged him. Tomorrow, he would talk to Dennis and ask him again, if he knew how that expense got on those portfolios. After all, they've been in his possession for more than six months. He must have some excuse as to why they were on there or how they got on there.

"Dad?"

Charles sat at the dining room table in a trance, not aware of anyone or anything around him.

"Dad. . .?"

"Yeah, son. Did you say something?"

"The Sox have a spring training game on TV tonight. Wanna watch it with me?"

***

Charles's first reaction was, baseball, already? He stared at Jack, thinking of the how soon they'll be able to attend a few Sox games this year. Jack was a big fan and really enjoyed going to the games with his father.

"Sure thing. Let's see who's new on this team this year."

"You know he loves being with you." Emily stood behind him, rubbing his shoulders.

"You're right. Things are going to change around here."

Charles stood up and hugged his wife.

***

The next morning at his office, Charles buzzed Alice, "Alice, could you tell Dennis I need to see him as soon as he gets in?"

"I don't think that will be possible, Charles. He's on his way to Switzerland this morning. Won't be back till Monday."

"Aah, I remember. Okay, thank you."

Chapter 13

The Truth Comes Out

When Dennis traveled overseas, majority of his contacts were in Switzerland. That's what Priority had and plenty of, big spending corporations that depended on huge tax write offs and Switzerland was the hot spot. There were only three cities in Switzerland that the agents traveled to, either Geneva, Zurich, or Bern. For Dennis, business days in those cities consisted of long, extensive hours involving negotiations and securing complicated contracts, leaving him scarce time to become a tourist. All were fantastic cities, but if Dennis had to select his favorite place, it was Bern.

On this trip, Sommerfeld Oil was the corporation he would be representing. They were new to Priority, a very wealthy Texas family that profited in the oil industry. Their portfolio was put together by William, but given to Dennis to negotiate. He always followed William's instructions and today, he'd find out. The meeting with Mr. Lans Schneider, Vice President of the Rothschild Bank in Bern, at times, an arduous person to negotiate with, would begin at eleven that morning. William instructed Dennis to be patient, courteous and remain quiet, sooner or later, Schneider would conclude the deal.

Although Dennis had visited the Rothschild Bank twice before, this would be his first encounter with the vice president. The delicate process of opening a new account, the process dealing with a new investor, and meeting with a very important person, made Dennis a bit uneasy. He was positive he had all his "I's" dotted and his "T's" crossed, but wanted to make a successful impression on Mr. Schneider.

When he arrived in Bern, he booked a room at the Warwick Hotel, a hotel he was familiar with. The amenities that the Warwick presented were impeccable, from their world-renowned restaurant, to the meritorious services, and even to the astounding wine bar. The plastic room key for room 1132 opened his door. He removed his suit coat, tie, and trousers, and hung them in the hall closet. From there, he moved to a small desk near the only window in his room where he placed the stack of papers that he'd present to Mr. Schneider. He was sure all the information and figures were solid and ready for Mr. Schneider's view. But, one more look wouldn't hurt. *Looks good to me.*

The wake-up call from the front desk rang twice on the room phone. It was 7:30 am, enough time to shower, shave and dress, then catch a quick breakfast in the restaurant before heading to the Rothschild Bank. The Warwick's restaurant offered its guests a Continental breakfast of German pastries, oatmeal and cereal, and a variety of toasts, coffee and tea. Once he finished his coffee, he secured his briefcase, and headed toward the presentation.

A brisk walk of about three blocks brought him to the entrance of the Rothschild Bank. He stumbled through the revolving doors and proceeded to the long, massive oak desk in the lobby. While standing, waiting, he read the small, gold- painted sign with bold black lettering, "Information Desk."

"Welcome to Rothschild Bank. How may I help you?"

"Could you please inform Mr. Lans Schneider that Dennis Reading is here to see him?" He handed the young lady a business card and watched her disappear around the corner of the lobby. Moments later she returned, walking side-by-side with an elderly, short, stocky man. Mr. Schneider was wearing a brown, three-piece tweed suit, a flashy yellow bow tie, and a noticeable gold chain dangling from a pocket on his vest. It was exactly what Dennis anticipated, typical Bavarian fashion.

"Mr. Reading, Lans Schneider here. So nice to meet you. And very punctual. Exactly eleven o'clock. I like that. Follow me and we can conduct our business in my office."

Dennis accompanied the vice-president with a brisk walk to his office. When Dennis entered the office, a quick scan of the office inculcated to Dennis that Mr. Schneider was a very well-organized person. Everything in its correct place, from the placement of his business cards to the neatly stacked books lining the shelves behind his office chair. Not a speck of dust, not a misplaced paperclip, nothing was out of order. He wondered if his proposal was as organized as Schneider was. He would soon find out.

"Well, now. Let me see your portfolio on your client."

Hearing that, Dennis reached for his briefcase and withdrew the accumulation of papers, handed them to Schneider, then settled back into his chair. He remembered what William warned him about Schneider. Be patient. It seemed that time stood still while Schneider looked over the papers. Dennis watched him meticulously reading every page, checking all the figures. He removed a calculator from the top drawer and punched in numbers from the papers in front of him. An hour passed.

Jesus. I wonder if Charles had dealt with him before? Talk about being thorough.

Dennis tried to hurry the meeting by keeping silent, not disturbing Schneider, and letting him finish his inspection. Another hour passed.

"Well done, Mr. Reading. Everything looks agreeable. I'll have my secretary make copies and get it sealed and notarized. How does that sound to you?"

"Perfect."

Schneider summoned his secretary and informed her to make copies of all the paperwork.

"Now that we've accomplished that, how about joining me for lunch today?"

"Mr. Schneider, I'd love to. But I have friends waiting for me at Interlaken. I promised them I'd meet them as soon as my meeting ended here."

"Yes, of course. I understand. Interlaken is a very beautiful place. Especially this time of the year. I take my family there a lot. They love it."

The secretary returned with the papers and copies and set them on Schneider's desk. Schneider began signing the documents, and passed each one to Dennis for his signature. Once the papers were finally signed and sealed, Dennis locked them in his briefcase.

"Very good. I know my clients have made the right choice in selecting the Rothschild Bank. As soon as I return to Chicago, I'll meet with them to explain everything. Just as soon as I get their approval, the funds will be transferred into your bank."

"I'll look forward to that. In the meantime, enjoy your time with your friends at Interlaken."

They rose and shook hands. The meeting was over. Dennis had the rest of the weekend to be a tourist, by himself.

***

From the Rothschild Bank, Dennis returned to the Warwick Hotel, dressed into a more relaxed attire, retrieved his luggage from his room, and checked out. The time was 2:25 pm and early enough for him to take his time driving to Interlaken, approximately one hundred miles away. Now that his business was finished, he had one more priority ahead of him, obtaining information regarding the real estate market in Interlaken. During the two-hour drive, Dennis had time to contemplate all the scenarios surrounding him. How would he benefit if William's plan paid off? How much money would be coming his way? He thought about Helen and if he asked her, would she come to Switzerland with him? All that depended on William's plan. He was well aware of the relationship Helen had with her brother, even telling Dennis numerous times that she would kill William if the opportunity presented itself. Dennis thought about that and started to think of a plan of his own. Let William do all the work, get the money to Switzerland, then eliminate William. It sounded logical and Helen would absolutely go along with it. The thought of money, escaping to another country, spending his life with Helen, it all spelled out...greed.

As soon as he arrived, he looked for the first available real estate office. There it was, settled a few hundred feet off the road, and built exactly the way Dennis viewed his house would look. An A-frame, with log cabin features with all the chalet motif characteristics of Switzerland. He went inside and met the only agent in the office. His name was Rodney Schintz, a middle aged, blond haired chap who guided Dennis to his office desk. They chatted about Dennis's job, how often he came to Switzerland, the usual gibberish before Dennis was ready to talk business. He explained to the agent what exactly what he was looking for, where he wanted to live and $400 thousand was his

comfort range. Within several minutes, Dennis had multiple listings and the agents card in his hand, he thanked Rodney and goodbye.

The Lindner Grand Hotel Beaurivage was the hotel Dennis saw when he left the real estate office. It was a building that you had to see in person to believe the allure, the elegant Swiss motif. It helped make Interlaken the city that swept you off your feet. Dennis felt like a king when he stayed there, because all the personnel treated him like royalty. Since the meeting with the real estate agent took longer than Dennis anticipated, there would be no time left to visit the surroundings so he decided to book into the hotel, catch an early dinner, then relax in his room. It would be a good time to sit in front of the fireplace sipping on a glass of wine and reading through the information the real estate agent gave him. There were numerous houses on the market, a good time to buy, the agent informed him, and a wide variety of price ranges. A small comfortable place would keep him happy and having Helen by his side, this would be his ultimate destination in life.

The fire from the fireplace kept the room warm and cozy, his glass of wine was empty, so Dennis decided to call it quits for the night. He pulled back the covers, climbed into the warm bed, laying there thinking... *how did Charles find out about I.C.E.?*

***

On his way to the office Monday morning, Charles knew that Dennis would be back from Switzerland. He wanted to meet with him as soon as he was available and ask him how the I.C.E. expense landed on his smaller accounts. If Charles had any way to prove William was illegally defrauding his investors, it had to be through Dennis. Charles wasn't sure about Alice, but he did remember her remark about getting information into the wrong hands. Why did she make that remark? If he could squeeze any incriminating information from Dennis, one little slip-up, then maybe a deal with William would be in order. With his normal morning routine over, Charles took his cup of coffee and headed toward Alice's desk to pick up his messages from the weekend. He briefed through his messages, sipping his coffee when...

"Alice, send Dennis into my office now." William's tenor voice blared out from her intercom.

"Yes, Mr. Fossett, as soon as he comes in, I'll send him to your office." Moments later, Dennis entered through the glass doors of Priority, holding a cup of coffee in his left hand.

"William wants you in his office. ASAP."

Dennis raised his right hand, acknowledging the command and headed for William's office.

Charles stood at the corner of Alice's desk, set his coffee down, and glanced through his messages. As soon as Dennis disappeared from sight, Charles turned to Alice.

"The other day, you mentioned to me about specific information getting into the wrong hands. What did you mean by that?"

"Well...I was just..." Alice stopped as soon as she heard William's voice blurting from her intercom box.

"Come in. Sit down." Alice looked up to Charles realizing that William forgot to turn off his intercom.

"I'm ready and I believe it's time to get the ball rolling. The seven million is there and I'm ready to pull the trigger. What do you think, are you ready?"

"Well. I'm ready when you are. You're the boss. But, there's something I think you should know. Charles knows about I.C.E."

"What!" William screamed. "How?"

"Yeah. He and I were looking over a couple of his smaller accounts on Thursday, and he asked me about it. I played dumb and acted as if I didn't know what he was talking about. I think he believed me."

"How'd he find out? It was Alice. I should've known better with her. That stupid whore. I knew she'd be trouble all along. I should've gotten rid of her when I had the chance years ago."

"Taking care of her will be much easier than dealing with Charles."

"You're right about that. He's smart, too smart. My plan didn't include him finding out about that money."

Alice and Charles stood motionless, shocked by what they were listening to.

"Did you hear him? He called me a stupid…?"

Charles said nothing, but put a finger to his lips. *Ssshh.*

They listened to the incriminating information leaking through the incriminating black box.

"Come over to the house tonight. By then, I'll have everything in order and I'll explain it to you. Say, about seven, okay?"

"I'll be there."

"I'll have to figure out how to shut up Alice."

Charles grabbed Alice by the arm and pushed her into the office storeroom behind her desk, then closed the door.

"What do you know about I.C.E.?"

"Nothing. I don't know anything about it. Honest. All I know is what William told me: Don't print out any Priority statements without his authorization."

"Something is going on here illegally. From what I saw on those statements, William is fraudulently charging all the oversea accounts and it's in the thousands. $200 thousand to the Kaiser account, alone."

"Holy shit."

"I'm not sure what I can do. I thought something smelled fishy when he hired Reading."

"What do you suppose he meant by "taking care of me?"

"And me!"

"Quick. Open Priority's financial page. See how much is in that I.C.E. account."

This time Alice didn't hesitate. She closed out her home page and opened Priority's yearly statement. She gasped!

"Jesus Christ. Nearly seven million. Close the page, Alice. I knew it. They're gonna steal that money and get rid of us. I'll bet ya."

"Get *rid* of us? How?" The terrifying look on Alice's face sent shivers down Charles's spine.

***

After filling his stomach with another fantastic dinner prepared by Emily, Charles rose from the table, collected the dirty dishes and began filling the dishwasher.

"Want to hear the latest gossip from the office?"

"What could be any better than the last piece of gossip you told me?"

"Well, this morning, I was standing next to Alice's desk gathering my messages and yesterday's mail when, over the intercom, William blurted out that he wanted to see Dennis in his office ASAP. Alice gave me that look, walked down the hall to Reading's office and told him William wanted to see him right now. As soon as she returned, William forgot to turn off his intercom and both of us began listening to their conversation. William was very adamant about starting the ball rolling after the signing Kaiser to a monster contract."

Emily just stood still, staring out the kitchen window as if she was in a trance. What was going through her mind suddenly? "Oh, did I mention to you that Carol wants me to help her putting up drapes in her bathroom tonight?"

"No. When did this happen? How come this Carol person never comes over? I don't think I've ever met her, have I?"

"Yes, you've met her. She stopped by for your mother and father's funeral. You were not yourself during that time. Besides, Carol hates men. Ever since her one-time relationship in college, she was sexually used and dropped. I feel so sorry for her."

"Okay, okay. I've got things to do on the computer. I'm waiting for Jack to challenge me on his X-box so he can laugh at me."

Chapter 14

The Meeting To Die For

A long time ago, on the north side of Chicago, there was an amusement park called Riverview Park. A place to go to play games, plenty of roller coasters and one in particular, the Parachute ride. This structure stood about two hundred and fifty feet in the air with people who were daring to ride it, loved it. It just looked scary, maybe it's height made it that way. Well, the life of William Fossett reflected the Parachute ride. You go up, you come down.

His life slowly began to rise just after graduating from college. He married his college sweetheart, earned his license to sell life insurance and worked strenuously to reach higher goals for them both. He stepped on people's feet, good or bad, because he wanted the best of everything. He needed to be the best. It didn't take him long to reach the top of that ladder, thanks to his persistent hard work and being in the right place at the right time. His persistence paid off when a windfall from one investment gave him the capital to establish a new venture and a prospering future.

He started his own business, becoming an insurance broker and small time investment consultant. The business, situated on the far north suburbs of Chicago, provided a predominately wealthy clientele and with hard work, the future was promising. As his practice grew quickly, so did the profits. William got a full blown taste of what it felt like to be rich. He was spending a lot of money, spending to much time away from home and creating problems with his marriage. His parachute was starting to float down. His wife filed for divorce, a bad investment here, a sordid affair there, then another affair, until finally, word got around within his clientele concerning his troubles and his profits turned into debts. His ride was descending toward bankruptcy, until his fortuity changed again.

He boarded the parachute ride again after another windfall fell into his lap. A sizable fortune from a quick pick lottery ticket allowed William to jump back into the investment game.

The second time around, William had to rebuild his reputation and a new business, an up hill battle all the way. He understood that and he learned from his past experiences, what he could and couldn't do. He had to reestablish the trust and prove to investors that they could trust him. In order to move forward, investors were his main urgency. He had a sister, named Helen, that was establishing herself in the real estate market and doing better than him. He hated Helen and even more, hated her success. William was the oldest of the two siblings, but during their early childhood years, William taunted her, played tricks on her and berated her at every chance. He set up a deal where Helen would receive more than double her initial investment within the first year. And that was exactly what it was. A set up. It was a scam from the start, set up to dissolve Helen's assets and fill William's pockets. The scam worked and she faced possible bankruptcy. She pleaded with him to help her gain enough money to crawl from under the rock pile that was on top of her. She was being pressured daily: settle the debt or serve time in jail. Helen never saw a penny from William.

The pressure forced her to sell her house and liquefy her few remaining assets, which left her penniless. But William didn't care, he just laughed. From that day forward,

William never saw or heard from Helen again, but he figured it was Dennis who saved her. Dennis borrowed the capital so she could move to California, she changed her name, then found employment and started a new life. She married, but not having full trust in men, the relationship dissolved in less than a year.

***

Not long after the ordeal with Helen, William partnered with another close friend, Samuel Hasid. Together they organized a company called Priority Investments, Inc., an investing consultant firm located in the Edison Building in Chicago's Downtown Loop. Samuel Hasid bank rolled the business and believed William was the right partner, overlooking William's past, William was a go-getter.

After six years of the partnership, Samuel died unexpectedly. So unexpectedly that people around the office and the business sector began wondering about the circumstances of his death. He was found sitting in his car, parked in his garage, with his brains scattered across the passenger seat. The FBI was called in, the investigation continued, but it died as questionably as William's partner. It was decided that Samuel Hasid committed suicide. The talk continued and many fingers pointed toward William Fossett. Associates believed his eagerness, his arrogance, his greed to power the very successful business to be the motive. It all filtered down to him. Somehow, William convinced the investigators that he had nothing to do with Samuel Hasid's death, and he had a foolproof alibi to prove it. No weapon was ever recovered, and there were no witnesses and no solid concrete evidence proving William killed his partner. Case closed. The corporation now belonged to William, the sole owner and the sole owner to collect all the profits.

Fossett continued to live alone in Lincoln Park, and kept to himself. His neighbors weren't aware of his history, but if they were, it wouldn't bother him at all. He always claimed he had nothing to do with his partner's death. Eventually, suspicion blew over and his life remained on it's parachute ride.

***

As Dennis drove to meet William, the day belonged to the snow Gods. All day long the snow filtered down from the sky, very light and you would think it would never reach the ground. But it did, producing nearly four inches of the white dust. The Escape turned on William's road and no sooner, Dennis noticed three middle-age women walking in the street in front of him. Immersed in their conversation, they were unaware of his oncoming car. He tapped his horn to alert them he was behind them and rolled down his window to apologize for startling them. One of the women began shaking her fist and screaming profanity at him.

Screw you too, lady.

"You came pretty close to hitting us, you asshole."

"Walk on the sidewalk where you belong. You were taking up the entire lane, idiot."

The screaming woman joined the other two as they continued their walk, keeping an eye on Dennis until the car pulled into William's driveway. He shook his head and shut off the engine.

The bellowing chimes notified William that he had a visitor at his front door. He set the newspaper down and peeked at his watch. Seven pm, it must be Dennis.

"Come in."

Dennis removed his light jacket, then followed William down the hall to his den. William picked up a pack of smokes and lit one. He poured some whiskey into a small tumbler and handed it to Dennis.

"I've been thinking this out. I know I can take care of Alice, that's not a problem. It's Charles I'm concerned about."

"What do we do with him?"

"Listen up. Here's what I'm thinking." William paced around his den still puffing on a cigarette and gulping down his whiskey.

"There's nearly seven million in that account. I can arrange for Charles to take a trip to see Adolph Kaiser in New York. I'll make up some lame excuse and tell him Kaiser needs his advice. While he's gone, that will give us time to transfer the money, schedule our flights, and get the hell out of here."

"I'm listening."

"While he's in New York, my connections there will see that Charles doesn't board a plane back to Chicago, ending our problem with him. I'll have them make it look like he was robbed. Once he's gone, we'll be gone. Also, I have an alibi. I was here in Chicago all the time with you."

"I get it now, an alibi. So you're the one who had your partner murdered. I've heard talk about that. Now, the truth comes out. So you did it, right?"

"You better keep your fucking mouth shut or I swear, you'll end up sleeping with Charles and Hasid. You hear me?"

"Yeah. Loud and clear."

"Once we land in Switzerland, you'll get your cut and I'll never see you again, understood? What you do with your money is your business. And me? I'm invisible."

William finished his whiskey, set the glass down and walked out of the den.

"Okay. Get out of here. Tomorrow, at the office, stay clear of Charles and Alice."

"What if Charles pesters me about I.C.E.?"

"Tell him to come and see me. I don't think he'll do that, but if he does, I'll handle it."

Dennis picked up his coat and headed for the front door. William stood in the doorway watching Dennis exit his driveway, closed the door and walked back to his den when the door chimes rang out again. William dropped his newspaper and opened the door.

"Jesus Christ. What did he forget now?"

BANG!!

***

The alarm from Charles's bedside radio sprang into action. The music was loud, loud enough that Charles hustled to turn it off without waking Emily. He sat up, scratching his head, and looked to see if Emily was awake. With no moving parts next to him, he was sure she was still asleep. Slowly, he moved into the bathroom, still scratching his body and still yawning. He put on the robe from the bedroom door and made his way to the kitchen. He dropped a pod in the Keurig, turned on the portable TV on the kitchen counter, and waited for his cup to brew. The voice from the TV news caught Charles's full attention.

"We have late breaking news. William Fossett, CEO of Priority Investments here in Chicago, was found shot to death at his home in Lincoln Park early this morning. With the latest on that, here is our correspondent, John Simmons, covering the news."

Did I hear that right? Charles's full attention was focused on the news broadcasting from the TV. He stood very still, his eyes glued to the TV screen and, somewhat, in shock.

"Good morning, Thom and Sharon. I'm standing in front of William Fossett's home in Lincoln Park. The police have secured the entire property and are continuing their investigation. Not much is known about the shooting, only that Mr. Fossett was found by his neighbor around six o'clock this morning. He was shot at point-blank range. A single shot to his skull. Also, police are not sure when the shooting occurred. So far, no weapon, no witnesses and no suspects. Until more information is available on the shooting, I'm John Simmons reporting from Lincoln Park. Thom and Sharon, back to you in the studio."

Charles's body was frozen. William was dead? He hustled into the bedroom to wake up Emily.

"William is dead." He shook her. "Emily, they found William dead at his home this morning."

"Whoa. What? William, who?"

"No. Come to the kitchen. It's all over the TV."

Emily hurried to the kitchen. As she kept her eyes glued to the screen, she fumbled with the Keurig.

"See? Watch the graphics at the bottom of the screen. It'll come up shortly."

They waited for the scroll of news to appear.

"I can't believe it. Who would want to kill William? Just what I told your yesterday, those two had something up their sleeve. And then hiring Reading, that itself was puzzling. Everyone in the office didn't understand why he was hired, but now I know why. Ed Weldon told me all about William and Reading, how they socialized together, wining and dining with whores, traveling around the world. It all makes sense now. Reading killed William."

"You think he did it?"

"Well, over the last several months, I discovered something that William was up to. Illegal stuff. I didn't want to make any waves, you know. I didn't want to start any trouble. Because I really didn't have solid evidence. So, I've been quiet."

"What kind of illegal things?"

Charles hesitated. Should he spell it out to her? Emily was his wife, his best friend. Of course he could trust her. He had no other choice, he had to tell someone.

"Sit down. It happened last December when I was getting all the paperwork ready for the year-end totals. I came across a figure on Kaiser's financial statement, an Imposed Custom Expense. I've never seen or heard this fee before. It was in the thousands. My jaw dropped, so I started checking it out. I had Alice open up Priority's financial pages, we counted almost seven million in Priority's secret account."

"How do you know it's illegal?"

"I don't. But everything I've checked points to it. Oh, and get this. I called Dustin Taylor. He's an investment attorney. He and his colleagues at work never heard of such a tax. It's bogus, it's illegal."

"Are you insinuating that Reading killed William for the money?"

"Kind of looks like that way, doesn't it? I'm not sure. I don't know who did it, but both were up to something big."

"Are you going into the office this morning?"

"I think I better. I want to see if Reading shows up."

***

A couple of hours later, Charles hastily walked to the Edison building. A few Chicago police cars were parked in front and after seeing that, Charles knew what was in store for him once he reached his office. He stepped out of the elevator on the twelfth floor and walked to the main entrance of Priority Investments. Inside, a crowd of detectives conducted interviews with whomever they could corral. As Charles entered, all heads turned toward him. He nonchalantly walked to Alice's desk, picked up his messages, and whispered to Alice.

"We have to talk, you understand me?"

Alice never looked up, but she heard him loud and clear. With the stack of messages and his briefcase in hand, Charles walked to his office, glancing around trying to locate Reading. No sign of him. He set his briefcase and messages on his desk and walked out.

First, he looked in Dennis's office. His door was wide open and his office was vacant. He looked up and down the halls, checking most of the offices, but unfortunately, no sign of Dennis. Charles's thoughts were starting to make sense. If Dennis was at William's house last night, then it would make sense for him to be elusive. Staying away from work and from all the interviews was not looking good for him. Charles grabbed a cup of coffee and made his way back to his office, anticipating a barrage of interviews that would inevitably be coming. In fact, before he had time to sit in his office chair, he heard a tap on his office door.

"You must be Charles Collier, correct?"

"Yes, you found me. And who might you be?"

"I'm Detective Mike Konrad, third precinct." He shoved a badge and card toward Charles. "If you don't mind, a couple of quick questions."

"Sure. Fire away."

"Where were you last night, between six and ten pm?"

"Do you think I did it? I was home with my son, enjoying a terrific meal and an outstanding Harry Potter movie."

"You have any idea who would want to murder William Fossett?"

"Not the faintest idea. In fact, as soon as I woke up this morning and turned on the TV, I heard the news and was completely in shock. I ran to wake up my wife to tell her. We both stood in front of the TV not believing what we were hearing."

"In the past several months, did you observe Fossett acting peculiar? Did he seem like he was troubled, doing or saying things that were unusual? Behaving abnormally?

Charles sat there, knowing that William had been acting abnormally. Should he keep his mouth shut? Thinking quickly, he thought he'd want to talk to Alice before he fully committed to the police.

"I haven't noticed anything peculiar with William. But, there were plenty of days when I would never see him at all. He traveled a lot, then stayed in his office. Nothing unusual I can think of."

"What about enemies? Any clients that he treated unfairly? Anyone who might hold a grudge against him?"

"Again, I'm just shocked that this has happened. I have no idea of anyone who would want to harm William. But, I believe Mr. Reading was meeting William at his house last night around 7 o'clock."

"Is that so? Really. All right. Thanks for your cooperation. If there's anything you can remember, please give me a call. The number on the card has a twenty-four-hour answering service."

Detective Konrad shook Charles's hand, but hesitated. "By any chance, would you have a recent picture of Dennis Reading?"

"I don't. But why do you need a picture of him?"

"Just a formality, that's all."

Charles escorted Konrad to William's office. They moved about the office looking at all the pictures William had accumulated over the years.

"Here, how about this one?" Charles handed him a picture of Reading and William. "I believe that was taken this past winter. They took a fishing trip to the Keys. Reading got lucky and landed that huge sailfish. They talked about that for weeks on end."

Konrad held on to the picture and both went back to Charles's office.

"This will help a lot. Ohh, one last thing before I leave. Reading's address. You know where he lives?"

"No, I don't. Ask Alice. They have records of all the employees at her desk."

"Okay. You've been a great help. Thanks."

"No problem. And good luck with your investigation."

Konrad didn't waste any time getting to Alice's desk. All the other detectives were standing in the lobby waiting for him. "Mr. Reading's address? Collier said you would have a record of where he lives."

Alice looked up, with disgust written on her face. Without saying a word, she opened the lower, right drawer and removed a record book containing the information Konrad wanted: 752 North 15th Street, in Oakville.

"Got it. Thank you." Konrad wrote the address in his note pad and waved to the other detectives. Their business at Priority was done for the day. They had a picture and an address of their prime suspect, Dennis Reading.

Chapter 15

Get The Show On The Road

Where in the hell was Dennis? As far as Charles could determine, there were only three people, including himself, aware of William's scheme. After all the commotion in the lobby had died down, Charles got up and walked out of his office. The lobby was empty, just Alice sitting behind her desk. He approached her desk, anxiously waiting for a response from her. She looked shaken and agitated. The other time Charles noticed that demeanor in her was the day before, when William used that vulgar word regarding her.

"You know something, right?"

"You'd be surprised."

"Well then, surprise me. Let's go have coffee. We need to talk."

Charles hustled back to his office, locked his briefcase in his desk, picked up his cell phone, and returned to the lobby.

Alice was leaning against her desk with her purse slung over her shoulder waiting. She accompanied Charles to the Starbucks coffee shop across the street. The crowd there was usually on the go, but some came to set up their laptops and finish business before they left for the day. Charles found two empty chairs and a small table in the back of the shop.

"Okay, Alice. Spit it out. All of it."

"Jesus. Where do I start?"

"The very beginning."

"It goes back a long time. I am so shameful of my life, especially when I was a lot younger. I met William when I was a prostitute, William and I had an affair that broke up his marriage and caused

William to loose control of his temper. I had an abortion. He became very physical with me, I was totally scared for my life, I had to get away from him. After his divorce, when William and Samuel partnered up and opened this business, he found me and, I think, felt sorry for me. I was living off the streets and, I too, became a very angry woman. I started working here, but the romance was over. I wanted to leave here in the worst way, but I needed the money. William was paying me well." Alice hesitated. "Did you ever hear of Samuel Hasid?"

"Hasid. Hmm. Oh, of course. I've seen his picture in William's office. One time he was William's partner."

"Samuel Hasid was William's partner who was murdered. William had him murdered, but…he never went to court about it. Money will buy anything."

"He told you that?"

"I was so much in love with him, I helped him murder that poor man. William paid a lot of money to keep my name out of it. I'm so ashamed about my life. I was pregnant with William's baby, but William became so enraged, he talked me into having an abortion. To this day, I hate myself for letting him talk me into that. I killed that baby, too." Alice covered her face with both hands and began to cry.

"Unreal. I can't believe what I'm hearing. So, what about I.C.E.?"

"Honestly, I don't pay attention to what William does anymore. I have no idea what that is. To me, he's just another boss. I keep to myself, but sometimes he tells me important stuff, like keeping the financial statements private. When he told me that, I had a hunch he was up to no good."

"Yeah. When I saw those financial statements, I compared them to my accounts. None of my accounts have that fee on them. Nearly seven million total, and $200 thousand just from the Kaiser account. The Kaiser account that has my name all over it."

"Unbelievable. Huh. I know that's why he hired Reading. Did you know that Reading was almost related to William?"

"What! How?"

"Not blood related. You knew William had a sister, Helen? Dennis and Helen became romantically involved, then were engaged to get married, which really pissed off William." Alice hesitated, then continued. "William and Helen fought like cats and dogs. Until that one day. Something happened between them causing her to move away. I don't know what it was about. William never said anything to me about it, so I never asked. Maybe it was the relationship between Helen and Dennis that caused all the trouble. I don't know."

Charles started to put the puzzle pieces together. From what he was hearing from Alice, it started making sense. He knew about Hasid, knew about the scam William pulled on his sister and knew what William and Reading were up to.

"This is incredible. What a life William had. What do you think we should do regarding the police and the investigation?" Alice answered. "I don't know anything. I tend to believe it was Reading all the way. He was there last night. It sure the hell wasn't me."

"Your guess is as good as mine, Alice. I don't have any information, other than what both of us heard yesterday."

"I wonder where Reading is?"

"We better get back to the office, maybe he's there."

***

The mood there was like any other day at Priority. Most of the employees who showed up were in their offices, continuing work as if nothing had happened. The police were gone, the lobby was empty, and the phones were quiet. Normal as normal could be. Except...there was Reading walking up the hall toward Alice and Charles.

"Sorry I'm late. I ate something bad for lunch yesterday." Dennis stood puzzled by the looks on their faces. "Is there something wrong?"

Alice and Charles contemplated the same questions.

Are you kidding me? Where have you been this morning? Don't you listen to the local news?

Charles spoke up, "You're not aware of what happened last night or early this morning?"

"This morning? No. Did I miss a meeting?"

"The police found William dead at his home. Cops have been here all day."

Dennis appeared stunned. "Dead? How?"

"From what the police are telling us, a gunshot, point blank to his head. Said the shooting took place between eight and eleven last night."

"You're kidding me. C'mon. What's really going on here?"

"The police said they have three witnesses. Three women walking near William's house around seven o'clock last night. They claim they saw a white male, driving a black SUV pulling into William's driveway. You own a black Ford Escape, don't you, Dennis?"

A ton of bricks had just fallen on Reading's head. Three witnesses, his black SUV, seven o'clock. They knew he was there.

"I wasn't even near William's house last night. I went straight home from work. Something I ate for lunch didn't agree with me. I felt sick, so I went to bed early last night, honest."

Charles shook his head, "If I were you right now, I'd be sweating bullets. Maybe it would be in your best interest to contact the police department."

"You haven't talked to the police yet, have you?" Alice asked.

"What am I going to tell them? I have no information at all. I didn't kill him."

They stood in the lobby. No tears, no signs of sympathy, no one having any solid information regarding William's death. Could it be that Dennis was telling the truth? Or could he be nominated for an Oscar?

He turned and raced to his office, then minutes later, Alice and Charles watched him, his hands full of papers, his briefcase under one arm, and his jacket half on, run to the elevator without a word.

When his Escape came to a sudden stop in his driveway, Dennis pulled the keys from the ignition, locked the doors, and hurried inside the house. Without closing the front door, he ran to the TV and turned on the local news. He knew it had to be Helen. She had the motive, she finally did it.

The TV pictured a pair of news anchors summarizing the top stories of the day. He sat down, waiting to hear the news of William's death. Nothing. He wondered if Alice and Charles were playing a joke on him. It was possible that William went away and didn't tell him about it. When he left William's house the night before, William was alive.

"We take you now to Susie Lu, our correspondent covering the death of William Fossett. What's the latest regarding the investigation, Susie?"

"The police aren't telling us much. What we do know is that William Fossett was murdered between eight and eleven last night. One shot to his head at very close range. And recently, three witnesses claim they saw a young white male, driving a black SUV, pull into Fossett's driveway around seven. So far, no weapon, no motive and no suspects. Reporting live, Susie Lu, WFN news, back to you, Marcus."

"We will keep you posted as we know more about this story. Now, the weather with..."

Dennis clicked the TV off and fell back into the sofa. Reality set in: *Three witnesses, a black SUV, a white male. I'm screwed. I'm being framed for this. Helen shot him after I left.* He began to panic. If the police checked his background, they'd find out about his arrest when he was a teenager for possession of a firearm without a valid registration. He had to make a decision and fast. If he stuck around, the police would surely find him. They'd interrogate him for hours upon hours, put him and his black SUV at the crime scene, his fingerprints on the whiskey glass. He had no alibi. They had him dead to rights.

Without any hesitation, he scrambled to his bedroom and crammed whatever clothes he could find into a large suitcase. He had stashed some cash in a shoe box in his closet for emergency situations, and this was an emergency. In a fast glance across the living room and kitchen, he saw nothing that would be incriminating, no evidence. Crazy thoughts raced through his mind, like…where am I headed?…Getting rid of the SUV…Stay off the freeways till I can get another car…Throw away my cell phone, my credit cards, anything that would leave a paper trail that the police could trace. But wait. Why am I running? I'm innocent. I didn't kill William. If I run, all fingers will point directly to me. Shit. What about all the money in the I.C.E. account?

Dennis knew for sure if he stayed in Chicago, the police would eventually pin the murder on him. Especially, when he was the last person to see William alive. He would be arrested, put in jail and remain there till his court hearing, which could take years. The more he thought about jail time, the more he was convinced that he had to get away from the Chicago police. Think, Dennis. Instantly, Helen's name popped into his brain. Of course. She was the only logical person he could trust to help him. Then he thought… *It was Helen that murdered William.* Jesus Christ. Panic was in full force for Dennis. There was no time to spare, he better hit the road now.

If Dennis flees now, what was going to happen to the seven million that he and William planned to steal and how could he get it if he ran? What bank was it in? Now, William was dead! The only logical conclusion was contacting Helen.

***

Dennis kept the Escape heading west. He drove what seemed like an eternity until his fuel gauge started beeping. He needed gas. When he stopped, he reached for the shoe box and counted the money. One hundred…two hundred…one thousand…one thousand nine- hundred and eighty-five bucks.

With the tank full of gas, Dennis walked inside the station to pay the attendant. The drive to California would take several days, so he supplied himself with enough snacks and water for the trip. He pulled a wad of money from his front pocket and was about to pay the attendant when he noticed a road atlas. It was just what he needed. He could study the maps, keep off the interstates, and travel the secondary roads. Once outside, as he approached his car, he burst out laughing. There, standing out like a sore thumb, it said it all, the shinny chrome emblem…Ford Escape. How appropriate, driving an Escape while escaping.

He reached across the console and picked up his cell phone lying on the passenger seat. He opened it and found Helen's number, but before dialing, he asked himself. *If Helen did kill William, am I safe looking for her?* Dennis didn't have time to fool around. He didn't have many choices, in fact, only one. He dialed Helen's number.

"I'm screwed. You know that, don't you? It's all over the news this morning, I'm guilty as hell. But you killed him. Why? What were you thinking?"

"What are you talking about?"

"I'm a dead man if I stay in Chicago, because of you. You killed him and now you've killed our plan. I can't believe it."

"Calm down, okay. Where are you now?"

"Hell, I don't know. Somewhere near Iowa, I think."

The conversation went quiet until, "OK. Don't do anything stupid, you understand. Keep off the freeways, in the meantime I'll think of something. Oh, most important now, get rid of your phone. The cops can GPS your phone. If you need to call, use a pay phone and I didn't kill my brother."

"Okay. Who did then?" Helen didn't answer, just dead silence, "It's gonna take a few days. I'll be in touch." The more Dennis thought about Helen, the more it didn't make sense to him. It totally shattered their plan about seizing the money for themselves. The only other person that knew of the money was Charles.

His strategy was to drive the entire night, staying along the back roads and away from all freeways. By now, he was sure the cops had an APB out nationwide, looking for a black Ford Escape with Illinois plates. The familiar sign of a Burger King appeared through the windshield. A time to stop, grab a burger, and plot his route to California. He opened the atlas and studied the map. *Wow. This is going to be a very long trip.* Dennis decided to stay north, away from traffic and crowded areas. He would travel through Iowa, into South Dakota, across Colorado, then Utah, Nevada, and end in California.

After driving all night, Dennis was leaving Iowa and entering South Dakota. The dashboard clock read five-fifty am. He needed to get out and stretch, grab a cup of coffee and look for an inconspicuous, cheap motel. He'd freshen up, take a quick nap, and study the atlas again. The life of living like a fugitive bothered him because he knew he did nothing wrong. Running away only made matters worse. As daybreak began to appear, a huge sign to the side of the road informed him he was now entering the town of Yankton, South Dakota. *Woophie!!*

He paid close attention to the surroundings, looking out for patrol cars and avoiding as much traffic as possible. Slowly driving and not causing any attention, he drove passed a used car lot. Yes, this would be the perfect place for him to buy a used car and get rid of the SUV. It was too risky to keep driving the Escape, the odds would definitely catch up to him. He'd ditch it somewhere, strip off the license plates, and toss the keys out the window in another town. About a mile from the car lot and the road leading out of Yankton, he spotted a small motel, The Lazy Day Motel. Slowly, he turned his vehicle onto the asphalt driveway, parked and entered the office.

"Howdy." A thin, frail old man greeted Dennis. The clerk's long salt and pepper hair with the matching beard was the by-product of old age, along with his missing teeth.

"You've stopped at the right place."

Hearing that, Dennis automatically imagined the famous scene from the movie, "Psycho."

"Good. I've been driving all night long and I'm tired." Dennis waited as the old man reached under the counter and slid a sheet of paper toward him, a registration form. *Shit, I can't sign my real name, the paper trail.* Realizing that, his eyes quickly scanned the area looking for help. Glancing to his right he saw nothing, but when he looked to his left, there was his new identity. A clear, plastic stand filled with brochures advertising vacationing in Mesa, Arizona.

Got it. Mesa...Dan Mesa. From now on, Dennis Reading does not exist. I am now Dan Mesa.

The old man, who probably couldn't read anyway, never looked at the register and said, "One room, single bed, $35."

Dan pulled out his money and spread the cash across the counter.

"Is there a restaurant or diner nearby?"

"Why sure. You can walk there from here. Just look out the window and across the street. Yankton's finest restaurant."

Dan looked through the window and across the highway were a row of small buildings including Yankton's finest. The old man handed Dan the key to room four, turned and sat down and puffed on his cigar.

Just what Dan expected. The room was old and so was the furniture. Even the smell was old, but the bed looked comfy. He dropped the duffle bag on the chair and collapsed on the bed, instantly falling asleep.

It was still light out when Dan awoke a few minutes after six o'clock. He lay motionless, trying to sort out his confusion. First, take a much-needed shower, get food in his stomach, and figure out where he was headed next. He stood leaning against the shower wall, relaxing to the soothing hot streams of comfort pouring over every aching muscle. He stepped out of the shower and looked in the mirror. The reflection he saw was blank. A face with no answers. A face that looked scared and needed to be changed, like growing a mustache and goatee. Now he was thinking as a fugitive would.

***

Dan was on his way to Yankton's finest, but as he walked toward the diner, his eyes searched the area, looking for the ideal spot to dump the Escape. The sooner the better for him, because his time was ticking away and he was pushing his luck. He strolled to the back of the buildings and found nothing but dirt piles, numerous stacks of chopped down trees, old cars, and plastic garbage bags scattered all around. Perfect, he thought. He could steal a plate off another car, remove the plates from the Escape, then park it behind the stores. It would take weeks or even months for the police to discover the SUV. By then, Dan would be hundreds of miles away.

***

The following morning, Dan took a walk and headed to the used car lot with one thing on his mind, buying a new set of wheels.

"A fine day to purchase a new car, right?" A salesman remarked.

"I think so. Depending on what kind of a deal you can give me."

Dan was standing in front of a blue, 2001 Chevy Impala, looking inside the windows, then inspecting the outside body and tires.

"You want to take it for a test ride?"

"Yeah. I've been looking at this car for weeks. I like Chevys."

"Wait here a second. I'll go get the keys."

Dan noticed the sticker listed the car for $1,100. He would offer the salesman $800. If he said no, there were other cars on the lot that sold cheaper. But the Chevy was Dan's car. When the salesman returned, they both jumped in, with Dan at the wheel.

"Are you from Yankton?"

"Yeah. I moved here a month ago. Still looking for work, though."

"This car had only one owner. An older gentleman who took great care of it. Unfortunately, he became ill and had to sell the vehicle."

Dan knew that story was a common sales pitch. He tested the radio, heater, and the air. All seemed to be working fine. With no oncoming cars in view, he stomped on the accelerator. The engine roared and the Impala leaped forward, reaching eighty-five miles per hour with ease.

"Fine machine, three-twenty-seven, huh?"

"Yep. You know your engines. Like I said, the owner took great care of it."

Dan couldn't care less even if it had five owners or been in several accidents, as long as the engine was running great. After a fifteen-minute test ride, he pulled the Chevy

back into the lot, lifted the hood, and started inspecting the engine. He knelt low enough to look under the car for oil leaks, but didn't notice any drippings.

"I'll give you $800 cash right now." Dan said, without looking at the salesman.

The salesman rubbed his chin and without hesitation said, "You got yourself a new Chevy, young man. Follow me and we'll start the paperwork, okay?"

Inside the tiny office, Dan waited for the salesman to produce all the papers. Finally, with the last signature inked, Dan counted out eight one-hundred-dollar bills and laid them on the salesman's desk.

"Excellent. I'll get your receipt and you'll be on your way."

When he returned, he handed the receipt to Dan along with the keys. "Your registration should come in the mail in about two or three weeks. Here's the title, fill in the spaces and sign it. This has to be sent to the state to be notarized. That may take longer than 2 weeks. Well, thank you and enjoy your new Impala."

As Dan drove back to the motel with his new machine, he thought about his next move. He'd study the atlas, write down the route he wanted to take, thoroughly clean out the Escape, remove the plates, and wait till dark and the mall closed. He stood looking out the window waiting until all the lights went off and all the cars left the mall. Quickly, he gathered his belongings, threw them in the Chevy, and hopped into the Escape. He pulled out of the motel parking lot, crossed the highway, and drove the SUV behind the row of stores. He knew he had to be quick to avoid suspicion, so he parked the Escape between a garbage dumpster and a rusted-out old pick-up truck. The spot was not conspicuous, and the car fit in with the other junked cars. He locked the doors, then picked up a huge rock and tossed it through the windshield, smashing the entire plate of glass. Then, using a sharp rock, he destroyed the VIN number the best he could. Finished, he stuffed the keys in his pocket and would dispose of them in another state. He stood and looked at the SUV, once his pride and joy was now abandoned and forgotten. Next stop, Colorado.

Chapter 16

Visions of $$$...Dancing In Her Head

"Jack. Pass me the butter, please."

Emily had cooked another great meal. It was not the award winning spaghetti that they loved, but roasted chicken, mashed potatoes, and kidney bean salad, along with homemade hot cross buns.

"Now that school is nearly over, Jack, what are your plans for the summer?" his Dad asked.

"Not a whole lot, Dad. Summer baseball is starting. I'm thinking of trying out for the Legion team."

"Now that's the spirit. Remember what I told you before, you have only one shot at life. Go for it. You'll never regret it."

"You've always liked playing baseball. Anyway, the exercise will do you good. It will get you away from the TV and all those Xbox games and movies," Emily barked.

The dinner was over. Jack and Charles let out a big belch and they both started laughing.

"I'm stuffed, Jack. Give me a hand to my recliner."

"Anyone for dessert?" Emily saw two hands rise into the air. She pulled out a bowl of cherry flavored Jell-O and a container of Cool-Whip topping.

"Ohh, boy. You know I always have room for that."

Emily scooped the Jell-O into small bowls, topped it with the Cool-Whip then set it down in front of them. Jack took his into the living room.

"Dad, I can't get the remote to work." Jack was standing in front of the TV pushing any button that might turn it on.

"Let me try." Charles duplicated the process. Same result.

"Let me check the wires and connections. Maybe one came loose or fell off."

Charles struggled to move the unit away from the wall, leaving room for him to squeeze behind the console and check the wiring. After a grunt here and there, he slid the entertainment center back to its original position.

"Everything looks good. Nothing loose that I could see. Give me the remote. Maybe it needs new batteries."

After a new set of batteries were installed in the remote, the TV remained blank.

"I'll stop at Loop Appliance on my way to work tomorrow and get someone out here to look at the problem."

"Crap. Can I use the computer then?"

"Okay, Jack, but be careful of my programs on there." Charles moved back to the kitchen table and joined Emily for another cup of coffee.

"I wonder what it'll be like at the office tomorrow? Now that William is gone, who's going to step up and run the show? Will the business keep going? I guess we'll all sit down, have a meeting, and discuss it's future."

"Poor William. You have any idea who wanted to kill him?"

"My guess? Dennis did. Anyone would do anything for seven million. When Alice and I spoke to him after lunch, he looked guilty to me. His excuse was pretty lame, too. Said he ate something bad at lunch and stayed in bed all night. But if he didn't kill William, why would he lie? Alice and I both heard him say he was meeting William last night at William's house."

"Amazing. From the news on TV, that's what they're inferring. Sounds like he's the only suspect." Emily's behavior seemed strange to Charles. He studied her and wondered why was she asking so many questions about William?

"Something just doesn't add up. Within the past year, William began charging his clients excessive fees, then he hired Reading, then the conversation Alice and I heard between them. There's gotta be more to it than just Dennis killing William. I know seven million is a ton of money, but there has to be more to this than what I know now."

"So, what's going to happen with that money? Does Alice know about it?"

"Yeah. We saw it on the financial statement. She told me that she and William had an affair years ago. It broke up his marriage. Now, she says whatever William is up to, she's wants nothing to do with him."

"Oh, really. That being said, then only you, Alice, and Reading know about the money, right?"

What is she up to? Charles set his cup down. "As far as I know. Meaning what?"

"William is dead, Reading has split, and only Alice is left. Why don't we sit down with her and make her a deal. We'll split the money with her."

"Emily, what are you insinuating? That we steal the money? Hold on, now. The money belongs to Priority Investments, dear. Other agents work there, too. Not just Alice and me. Besides, I'm not a thief."

On his way to work that morning, Charles stopped at the Loop Appliance store where he purchased his entertainment center. He walked up to the service counter and waited for the available technician.

"May I help you, sir?"

The name tag on the service man's shirt read Nick. Nick was a short, rotund fellow with black hair, wire-rimmed glasses and, of course, like all computer geeks, he had a plastic pocket protector filled with pens and pencils.

"Yes, I hope so. I purchased a Sony entertainment center from your store about two months ago. Last night, my son tried to turn on the TV and nothing happened. Nothing works, not the plasma TV or the DVD player. I replaced the batteries in the remote, checked all the wiring and connections, but still nothing."

"Your name, sir?"

"Collier, Charles Collier. One-o-five East Cedar Street, here in Chicago."

Nick punched the keys on the keyboard while keeping his eyes on the screen in front of him.

"All right. Forty-six-inch Sony plasma TV, a Sony Blu-ray HD DVD player and the Sony one-thousand-watt, five-point-one home theater system. The warranty is still in effect. According to all the data, looks like we need to pay your system a visit."

"Sounds good to me."

"Mr. Collier, when would be the best time to set up your appointment?"

"My wife is usually at home during the day. Whenever you can get there as quickly as possible would be appreciated."

"Okay. Let me check the maintenance log." Nick reached for the book under the counter and thumbed through the pages. "I believe we have a technician available this afternoon, around two o'clock. How does that sound? Is there a phone number where you can be reached?"

"Yes. Here's my card with the number. I'll make sure my wife is home."

Nick printed a work order and handed the yellow copy to Charles. Now I can get Jack off my computer and let him play with his Xbox.

Chapter 17

Get the "Hack" Out of Here!

When Charles entered the doors of Priority Investments, he was greeted by Detective Konrad. "Mr. Collier. You mind if I take a few minutes away from your busy schedule?"

"Now what?"

"I think we'll have more privacy in your office, okay?"

Charles went first, followed by Konrad. He saw Alice sitting by her desk talking to another officer. The constant interviews, the same questions, over and over again. He wondered when it would stop.

He put his briefcase down and removed his sport coat. "You want a cup of coffee, Detective?"

"No, thank you. I've had too many cups already this morning."

"Now, what's on your mind?"

"When was the last time you saw Dennis Reading?"

"Yesterday. Just after lunch. Alice and I got back from lunch, saw him in the lobby, and informed him about William."

"As far as you could tell, did he seem bothered? Do you think he knew about Fossett's death?"

"Well, he claimed he didn't. He thought Alice and I were playing a joke on him. Then we told him about the police having witnesses. He said he ate something bad for lunch and spent the entire night at home in bed."

"You have any idea where he could be right now?"

"Nope. The last time I saw him was yesterday around noon. He was in a big hurry leaving the office, tho. Haven't seen or heard from him since."

"One last thing. Was Fossett in any kind of financial trouble? I mean, did he ever discuss with you fraudulent stocks or trades?"

"No. Absolutely not. That's a no-no in our office protocol. William was a very private individual. If he had any money problems, he wouldn't discuss that with me or anyone else here."

"We'll need to see the financial statements for Priority over the past five years. Who would have those?" Konrad pushed.

Christ! Charles knew that handing the statements over to Konrad could be the death of the seven million.

"I sure don't. You could ask Alice, but I think William had control of all that," he lied.

"Yes, Alice, you think?" Konrad was recording all the information on his note pad.

"Very well. I won't take up any more of your time. Thanks again."

Konrad's last stop was Alice's desk. When he arrived, Alice was gone and another woman was sitting in her chair.

"Is Ms. Oliver around?"

"She fell ill and went home for the day. Is there anything I could help you with?"

"No. No. I'll stop back later this week. Nothing important."

After Konrad left Priority, Charles remembered that he needed to call Emily and tell her the Loop was sending out a technician.

"Hello."

"Emily, I stopped by the Loop this morning. They'll have a technician out there around two o'clock this afternoon, okay?"

"All right. I'll be here. How is work going?"

"Unthinkable. Unreal. Detective Konrad was waiting for me when I got here. They can't find Reading."

"That's no surprise."

"Well, I better get moving. Going to try to set up a meeting. See what direction we all want to go. This ought to be fun. I'll see you when I get home. Love you."

"Good luck."

***

Dong! The chimes on the grandfather clock echoed through the hall leading to the living room. Emily knew it was one o'clock and she had one hour to clean the condo before the technician arrived. Then the phone rang.

"Yeah. My name is Andy Majewski. I'm from Loop Appliance. I'll be there in about fifteen to twenty minutes, okay?"

"Fine, I'll be here."

Precisely twenty minutes later there was a knock at the door. Emily looked through the peep hole and saw the uniformed technician. She unlocked the deadbolt and opened the door. "Hello."

"Howdy. I'm here to look at your entertainment center." He produced his photo ID card verifying he was Andy Majewski. His shirt had the tag "Andy" just above the left pocket. He entered the condo carrying a gunnysack and a large, square black case loaded with tools.

The huge oak entertainment center was filled with books, movies, knickknacks, and pictures. It engulfed the entire back wall of the living room.

"Wow. I bet this baby took some strong men to get it up here."

"Oh, gosh. You should've been here. They could've used you. It took them all morning to get the unit up and assembled."

Andy fiddled with the remote, but nothing appeared to work. He moved to the corner of the unit, lifted it very slowly and eased it away from the wall.

"How long have you been doing this?" Emily questioned him.

"Too long. I started out working for my brother-in-law. He had his own TV repair shop. Then the computers surfaced, we took that on too."

"Your brother-in-law owns the Loop?"

"No, no. I started working at the Loop about four years ago." Emily could hear the technician grunting and unsnapping wires, then snapping them back. He squeezed out and away from the back of the unit.

"My brother-in-law is a genius with computers. Like he was

born to repair them. He can take them apart, rebuild them, program them, anything…blindfolded. Even to this day, I'm awed when I watch him work. He could do it in his sleep."

"Would you care for a cup of coffee? I just made a fresh pot."

"Yes. Thank you. Just a touch of cream and sugar."

Andy pulled some more tools from his case, including an electronic tester with cables extending from it. He squeezed back behind the unit.

"Here you are. Does your brother-in-law work for the Loop too?"

Carefully, Andy maneuvered from behind the center and gently slid it back to its original spot.

Andy began to laugh. "I'm afraid not. Old Ronnie boy was released from prison about five or six months ago. Because he was such a genius with computers, he started hacking into places he shouldn't have. He got caught and away he went. He spent four years at Stateville Prison."

Emily almost choked on her coffee. A hacker! She wanted to hear more from Andy.

"That's strange. I think I remember something about that. I was working at the Federal Building at the time, because we had a seminar regarding computer security. What was his name?" Emily was really pushing her luck. She never worked there, but grasping for straws was her only chance to get more information from Andy.

"Ronald Dugan. I run into him on occasion. Especially at family gatherings. He still lives around the area, never got married or had any kids. He's a simple drifter."

"Have you seen him recently?"

"No. Maybe it was three months ago. Let me think." Andy stood looking at the ceiling, his hands scratching his head. "Prairieville. I believe he lives near Prairieville."

So far, so good. Emily had a name and a location. All that was left was for Andy to finish fixing the TV and split. Then she could log onto the computer and look up Dugan.

He packed away his tools, then picked up the remote and pushed the "on" button. The plasma sprang into action. The sound was sharp and clear, better than before.

"Okay. You're up and running."

Andy kept changing the channels, raising and lowering the sound, the contrast of the picture, everything he could to make sure the system was running at one-hundred percent. Satisfied, he set down the remote and retrieved his clipboard to fill out the work order. He jotted down numbers, looked at his watch, and said, "Your total is $13.60. Two connectors shorted out. I replaced those at no cost because they're under warranty. I put in some new wires on the back of the unit that weren't covered by the warranty. Everything looks good now."

Emily reached for her pocketbook and handed Andy a twenty dollar bill. In return, Andy counted out $6.40 back to Emily. He handed her his clipboard with the work order on it, showing her a line she must sign, then tore off the receipt and handed it to her.

"Thank you, Mrs. Collier."

"Do you have any business cards? In case we have another problem."

"Sure. Here are a couple. Call us if that happens."

Emily said goodbye and after closing the door, she dashed to her computer and logged on. She entered Google's home page and from there, she typed in "People Search", pushed the Enter key, and within seconds a list of available sites were at her fingertips.

FindPeople.com sounded like the right spot. If not, she had plenty of other sites in reserve. Once the page opened, she followed the instructions and inserted the name Ronald Dugan from Prairieville, Illinois. Several Ronald Dugans were listed, but only one from Prairieville, Illinois. That had to be the one. She clicked on his name and waited for that page to appear. There he was, with a picture. Such a handsome hacker.

She scrolled down and read the skimpy information about him. When she reached the bottom of the page, she saw that for only $19.99, she could download his entire background. Everything recorded about him, his birth date, phone number, credit scores, even his criminal past. Emily hurried to get her purse and her debit card to acquire the necessary data of Mr. Dugan. She typed in her vitals, double-checked the information and hit the "Submit" icon.

In a matter of seconds, the site began to download her request. Amazing. Staring back at her was all the information she wanted. The complete history of hacker Ronald Dugan.

She moved the cursor to the print icon, her printer reacted and within a few moments, Emily had her ticket to the seven million dollar jackpot. She printed out several copies,

just to be on the safe side. She was so excited that she wanted to call Charles right away, she picked up the phone and dialed the number of Priority.

The phone rang five times, six times. Finally, "Priority Investments," a man's voice answered, one not familiar to Emily.

"Is Charles available?"

"I'm sorry. Everyone's at an important meeting right now. Can he call you back?"

"I'm his wife, Emily. Just tell him to call me when he finishes, okay?"

"Will do. Goodbye."

***

It was another day of interrogations for the Priority employees. But when the detectives finished their business, the office became still and quiet. All the agents who showed up that morning were in their offices, except for Charles. He waited until the halls became empty, then walked over to Alice's desk. She was playing solitaire on her computer screen, completely bored.

"I think we should call a meeting with everyone here. I don't know about you, but we need some questions answered as soon as possible."

"I don't know myself. I'd hate to lose my job, but it's not the end of the world for me, you understand?"

"Well, call everyone to the lobby and let's get this over with."

Alice leaned closer to her intercom, pushed the Send button and spoke out, "Would all employees please come to the conference room. Thank you."

She and Charles walked a few feet to the empty room, waiting for the agents. One by one, they arrived. Most had puzzled looks on their faces, concerned about what to expect.

"Well, many of you, like myself, probably have questions regarding the future of Priority. I wish I had an answer to that, but I don't. William is gone. So I ask you, do we pack up and move on, or establish a new CEO and continue with what we have?"

Hank Klaus, a senior agent who had been at Priority as long as Charles, spoke out. "As for myself, I wouldn't want to move. Just because we lost our leader doesn't mean we have to fold up our tent. It may be awkward the first few months, but if we all work together, we can keep this ship afloat."

The rest of the employees began clapping. There were a few whistles and shouts of "Yeah, yeah." Charles raised both his arms above his head, indicating silence. "That sounds good to me. We'll work even harder to succeed. So, what about this? Write down what you suggest we do. Who would you like to see as CEO? Take the weekend to digest your questions and on Monday, we'll meet back here and hash out the pros and cons to see what we come up with."

He scanned faces. Most of the agents seemed to like the idea he presented. Some faces looked positive, some gave him the feeling of "get me the hell out of here!"

There was still no sign of Dennis. Charles had the confident feeling that Dennis would never set foot again in the offices of Priority. In fact, Charles believed he was miles from

Chicago, running for his life. When the employees emptied the conference room, Randy, one of the younger agents said, "Charles, your wife called. I told her you would call her back as soon as the meeting ended."

"Thanks, Randy. I'll call her right now."

Alice and Charles walked back to the lobby. "That went over like a fart in church, Alice. As I looked around, I saw plenty of disgruntled faces. Tom, Louis, and Michelle didn't look happy. I can't wait to hear what they have to say. Jesus Christ, what a mess we have here."

Alice said nothing. If Charles could read her face, he would have seen only two words on it. *Who cares!*

Charles retreated back to his office, picked up his phone and dialed his home phone.

"You aren't going to believe what I'm going to tell you."

Charles heard the anxiety in Emily's voice.

"I hope this is better news than what I encountered at the office meeting."

"Can you get away from work right now?"

"Sure. You can't tell me over the phone?"

"Gosh no. I want to see your face when I tell you this. I'll meet you at the Starbucks across the street in thirty minutes."

"Okay. If it's that important."

"Charles. It's that important!"

Their call ended and Emily hurried to collect her coat and purse, but before that she opened the lower desk drawer and selected one large manila envelope. Large enough to carry the history of the person who will make them rich. Slamming the door behind her, she scurried to the elevator. She pounded the elevator button. *Shit, C'mon, C'mon...* Finally, the bell sounded and the door opened.

Charles arrived before Emily did. At two o'clock in the afternoon, there were plenty of empty booths, so Charles sat at the first empty one. A few minutes later, the taxi dropped off Emily. She rushed through the doors, spotted Charles, slid into the booth, and handed him the large envelope.

Emily whispered, "This is it, Charles. This is the guy who's going to open the door to our fortune."

He looked over the information. After he finished, he appeared confused.

"What is this? Where in the hell did you get this?"

"It came from Andy. Andy Polish-something. The computer geek who repaired our TV this afternoon. I began to talk to him, thinking he might be the guy we're looking for.

After a few cups of coffee, he didn't shut up. I mean from how he got into electronics to Ronald Dugan."

"So who is this Ron…what's his name? "

"He told me he began working for his brother-in-law, Dugan. Dugan owned a small TV repair shop, but when all this computer stuff started, he jumped into repairing them. Andy believed he was a genius with computers. So good, listen to this…he ended up in prison for computer hacking."

"Emily. Emily. Hold on a minute."

"So, when this Andy guy left, I jumped on the computer. I found a people locator site on Google and looked up Ron Dugan. Look at all that information about him! The best part of it all? It cost me only twenty bucks. I got a complete history of the man. A picture, where he lives, his phone number, even his criminal background."

"Well, this is incredible. But I still work for Priority, Emily. I can't take millions from them. Not until I find out about the future of the company. I'm just another employee.

"Charles. Think about it. Only three people in the entire office know about the huge chunk of money. It's there for the taking. If William were still alive, he'd have it in his pocket by now."

"Emily, believe me, the temptation is overwhelming. But now, my hands are tied. Besides, there are cops crawling all over the office every day."

Emily slouched back into the booth, as if Charles himself punched her in the stomach. He had let all the air out of her seven million dollar balloon.

Chapter 18

A Long Way From Home

Dan's checkbook kept reminding him of the seven million remaining in a Chicago bank. Now that William was out of the picture, the money was there for the taking, but how would he go about getting it? He had to get it before Charles did, also he knew he couldn't set foot back in the Windy City, at least not for awhile. Every detective in that city would be looking for him. In fact, he knew that from now on he would constantly keep looking over his shoulder for any suspicious cop ready to arrest him. The more he thought about the killing, all his fingers pointed to Helen. She, definitely had a motive, revenge, he was sure she pulled the trigger.

All through the night he kept driving, stopping only for gas, a quart of oil, and a quick bite. He made it through Wyoming and Utah, heading to northern Nevada. The Impala was running like a champ. Not a bad investment for only eight hundred bucks. With gas and a little oil, it would take him to wherever he turned the wheel. He stayed on the back roads as long as possible, but when he studied the maps, he sometimes couldn't avoid jumping onto the freeway. It was his only option. He was traveling on Interstate 80 through Salt Lake City, heading south until he reached Route 6. That route would take him all the way through Nevada and into California. According to the maps, Route 6 ended at the California border and from that point Route 395 was a direct shot into LA. His cash was running low and no way to withdraw funds from his bank in Chicago, fully aware that the cops were looking for any mistake he'd make, mostly a paper trail would certainly lead the cops directly to his location. *Damn it, I gotta stop doing that. It's Dan now. I have to keep remembering to use the name Dan, Dan Mesa.* He slammed his fist on the steering wheel, knowing the trouble he'd be in if he slipped up and used his real name.

The clock on the dash read 4:25 am. Dan felt sure he had been driving on Route 6 for years. Nothing but the dark road, no headlights, no animals, just an endless road through the barren, lifeless plains of Nevada. As soon as he crossed the California border, a sign greeted him—The State of California Welcomes You. Finally. It would be about another 350 miles before his drive was over, but not his worries.

As the sun peeked over the horizon, it was time for Dan to catch some much needed sleep. The trip from Illinois was long and tiresome, but it did give Dan the chance to sort out whats been happening over the past several days. The idea of Helen killing William never set right with Dan. It didn't make any sense. Why would she fly to Chicago, kill William and immediately fly back? Why would she jeopardize their scheme to confiscate the money when they needed William alive? The whole idea stunk. When the time came, meeting Helen, he'd have to find out the truth from her.

Dan exhaled a long gust of air from his tiresome lungs. He had gotten himself in a complicated mess all right. He sat behind the wheel shaking his head and asking himself. *This can't be happening. Jesus!* The only thing on his mind was the money, knowing William was the only person capable of moving the money from the bank in Chicago to an overseas account. His thoughts shifted from William to Charles. Charles was still in Chicago, still had the opportunity to claim the money or has he already done it? Dan's head was spinning out of control. There were to many questions on his mind and not one solid answer.

The eight hundred dollar, trustworthy Impala was cruising south on route 6 when Dan read the sign planted on the side of the road, *Entering the State of California, We Welcome You.* Finally, he was nearing the end of his innocent escape. The first town he came to was Bishop, where Route 6 ended and Route 395 began. He glanced at the dashboard, the digital clock glowed, 6:10 in the morning. The town of Bishop was desolate and quiet which pleased Dan, but he was tired and hungry. He approached the Travel Motor Inn and entered the small parking lot and parked in front of the lobby. It was definitely small, twelve rooms with an adjoining breakfast-lunch cafe. Awesome. He walked in and sat at the counter where an old, short gray haired waitress took his order of ham and eggs with rye toast and a cup of coffee. The meal hit the spot, Dan had a full stomach with a cup of coffee to go. He strolled across the diner parking area to the entrance of the Motor Inn. He signed the register under the name of Dan Mesa and paid the clerk, in return she handed him a room key.

"Is there a pay phone handy?"

"Yes sir. To the right of the diner, on the outside wall."

"Thank you."

He thought about dialing Helen's number, but realized what time it was. He decided to catch a few winks and make the call later in the afternoon. He was tired. Tired of driving, tired of thinking, and already tired of running. The fact became more surreal to Dan. He could be running for the rest of his life.

He parked the car in front of room seven, grabbed the duffle bag along with the atlas, then locked the car. The room appeared just like the one in Yankton, old, reeked of cigarette smoke and desperate for remodeling. He closed the drapes, plopped on the bed, and within minutes, was dead to the world.

The sound of the screeching siren startled Dan. He leaped from the bed and quickly, peeked through the drapes. At first, thinking it was the cops surrounding his room, but was relieved to see a hustling ambulance traveling north toward Bishop. He caught his breath, rubbed his eyes and walked to the desk, it was twenty past one. Time to call Helen.

"Yeah, it's me. I just got into California, some small town...Bishop, I think. I'm going to need some money when I get there." The long drive put Dan in a sour mood. "Listen, Helen, you're the reason I'm standing in some stupid small town in California running for my life."

"This is no time to panic. You panic, you make mistakes, so calm down and put your head on straight."

"Well, I'm already tired of running. I didn't kill Fossett so why am I running? What's happening back in Chicago?" Dan leaned against the wall listening for Helen's response.

"I'll find out. I haven't heard from my people out there, so I guess pretty much the same. I'll check the Internet, look up the Chicago papers. They'll have the up-to-the-minute news. When do you think you'll get here?"

"I don't know, I think I'll stay here for the night and get an early start in the morning. I'm going to need some money, soon. I'm nearly broke."

"Okay. Just call me when you get here. I'm in Pasadena."

Dan hung up the phone, adjusted his sunglasses, and took another swig from his bottle of beer. *Shit, what a fucking mess."*

***

Charles returned to work, anticipating good results from his co-workers about the direction Priority was about to take. Becoming the new CEO of Priority had many advantages for him. Definitely a pay raise, overseeing the development of all the clients' accounts, and the best possibility, maybe owning Priority Investments, Inc. In other words, the top of the corporate ladder. He was sure that was what the other agents thought too, but when he entered the lobby, Alice was waiting for him with bad news.

"Hans, Mike, and Kathy handed in their resignations this morning," she said, looking disgusted.

"Why! Even Hans?"

"And from what they're telling me, there will be two more. Michelle and Louis are leaving the end of this week. So, I can see where Priority is headed. We're down to just four of us. If that's the case, I will be leaving also."

"Come on. Hold on a sec. Let's think this out. They're all jumping the gun here, and...we haven't even sat down to hash this out."

"The handwriting is on the wall, Charles. No one sees a future here, now that William is gone. Are you going to be the next CEO?"

"If that's the case and if I can get everyone to reconsider, hell yes. I'll do it."

The door of the front office opened and Detective Konrad with his partner Detective Fritz stepped in.

"You people look so happy this morning. I'll make it even happier for ya. You wanna hear the latest?"

Alice stood and walked to the front counter to join Charles.

"Oh. This must be our lucky day, huh Alice?"

"We found footprints in the snow across from the front door, a man's print size 11 along with another print. We believe the footprints belong to a woman. Size nine shoe, approximately 135 to 150 pounds. Also, a .38 caliber spent shell casing."

"A woman? Come on. You're telling us it was a woman who murdered William?"

"A very strong possibility. And that's not all."

"Bring it on, Detective."

"Cops found Reading's SUV. He hid it behind a shopping mall in Yankton, South Dakota.

"Hold on a second. You think that Reading had a partner? If he did, it had to be William's sister. She definitely had a motive."

"After Reading ditched the SUV, the police in Yankton talked to a local used car dealer. They showed him a picture of Reading and learned that he sold a 2001 Chevy Impala to a curly brown haired fellow just a few days before the cops found the SUV. Even paid cash."

"This is incredible."

Alice didn't react to what she heard. When Detective Konrad

mentioned the lady's footprints, he looked directly at her. And if looks could tell a story, he was assuming the possibility Alice was a suspect. She fit the description, size nine shoe, weight between 135 to 150 pounds.

"What size shoe do you wear? And your weight? Where were you the night Fossett was murdered, Miss Oliver?" Konrad's biting eyes scared the shit out of Alice.

"I get it now. Because I work here and know Fossett, I'm a suspect now?"

"Until we find the real killer, everyone is a suspect. And by the way, we want to see Priority's financial statements over the past five years."

Alice was furious, standing with her arms folded across her chest. "You got a warrant?"

"As a matter of fact, right here in my hand."

Disgusted, Charles said nothing and walked back to his office. Alice returned to her desk too, as the phone rang.

"Priority Investments. I'm sorry, Mr. Klaus is not employed here any more. You're welcome."

"The statements, please." Konrad tapped his fingers on the reception counter, agitating Alice even more. He sent his partner, along with another policeman, to search Reading's office to look for any evidence Reading may have left behind. Alice took her time gathering the statements off her computer and making copies for Konrad. When she finished, she handed them to him. "Choke on these, asshole." Konrad laughed.

Ever since the death of William, it was pure chaos within Priority's community. Pointing fingers, employees quitting, everyday presence of the police. Charles sat motionless in his office, pondering the thought if Emily was right. Does he have the opportunity to take the money and run? The more he thought, the more devious his thoughts became. First come, first serve, meaning... get it before Reading does.

"Look what we found in Reading's desk drawer, Mr. Collier."

Fritz showed him a picture of four individuals standing on a golf course, all holding a golf club and arms around each other. Two men and two woman, all smiling and about to participate in the Woman's Cancer Research golf outing, according to the caption on the photo. Charles studied the photo. It was William, Reading, Helen and…Alice.

"I'll be goddamn. That's Reading, all right." Charles had never seen this picture before. Of course, he avoided Reading's office, nothing in there interested him. But, here was the proof that all four of them were friends.

"You object to us keeping the photo?"

Charles said nothing, but detective Fritz removed the photo from the frame, then set the empty frame on Charles's desk.

"I'll keep in touch. Have a nice day." Both detectives walked to the lobby, where Konrad was waiting. Konrad had what he came for and more.

Charles was furious. Not about the detectives, but the photo they found. He darted out of his office to confront Alice face to face.

"They found a picture in Reading's office. You, William, Helen and him at a golf outing. You knew him, didn't you? Before he was hired here. When was that picture taken?"

"Cool down, Charles." Alice sensed that Charles was beginning to realize what she feared, she did know Reading. "A long time ago, I can't remember. And, I didn't know who Reading was. Just a friend of William and Helen. I think he was dating Helen at the time."

"Things are adding up, Alice. You think Reading is scared? You better look in the mirror. You and that Helen. You're the only two women that had reasons to do this. Did you kill William?"

***

The financial papers were now in the hands of the police. It wouldn't be long before they put everything together and found out about the seven million. Charles dashed back to his office, grabbed his coat and briefcase, and left Priority's offices.

Chapter 19

There's No Place Like.. A New Home?

"You're home early."

"Sit down. You remember what you said to me a few days ago? At Starbucks?"

Emily thought fast, shaking her head. "I said a lot of things. You mean about the hacker, Dugan?"

"Priority is folding like a tent. Three quit today and two more will leave on Friday. And…the cops were there again today. They found footprints at Fossett's house. A woman's footprints and a bullet casing. Also, they found Reading's car in South Dakota. I think Alice, Reading, and his girlfriend were all in this together."

"Jesus." Emily looked scared. All she heard were the footprints found at William's house.

"That's not all. The cops found a photo in Reading's office. The four of them golfing together. I asked Alice about it and she denied everything. She said the photo was taken years ago. I don't believe her."

"Seven million, Charles. If we don't get our hands on it, they will."

"I have to think."

Charles went into the living room and sat in his recliner while Jack continued playing games on his Xbox. He and Emily sat with him, they watched TV, and talked about Jack's plans for the summer. He would be a senior this fall and soon would graduate and leave for college.

"So, have you thought any more on what college you'd like to attend?" Just to change the subject and get his mind away from the woeful events, Charles put his arm around Jack.

"Yeah. I think so. I want to get my degree in computer graphics or computer animation. You know, get into the movie industry."

"Really. That's cool. I mean, the things they can do with computers these days. Almost every movie we've seen, there's some kind of trick animation to it. It sure makes it look so real."

"Yeah, that's what I wanna do. Look at every Harry Potter movie. I've been on the internet and checking out colleges that have the programs I'm interested in. Most of them are out west tho, like USC, UCLA, or Stanford."

"We'll always be behind you, son. Whatever you decide, we're sure you'll make the right decision. Besides, you're old enough to start making important decisions on your own."

"You think we could we take a vacation to California this summer and visit those schools?

"Sounds okay to me. What do you think, Hun?"

"It does sound exciting. Kind of wish I was your age and had that in front of me."

The chimes from the grandfather clock echoed through the condo. Ten o'clock and time to start getting ready for bed. Jack said goodnight, kissed his mom, and headed for his bedroom.

Charles turned off the TV and the kitchen lights, then make sure the doors were all locked. When the lights were off in their bedroom, Emily snuggled up to him.

"Only the three of you know about the money, and one is…well, God knows where Reading is. This is something we can do, Charles. I'm sure if William and Dennis could get away with it, so could we. Tomorrow, let's sit down and plan something out. Be ready, if we need to."

"This is a huge step, Emily. Its embezzlement. You must look at the consequences? If I get caught, I'd be spending a long time in prison and away from you and Jack. I'm not sure I want to do that and besides, sitting in a desolate prison cell the rest of my life, getting butt-fucked. No way."

Emily laughed, "That's why we really have to study hard, think of all the angles, cover all our bases, and plan a backup if anything backfires."

"When I go to work tomorrow, and if Alice isn't there, I'll check all the financial data on Priority to see if the seven million is still there. If so, then we can start thinking, okay?"

Emily inched closer to Charles, snuggled and kissed his cheek. "We can do this, Hun."

***

It was a little past seven am. when Dan left the cafe. With his belly full, and ready to hit the road, he walked to his room, double-check to see if anything was left behind, then check out. According to the map, it would be about a four drive to Pasadena. Once he arrived there, he wanted to ditch the Impala, therefore, erasing all connections that would tie him to California. He was a full-blown fugitive at this point, knowing every police officer in America would be looking for him. From this point forward, Dan would be constantly looking over his shoulder for danger. He had to avoid crowds, keep low and, if possible, stay out of sight. But, for how long?

As he got closer to LA., the traffic became more congested, there were more people, meaning more cops. He exited the interstate, drove a few blocks till he came to a shopping mall. He pulled in, parked the Impala and sat in the car figuring what he can do with the Impala. When he looked up, he solved the solution. Standing on the corner, about thirty feet from him, were a group of teens. He got out of the car and approached them.

"Yo…anyone of you want a free car?"

Five of them, all dressed like they belonged to a gang, all wearing hooded sweatshirts and pants that buckled around their thighs, exposing plaid underwear. They looked at Dan, wondering if he was high on something.

"Say what?" The tallest member moved closer to Dan.

"I said, if you want a free car, here it is. I don't need the car anymore, and I don't have the money for insurance and gas. You want it, take it." Dan dangled the keys from his right index finger.

They started high-fiving each other and without any hesitation, snatched the keys from Dan's finger.

Dan vacated the area as fast as he could and disappeared into the swelling streets of Pasadena. But, first things first, he must look for a place to stay. He reached into his pocket and removed his remaining money, unfolded it, and began counting the bills. He counted $822, enough for him to rent a furnished apartment until more money came. He walked the streets, carrying his bag, and looked for a local newspaper. Finding one, he went into McDonald's, ordered a Big Mac, fries, and a Coke, then sat down to check the available apartments.

There were hundreds of places to rent, with prices ranging from $600 to $2000 a month. Okay, but where was he? He needed to find someone familiar to the area who could help him find an apartment. On the same page as the rentals, he saw several ads representing real estate agencies. Sure, that had to be the answer. They would definitely know how to help him. When he finished his Coke and Big Mac, he hurried out of the restaurant looking for one of the real estate offices. He kept walking until he saw the red sign for Capital Real Estate. He crossed the busy street and entered the office.

"Hello. May I help you?" asked a very well-dressed, young brunette woman. She was wearing a white blouse, tan skirt, and a dark red sport coat with her ID badge pinned to it. Her name was Mary Clemons.

"I'm new to LA. and looking for a furnished apartment. Somewhere in the range of $500-$750 per month and somewhere close by."

"Sure. Please, sit down and let's take a look."

"Where am I now?"

"You're in Pasadena. A little northeast of LA. It's beautiful here."

Dan watched as Mary surfed the computer for rental properties in his price range, typing information, and moving from one page to another.

"There are a number of places to rent, so we have a wide variety to select from. Give me one more second here and I'll print out some properties that are close by and all within your price range."

As she finished, the printer had produced a few pages for Dan to review. She collected them and handed them to him.

"Now these are all furnished apartments. Most require a security deposit and a credit background check. They all depend on the price of the unit and the location. The higher the rent, of course, the more the deposit and more stringent the credit report."

Ooh, a credit report. Dan looked at the rentals, wondering how he could rent an apartment without a security check. There was no Dan Mesa.

"Gee. A security check. I'm not sure I can do that. I mean, I don't have a good credit rating but I have the money. I was hoping I could find something today."

"Well. That could cause a problem. Let me get back on the site and see if I can locate some cheaper rentals for you."

Mary continued to punch the keyboard and study the information.

"Here we go. There are two rental properties close by that do not require a deposit or a security check. I'll print them out for you. You can walk there and check them out for yourself. How does that sound?"

"Excellent."

Seconds later, she handed him the latest page along with a street map of Pasadena.

"I think you'll need this too."

"Do I owe you anything for this?"

"Since you're new to Pasadena, consider this a token of our hospitality. Good luck in finding a place. If you ever need help in purchasing a home, I'd be delighted to help you." She selected a business card from her tray and handed it to him.

"You've been so kind. Tell you what. Whenever I'm back in this area, lunch is on me, deal?"

"That's very kind of you. Deal."

The first property was located on Forest Drive, and the second on Truman Avenue. He unfolded the map of Pasadena to determine where he was, and where to find the closer of the two rentals.

Got it. Truman Avenue is only four blocks away. He crossed the street, found Truman Avenue, then turned left toward the apartments. He passed plenty of stores on his way down Truman Avenue, including a drug store with outside pay phones.

He continued walking for two more blocks until he came to 4455 Truman Avenue. The Casa Truman Apartments. It was a three-story, old brick building, with concrete front steps leading to the second story, the main entrance to the apartments.

He climbed the stairs and on his right he saw a row of six door bells and mail boxes. Apartment 3 was labeled Manager. He pushed the white button, waited a second till the buzzer answered back, allowing him to enter the building. Apartment 1 and 2 were located on the lower level, 3 and 4 were on the second floor, and 5 and 6 on the top floor. When he located apartment 3, he rang the doorbell and waited for an answer. Minutes later, a short, older woman with gray hair pushed back into a pony tail greeted him.

"Hello. I'm here to look at the vacant apartment."

"Very well. Let me get the key and I'll show you the apartment."

When she returned, she told him apartment 2 was for rent and they had to go outside. The pair walked to the entrance, down the concrete stairs and turned right to apartment 2. Both lower apartments had outside doors, a private entrance which meant better security for Dan. As soon as the door opened, Dan anticipated what he was ahead of him. The place was old, but furnished, the kitchen was small but adequate, and there were two bedrooms, and a reasonable area for the living room. The apartment didn't furnish a TV, so if Dan was going to live like a hermit, a TV was necessary. It was what Dan expected, nothing to get excited about, but a place to call home. Anyway, he needed a roof over his head right now.

"The rent is five hundred a month. All the utilities are paid for except your phone and cable. You're responsible to keep the apartment clean, no excessive noises, and no pets. There is no lease to sign. You live here from month-to-month, agreed?"

"Okay, sure. No problem. I'll take it." Dan handed her the first month's rent leaving him 300 dollars in his pocket.

"How close is the nearest grocery store?"

"Down a few blocks. Right across the street from the drugstore."

"Cool."

She handed the key to Dan, then headed back to her apartment. *So, this is home for the next... oh boy. Jesus, I hope not.*

He began casing out the apartment. The bathroom, the shower, then the bedrooms and the softness of the mattress. From there he went to the kitchen. He opened all the cupboards. He found dishes and glasses, pots and pans, and silverware. The refrigerator was empty, and the kitchen had a small microwave. Dan left the kitchen and looked to the living room, still no TV. How was he going to live here, secluded from society and not have a TV? As soon as he got some money from Helen, the first thing on his list would be to buy a new TV.

Well. I better get some food. On his way to the grocery store, Dan passed the drugstore, and on the outside wall was a row of three pay phones. Pretty rare to find these days since cell phones were introduced. Finding a pay phone close to the apartment was a bonus for Dan, so why not call Helen.

"Hey. I found a place to stay. It's perfect. An old, brick house with six apartments. Has its own private entrance. Pretty quiet and not far from a grocery store and drug store. I believe it's in Pasadena. It's called Casa Truman Apartments on Truman Avenue. You know where Truman is?"

"I've heard of that street, and its close by. I've got news from Chicago. The police found your car."

"Oh, cut it out! Seriously? They found the Escape? Shit. I can't believe that. It's only been two days. I thought it would be months till they found it. Listen, we need to talk soon. A lot has happened since William was murdered. Cops have been at the offices every day and worse case scenario, Charles and Alice know about the money, too."

He stood, listening to Helen as people walked by him, "I don't know what to do, we need to sit down and discuss this. I don't want to loose that seven million. Well, get me five thousand, that should hold me over for a few months. Yeah. Okay, I'll talk to you later."

He crossed the street and walked into the grocery store. He loaded up on familiar junk food, picking up items that looked good. Since there was no TV, Dan purchased two books, a puzzle magazine and a case of beer. If boredom showed it's face, he was ready for the battle.

Chapter 20

Getting the Ball Rolling

What was the purpose of going to work today? Charles tossed that around as he made his morning coffee and listened to the latest news. His mind was heavy with uncertainty. Whether to stick it out with Priority, although only three of the original nine agents were still working there, or listen to Emily and take the risk of pocketing the seven million on behalf of William Fossett. If he decided on the latter, what would happen with his clients, especially Adolph Kaiser? Should he tell Adolph that the company was closing it's doors?

He was sure that Adolph would understand, but all his months of hard work and his persistent struggle to achieve the best for his clients would be thrown out the window. Although, on second thought, having all that money to himself could open a lot of windows. There was one more thing to do before he made up his mind. He had to check the figures on the current Priority financial statements. If they were the same as when he last saw them, it would be another plus for him—proving that no one had the ability to manipulate and withdraw the money.

"Good morning. You want a cup of coffee?"

"Just watching the news. I think I missed the current news, now the weather and sports are on."

Emily sat at the table across from him holding her cup of coffee.

"Can't get your mind off of it, can you? Well. I had a hard time sleeping and thinking about it too. I'm damned if I do and I'm damned if I don't. You know what I mean?" Charles sat aimlessly staring at the TV.

***

"Yes. There were so many things running through my mind last night. Like…what about Jack? There's no way we could still live in Chicago. Or how hard would it be to hack into that account?"

"Those questions might be answered after I stop in the office. If Alice isn't there, and if I can find her password, then I'll have a chance to review the current financial statements. Charles exhaled a deep breath. "Hoping that all works out and the money is still there, our next obstacle…finding Mr. Dugan."

"Our lives could change significantly. If we had the seven million, Charles, we could live anywhere. More than likely, outside the states."

"Don't get ahead of yourself, Emily. First things first." Charles got up and dressed for the office.

***

He left the elevator and walked the short distance to the doors of Priority Investments. The doors were locked, apparently, nobody showed up for work that morning. He let himself in, locked the door again, and went to Alice's desk. All the information he needed was on her computer. He needed to open Priority's site, submit the password, and print out the pages. *What's her god damn password?* He then remembered the last time he asked Alice for information regarding his accounts, Alice logged into the home website and punched in the password. She chuckled and inadvertently, spit out the password. It was Y-T-I-R-O-I-R-P. Of course, Priority spelled backwards. He entered the password and instantly, the main page to Priority came to view.

He opened the financial page to find everything as it was the last time he saw that page. What a lucky break! His eyes focused on one line. The seven million was still untouched. He printed out the results, closed down the computer, and straightened Alice's desk. He went to his office, sat in his chair, and stared out the window toward Lake Michigan, where he did all his needed thinking. He thought about his clients. What should he do about them? He remembered his meeting with Ed Weldon. Yes. He'd hand them over to Ed, knowing full well that Ed would do a good job. He reached for his Rolodex and called Ed's number.

"Ed Weldon."

"Ed, it's me again. Charles."

"All right. You want to go out for lunch again?"

"Not today. But I have an interesting proposition for you."

"Really. How interesting?"

"Well, since the death of William, the office is in complete turmoil. Six agents have quit and moved on. I'm up-in-the-air about my plans here, but Emily and I are thinking of moving to California."

"Really? A Midwestern boy going west? Ohh…all of us here are truly sorry to hear about the death of William. It was a real shock."

"Me, too. We're still puzzled about who would want to kill William. But, putting that aside, my son Jack will be attending college in California next fall. So we thought the best plan for all of us is to move with him. My proposition to you is taking over my accounts I have at Priority. Would you be willing to do that?"

"Wow! That's extremely generous of you. Although, its been a few years since I worked with stocks. I know I'll do good with them, Charles. Maybe not as good as you, but I'll work hard for it."

"That's why I thought of you. I'm about ninety-five percent sure this is what our plans are. But, you can never predict the unforeseen. I should know in one or two weeks, all right?"

"Absolutely. Call me when you're ready?"

"One more thing before I hang up. Don't mention this to

anyone. I mean, with all the police running around, they may jump to the wrong conclusions."

"No problem, Charles. I understand, and I won't say anything to anyone."

"I'll talk to you soon, Ed. Goodbye."

***

Emily and Charles woke up the next morning with one thing on their minds. Find Ronald Dugan. They sat at the kitchen table, coffee cups in their hands, as Charles looked over the life history of Mr. Dugan. The twenty-dollar report contained his last three known addresses, places of employment, his criminal background, and other less valuable stats like age, single or divorced, a credit report, even his current phone number. The TV was on, tuned to the local news station. As they watched, the broadcast mentioned no late news regarding the investigation into William's murder.

"I think we should try this number. If it's his, then we talk. What do you think?"

"Sounds exactly what I would do, Charles. You know, once a criminal, always a criminal." she laughed.

"Don't say that, Emily. Don't ever say anything you'll regret later. And that's not funny."

"Have you thought about what you might offer Dugan if he cooperates with us?"

"He'll do anything if the price is right. Fifty thousand I thought was a nice round figure."

"Jesus. This is scary. I mean getting another person involved. How can we trust him?"

"Morning." Jack came in, sat down and began eating his breakfast.

"What costs fifty thousand?"

Charles thought quickly and the first thing that popped into his mind, "Probably your college tuition."

"Holy crap, that's a ton of money."

Jack finished his breakfast and returned to his bedroom.

"Well, let's wait till eleven o'clock. It'll give me time to think what I'm going to say and how to approach this."

There was no reason for Charles to go into work, because there was no real work to do. Sit at his computer reviewing the stock market? What would be the sense of that? Now, it all depended on Ronald Dugan. If Charles could persuade Dugan, there would be more important issues to consider than the latest stock quotes.

It was time. Emily handed Charles his cell phone. "I'm keeping my fingers crossed."

Charles picked up Dugan's history sheet and punched in the number from that. He took a deep breath.

"Yeah? What do you want?"

"Am I speaking to Ronald Dugan?"

"Who the hell wants to know?"

"If you are Ronald Dugan, I have a proposition you may be interested in. So, let's talk."

After a dead silence, the voice spoke. "Yeah, that's me. What's this proposition about?"

"It's not something I want to discuss over the phone. But I will say this. The monetary rewards are highly in your favor. Tomorrow, I'll be at the 5th Street Deli, Chicago. The corner of 5th Street and Wells at two o'clock. If you're interested, you'll be there. If not, I'll find someone else who could use the gift. Good day." Charles closed his cell and sat down. Emily was biting her nails, shaking. A minute later, his cell phone rang.

"Mr. Dugan?"

"Okay. I'll be there. How do I know who I'm looking for?"

Charles thought fast, his eyes focused on Jack's black White Sox baseball cap hanging on the coat rack.

"Look for a black White Sox baseball cap. I'll be in the rear of the deli. Two o'clock."

Charles hung up. His life as a criminal has just begun.

"Whew. He sounded like a criminal and I was scared. Jesus!

No more cell phones. Anytime we need to contact Dugan, we have to use untraceable phones, all right?"

"Do you think I should go with you?"

"Let me think. Yeah. You should go. But sit in a different place. Get a good look at him. Maybe take his picture or something of that order. If this backfires, we could say that Dugan blackmailed us, right?"

***

The next day, Charles prepared mentally to meet Dugan. The amateurish pair thought hard about what they could do and what they couldn't do, what they would say and couldn't say. All they hoped for was Dugan showing up at the deli. They walked to the deli instead of taking a cab, they dressed like vagrants keeping a very low profile. Now that Charles knew the money was untouched, he felt more confident about meeting Dugan. The rookie "thiefs" discussed their plan constantly, how critical each and every move would determine their success. They must take everything in stride, avoiding mistakes, take their time, think everything out, and go forward from there. Hour after hour they devised their plan. They even established a plan "B."

The deli had emptied after the noon lunch crowd left, so two o'clock was an ideal time to meet Dugan. Charles entered alone, wearing the black baseball cap. He walked to an empty booth near the rear of the deli and began his wait. Minutes later, Emily entered. She winked to Charles as she passed, and sat at a table behind and to the left of Charles's booth. She took a book from her purse and acted like an innocent patron. Approximately ten minutes after two, a man entered through the revolving doors and stood motionless. His eyes scanned a handful of patrons, then spotted the black White Sox hat on the head of a man staring at him from a booth at the back. With no other Sox hats in view, he headed to that booth. He looked at Charles and sat down facing him. It was the perfect angle for Emily to take his picture.

"Mr. Dugan, I presume?"

"At your service. So, this better be good. I had to drive from Prairieville. Fucking traffic and it cost me twenty bucks to park my car."

"Indeed it will be good. Does fifty thousand sound inviting to you?"

"Fifty thousand, huh? Start talking. What do I have to do?"

"I'm not going to get into the finer details with you now. You don't have to know what, who, or where, okay? There's a huge sum of money sitting in a Chicago bank, unknown by some people, but I know it's there. What I need from you is to acquire the passwords and codes from that account and transfer the money to an account in Switzerland. Should be a piece of cake for you."

"How did you find me?"

"I have my sources. So, do we have a deal or not?"

"You think it's a piece of cake? Then why don't you do it yourself?"

"Simple. I don't have your capabilities and I can't get my name involved with this. Plus, there are passwords and codes I don't have access to. You, being a genius hacker, can get them for me. Correct?"

Dugan studied Charles. His arms were folded across his chest and he was thinking, *This could be messy. Is the fifty thousand worth it? Or ten more years in prison? If he can pay fifty thousand, he surely can pay a hundred thousand.*

His wrinkled face looked as though he'd endured a struggled life, much resembling that of an old man.

"I'll do it for a hundred thousand, no questions asked. After we're done, you've never heard of me or met me, understood?"

Without any hesitation, Charles reached across the table to shake Dugan's hand.

"Agreed. In return, you never saw or heard of me either. You'll get your hundred thousand the minute we successfully transfer the money to the Swiss account."

Was Charles playing with fire? He'd never experienced dealing with a convicted criminal, but was he becoming the same person Ronald Dugan was?

Dugan rubbed his chin, gritted his teeth, then extended his hand to meet Charles's hand.

"I'll agree to that. When do we start?"

"I will contact you in a few days. I'll have a place where we can meet and complete the transaction. Safe and easy to find."

Dugan slipped out of the booth and vanished from the deli.

Charles turned toward Emily and saw her thumb pointing upward, indicating…*good job, Charles.* He went to pay the bill and left the deli. Emily stayed behind for several minutes, remembering to cover their tracks, in case Dugan was watching Charles.

Charles arrived at the condo before Emily, still nervous and shaking from what went down with Dugan. About thirty minutes later Emily arrived, ready to hear the deal Dugan made.

"Boy, he looked scary. Do we have a deal with him?"

"Honestly, I was shaking in my boots. It's not like I've done this all my life."

"He looked nervous too. If I didn't know anything about him, I would've never guessed he spent time in prison."

"Well, he agreed to do it, but not for fifty thousand. Now it's one hundred thousand. I didn't want to barter with him or scare him away. He's our only chance to get this done."

"Charles, he could've asked for two hundred thousand and we would've agreed to get it done and over with. He's our only key to open the door to that money. Besides, he's a crook." Emily hung up her coat, then removed her cell phone from it, hit a couple of buttons, and handed the phone to Charles. She had taken six pictures of Dugan, all showing the cute, innocent face of their hacker.

"Just let him try to double-cross us." Emily said.

"While I was walking home, I thought how easy it would be for Dugan to hack into Priority's account. Then I realized how easy it would be for him to hack into our Swiss account."

"Holy shit. Now that is scary. I never thought of that. How do we protect ourselves?"

"I have no clue."

Chapter 21

How Does Costa Rica Sound?

With the first step in place, Charles and Emily had additional planning to do. Next he would contact Franz Schindler at Clairden Leu Bank in Geneva to set up a new account. He had worked with Franz several times in the past and getting new accounts open took only a few days, thanks to the fax machine. He'd explain to Franz that the account, near seven million, was created by a very important client, so speed and security were vital. Then it would be on to step two.

With a heavy load on his conscience, Charles worried about his clients. Would Ed Weldon be capable of handling this work load, especially the Kaiser account? It took him eighteen years of hard work to accomplish his success. Handing them over to a person that didn't have the experience, Charles felt guilty to those clients. But, grasping his paws on the pot of gold, he didn't care what happened to his accounts.

His plan had to be flawless. Yet, there were many obstacles needed tending to and seriously thought out by the pair. His plan rehearsal with Emily, his meeting with Dugan, handing over his accounts to Ed, obtaining his passport, closing his office at Priority, avoiding Detective Konrad, and most important, their son, Jack. What were they going to tell him? It all rested on the shoulders of Mr. Dugan.

Jesus. So much to do.

"Mom, right after dinner Tom and I are going over to Lincoln Park. Some kind of party with Tom's family." Jack spoke.

"Okay. What time do you think you'll be home?"

"I'm not sure. But if its getting late, I'll call you."

"Sounds good. Be careful, Jack."

After dinner, and with Jack out of the house, Emily and Charles started fine-tuning their plan.

"You know, I'm still having second thoughts about this. Getting caught scares the hell out of me. I hope you realize that if I get caught, our lives are over. You understand?"

"I'm scared too. But we can't think that way. We have to think positive. The hardest hurdle is getting Dugan to hack the money. After that, we're home free. We can do this, Charles, we can do it."

"I hope you're right. Once the money gets transferred, we won't have much time to decide where we're going. We can't sit around and wait for Konrad to discover when or where the seven million went."

"Yes. Here's what I was thinking. We have a slight problem with Jack. We can't deny him the opportunity of attending college. Right?"

"Yes. I'm listening."

"This may sound off the wall, but let me finish. We need a foolproof excuse for you quitting Priority and moving away. Say we file for divorce, then you move to Mexico or some other country. I'll move back to Manford with Jack as if nothing has happened. Doesn't that make sense? Think about it. We have to stay one step ahead of everyone else. We have to make them believe all this."

"Boy, that is off the wall. A divorce?"

"Yes, but living with seven million in our pockets is off the wall. I'm sure it will create a load of problems, but we can't crack, no matter what. How could they prove that we didn't have marital problems? Millions of people do. Get a divorce, then we split. I'll go on living in Manford with Jack, get a job, and live like we're average middle-class people. We have to keep low for a year or two. When everything settles down, we get back together and live where no one can find us."

"Does sound logical. How do we explain all this to Jack?"

"That I haven't thought about yet."

Charles moved to his living room desk containing the computer and logged on to the Internet. He typed "California" in the search box and pressed the Enter key. Up popped a page listing numerous sites that contained topics about California, from vacationing to the real estate market. He scrolled down to a link showing real estate in Southern California. Once on the page, he found a lot of information about houses for sale, houses to rent, and descriptions of communities.

"Do you have a particular city you want to move to?"

"What's showing, Charles?"

Emily crouched behind him, looking at all the information as he moved from page to page, and house after house.

"Look at those prices. Unbelievable."

Charles's eyes caught a small advertisement on the far right border of the page. "Costa Rica. The new excitement in living."

He clicked on the Costa Rica link. The site showed glamorous pictures from all parts of Costa Rica. The ocean, the tropical forests, the isolated sandy beaches, the colorful foliage, and most important, real estate. He was awestruck. He selected the link for real estate and found page after page of houses for sale in every locale. It looked like Costa Rica had it all.

"Emily. Look how much cheaper it is to buy a house in Costa Rica."

The more he stayed on the site the more his interest grew. He began reading about the history and government of Costa Rica, and how they affected the residents and the tourists. He came across a paragraph regarding laws governed within that country. He saw the "search" box at the top of the screen, then typed in "Extradition". A new page opened up and Charles began reading the paragraph. In the 1940s, the government of Costa Rica passed laws denying extradition of new citizens of Costa Rica back to their original country. *No extradition laws.* He opened the desk drawer and removed the Webster dictionary.

Extradition: surrender of criminal to another authority: The process of returning somebody accused of a crime by a different legal authority to that authority for trial or punishment." How interesting. So, if he moved to Costa Rica and became a citizen, then was accused of a crime in Illinois, that state could not extradite him back to Illinois for a trial. Outstanding.

Charles definitely knew Costa Rica was the place he'd go. With pen in hand, he started jotting down several places that drew his attention. *What would it cost to fly there?* He Googled air flights to Costa Rica. He found a website posting one-way flights to Liberia, at $550, and four-star hotels at $80 a night. The prices seemed cheap to Charles, but he hesitated to book anything. He began jotting this information down in his notebook, his itinerary was shaping up.

He prepared a list of priorities. One…move the money. Two…get his passport. Three…book his flight and hotel. Four…complete the divorce. Five…quit Priority. Six…meet with Ed. Last…talk to Jack. His timetable was set.

Satisfied that he had everything in order, Charles shut down the computer. It was 2:30 in the morning, Emily and Jack were fast asleep and that's where he was headed.

***

When Dan opened his eyes, *Where am I? Did I get lucky last night?* He turned his head to the left, then to the right. He was alone and in an unfamiliar environment, a place he didn't feel comfortable. His luck hadn't changed and there wasn't seven million dollars in his pocket when reality set in. *I'm in a shit-hole, fleeing for my life and no clue where the money is.* He lay motionless with his eyes focused on the peeling plastered ceiling. He realized his life was spiraling out of control, running for his life for a crime he never committed.

After he ate breakfast, he sat at the table trying to understand how long this was going to last. Day after day, the constant gut reaction of looking over his shoulder. The unalterable feeling that everyone was gunning for him. *It's called paranoia, Dan.*

Dan left the apartment, walking west on Truman Avenue toward the drug store. He was hoping to find a Chicago newspaper. There was no sign of a Tribune on the rack, instead, a local paper would do. He slipped his hand into his pocket for change, but in that pocket he also found the business card of Mary Clemons. Yes, today would be a fantastic day to take that young lady out to lunch. That's where he was headed.

From the change he pulled from his pocket, he paid for the paper and also bought a pack of Dutch Masters cigars.

"Do you know where I can get a Chicago newspaper?" asking the counter person.

"Try the news stand on the corner of Truman and fifth street, about four blocks west." the clerk told him.

"Thanks."

Dan found the corner newsstand and the Chicago Tribune. He scanned the headlines, paged through the first section and found nothing regarding William's murder. He folded the paper under his arm and walked to the nearest coffee shop. He purchased a cup of coffee and moved to a table to finish reading the paper. On page twelve at the very bottom in small print, a headline read, "No New Leads in the Fossett Murder." The article talked about witnesses, footprints, the .38 caliber pistol, and the black SUV. The article went on to explain that the SUV had been found and was registered under the name of Dennis Reading.

So, there was nothing that Dan didn't already know. There was no mention of Charles or Alice and nothing about the seven million, but what he did know, the police labeled him their number one suspect. He finished reading the paper and coffee, then proceeded across the street to Mary's office. He entered the office but was told that Mary's was attending a closing and wouldn't be back in the office till Friday. *Just my luck. Mary, you don't know what you're missing.*

The rest of the afternoon was boring and he still didn't have a TV. He struggled with the crossword puzzle in the Tribune, only guessing at the answers, frustrated, he stopped guessing. If this was just his first week in seclusion, how would he survive months of isolation? The walls in his apartment started looking like cold, steel bars, like he was in prison already. Without warning, there was an unexpected knock at his door. Dan's heart raced. Already? Were the cops standing outside his front door? He cautiously moved toward the door and peeked out the small side window. It was Helen.

"You! I was scared shitless."

"Welcome to Pasadena, Denny boy."

"I'm not Denny anymore. You better get used to calling me Dan. Your Denny boy has vanished."

"Denny, Dan, what's the difference." Helen, nonchalantly, scanned the apartment.

"Anything new?"

"Well, cops still don't have any new evidence. Shortly, and if we play our cards right, we'll have our money."

"The money! If we don't think of something fast, there will be no money. Without reason, you screwed our plan. All we had to do was wait two or three weeks and we'd be in Switzerland by now. But no, no. You had to kill William."

"Why do you keep thinking I killed my brother?"

"Okay, smart-ass. Then who was it? Only five of us knew about the money. Now its down to four. Jesus Christ! How are we going to get that money? I can't believe you did that."

"Leave it to me. If Collier steals the money, I'll know about it. When he does, he can't stay around Chicago. He'll have to hide somewhere. My people will find him."

"Your people? Who are "your" people? Are you telling me there are more people involved I don't know about? That know about the money?"

"I said, leave it all to me."

"Why do you think Charles will leave the country? You have any idea how big the United States is, Einstein?"

"Listen...if I was Collier, I surely wouldn't stay in the states."

Helen walked into the kitchen and dropped a white envelope containing the money Dan needed to stay afloat.

"Here's five thousand. That will keep you happy for a while. And keep your mouth shut, you'll blow the lid off this whole plan."

"I gotta find something to do. I'm not going to sit in this fucking room for months staring at the walls."

"Hold on, hold on. Don't get your underwear in a bunch, you'll definitely cause suspicion. Give me a few days, I'll find something at the office." Helen looked around his apartment, his prison cell, amazed. "And go buy a TV."

Chapter 22

Three Down.. Two To Go

Adhering closely to their plan, Charles and Emily drove to the local post office to apply for Charles's passport. When Emily suggested, "We still need to think about the divorce." Charles was concentrating on his driving, but wondered why a divorce was necessary? What were Emily's reasons? And why was there a rush? Was she hiding something?

"Whatever."

"We aren't jumping the gun here, are we, Charles? I mean getting the passport before Dugan even hacks the money?"

"It doesn't make any difference. It may take weeks to get the passport."

"Okay."

The nearest post office was on Clark Street in Lincoln Park. Too far to walk and to confusing if they went by bus, so Charles chose to drive.

"Yes, sir. How may I help you?" asked a middle-aged man dressed in his blue and gray postal garb.

"I'd like to apply for a passport today."

"Very well. Please fill out these forms and return them here. Then we will need to take your photo."

Charles and Emily moved to the nearest counter and Charles began filling out the forms. He hesitated. *Do I use my real name? I'll have to.* He'd have to show the clerk some sort of ID. He couldn't put down a fictitious name. Charles filled out the form with all the correct information.

"All right. May I see a valid form of identification, please?"

Charles had his driver's license ready and handed it to the clerk, who took a copy of his license.

"There you are, sir." he handed the ID back to Charles. "That will be $145, please."

Charles filled out a check and handed it to the clerk.

"If you will move to that door, I'll be with you shortly."

The ordeal was over. After his picture, the clerk informed Charles and Emily that he would contact them as soon as the passport arrived at the post office, approximately seven to ten days.

On their drive back to the condo, Emily brought up the subject of a divorce lawyer, again.

"We better take care of this, soon. If the passport takes ten days, I'm sure the divorce process will be just as long, if not longer."

"I'll drop you off at the condo. Start looking for a lawyer in the area. I'm going to drive downtown and look for a meeting place for Dugan."

"All right. I'll ask them how long the process will take."

Charles remembered two major hotels off Michigan Avenue, the Congress Plaza and the InterContinental Chicago. He wanted to check out each hotel: the size of the lobby, security cameras, wireless Internet connections, and a side entrance to the hotel. This was the most critical step in their plan. Their backup plan, if imperative, would depend on the hotel lobby they selected.

He stopped at the InterContinental first. He walked slowly through the lobby with his Panasonic video camera. Acting as a tourist, he started capturing the layout of the lobby.

The area was small but wide open. He made his way to the reception desk and asked about wireless connections.

"Yes, sir. Every room is equipped with Wi-Fi connections."

He didn't notice any side entrances, therefore the main front doors were the only options to enter and leave.

The Congress Plaza was five blocks south of the InterContinental. Once inside the lobby, Charles knew this was a better fit for their meeting. Out came his camera, recording as much as he could. Security cameras were in good locations, the lobby was large and lit very well. This was the place, no doubt in Charles's mind, where he would meet Dugan. He approached the desk and saw a sign indicating that every room was equipped with Wi-Fi, he spun around and left the premises.

By the time he got back to the condo, Emily and Jack were there. Charles handed the camera to Emily to look at the footage he took, explaining to her the important details of each hotel.

"It's the Congress. That's where we'll meet. It's huge, very discreet, and I feel very comfortable there."

"Great. I located a lawyer nearby, a Mr. Potter. No, not Harry, but Robert Potter. I scheduled a meeting tomorrow afternoon. Is that okay with you?"

"I guess. But I'm not overly excited about getting the divorce. I don't understand why we need to do that?"

"Listen to me. Once we get the money in our hands, I cannot stay here. As I've suggested, I'll sell the condo and move back to Manford with Jack. Also, I was thinking, what if we transfer the money under my maiden name? If they traced Charles Collier, there would be nothing on record."

"Hmm. Good idea, you're right. Cops would never find that."

"Do we wait the ten days and meet with Dugan or do we meet with him now?"

"If we wait, he may panic and never answer his phone. I say we meet with him ASAP."

"It's risky, you know. But I think you're right. Do it now and get it over with, then we forget about Dugan."

Emily hugged him. "I love you."

"When do we talk to Jack?"

On the drive to meet with Robert Potter, Emily alluded to, "This divorce is only to cover our tracks, part of our plan to keep suspicious cops away from you. Right, Charles?"

"I guess. It was your idea. But after I thought about it, it made sense to me. It's the best for all of us. Any type of diversion will help separate us from the cops. All I can do is pray nothing happens to either you or Jack. Well, here we are."

Emily informed the receptionist that the Colliers were here. Charles looked around Potter's office. Old oak paneling separated from each other, dirty carpeting, and out-of-date magazines gave Charles the impression that Potter was an ambulance chaser.

"Mr. and Mrs. Collier. Mr. Potter will see you now."

They followed the receptionist down the hall, the old oak panels accompanying them. Charles thought Potter either liked the looks of the oak or he got one hell of a deal when buying it. The conference room held the usual furnishings and framed degrees. He saw one wall shelved with hundreds of legal reference books. *There's no way this lawyer has opened every book on the shelves, let alone read them.*

Robert Potter entered the conference room, shook hands with Charles and Emily, and introduced himself. This lawyer didn't make a good impression with Charles; in fact, he was a slob. He appeared as old, seedy, and outdated as his office. But, time was critical and how could he screw up a simple divorce.

"My name is Charles Collier and this is my wife Emily."

"I see. According to my secretary, you're seeking a divorce?"

"Yes. We just want a simple dissolution of marriage."

Potter's eyes turned to Emily, looking for any resentment. "Are you in accordance with his declaration, Mrs. Collier?"

"Oh, yes. We're not bitter toward each other, not in any way. Our interests are traveling in different directions and after hours of discussion, we thought the best for both of us is to get divorced."

"Do you have any children, real estate, liabilities, or any assets?

"Yes, sir. We have a son, Jack, who is eighteen years old. Like we said, we've talked about this for some time now, even with Jack. Everything was explained to him and he seems to be at ease with it."

"Well, what about your assets and liabilities?"

"Everything will be split down the middle. We have everything written down, who gets what."

"Very well. Sounds simple enough. I'll have my secretary compile the settlement. When it's ready we'll contact you and have you stop in to sign the papers. Once they're signed, I'll present them in court, get a date for the hearing, and after that it will be final. Any questions?"

"How long will this take? Do I have to be in court when the settlement is read?"

"Mr. Collier, I would think no more than three to four weeks. Let's see, today is May 15th. We could possibly plan on the first or second week in June. And as far as your appearance, just one of you has to be present. Either you or your wife."

"Excellent." Charles shook Potter's hand, thanked him, and he and Emily headed for the door.

"We'll be in touch as soon as possible."

Driving home, Charles said, "Three down and two to go."

"That might be the easiest of the five."

"You're right. Getting Dugan to do his job, getting to Costa Rica, then getting Jack to understand. All this for a measly seven million." Charles looked across to Emily, who was thinking the same thing. They burst out laughing.

Chapter 23

Charles... Now A Millionaire

As soon as Alice looked up from her desk, she saw Detective Konrad and his pestering sidekick Fritz entering through the glass doors.

"Miss Oliver. How is your day going?"

"Very well, until I saw your face. Then my stomach started to turn."

"Really. Well, we won't take much of your time. Just a follow-up on some questions we need answers to."

"Gee. As good as you detectives are, I would've thought you caught your man by now." She turned back to her computer.

"Miss Oliver. You're forgetting your facts. I told you last time that we found footprints. I never implied it was a man who murdered Fossett."

Alice ignored his remark and gazed at her computer screen.

"We believe it was a woman, about your size. How well did you know William Fossett?"

Still, Alice didn't respond. The dynamic duo were beginning to make her furious, questioning her as if she were the one who murdered Fossett. They were pushing her hard, they needed answers, and they wanted a conviction quickly.

"We know Fossett had a sister named Helen. Did you know her? Come on, Miss Oliver, you better start co-operating with us."

"Next time you want to talk to me, call my lawyer. Now get the hell away from me."

"If I were you, I wouldn't leave town. You hear me? Because the next time I see you, I might take you downtown. Have a nice day." To Konrad, Alice was beginning to be his prime candidate in solving Fossett's murder. He needed more proof.

Alice was shaking. She opened the bottom drawer of her desk, pulled out the bottle of Chivas, unscrewed the cap, and swallowed a long gulp. Then another, to calm her nerves. Why did she ever come to work today? With all the pressure the cops were putting on her, it appeared she was their number one suspect and not Reading. Now, she understood how Reading felt. He had to be the one who murdered Fossett. What now? She was becoming desperate and she knew that when you're desperate, you do desperate things. Yes. It was a risky move, but an email to Helen was the only option open to her.

> Helen: The cops were here today. Asking me questions about you and William. I didn't say anything. What should I do now? If I stay here any longer, I'll be in handcuffs. Get back to me ASAP. I'll stop back in the office tomorrow afternoon, if I'm not in jail. Do you know where Reading is? And get this, Charles thinks I did it.
>
> Help!!

While Emily finished the dishes from dinner, Jack hustled his way back to the TV, continuing his game against the terrorists on his Xbox. Charles stayed in the kitchen and whispered to Emily so Jack couldn't hear.

"I'll call Dugan and have him meet us around two o'clock tomorrow. In the morning, I want you to go to the bank and withdraw two thousand. I'll need a new laptop and money for the room, all right?"

Emily nodded.

Charles walked to the front door on his way to the condo lobby. There he'll use the pay phone and make his call to Dugan.

When Charles reached the pay phone in the condo lobby, he removed several coins from his pocket and dropped them into the coin slot. "Dugan, it's me. Tomorrow. Congress Plaza hotel, two o'clock. I'll call you again tomorrow and let you know what room number."

Finished with his call, Charles stepped into the elevator and made his way back to the condo.

"Okay. I've got the meeting set up with Dugan. I'll have to call him tomorrow and let him know what room I'll be in." He left the kitchen on his way to the computer when… a loud knock on the front door. Charles opened it to find Detective Konrad in his face.

"Collier. You got a few minutes?"

"I…aah, yeah. What's on your mind?"

"We've noticed you've taken some days off work. Seems all the employees are taking days off. You hear from Reading yet?"

"Now why would he call me?"

Konrad's eyes were fixed on Charles, holding his keys in his hand, waiting for him to say something stupid, like… *Alice killed William, she told me.*

"You sure you don't know anything about Fossett's financial problems? Who he owed…?"

Before Konrad could finish, Charles blurted, "Look. I've told you all I know, okay? Now leave me alone and go find your killer."

"You planning on quitting your job, Collier?"

"What's going on? Why are you harassing us, Konrad?" As Emily joined in.

"Good morning, Mrs. Collier."

"Yeah, Konrad. If you're so sure a woman killed William, why are you bothering us?"

Charles slowly closed the front door, staring back into the detective's eyes. A pair of cold, beady eyes that sent a message back to Charles. This won't be the last of Detective Konrad.

***

The next morning, Emily and Charles walked to the Congress Plaza. Charles approached the registration desk.

"A room for the night, please?"

"Do you have a reservation?"

"No, I don't."

"Kindly fill out the registration form."

Charles filled it out the reservation using Dugan's information. His name, address, city, and his phone number. Charles guessed at the other data, but how would she know? The woman typed the information into the computer, "One single room, no premium channels, open bar…$245, please."

Charles counted and handed $250 to her. In exchange, she handed him a five-dollar bill and the plastic key to room 1034.

"You can take the middle elevator to the tenth floor, turn right and your room will be the first door on your right."

"Thank you."

Next, he called Dugan. "Dugan, room 1034, two o'clock. Don't keep me waiting."

"I'll be there."

Charles entered the elevator, but a group of six crammed in shouting different floor numbers for him to push. How would Emily know what floor he got off on? In the lobby, Emily watched the elevator rise, stopping at several floors. Now what? When the elevator was descending, it stopped, the doors opened, and there stood Charles. "Get in, quick."

"Push number ten."

Out of the elevator, they turned right to room 1034. Charles inserted the plastic key in the slot, a green light glowed, and the door opened.

"How long do you think it'll be till Dugan gets here?"

"If he's coming from Prairieville, probably about an hour. But, he may be in Chicago as we speak. You better leave now."

"Right. I'll sit in the lobby and watch for him. I'll text you when he arrives. I still have his picture on my phone."

"Okay. In the meantime, I have a lot to do to get this laptop set up."

Settling on that, Emily grabbed her jacket, purse, and left the room. She positioned herself in the lobby close to the main entrance waiting for Dugan. When the critical connection was completed and his business with Dugan over, Charles would text her informing her he was on his way down. Next, it was all up to Emily. It was her job to finish off Dugan. Get him to smile for the hotel's security cameras and keep their plan working.

An hour passed, then Emily spotted Dugan walking through the main entrance. Since his prison time, Dugan had become more cautious. Once inside, he shrewdly scanned the entire lobby, like a hungry coyote looking for plump rabbit. Emily noticed the lobby had cleared out considerably. She saw a couple of women working the registration desk, a woman reading a magazine near the entrance, and a small group in the middle of the lobby picking up their luggage. Satisfied that nothing was out of the ordinary, Dugan headed straight to the elevators. Being inconspicuous as possible, Dugan pushed the eighth floor button, exit there and walk up two flights. No surprises for him.

Emily texted Charles, "On his way up."

Knock…Knock…Knock.

Charles inhaled deeply. He was about to commit the perilous crime of his life. He greeted Dugan, closed and locked the door.

"Over here. Everything is set up and ready to go."

"A brand new Dell, excellent choice." Before Dugan began, he noticed the open bar. Not a stranger to the liquid comforts, Dugan helped himself to a shot of whiskey.

"I need something to loosen me up." He downed the shot, shook his body, and plopped down in front of the new Dell.

"And one last thing, I'm not walking out of this room until I see my $100,000 in my account, you understand that?"

"You've got to trust me, Dugan. Once you log on to where the money is, you'll see what's in front of you and you'll understand."

Dugan adjusted the laptop and cracked his knuckles, ready to put his genius computer mind to work. Now, it was up to Dugan. Charles watched him rapidly punching the keys, pages sweeping across the screen, devising password after password.

"I'll get it. It's time consuming but I'll get it. Just a bit rusty."

Charles paced the floor, keeping quiet. He walked to the small open bar, to a collection of small alcoholic bottles, vodka, gin, brandy, whiskey and the last one…Chivas Regal.

Dugan kept his fast pace punching the keyboard, back and forth. Random ideas crossed his brain, from page to page, names to numbers, but the hacking experience paid off. Finally, bingo. Dugan slammed his fist on the desk, "you're home, buddy."

Charles leaped off the bed and began guiding Dugan through the pages of Priority's financial statements until they came to the page and the figure he was looking for.

"That line, there. We need to transfer that figure only." excited, Charles pointed to the screen.

When Dugan saw the number, he yelled, "What the fuck…! Seven million bucks! Well, well, well, my friend. The price of my services has just sky rocketed."

Charles wasn't surprised at all, he'd expected it. If he wanted a million, Charles would gladly give it to him. For a second or two, he felt like Adolph Kaiser.

"It'll cost you $500 grand. Understood?"

"If and when I see the seven million safely in my Swiss account, Dugan, we have a deal."

Dugan was back, ferociously snapping at the keyboard. "Okay, done here. Give me the other page to transfer this to."

"I'll handle that. Go have another drink."

Within minutes, Charles had logged into the Clariden Leu home page and opened up his new account.

"You're up. You get that money transferred and I'll work on the codes and passwords."

It didn't take Dugan but a few seconds to get the seven million safely into the account of Emily Dearborn.

"Excellent. Now transfer the $500 grand into your account."

Done. Charles had his money and so did Dugan. They celebrated by having a drink.

"A toast. One man's greed turns into another man's fortune," quoted Charles. He poured them another drink.

"Okay, we're finished. I hope we never cross paths again. We both got what we wanted, so let's not do anything foolish, right?" Charles put his hand out to shake Dugan's.

"You never saw or heard of me, either." Dugan didn't shake hands. He grabbed the bottle of Chivas and left room 1034.

Charles immediately texted Emily. "Your turn, Sweetie."

She stood close to the elevators waiting for a door to open. Out walked Dugan carrying a bottle and wearing a very contented look. Near the middle of the lobby and under the security camera, Emily approached him.

"This could be your lucky day, baby." The look on Emily's face kept Dugan interested.

"Yeah? Why do you say that?"

"You could use a lady like me tonight. Help you with that bottle? My favorite, Chivas." Emily took a small swig.

Dugan was never a person to pass up a free deal. Especially when it pertained to beautiful women and the possibility of getting lucky. All free.

"What's your deal, lady?"

"We can talk about that later. Right now, I'm horny as hell and looking for a man like you."

"Let's go. God knows I sure could use a woman like you tonight."

Dugan took Emily's arm and ushered her toward the elevators.

"Wait. Don't you think we need a room?"

"I have one already. For the entire night."

Oh boy! How was Emily going to get out of this predicament? All she wanted from Dugan was his face on the security camera. She found herself in a position that she was altogether quite familiar with. In a strange room with a strange man, giving him what he wanted. The demented thought crossed her mind, *What any woman would do for money!*

It was Dugan's lucky day. As he and Emily got off at the tenth floor, Charles was about to leave the room 1034. Dugan walked up to Charles, grabbed the plastic card from him and said, "Think I'll stay here for the night. I've got company."

Charles didn't look at his wife. He had to swallow his pride and keep going.

Moments after the door closed behind them, Dugan was sitting at the edge of the bed. He knew what he wanted. He dropped his pants and pulled out a hard present for his guest.

"Time to get on your knees, honey."

Her performance was terrific. She grabbed her purse and ice bucket and excused herself from the room, telling Dugan that they needed ice for their drinks.

"Hurry back. I want an encore performance from you."

She had her purse and ice bucket and hurried to the door. She purposely left her jacket, letting Dugan believe she was coming back, but by the time Dugan zipped up his pants, Emily was long gone.

"Keep it hard, big boy."

The door closed and Emily dashed into a waiting elevator. She ran as fast as she could to the front entrance and into the first available cab. "One-oh-five Cedar Street, please."

Chapter 24

Anything New On TV?

Dan had to find a way to control his paranoia after being trapped inside four walls for only a few days. With money in his pocket after Helen's visit, and the local appliance store within walking distance, he would solve that dilemma. He'd purchase a new TV. He pulled his baseball cap over his head, barely covering his eyes, sensing that everyone he passed, would recognize him. He was in no rush to get to the appliance store. After all, time was on his side. He remembered the old saying his Dad always told him, *I've got more time than I have money, son.*

The lackadaisical walk allowed himself to familiarize the businesses around his apartment. He took his time, occasionally stopping to look in the windows of the stores, and what they were selling. He came across a dentist, a hobby shop, a music store, a Tarot card reader, and a smoke shop. Anything he needed was within walking distance from the apartment. When he reached Goodman's Home Appliances, he saw that their selection wasn't anything close to a Best Buy. But, Dan wasn't fussy. All he was looking for was a flat screen with HD features. He settled on a 36-inch LG listed at $399.99. The salesman carted the box to the checkout counter while Dan was thinking how to get the large box to his apartment.

"You have delivery service?"

"Yeah, we do. Where do you live?"

"The apartment building on East Truman. About six blocks east of here."

"Hold on a second. John, you got time to drop off this TV?

It's just six blocks down Truman," he shouted to another employee.

"Yeah. We can do that."

"He'll pull the van around to the front of the store. You can ride with him. He'll set it up while he's there. How does that sound?"

"Terrific."

John loaded the TV into the small van. Five minutes later, they were parked in front of Dan's apartment building. He hurried to unlock the door and held it open for John, who was a stud, carried the box by himself like it was a box of Kleenex. It was a minor struggle to get it through the door, but once inside, John set the box down on the living room floor, extracted a box cutter from his pocket, and started cutting the cardboard all the way around the box until the TV was free.

"Where do you want it?"

Dan pointed to a table in the corner. He removed a lamp and John set the TV down.

"You know where the cable outlet is?"

"Gee. I'm new here, I have no clue."

They searched the walls until John found it behind the sofa.

"We can leave the TV there. I have extra cable in the truck." John left and returned carrying a coil of coax cable. Once everything was in place, John turned on the TV. Nothing happened.

"Your cable is out. Do you have cable?"

"I bet I don't. I'll have to call the company. You know what company supplies the cable around here?"

"I think South Cal Cable would be the one. At least they're the most popular one."

"Cool. I'll give them a call. See how fast they can get a serviceman out here."

"Okay. You're all set. Enjoy the TV."

"Oh, I will. Thanks again for helping me." Dan reached into his pocket and tipped John twenty bucks.

"Hey. Thanks."

Dan stared at his new toy. *This will keep me from going crazy.*

Well, now that he had his new friend, it would be off to the pay phones and give South Cal Cable a call. He jogged to the drugstore, looked up South Cal Cable and dialed the number listed in the phone book.

"South Cal Cable. How may I direct your call?"

"I need to set up a date to get my cable hooked up."

"One moment, please. Your name, sir?"

"Mesa, Dan Mesa, 4455 East Truman Ave., apartment two."

"The earliest would be Thursday. Morning or afternoon?"

"The morning would be better."

"Very well. We have you set for Thursday, anywhere between nine am and one pm."

"Excellent, thank you." After the phone call ended, Dan thought, *Shit, that's still three days away.*

The phone was still in Dan's hand when he decided to dial Helen's number and find out the latest news from Chicago.

"UniCell Wireless."

"Helen, it's me. Why are you answering UniCell Wireless? What's UniCell Wireless?"

"That's my business and I'm still at work. A force of habit, I would think. What do you want?"

"Any news about Chicago?"

"Got an email from Alice this morning. The cops got her in the frying pan. She's getting scared. We might have her move out here."

"Absolutely not. Are you stupid? You bring anyone out here and, for sure, it'll lead the cops right to us."

"If we don't help her, she'll crack. She'll tell the cops everything. Do you want that to happen?"

"Jesus. What about Alaska or South Africa? Any place except here."

"Let me worry about Alice. Anything else you need?"

"Yeah. A job. Ohh…what I really need is some IDs. Something to prove I'm Dan Mesa. A driver's license, Social Security card, credit card, anything, and quickly."

"I'll see what I can do."

"Okay. You know where I'm at." Dan hung up, walked back into the drugstore to purchase a couple packs of Dutch Masters cigars and a bottle of Jack Daniels. Two more days of staring at the walls, but he'd have company until then, his old friend Jack.

Alice knew the proverbial handwriting was on the wall. That the cops were content she and Reading were their only viable suspects, and he had vanished leaving her to take all the heat. If she could only find Reading and talk to him, maybe he had the answers she desperately needed. But, what if the police couldn't find him or what if he was dead?

Konrad dug deep into the backgrounds of Dennis Reading and Oliver, even William Fossett. He learned about the relationship Alice had with Fossett and the digging didn't stop there. Konrad found out more about William Fossett. How he had won a large sum of money, and how he cleverly scammed his own sister, Helen. And what about this woman, Helen? Where was she living? From the digging Konrad uncovered, this Helen woman had a valid motive to kill her brother. He knew William Fossett was a shrewd, egotistical, son-of-a-bitch who thought only of himself and didn't care about family or anyone else. He had only one goal in life…making a fortune by stepping all over people.

***

Alice was on her way to the office, hoping this would be her last time there. All she wanted to do was collect some personal items, drop her keys on her desk, and if anyone was around, good riddance. She went to her desk, opened every drawer, and removed everything of value to her. Satisfied that she had everything, she thought about the money. Was the money still there? She logged into Priority's home page and typed in her password. A few seconds later, she scrolled down to the only line that had her interest.

"*AAH!*" In disbelief, she stared at the line of zeros where the seven million was supposed to be.

No... No...This can't be right. She rebooted the computer, typed in her password, returned to Priority's financial page, the last page of its financial statement, line 11, Custom Imposed Expense...$0.00.

"It's gone. Instantly, her thoughts raced through her brain... a murder suspect, then the money... my life is over." She could not hold back her tears.

She knew it had to be Charles. It was definitely him. She started to panic. Her mind shouted to her, *Call Helen, immediately.* She closed out Priority's website and moved to her own personal page. She found Helen's address and opened it.

> Helen: it's over. The money is gone. I just checked the statements, no money...zero. I bet it was Charles. My life is over...don't know where to go or what to do. I'm thinking of turning myself in. I can't hide anymore. Don't try to email me back. I'm going to destroy the hard drive, pick up what's mine and leave...So sorry.

Chapter 25

How Do I Explain It, Jack

Friday afternoon Charles stayed away from the office again. He figured whatever he needed to work on, he could do at home—away from the tormenting Detective Konrad. Costa Rica had become more important than any of his clients' portfolios, even the Kaiser account. He pulled up the website again, to learn as much about that country as he could, he was possessed with Costa Rica.

The front door bell rang. Charles stepped away from the website, looked through the peephole, and saw that it was Emily, both arms clutching bags of groceries. He opened the door.

"Why didn't you buzz me from downstairs? I would've come down to help you."

"I figured you were busy. That's okay, I'm home."

She set the bags on the counter, took off her coat, then began to remove all the groceries from each bag.

"The cops are still sitting outside the condo."

"Unbelievable. Why are they thinking Reading would come here? They'll stay out there every night until they find Reading."

Charles kept tract all the information that would be essential to him when he landed in Coata Rica in his notebook. He had his flight to Liberia, Costa Rica nailed. All that was left is finding a place to hide. He switched his computer page to a map of Costa Rica and surveyed the towns that surrounded Liberia. Looking toward the ocean, he noticed the town of Ocotal. From what he gathered, Ocotal was right on the ocean and from the map, other villages were a comfortable distance away, only the ocean and national forests were close by.

"Any luck?"

"I have a flight picked out. Get this. From O'Hare to Liberia is around $475. It's a seven hour flight with one stop in Houston."

"You're not flying straight to Costa Rica, are you? Remember we talked about that."

Charles turned and looked to Emily, "You have a better place for me to go?"

"Charles. Remember what we discussed… diversion? You're not going to Costa Rica for a vacation. You're going there to hide from people who will be looking for you. Fly to some obscure country, then catch another flight to Liberia. Mix it up."

"Christ. This is getting so bizarre. You're right, I forgot. I better check into that."

Later that afternoon, Emily was sitting in the living room reading until Charles spoke out.

"Check this out, Emily. Mexico doesn't require a passport when leaving the country. So, I could fly to Mexico, board another flight with a false identity, and land in Costa Rica under my own name."

"See? You have to start thinking like Dugan. Not behaving like him, just thinking like him."

"Tomorrow's going to be a busy day for me. I have to contact Ed, meet with him and go over all my portfolios. That shouldn't take too long and I suppose I should call Adolph Kaiser and explain to him that Ed will be handling his account."

"Do you need me to help you?"

"You know what? Could you stop at Macy's and purchase a set of luggage for me?"

"I can do that. That will be fun. You know me and shopping. I'll take Jack with me."

"Ooh, Jack. We have to sit down and explain everything to him. We'll do that after dinner tonight. In addition, you and I have to decide how we can move the money around. With me in Costa Rica and you here, that will take some serious thought."

"I won't need anything. We have enough money in our savings to keep Jack and me safe."

"Really?"

"Of course. When I sell the condo, I'll have enough money to buy a small house in Manford. Don't forget, I'll be working and living the low life. You just worry about yourself."

The thought of being away from Jack bothered Charles. He didn't know how long he'd have to stay in Costa Rica, but the distance between them would distress him. With that on his mind, he'd spend as much time as possible with Jack before he left. They could watch a few movies, he could challenge Jack to his Xbox games, talk about school, go to a White Sox game or even discuss the trip to California. The most important thing to Charles was keeping Jack in an upscale frame of mind about him moving away and not seeing his son.

The dinner was great, the dishes were done, and it was time for Charles and Emily to discuss the move with their son. Jack was watching Double Dare You, one of his favorite reality shows, when Charles and Emily approached him. Charles took the remote and turned off the TV and like bookends, they both sat with Jack on the sofa.

"I know that you know I'm leaving for a new job, but I want to tell you exactly the circumstances behind my decision to leave, okay?" Charles fidgeted, getting the words out was difficult.

"With the death of Mr. Fossett, the remaining agents in the office decided to employ their skills elsewhere. Meaning, there will no longer be a Priority Investments. One of my clients, very wealthy Adolph Kaiser, has offered me a position as consultant to his Kaiser Foundation. I have accepted the position, but I must begin my work in Cozumel, Mexico. Now, that being said, I don't have a clue as to how long I have to stay in Mexico. It could be a month, a year, or longer. I simply don't have an answer for that."

Emily put her arms around Jack. "We'll be fine. We can call

him, or we can use the computer and email him. We'll always be in contact with him, only not in person."

"Mom, Dad, I'm eighteen years old. I'm not a baby anymore. I understand the situation Dad is in and I respect what he's doing. He has to do what he has to do. I just hope he's back in time for all of us to visit the schools in California together."

Charles embraced his son, "I love you and I'll really miss you. Your mom and I will never stand in the way of your success. We'll always be behind you one-hundred and ten percent."

"That's how it is, Jack. That being said, what new movies have you bought that we haven't seen yet?" Emily said.

"Do you have to ask?"

They began chanting "Harry! Harry!"

Chapter 26

Alice's Last Dance

Depression entered Alice's life at an alarming rate. She could not function or concentrate on positive thoughts, thinking the worst was going to happen to her. She hadn't left her one-bedroom bungalow in Covington since the money went missing. It's been two days and still no response from Helen since her email. Had Helen abandoned her? Was she letting Alice take the fall for the murder of Fossett? Certainly, Alice was believing that.

She opened the cellophane wrapper from a loaf of whole wheat bread and dropped two slices in the toaster. She poured a tall glass of milk and placed the glass on the counter, then reached into the drawer for a butter knife. Accidentally, her elbow hit the glass of milk. The glass smashed as it hit the floor, spilling the milk and shattering pieces of glass across the kitchen floor.

Alice exploded with tears. Nothing was going right. She dropped to her knees, but her left palm landed on a sharp piece of broken glass, cutting her. Blood trickled down her arm. She grabbed a dish towel and wrapped her hand tightly for several minutes to stop the bleeding. Carefully, she removed the towel and noticed that the cut wasn't bad after all. No need to call the paramedics, no need to get stitches. Two Band-Aids would suffice, problem solved. Or was it? Distraught and confused, Alice examined the mess in front of her. Sighing, she pulled several sheets of paper towels from the dispenser and began to mop up the pool of milk and pieces of glass. Within her mind, she asked herself, *what else could go* wrong?

Unexpectedly, the chimes from the front door rang out. Could it be the cops again? Alice became frantic, silently standing, thinking. Should I answer or just hide? Slowly, she advanced toward the door, slid the curtain from the small window and discovered it wasn't the police after all. It was a man dressed in casual wear. She didn't recognize him, but maybe it was someone who was lost or selling something. With the chain security lock still attached, she opened the door.

"Yes?"

"Alice Oliver?"

Alice didn't respond. How did this stranger know her name? Maybe he was a cop after all. Maybe he was dressed that way to fool her. She was scared, about to slam the door when the stranger spoke, "Helen Kruger sent me. To help you."

She dropped her head in relief. Thank God. Helen sent someone to help her.

"Come in, come in." She unhooked the chain from the track.

"My name is Bill Wilson. A very dear friend of Helen's."

"I was getting worried. The cops have been stalking me, constantly asking me all kinds of questions. I was at the end of my rope, you understand?"

"Of course. But now I want you to pack some clothes. Helen wants you back in California. There you'll be safe and away from the police."

"Yes. Just give me a few minutes. I won't take long." Alice couldn't move fast enough.

Wilson followed her into the room. She opened her closet doors, reached for her suitcase when…Wilson had his hands around her neck, choking her.

"Get on the bed, now!"

He released his grip and threw her onto the bed. He reached into his pocket and removed four pills from a small brown pill container.

"Swallow these."

Frightened for her life, Alice rejected the pills. She tried to escape, rolling to the opposite side of the bed, the bed separating her from life or death.

"Don't make this any harder than it is. Take them. They're only sleeping pills."

Sleeping pills, my ass. He wants to kill me.

She was backed into a corner, the monster between her and the door. How could she get to the door without struggling with him? She decided to fake crawling under the bed. If Wilson fell for her trick, she could leap across the bed, pass him, and run out the door. It was her only chance to save her life.

At first, Wilson fell for her trick. He was lying on the floor, but as she reached the end of the bed, he lunged for her leg and grasped it, holding a tight, steady grip on her left ankle. Alice kicked and fought hard to release his grip, but it was no use, both were lying on the floor, Wilson on top of Alice. He began to force the pills down her throat. Alice's life was on the line, she continued to fight. Wilson put both hands around her neck, not tightly, but with enough strength to keep her from freeing herself.

"Swallow the pills, god damn it."

Alice never had a choice. With his grasp around her neck, he could feel her swallowing the pills. He spun her around and inspected the inside of her mouth. They were gone. Wilson let go as Alice's limp body laid motionless. He stood and watched her body, minutes passed, she was lifeless, no pulse, no breathing, her life has ended. He was certain she was dead. His instructions from Helen were to make sure the poisoning looked like a suicide, so he situated her body on the bed, straightened out the covers to hide any signs of a struggle. In his haste, he forgot one very important assignment: leave the pill container in her hand. During their struggle, the pill container fell to the floor and rolled under the night stand. Wilson never realized his mistake. Satisfied everything was back to normal and the scene looked like a suicide, he put the suitcase back in the closet and left the house.

As fast as he could, Wilson jumped into his truck, started the engine, and sped away. He flipped open his cell and dialed

Helen's number. With all his attention centered around the call to Helen, he never noticed the old man standing next to his mailbox. The truck swerved hard to the left, barely missing the mailbox and the old man. Instantly, he looked to his rear view mirror. The old timer was jumping around swinging his cane at the vanishing truck.

"Finished, done. She won't be singing another word."

Chapter 27

I Wish I Were Single Again

Charles and Emily had just finished their coffee when the phone started ringing.

"Hello."

"Mrs. Collier, this is Denise from Mr. Potter's office."

Emily tried to recollect the name Potter.

"Your divorce papers are here and ready to sign."

"Oh, oh yes. I was caught dumbfounded for a second trying to recall the name Potter. Very well. We'll be in later this afternoon to sign them. Thank you."

"Our divorce papers are ready."

"Okay. Now, I'd better get to the office and meet with Ed. As soon as I finish with him, I'll call you and meet you at Potter's office, okay?"

***

He opened the doors to an empty Priority Investments office. When he passed Alice's desk, he noticed something very peculiar. Her computer was smashed as if someone took a baseball bat to it. Everything else on her desk was intact.

Puzzled, Charles continued to his office. "Hello, Ed. I'm in the office today. Can you free yourself and come over?"

"Sure. I'll be there right after lunch, okay?"

"Fine. I'll wait for you."

Since William's death, showing up at the office was risky, but in order to advise Ed about his clients, he had to take that chance.

He didn't need an unannounced guest popping in at the most inappropriate time, the likes of Konrad. He theorized Konrad was putting his numbers together, and for every day that passed, Konrad was inching closer to solving the crime and the whereabouts of Dennis Reading.

While he waited for Ed, Charles probed the entire office. First, he searched William's office, then to Reading's, nothing out of the ordinary, nothing Charles wanted to take. He thought it better to leave everything in place and nothing for the cops to confiscate as evidence. He ventured back to Alice's office, still puzzled about her smashed computer and the reason for it. Why would Alice want to destroy her computer? What was she hiding and did she tell Charles the entire truth? Charles, at this point was stymied, because Alice could've had a motive to kill William just as much as Helen did. As Charles glanced around her computer, he noticed a memory stick still inserted into the hard drive. He removed the stick and went back to his office, put it into his computer and opened it's contents. Most items were trivial company stuff, except for Alice's personal emails, how interesting. He opened that page, remembering her clever password…CHIVAS, which opened her entire email history. He started at the bottom and worked toward the top, from a week ago to the most recent and the most recent email said it all.

> Helen: The money is gone. I just checked the statements, no money…zero. I bet it was Charles. My life is over…don't know where to go or what to do. I'm thinking of turning myself in. I can't hide anymore. Don't try to email me back. I'm going to destroy the hard drive, pick up what's mine and leave…So sorry.

Shit. They know everything now. Contemplating what to do next, Charles sat silent looking out at Lake Michigan. The secret about the obtainable seven million was not a secret anymore. He knew it would only be a matter of time before outside interests began to surface, meaning that Helen and Dennis could find a hacker themselves. The only logical explanation was all four of them had there fingers in William's scam. But, William hated his sister. Was it possible that Dennis and Helen had a plan of their own. Possibly revenge? Finally, it dawned on Charles where Dennis had gone, to find Helen. Whatever was dancing through his head, the race was on, who would capture the jackpot first. Charles also knew that Reading knew what bank the money was held. That too, was a disadvantage to Charles. Was there a way to stop Dennis and Helen?

I'll destroy everything. That's right. I'll shred all the documents within the office. How would anyone ever know or prove that money actually existed? Charles began laughing, thinking he had solved everything and had both Dennis, Helen and Konrad over a barrel.

Charles jumped at his Rolodex and quickly found Ed's card.

"Hello?"

"Oh, Ed. I'm glad I caught you before you left. Listen, something important with the investigation just came up. I can't meet with you today. I'll call you back as soon is this is over, okay?"

"Yeah. No problem. I'll wait for your call."

Just as soon as he hung up with Ed, he remembered the meeting with the divorce lawyer. He called Emily and told her he would pick her up in twenty minutes, the shredding would have to be put on hold until other matters were taken care of.

***

They reached their lawyer's office and went inside where Denise escorted them back to Potter's conference room.

"Mr. Potter will be with you shortly."

And so it was. The rotund Robert Potter strutted into the room carrying a handful of papers. "Good afternoon. How is everyone today?"

Charles nodded and Emily smiled.

Potter sat down, wet his fingertips with his tongue, and ruffled through the papers, separating and distributing copies to Charles and Emily to sign.

"Take your time and read through the decree. If you have any questions, please don't hesitate to ask me."

After several minutes, the Colliers finished reading the decree and looked at Potter.

"Everything look satisfactory?" Complete silence. "Great. You'll see on the bottom of each page, lines highlighted in yellow. Each line has your legal name. That's where you'll sign."

About ready to sign his name, Charles began thinking whether there was really a need for a divorce. It was Emily's idea. What were her plans when he moved to Costa Rica? It was stuck in his mind, why she was so persistent about getting divorced. He felt something eerie. Charles stared at the yellow highlighted lines, debating whether to sign or not. He looked at Emily and then to Potter, who were watching him. *Sign your name, Charles, all eyes are on you, waiting.* Charles gave in and signed all the documents and pushed them to Potter.

"Very well. By the end of the week, I'll have a court date. My secretary will call and let you know the day and time. Once the appearance is over and the judge signs off on the decree, the divorce will be final."

"I'll be the one who will meet you in court." Emily spoke.

"Very well, Mrs. Collier."

They shook hands and left the office.

In the car and driving toward home, Charles said, "Four down and one to go."

"How come you hesitated before signing the papers?"

"Actually, I was thinking of Jack." Charles lied.

"Jack is all right with your leaving. He fully understands."

"It's not about Jack, it's about me. I'll miss him a lot."

"He can come and visit you. Wait. That would be too risky. The police will be watching. Shit, we don't have any choices. We must to stick to our plan."

"It's going to be tough."

The rest of the way home, they sat silent, contemplating everything that had transpired over the past several weeks.

"Macy's, Charles. We have to stop off at Macy's and get your luggage."

"You and Jack didn't go this morning?"

"Your son had other things planned today."

***

Charles turned into a downtown parking garage, grabbed the ticket and parked in an empty stall. They walked two blocks to Macy's department store, took the escalator to the fourth floor and headed to the luggage department. After circling the selections, Charles focused on a solid black three-piece set by American Luggage for $589. Kellye, the sales clerk, explained the features the set offered and the best one being, when empty, the two smaller pieces would fit inside the larger piece. Very convenient when storing the luggage. That sold Charles. As they neared the front entrance, they came across crowds of people hustling and scrambling for cover. A front had moved in, producing buckets of rain, forcing Emily and Charles to sit it out in Macy's coffee shop.

"Well, what do you say we have a cup of coffee and wait this out?"

"Might as well. We have more time than we have money."

"Ohh, you're so funny."

***

Early the next morning, Charles called Ed to set up a meeting that afternoon. But before Ed came, Charles continued in Alice's office, shredding every piece of paper he could find. From file cabinet to desks, nothing was spared. When the shredder became full, Charles dumped the contents in the middle of the floor, producing a small mountain of paper.

Then he heard a loud rap on the office front doors. It must be Ed. He closed the door of Alice's office and let him in.

"Ed, glad you're here."

"I really appreciate what you're doing for me, Charles. This will boost my salary a ton. My wife is extremely happy."

"It did that for me. To me, it's sad to leave this, but I have to put my family first. Besides, I couldn't think of a better person to take over these accounts. I have no doubts you'll do a terrific job."

Two hours later, their meeting ended after Charles explained everything to Ed about each client, their portfolios and the people to contact. They walked to the main entrance, said their goodbyes and the doors were locked. Charles reverted back to the paper pile left in Alice's office. He worked like a slave, office by office shredding every piece of paper that came in his eyesight. Now he was positive that the cops wouldn't be able to find any evidence regarding the I.C.E. account and no seven million dollars. By seven pm., his mission was over. Every office contained a small mountain of nothing. Satisfied, he walked back to his office to gather the cardboard box containing awards, plaques, and miscellaneous artifacts he earned since his start at Priority. As he picked up the box, he saw Alice's memory stick connected to his computer. *The computers. Of course. I have to destroy them.* All the computers had hard drives that had to be destroyed. He unscrewed the covers and removed the hard drive of every computer, dropped them into his cardboard box, where he would destroy them at home. Like the cat that swallowed the canary, mission completed.

He locked the front doors and was about to discard his company keys. *Wait. Those keys may come in handy, I better keep them.* Charles slipped the keys into his coat pocket and hurried to the elevator. The elevator dropped him off at the parking garage where the Escalade was parked. He unlocked the car, set the cardboard box in the back seat and slid behind the steering wheel. The Cadillac stopped at the security gate, he inserted his ID card into the slot, the gates opened and the Escalade roared onto Whacker Drive. Would this be the last time he'd ever set foot in that building again, he wondered. Charles felt more relaxed about his mountains of paper until, sitting at the traffic light on the corner of Whacker and Michigan, he spotted Detective Konrad and his partner getting out of their squad car, about to enter the Edison building.

Unbelievable! Charles knew they were there to find him and pound him with questions. Was it possible they discovered the I.C.E. account? He pushed the accelerator down, turned left onto Michigan Avenue and sped home, constantly looking in the rear view mirror.

Chapter 28

Will The Real Dan Mesa Stand Up

Dan locked the door on his way out, taking his time walking to the newsstand for his daily Chicago newspaper. He stopped at the Starbucks and ordered his typical large cup of Columbia decaf coffee with a splash of cream. Trying to fall asleep every night was a dilemma because his mind spun in all sorts of crazy visions. Mainly, the money and how soon he could get his hands on it. Was it still in the Chicago bank or has Charles beat him to it. Why would Helen want to kill her brother when they had a plan of their own? He still didn't have any solid answers and Helen was no help.

He reached the newsstand, picked up the Tribune and dropped four quarters on the wood counter. Nothing about the murder on the front page, nothing but the local mayoral elections coming up in November. Dan rolled up the paper and stuck it in his back pocket, found a phone and called Helen.

"What's going on?"

"I was about to drive over and pick you up. I have a job for you."

"Well, it's about time. I'm sick and tired of watching TV and working stupid crossword puzzles."

"Sit back and relax. I'll be there in about an hour."

"All right, later." Dan hung up, sipped his coffee and shuffled his way to his apartment. An hour later, Helen was at the side door.

"Let me grab my jacket and smokes."

They walked down to Helen's car—a bright yellow Mercedes-AMG GT.

"Nice. When did you get this?" He asked himself, *Wow, what kind of business is she in to afford a car like this?*

Helen was quiet. Dan closed his door and fastened his seat belt as Helen stomped on the accelerator, burning rubber in her wake.

"Jesus. You in a hurry this morning?" From past experiences, Dan was accustom to her frequent mood swings. "Any news from your sources in Chicago?"

Helen took her eyes off the road and looked directly at Dan. "About Alice. We found a place for her. No need to worry about her anymore."

"Cool. Where did she go?"

"I said I took care of it, didn't I?"

"All right, all right. I was just asking."

Dan remained silent until they reached Helen's destination. She parked the race car in front of a red brick, two-story warehouse building. In large white letters above the main entrance, a sign spelled out "UniCell Wireless, Inc."

"So, this is how you can afford this car, huh?"

Still nothing from Helen. He followed her into the building and into her office.

"Sit."

Dan sat. He removed a cigar from the package and lit it.

"I received an email from Alice. The money is gone from Priority's account. She believed that Charles took it and so do I. My connections are looking into this and when they find the answer, then I can implement my new plan."

"Really. You have another plan? Since when are you taking over? See, I told you this was going to happen. You fucked up by getting William killed. Our original plan was solid, remember? Of course Charles took the money. He's the only one left who knows about it. My guess is he found a hacker, transferred the money to an offshore bank, and plans to flee the country. Simple as that."

"Is that your guess?"

"That's what I would do. You have a better suggestion?"

Helen sat at her desk, knowing full well that Dan was right.

"Well, Charles is still in Chicago. I believe he won't be there long. So, this is what I'm thinking. His family is very important to him, especially his son. I think he knows whats going on and he's vulnerable. How old is the boy, you think?"

"Jesus. I guess he's in high school, maybe fifteen or sixteen."

"Great. I have something in mind, but first I need to hear from my people in Chicago."

Dan threw his hands in the air, fed up with Helen and her people in Chicago. "I give up. It's not just you and me and the money, now, you have other people we have to share the money with, right?

All to well, Dan was well aware of Helen's mood swings and this was the time to not say anything more."I should've never left Chicago. I'm innocent." Dan stood up and began to the door, then turned around, "You said you have a job for me?"

"Yes. I'll show you what you need to do."

She circled the desk, signaling him to follow her to another room, Dan's new office. When they entered the small office, Dan's new IDs were spread across his desk, a California driver's license, a Social Security card, and an untraceable Visa credit card.

Now it was time for Dan to switch moods, looked at Helen and smiled. He was a happy camper knowing from now on, life in California just got a whole lot easier.

"Just what I need. Now, there is a real Dan Mesa."

Chapter 29

One Less Egg To Fry

"Covington Precinct Police Station, Officer Smith speaking, how may I direct your call?"

"It's about my neighbor. I... I...I haven't seen her since Tuesday. She's always outside doing something." A man's trembling voice led the officer to believe the caller was old.

"What is your address, sir?"

"…one—one—seven East Sheridan in Covington. I'm worried about her."

"We'll send a car out there shortly, okay?"

"…very well." Another long pause, "Very well."

The officer dispatched the nearest squad car to the old man's address, guessing the woman probably went on vacation and never told the neighbor. Those calls are common and usually end up as that, just a phone call. The Covington squad reached the address, and the patrolman went to the entrance of the old man's house. He knocked on the door. There was no response. He pounded harder, until the door opened. Then he understood the long delay. The elderly man walked with a walker and wore hearing aids in both ears.

"You said you thought your neighbor is missing?"

"Yes, I haven't seen her. That house there." He pointed to a small bungalow to the right.

The patrolman retrieved a pad and pen from his shirt pocket, "Your name, sir?"

"Xavier Cromwell Pennington. I'm seventy-six years old, been living here since I was born."

"I'll go over and investigate. You stay inside."

The patrolman rang the doorbell, but there was no answer. He knocked hard on the aluminum screen door, still nothing. He peeked in the window and saw no movement inside, no sign that anyone was home. When he reached for the door handle and gave it a turn, the door opened and entered.

"Hello...anyone home?"

The house was silent. He pulled his revolver from its holster just in case he came upon a sudden surprise. He moved slowly through the house to the only bedroom, where he noticed the body of a woman lying on the bed. He thought she was asleep. He spoke, but the body remained motionless. He replaced his revolver, then checked her pulse. The woman was dead. She was young, 45 or so, apparently a suicide, he thought. He looked around the room, saw nothing out of place and no signs of a struggle. He bent to one knee, looking under the bed, it was clean. His trained eyes searched the floor. He saw something lying on the floor under the night table. Using a pencil, he touched the object to determine what it was and saw that it was a round, brown container with a white cap. A pill dispenser. His police skills immediately suggested that the young lady had committed suicide. Throughout his long service as a patrolman, the container was evidence he didn't want to disturb, so he left it as is. He left the bedroom, went to his squad car and called in for the ambulance and coroner. He stayed in his car, filling out the report and waited for the ambulance to arrive. Soon after, Detective Johnson and Detective Stillwell showed up, along with the coroner.

"Possible suicide, you think?" Detective Johnson asked.

"Looks like it to me. I found a pill dispenser is lying under her night table. "

"I'll take a look."

Detective Johnson, wearing rubber protective gloves, picked up the brown pill container and carefully examined it. "No label on it, no name, nothing." He unscrewed the top and took a sniff of its contents, shook his head, and put the container into a plastic bag.

The coroner, Dr. Thomas Clancy, took his time looking over

the body. He examined the inside of the mouth with a small flashlight, strained his eyes to focus on an exposed tiny blue object partially stuck under her tongue. With tweezers from his medical bag, he removed it from her mouth. It was a pill, still in original form, one she never swallowed. He pulled a plastic bag from his pocket and dropped the pill into it.

"Cut and dry. Sure looks like a suicide to me, gentlemen."

He removed his rubber gloves and picked up his medical bag, ready to leave the scene. The room began to get crowded with the paramedics there with the stretcher, ready to remove the body after a nod from Dr. Clancy. As the coroner made his way out, he motioned to the paramedics that the body was theirs.

The detectives remained on the scene to investigate the crime, looking for possible clues why the woman took her life. They checked her closets and her dresser, finding everything in order. They never found a suicide note. They searched the rest of the house, but nothing of significance caught their attention, satisfied, they left the house.

The Third Precinct of the Chicago Police Department had jurisdiction on the north side of the Loop, including Lincoln Park. The crime rate was very low in that area: an

occasional street fight, a shoplifting, a robbery, and less than rare, a homicide. It was the home for Detectives Konrad and Fritz for the past six years.

***

Mike Konrad entered the office and set his cup of coffee on his desk.

"Yo, Mike. Captain wants you in his office right now." bellowed out from another detective.

Mike had just enough time to take the lid off of his coffee and "Right now" meant you should've been there yesterday. His partner Billy Fritz was sitting in a chair waiting for him in the captain's office.

The captain was Fred Dailey, who had dedicated forty-one years of his life to the Chicago Police Department, soon to retire. He stood behind his desk, holding papers and signaled Konrad to sit down.

Captain Dailey removed his glasses. "Alice Oliver, that name ring a bell with either of you?"

"Yeah, it does. The Fossett case. A possible suspect.

"Not anymore, Konrad. She was found dead yesterday morning in her home, apparent suicide. I repeat, apparent suicide. Apparently to the coroner Dr. Clancy it may not be a suicide after all. He found a pill left in her mouth, arsenic...a quick and easy way to commit suicide, don't you think."

Konrad and Fritz sat there, waiting for Dailey to get to his point. If Dailey was part of the investigation, then something serious was about to happen.

"Well, I got a call from Dr. Clancy early this morning. He's telling me that Oliver had severe bruises around her neck, deep bruises. I think our investigation has gone from a suicide to a homicide, gentlemen."

"That's understandable. Somebody had a reason to shut her up. But who?"

"That's why you're in my office, Fritz. Find out. Check her neighbors, her friends. She must have known something about Fossett that nobody wanted leaked out."

"Captain, we've done that already. This woman was a loner. We checked her phone records and the name Helen Kruger, Fossett's sister, popped up. As of now, the calls came from a California area code near Pasadena. We're trying to locate her. We also have proof Kruger and Fossett had a very violent brother and sister relationship. Could be the motive, but through our investigation, we believe a woman murdered Fossett. It could be either Kruger or Oliver." Konrad said.

"Have you put out an APB on this Helen...?"

"Not yet. We're trying to put this all together. Our belief is that Oliver, Reading, and Kruger were all in this together."

"If she is still going by the name of Kruger, she should be easy to find." suggested Dailey.

"We have some leads. Right now we're watching Charles Collier, another employee of Fossett's. But I think he's clean."

"Very well. Keep me abreast on any new results. You can go now."

Chapter 30

Just Vacationing In Costa Rica?

Things appeared to be falling into place for Charles and Emily. The money was safely deposited into a Swiss bank account, they finalized their divorce, and had their talk with Jack. The only thing left, waiting for his passport. When that moment arrives, Charles could begin booking his flight, his hotel in Liberia, and start packing his bags. He hasn't seen or heard from Detective Konrad in more than a week, knock on wood. He was relieved about that, but there was still a chance he'd show up at the most inopportune time. And as fate happens, he'd be knocking on Charles's door the minute he was ready to board the plane. He sat with Emily on their bed, checking his list of important issues that they discussed earlier.

"Emily, I wrote down the password that will get you into the Swiss account under your name. If everything goes as planned, you won't need to withdraw any money from that account. The less we do, the better our chances of not getting caught. When I get to Liberia, I'll check the banks down there. I feel better doing it there, in person, than over the Internet."

"Charles, I'm not going to take anything out of that account. I've already told you there's enough money from the sale of the condo and your parents' house, that will be enough money to settle in Manford. Houses are cheap now and a great time to buy and besides, it'll just be Jack and me. If I start taking money out of the account, I'm sure the police could trace any activity I engage in, which is scary."

"Damn it. This has been nothing but mass confusion for me.

So much to think about, so much to do and keeping away from the police. When is the real estate lady coming to appraise the condo?"

"She hasn't called me. I'll call her today, get her butt in gear. The sooner the better."

"Let me think. I believe I haven't forgotten anything." Charles checked his list. "All I need is my passport and toothbrush."

"We can start packing some clothes tonight. If there's anything you need, you can pick it up tomorrow or I'm sure they have stores there, too. Whatever you forget here, you can buy down there, right?"

Charles sat still, remembering, "I destroyed every piece of paper I could find in the office. I mean everything, from calendars to business cards. Gone. I even took the hard drives off all the computers. Now, how could anyone find out about the money? Who would know about the clients we had? It would be as if Priority never existed."

"You're forgetting that Konrad confiscated the financial statements of Priority. It has the seven million figure on them." Emily rose from the bed and walked out the bedroom.

Charles sat, still thinking about what Emily mentioned when his cell phone on his dresser began ringing. He hesitated. He looked flipped open the phone and looked at the number. The number on the screen was not familiar to him as the phone kept ringing, Charles panicked. He didn't know what to expect every time his cell rang. What went through Charles's mind was frightening because every time his phone rang, he expected the worse on the other end, like the voice of Detective Konrad. As each day began, he realized the inevitable would happen sooner or later, by some means, Konrad would appear with handcuffs and arrest him and Emily. Now, his life was a game of chance, the phone kept ringing. He chanced it.

"Mr. Collier, Charles Collier?"

"Yes."

"I'm Cheryl Sitton, from the Lincoln Park Post Office. Your

passport is here. You can stop in and pick it up at your convenience."

Charles glanced at his watch, three-thirty five, "Oh, thank you." A big relief escaped Charles's lungs, "I've been waiting for that. What time do you close today?"

"Five o'clock."

"Great. I'm on my way. Thank you, again." Charles closed the lid on his cell. "Talk about perfect timing. My passport is ready."

From their condo, the Lincoln Park Post Office was a Twenty-minute ride. Charles started the engine, letting it warm up as he fastened his seat belt. Without warning, a sharp tapping on the driver's side window scared the daylights out of him. *I knew it, I knew it. It's that asshole Detective Konrad, with that shit-eating-grin on his face.* He put the Escalade into park and rolled down the window.

"Are you in a hurry, Mr. Collier?"

"A matter of fact, yes. What is it now, Detective?"

"Reading. Have you heard from him lately?"

"Jesus. Are you for real? Do you honestly think Reading wants to contact me? I have no clue to his whereabouts and quite frankly, I couldn't give a rat's ass."

"What about Alice Oliver. You seen or talked to her lately?"

"No."

"Of course you haven't. She's dead, Collier. Apparent suicide. Her neighbor found her dead in her house yesterday."

"What! What the hell is going on? This is so crazy. I gotta go."

"That's what we want to know, Collier. Who killed Fossett? If I were you, I'd be talking like a Chatty-Cathy doll. Level with us, Collier. Let's get this over with and move on."

"I can't help you. I don't know anything. Sorry." Charles rolled the window up and backed out of his designated parking spot. As the engine roared, the view in his mirror said it all. Good riddance, Konrad.

Charles entered the post office and stood at the end of the long line of perplexed customers. There was just one clerk working the counter and eight people waiting to being taken care of.

"Next," shouted the clerk, an African-American woman, standing about five-foot-six, long dreads, with excessive makeup on her face and, a definite weight problem.

"May I help you?"

"I'm here to pick up my passport."

"Your name, please?"

"Collier, Charles Collier. C-O-L-L-I-E-R."

The clerk slowly retreated to the rear of the service counter, stopped at the doorway of an office and spoke to another clerk. Charles recognized the man. He was the same clerk who took his application and his picture. Charles was in a hurry, but not the postal clerks and his patience was running thin. *What's the problem?* The man got up from his chair and approached Charles.

"May I see any identification you have?" Obviously, he didn't remember Charles.

He searched his back pocket, removed his wallet and produced his driver's license.

"Very well. Excuse me for a second." He retreated to his office.

Now what? Simmer down, Charles. Don't create a scene in here. Relax. It irritated Charles on how a simple transaction, just picking up a passport that he already applied and paid for, was taking so long to accomplish. He watched the clerk searching through the papers on his desk. The clerk returned with several of the papers in his hand. He scanned through them, located Charles's application, and handed them to him.

"Please look over the information on your passport. Make sure everything is spelled and printed correctly."

Charles scanned the passport, verifying all the information.

"Fine. Everything looks fine. Thank you."

***

Once Charles arrived back at the condo, he opened his paper notebook and reviewed all the data he had written down about Costa Rica. He open the Internet and located the page regarding air flights and booked his flight to Cozumel, Mexico. If and when they traced his credit card transactions, it would end there, in Mexico. When the scheduled flight landed in Mexico, Charles had to hurry. His connecting flight to Liberia was less than ninety minutes, only time to collect his luggage, find the air carrier to Liberia, pay for his flight and then rush to the departing gate. All that in less than ninety minutes.

Charles sat motionless, his arms folded across his chest staring at the computer screen. But before he was ready to shut down the computer, Charles turned the printer on and printed the itinerary of his flight. All the data had to be precise and accurate, no foul ups, no delays, no time to waste. Anyone looking for him would believe Charles fled to Mexico as his plan indicated. Next, as soon as he set foot in Mexico, all his purchases would be paid in cash.

Done. He closed down his computer and deleted as much as he could find on his hard drive regarding Costa Rica. This is when he remembered all the computers at the office, all destroyed. He marched to the closet in the kitchen, picked up a hammer and screwdriver and went back to his computer. He took the cover off, dismantled the hard drive and smashed it to a thousand pieces with his hammer.

"Emily, I think you and Jack need to buy a new computer. We can't take the chance of Konrad confiscating this and finding out about my being in Costa Rica or the money in Switzerland."

"Can we afford another computer?" Emily laughed. "Good idea. And speaking of smashing things, you better destroy your credit card and maybe your cell phone, too. Don't even take the chance of using it. How much money are you planning to take with you?"

"I think eight thousand will be enough. Once I'm situated, I'll find a bank near Liberia and open an account. I'll deposit a thousand dollars right away. Then I can start moving the money around whenever I need it."

"Sounds good. Now let's go over everything, starting with your flight."

He picked up his notebook and read the data to Emily. "I leave O'Hare on Sunday morning at nine am., land in Cozumel at two pm., board the connecting flight to Liberia, and land there around six that night. I'll find a hotel near the airport and stay the night.

The next day, I'll rent a car and drive to Villa del Rico. The place looks awesome. A one-bedroom villa, nestled on the side of a mountain, surrounded with trees and tropical plants. I can't wait to get there. According to it's website, the resort offers numerous amenities, like golf, tennis, scuba diving, sauna and spa, the whole works, even a restaurant. Looking at the map on their website, its fairly close, too."

"Honestly, I wish I was going with you. It sounds and looks breathtaking and I'm going to be very jealous, knowing you're down there, but I can't talk to you."

"If we have to talk, I wrote down the number on the desk phone in the downstairs lobby. As soon as I get to the Villa, I'll look for a pay phone there. All the calls will be by chance. You know that."

"I know. As hard as it's going to be, we can't waver from our intentions. Maybe in a short time, they'll find Reading and Helen and convict them of killing William. Case closed. No more looking for Charles Collier and you can come home."

"Wouldn't that be sweet. These next two days are going to be a struggle for me. I want to spend as much time as possible with Jack. I'll check and see if the Sox are in town and if so, we'll go to a game on Saturday. He'll like that."

***

The time with Jack whisked by and before Charles knew it, the alarm clock was ringing... five am. He learned over and turned the clock off, laid back for a moment to reminisce about last night. His last night with Jack. He had a lengthy talk with him before they all retired, assuring him that when he was in Mexico, he would keep in contact with him. Jack was very happy about that. Charles made a promised to him, to call every Saturday at around six pm., Chicago time.

Now, it was a rush to shower, dress, and flag down a taxi to the airport. Emily was up and had his coffee made. Charles entered the kitchen, sat and sipped on his hot coffee.

"You know you can pinch me. Can you believe this is actually happening?" said Charles.

"Think of the rewards, darling. Before you know it, Konrad will have solved his case, put the crooks in jail and then we can start a new life with Jack."

"I can't wait. Gosh, look at the time. I gotta hustle."

Charles moved into the living room, picked up his luggage and headed to the front door. "Remember, Jesse knows about me using the lobby phone to call you. So, when I call, he will contact you. Well, I guess that's it. I love you, I'll call as soon as possible, okay?"

"Please be careful. I love you too." They embraced and Charles was on his way to a long vacation.

***

"Good morning. Welcome to flight nine-nine-six to Cozumel, Mexico. I'm Captain George Eagan. On behalf of myself and the entire crew, I invite you to sit back, relax and enjoy your flight. Presently, the temperature in Cozumel is a tropical eighty-two degrees. We should be landing at approximately two o'clock this afternoon. Persons connecting to other flights, inform your cabin attendant. She'll be happy to guide you to the correct gate. Once again, thank you for flying Tropical Airlines."

The four-hour flight would give Charles enough time to rest and coordinate his criteria. He'd book his connecting flight under the name of Russell Swanson from Detroit, pay cash for the flight, and be on his way to Liberia. During the flight hours, Charles caught a quick nap, but woke when he felt the jet slowing and the plane begin its descent into Cozumel. Finally, the aircraft touched down. The wheels screeched along the long asphalt runway as the engines roared, slowing them for the journey to the terminal. Everyone disembarked the jet in single formation. As he walked through the waiting area, the overhead flight schedule let Charles know that flight 1516 was boarding at gate 3E. He had to hustle to collect his baggage, obtain his ticket at the ticket counter, pass through security, and then locate gate 3E. All within ninety minutes time.

***

"One way ticket to Liberia, please." Charles was nervous and it showed.

"Your name, sir?"

"Russell Swanson. I just got off a flight from Detroit." *That was stupid, Charles. Keep your mouth shut.* He watched as she punched the keyboard, fearful that she might find that out.

"Coach or first class?"

"Coach, please."

"One way to Liberia, Costa Rica. That will be four hundred ninety-five dollars, Mr. Swanson. Are you paying by credit card?"

"No. I have the cash." Charles removed the money from his wallet and handed it to the registration clerk. She tagged his luggage and gave him the receipts. *Shit.* His name, Charles Collier was printed on all the luggage tags. *Would she catch that? Look the other way, Charles.*

"There you are Mr. Swanson. Your seat number is 27 F and you'll be departing at gate 3 E. Enjoy your flight."

Unbelievable. She missed it. *This is the way it's going to be, Charles, so get used to it.* He went through security with no setbacks and made it to gate 3E as the last passengers were boarding. Charles boarded the jet and when he reached his window seat, his hands were shaking and his stomach became queasy. He removed his handkerchief from his back pocket and wiped the sweat from his brow. What he needed was a stiff drink to calm himself down and relax. One thing for sure, life will not be the same as living back in Chicago.

The announcement over the intercom informed the passengers they would be landing in fifteen minutes. Once they landed, it was another rush for everyone to exit the plane and hurry to get somewhere else, but not Charles. He sat there, patiently waiting as the plane emptied. Why would he need to rush? He had all the time in the world to becoming a life long tourist.

***

The next morning, Charles checked out of the airport hotel, rented a four-wheel-drive, black Toyota 4Runner and headed west out of Liberia, toward the ocean. The rental agency supplied him maps and other brochures that offered points of interest, food, lodging or whatever he needed. His next stop was Villa del Rico. From what he learned on the Internet about the Villa, it sounded and looked like the ideal location to hide. Now, he had to see for himself.

The Villa was located in the Guanacaste Providence of Costa Rica, approximately thirty miles west of Liberia. The drive was beautiful. The road twisted throughout the dense vegetated terrain populated with colorful plants and various species of trees. The open-aired 4Runner allowed him to breathe in the fresh air and smell the fragrance of the blooming flowers lining the roadside. He'd enjoy the ride, took his time, and remember his arrangement. A sign for Villa del Rico emerged along the roadside, informing him to turn right one mile ahead. He found the entrance, driving along a narrow asphalt road leading into the thick forest of the Guanacaste Providence, approximately one mile to the resort. All the pictures on the website came true. The radiant colors, the sounds of the birds, and the aromatic smells of the blooming vegetation. The Toyota came upon an opening one mile in, where Charles found the main office. Inside, the motif reminded him of an old Tarzan movie. Grass and bamboo decorated the walls and ceiling, and the fragrance of incense drifted into his nose. Behind the bamboo-built counter stood a Latin-American gentleman, dressed in a khaki-colored suit with a vibrant red, yellow, and green striped tie. His face was well-tanned and his hair was jet black, along with his mustache.

"Good afternoon, sir."

"Hello. Do you have any vacancies?"

"Oh yes. 'Tis the end of our busy season, mind you."

"Fantastic. I just flew into Liberia last night. I found your resort on the Internet and it looked like an exciting place to stay."

"Oh yes, you'll love it here. Let me call Carlos. He will gladly show you around the property. We have four different-styled villas, each set in the foothills of the mountains and all have extraordinary views of the ocean."

The clerk slammed the bell sitting on the counter and within seconds, Carlos appeared.

"Carlos, show this gentleman around. Have him view the villas and feel the ambiance for himself."

Carlos led Charles along the wooden paths and signs to the four different villas, each floor plan upgraded to accommodate more guests and each more expensive. What Charles liked most was the distance between them. The villas were spread far apart, very private, and built within the forest with plenty of trees. Carlos mentioned to Charles to keep an eye out for monkeys that climb through many of the trees. The wooden paths rose higher into the foothills, a lengthy walk from where he parked the Toyota, but produced incredible views of the ocean. From there, they continued until Charles saw the entire resort.. The amenities were endless: fishing, snorkeling, golfing, hiking, surfing, a spa and a place to enjoy every interest. When they reached the main office, Charles asked the clerk about Villa Sixteen. He loved the views, especially from the outside deck. He couldn't wait to see himself lying in that hammock, sipping on a margarita and watching the sunset over the Pacific Ocean.

"Yes. That villa is very popular. It's rare that even today, it's vacant. Very unusual."

"Superb. I'll take it. I'm a writer, so I'll be here for a considerable length of time."

"Really? The lady in Villa Eighteen is also a writer. Well, our summer rates have taken effect. Normally, during our peak months, that villa would rent for eleven hundred a week. Now, it is renting for eight-fifty a week. But, if you want to rent the villa by the month, I can offer you a better rate. How does twenty-seven hundred a month sound?"

"Splendid." Charles counted out $2,700 in cash and handed it to the clerk.

"You do have a restaurant on the property, don't you?"

"Of course. The Mai-Kai. Great food and tasty, refreshing drinks. Prices are very reasonable and I'm sure you'll like it. In fact, I'll give you a voucher for one free meal. Compliments of the management."

"Thank you. Oh, just one more thing. A food store. Do I have to drive back to Liberia?"

The clerk reached under the counter and handed Charles a brochure indicating various stores and shops close to the villas. The brochure offered many discount coupons, from dining to fishing, and included a map of the entire Guanacaste Providence. The towns, places of interest, and roads.

"Perfect. Just what I need."

He hopped into the 4runner and slowly climbed the trail until he came upon a sign: Villas 15 to 20. He guided his car into the lot and began to unload his baggage. It would be a hike to his villa and one that he wouldn't make in one trip. Inside and to his right he found a spacious living room equipped with a sofa, lounge chair, and TV. The bedroom was average in size, containing a large dresser, two night tables, and a king-size bed. The small kitchenette contained plenty of cabinet storage, a sink, a small refrigerator, a stove and a microwave. A tiny table with four chairs sat in the middle of the room. It was perfect, after all, it was just him staying there.

The back of the kitchen, sliding glass doors led to an outside deck equipped with a hammock, small table, and two over-sized bamboo chairs. He opened the glass doors and walked to the deck railing. He stood in amazement, viewing the extraordinary post card views of Costa Rica and the Pacific Ocean. This was the ideal spot for him: Charles Collier, writer and multi-millionaire.

Chapter 31

Time To Move On

Emily sat at her kitchen table sipping her third cup of coffee, thinking with mixed emotions how her life has changed since Charles was no longer in the picture. Charles was out of her life and Sergio was in. After all, she was a single divorced woman and needed affection on a daily basis, something she did not get with Charles. Sergio gave that to her. Her desire was to spend more time with him, devour his love, and avoid thinking about Charles. But, as crazy as relationships go, Emily had fallen in love with Sergio. It was her idea to divorce Charles because it was the only obstacle standing in her way of being with him on a steady basis. Not to forget that she was a millionaire.

During the past several months, Emily spent as much time with Sergio as time allowed her. Although living with Jack had it's struggles, because his unwillingness to accept Sergio, Jack rebelled with Emily every time Sergio showed his face. Maybe she did believe in fate. If William hadn't been murdered and if Charles had never come across the seven million, there would never be a future with Sergio. But, now, there was hope. Charles was living in another country, they were divorced and, soon, Jack will be attending college on the west coast. All Emily had to do was sell the condo, move to Manford, and fall asleep in Sergio's arms.

The telephone rang, bringing her back to reality.

"Hello."

"Mrs. Collier? This is Jan Sturtevant from Chicago Land Realty. How are you this morning?"

"Just sitting around, waiting for my ambition to kick in."

"Believe me, I've had days like that. I was hoping we could meet this afternoon. Get started on the listing and take some pictures."

"Yes. I'll be home all afternoon. Give me a call when you're on your way."

"Fine. I'll see you around two this afternoon."

Emily set the receiver down and glanced around the condo. It was an adequate sized condo—a spacious living room, two bedrooms, two baths, and a workable kitchen with a small area set aside for dining. It wouldn't take Emily long to clean, make the beds, and wash the living room window to make the condo suitable for pictures.

A few minutes after the grandfather clock struck two, her phone rang again.

"Hello."

"It's Jan. I'm downstairs. What floor is your condo on? For some reason I never marked that down."

"We're on the ninth floor, nine B. When you exit the elevator, it's the first door on your right."

"Okay. I'm on my way up."

Emily opened the door to greet her Realtor and as she entered, Jan handed Emily her business card.

"This shouldn't take too long. I'll go over the listing agreement with you, then I'll take some pictures and that will be it."

"Would you care for a cup of coffee, Jan?"

"Yes, thank you, with cream, please." Jan sat at the table, removing a stack of papers from her brown leather carrying case.

"I'll explain the process of listing your condo, okay? Have you ever sold a house before?"

"Yes, my in-laws' home after they passed away, but this is our only house. My husband's job got him transferred to Mexico. So, we want to sell as quickly as possible. If we can close by the end of July or August, it would be terrific."

"Well, let me explain what we need to do. When I get back to the office, I'll look up places that are for sale within your location and see what they are listing for. Then, we can determine the value of your property and settle on a marketable selling price. It's called "comparables". Simple as that."

"Awesome."

Jan concluded her business, taking pictures of the interior of the condo and some measurements. "I should have everything loaded onto the computerized multiple listing service later this afternoon. As soon as I do that, I'll call you and suggest a reasonable listing price. Your location is excellent. It wouldn't surprise me if your condo sells very quickly."

"All right. I'm keeping my fingers crossed."

***

It was ten minutes after four. When Jack got home from his game, Emily planned to ask if he wanted to drive to Manford on Saturday to look at houses with her. Saturday would be a family day, just her and Jack.

"Mom?"

"Yes, I'm in here."

Jack tossed his glove and backpack on the kitchen table and took off his windbreaker. Like most active teenagers, it was a habit of his every day when he arrived home to invade the refrigerator.

"What's for dinner?" Jack saw one red apple, took it out and began munching on it waiting for Emily's answer.

"Chicken cacciatore. You'll love it."

"Have you heard from Dad yet?"

"No. It may take a week or so. Let him get situated there. With his new job, he's going to be quite busy, but remember, every Saturday, six pm."

Jack headed to the living room for phase two of his routine—continue hunting for terrorists on his Xbox.

"You don't have anything planned for Saturday, do you?"

"Yeah. Timmy and Josh wanted to sneak over to Lincoln Park. Something about a basketball tournament."

"I was hoping to go to Manford and look at houses. I wanted you to go with me."

"I'm not doing anything on Friday. We could go Friday."

"Okay. Let's do that."

Emily sat at the computer desk. She needed to find a real estate agent in Manford and try to schedule a meeting on Friday to view a houses on the market in Manford. The page opened to Manford Real Estate, showing a list of houses and the list of available agents. The name Jenna Findlay sounded appealing to her. She dialed the number listed on the website and waited for an answer.

"Manford Real Estate."

"Yes. I'm looking for Jenna Findlay?"

"One second, I'll transfer your call to her."

"Hello. This is Jenna."

"Hello, Jenna. My name is Emily Dearborn. I'm looking to purchase a home in Manford. I was thinking two or three bedrooms, two baths, a large open kitchen, and hardwood floors. My budget is around one hundred seventy-five thousand."

"Well, now is an excellent time to buy a house because of the economic market. I know of three or four houses on the market that fit your requirements to a "T".

"I live in Chicago right now and have my condo on the market here. I was hoping we could meet Friday and look at some houses."

"Emily, is there a number where I can reach you?"

Emily gave Jenna her cell number rather than the house number.

"I'll put together a list of houses that meet your criteria. I'm looking at my agenda right now. How does eleven o'clock Friday morning sound to you?"

"That would be fine. I'll look forward to seeing you, Jenna. Goodbye."

Emily browsed the pages still open on her computer and saw two houses that caught her eye. A two-story brick house on South Street, and a newer two-story house on Devlon. Both were easily within her price range. She wrote down the addresses for Jenna when they meet on Friday.

She sat back in her chair, thinking about the move to Manford. It was a move back to where she grew up as a child. Although her parents moved from Manford years ago, she still had the feeling that Manford was the right place to live. She noticed she still had her cell phone in her hand, thinking the right place for her to be was with Sergio. She dialed his number.

"I had a feeling you would call today."

"Really. I put the condo on the market today and I'm going to Manford on Friday to look at a few houses."

"You're moving pretty fast, young lady. You need to slow down a bit."

"I'll slow down when I'm in bed with you, like later this evening. Are you ready for that?"

"Lady, you know me, I was born ready."

Chapter 32

Could She Be Ms. Universe?

It was an ear-piercing, shrilling scream that, instantly, woke Charles up. He leaped from his bed and sprinted to the living room window. At that moment, he thought a woman was, possibly being attacked. There was nothing out there. Again…that scream, this time it sounded like it was coming from the back porch. Sprinting again, he rushed to open the glass sliding doors, ran onto the deck, but no sign of a desperate woman. Again, the high-pitched screechy noise. When Charles turned around, he burst out laughing. There, sitting on his roof were two innocent looking holler monkeys. They weren't being robbed or being raped, just calmly going about their business, eating nuts. Charles plopped his butt on the hammock, sat for a bit and asked himself…*why do people commit crimes?* He though hard about that question. If he had won the seven million in a lottery, or a windfall from a stock sale, the money was his legally. But he did commit a crime, he stole someone's money. His brain didn't have an answer he wanted. To clear his mind, he strolled back into the kitchen, turned on the cold water and doused his face with the cold water. *There, it's over and done with. Think positive, think of Emily and Jack.*

One thing that could settle his mind was getting out of the villa and becoming a tourist. So, he decided to explore Ocotal. He dressed for the perfect weather that Costa Rica offered: a pair of khaki shorts, a blue tank top, and Croc flip-flops. He dove the Toyota out of the resort and headed west toward the ocean and Ocotal. The sun sent warm rays of sunshine across his face, a feeling he could embrace every day. He smelled the ocean, tasted the salt in the air, and felt the warm breezes swirling around his face.

Entering the town of Ocotal, he was quite surprised to see how modern the settings were, new buildings mixed with some old ones. Several strip malls scattered along the highway leading into the town. He saw a Starbucks, a Burger King, and a Post Office. Whatever he would need, this town could provide. Slowly driving down Main street, Ocotal Providence Bank was right in front of him, so what better time to set up his checking account than now. He pulled into the parking lot, entered the bank, and approached the counter.

"I'd like to start a checking account, if I may?"

"Certainly." She pointed to a gentleman sitting at a small desk to his right. "He will help you."

As Charles approached the desk, the man rose from his chair and introduced himself as Antoine Vargas.

"Sit down, please. How may I help you today?"

"I just moved into the area and I need to establish a checking account."

Mr. Vargas opened his top drawer of his desk and removed a file with papers in it. "Would you kindly fill out the application Mr…"

"Charles Collier." At first, Charles hesitated, then remembered that using an alias would create more trouble.

"Mr. Collier, please fill out the application, read the information and then sign on the line at the bottom of the page."

After Charles signed the document, he thought about the paper trail. It was a thought that will never go away, the dreaded paper trail. But he needed a bank to transfer his money, so it became unavoidable. Also, Charles had to prove who he was, the real Charles Collier.

"I'll need to see your passport and driver's license. Will you be making a deposit today?" Charles handed his license and passport to Vargas.

"I'll be depositing one thousand dollars. I'm a writer, working on my third book. I should be receiving royalties sent to me monthly and deposited into this account."

"I understand. Will you be needing a credit card or debit card?"

Warning!! No paper trail, Charles.

"No, no. I won't need them."

"Very well. Excuse me while I get you a receipt for your deposit."

Charles noticed that Vargas took his license and passport with him. *This is a paper trail, Charles!* It was a risk, a very high risk, but he had no other options open to him. Vargas returned and handed the license, passport, and receipt to Charles.

"This pamphlet will show you several options about ordering checks. You can order all this over the Internet. Here are five blank checks that will be honored until you receive your personal checks. Any questions?"

"One more. Where could I go to apply for citizenship in Costa Rica?"

"Well, I'm not sure, but try the Post Office."

"Thank you."

Charles remembered to keep it fast and simple. The less he talked the more he felt secure using this bank. His next stop was the grocery store. The drive through Ocotal allowed him to acknowledge other stores and shops, some restaurants, and nightlife bars.

While still driving through the town, a grocery store appeared, the same type store you would see back in the States, except the name was Hispanic, the Cortez Brothers Supermercado. Charles came out of the store with nine bags full of groceries, and $156 donated to the Cortez brothers. From fruits, coffees, snacks, beer, liquor, and microwave dinners, he had enough food to last him a couple of weeks.

The grocery store pointed him in the direction of the ocean. The drive was less than a half mile and as he got closer, he could hear the waves and people shouting. The narrow asphalt road ended at Playa Ocotal beach parking lot. Exiting the Toyota and what

Charles saw was a picture on a postcard. The light aqua blue ocean water, the long soft white sandy beaches, crowds of people either swimming, tanning or surfing the waves, it was awesome, breath-taking. The cove held several anchored sailboats bobbing with the semi-calm waves, and to his far left, he noticed a rocky island several hundred yards from the shore. He started to walk in that direction and as he came closer, there was a group of snorkelers swimming around the small island. That was something that caught his interest and a challenge he must try.

He reached into one of the grocery bags and removed a six-pack of beer. He popped open a can, took off his flip-flops and walked toward the bench area, sipping on his beer. Tourists, some with children, walked the small beach, testing the waters and saying hello.

Then Charles spotted a woman alone, wading in ankle high water and walking toward him. She wore a bright red bikini with a multicolored wrap around her waist. As she neared, he focused on her. She had strawberry blond hair down to her shoulders, and a bodacious tan on her sexy, ultra- slim frame. He thought she had to be a famous celebrity or model, taking time off from her busy schedule to enjoy her free time on the beach. The closer she got, the more stunning she became. So close, he wanted to reach out and touch her, embrace her. Her stunning eyes were framed by long black eyelashes and black eyebrows, her breasts filled the tight red bra, barely covering what Charles wanted to see. Their eyes met, they both smiled. Then she passed by, nothing said, no hellos, no exchanging phone numbers, just gone with the wind. *You could have offered her a beer, you idiot?* Charles watched her fade away, walking aimlessly into the parking lot. Was she by herself? Maybe she lives around Ocotal, why else would she choose this beach? He was determined to find out, but how?

To salve his disappointment at letting "Miss Universe" get away, he finished another can of beer. On his way back to the parking lot, he noticed a small shack toward the end of the lot. It was a concession stand, offering sandwiches, snacks, and drinks, a place he wanted to find out about. He had a taste for a hot dog, in fact, he bought two. The quick lunch was just what he wanted, but not like a "Chicago" style hot dog, but it hit the spot.

It was time to head the Toyota back to the villa. He turned the 4Runner into the Villa Rico's entrance and followed it till he came to the office. He needed to know about Internet settings, something he forgot to ask when he first arrived.

"Are the villas equipped with Internet capabilities?"

"Oh, yes, Mr. Collier. Every villa has a Wi-Fi connection. Even if you are lying in your hammock on your deck."

"Excellent. Thank you."

When Charles left the office, he looked to his left and saw the Mai-Kai, the restaurant that would provide his free dinner tonight. *Well, I wonder what they serve?* His curiosity got the best of him, so he walked to the entrance. The place was closed, but he saw a menu encased in a wooden frame near the front entrance. They served steaks, chicken, and several tropical seafood dishes. It all looked good. What also looked good was a pay phone near the entrance. He thought about calling Emily, then remembered he left the number in his briefcase. Anyway, it wasn't six o'clock Chicago time and it wasn't Saturday, but it was the perfect place to make his calls.

***

He finished the chore of getting his groceries to his villa and stored in the cabinets. His laptop sat on the small, circular kitchen table and what better time to check out a few things over the Internet. He flipped the power switch and waited a few seconds.

"Yes!" He slapped his hands together, then walked to the small refrigerator and took out a can of beer.

"This calls for a celebration."

He logged into the Clariden Leu website and entered his password. There it was. Nearly seven million sitting on one single line, all his. His next step was logging on to the Ocotal Province

Bank website and setting up his account. Once that was done, Charles would test the waters by transferring five thousand to his new account. Hopefully, within minutes, he would have his answer. Bingo! His balance was six thousand dollars, it worked.

***

Later that afternoon, Emily was preparing dinner for Jack when her phone rang. It was Jan Sturtevant, her real estate agent, informing her about the CMA report. Several condos similar to Emily's were on the market and selling for around $210 thousand. Emily felt comfortable listing her condo for the same price. The sooner the property became available, the sooner it would be sold. She told Jan the price was fair, but she would drop the price if it meant a quicker sale. Jan encouraged Emily to leave the price at $210 thousand, at least for a while, because of the condo's excellent location. With Jan's experience, it shouldn't stay on the market very long, because it was true what they said about real estate…location, location, location.

Friday came, and Emily and Jack headed for their appointment in Manford. Just before hopping on the freeway, Jack was hungry and asked her to stop at McDonald's to get him an Egg McMuffin and an orange juice, Emily ordered a cup of coffee. The silver Escalade headed south on I-67 and within an hour they would be in Manford. Emily programmed the car into cruise control and then opened her cell phone to call Jenna Findlay.

"Manford Real Estate, Jenna Findlay speaking."

"Jenna, Emily Dearborn here. We're on our way and will be there in about an hour."

"Very good. Just exit off I-67 and go east. As soon as you enter Manford, you'll see our office on the right. You can't miss our one huge sign."

"See you in a bit."

"Emily Dearborn? What was at all that about?" Jack stared across the seat.

"Did I say that? Gosh. What was I thinking?"

"You've been acting strange ever since Dad lost his job. Even more since he's gone."

"Too much on my mind right now. Worrying about him, selling the condo, taking care of you."

"And taking care of Sergio, too. You still haven't told me why we need to move down here?"

"Simple. I don't like living in the city, to busy, to crowded. Besides, this is where I grew up. I've always wanted to move back here."

Jack sat there, thinking about moving away from his friends with only one more year of high school left. "I only have one more year of school left, you know."

"Wait till you see this town. You'll love it there. Trust me."

"Does Dad know you're moving down here?"

"Of course. He's all for it. He understands me and knows that I don't like living the city life. It's a lot slower here, and people are more friendly here. That's the way I like it."

***

Emily turned off I-67 and onto the exit ramp for Manford, heading east. A mile or so later, Jack saw the white neon sign for Manford Real Estate.

"You made it. Terrific. Let me get my listings together and we'll be on our way." Jenna said.

Seated in Jenna's Chevy Tahoe, she handed the listings to Emily to look over, in case she had any questions about them. Emily noticed both the properties she saw on the website were included in Jenna's listings.

"Could we see the house on South Street first?"

"Sure. It's vacant right now. Been on the market for nearly four months. I think you'll like this one. It has everything you're looking for."

It didn't take long to reach South Street, a long and straight concrete avenue. The house, located at the end of a cul-de-sac, appeared very private and very well landscaped. That's what Emily liked about it. No busy traffic. From the moment they opened the front door until they left, Emily felt that this was the house for them.

"This house is listed at one hundred eighty-eight thousand, completely renovated, with new kitchen appliances and all new carpeting. No one has lived here since it was renovated. It would be like moving into a new, older house."

Emily and Jack explored the main floor. But when Jack saw the bedroom upstairs, he was sold too.

"Mom. You gotta see the bedroom upstairs. My bedroom."

The entire upstairs was one large attic converted into a bedroom, including a complete bathroom. Emily agreed it was perfect for him, his own domain.

"Well, Jack, you think this is the house for us?"

"I like it, Mom. It's perfect for us. Just the right size, and nothing we have to do. Just move in."

"I think so too. Well, Jenna, shall we drive back to your office and write an offer?"

"I can't think of a better thing to do."

When they were back in Jenna's office, Emily wrote an offer for $175,000.

"Let me call Diane, one of my best friends and also the listing agent and give her the offer."

After Jenna made the call, they sat in her office talking about living in Manford. The rural community was mostly farming country, but Jenna informed Emily of the new shopping center that included Macy's, Sears, and Bed Bath & Beyond. Emily told Jenna she was born here, lived on Chestnut Street and attended Columbia High School, but moved to Chicago to attend college. Their conversation was interrupted when Jenna's phone began ringing.

"Yes, Diane. Excellent. I have them in my office as we speak. I'll tell her the great news. Very well. I'll call you tomorrow."

"Emily. You have a new home in Manford. Congratulations. They've accepted your offer."

"All that's left for me to do is sell the condo in Chicago."

Chapter 33

Waiting For Godot?

The next day, Charles drove back to Playa Ocotal, hoping he would see his dream girl again. He sat on the hood of the Toyota, watching people entertaining themselves on the sand beaches or in the ocean waters, but there was still no sight of her. He looked at his watch and thought it was about the same time he saw her the day before. Charles still had his hopes up, assured he would see her again.

As he sat, he wondered, maybe she worked in town or maybe it was her day off? He jumped back into his rental and headed toward town, where he could spend time walking the sidewalks looking in the stores. He took his time strolling from shop to shop, keeping a close eye out for her, but also discovering the culture in Ocotal. Two hours dragged by, but his dream girl was nowhere in sight. Charles decided to grab a quick sandwich and after that, look for a phone to call Emily, because it was Saturday and close to six o'clock Chicago time. It was a short walk where he came upon a pay phone, pulled the card from his pocket and started dialing the lobby number.

"Hello."

"Yes. I'm calling long distance trying to reach Emily Collier in condo nine B."

"Is this Mr. Collier? This is Jesse, the doorman."

"Oh, Jesse. Yes, yes I remember you. Could you do me a favor and see if Emily is home? I'm going to hang up, but I will call back in fifteen minutes, okay?"

"Okay. I'll check and see if she's in. Goodbye."

Charles watched the passing cars, keeping a close eye out that his Miss Universe would miraculously pass by. No such luck. The fifteen minutes passed and Charles redialed.

"Hello, Charles."

"Emily, it's me."

"Charles, I was on my way down to wait for your call. How are things going down there?"

"Everything is fine. It's so beautiful here. You'd fall in love with Costa Rica. I wish I could send some pictures so Jack could see them."

"Definitely. Our divorce is final now. I went to court on Thursday with Potter. It was quick. I was in front of the judge for only five minutes and that was that. Also, I've bought a house in Manford. Jack likes it so much because the entire upstairs is his bedroom, his man-cave he calls it. Our agent here told me our condo should sell quickly because of the location. I sure hope so. It would be awesome if I got an offer by the end of the month. That way Jack and I can move as soon as possible and get away from the nagging police."

"Are they still hanging around the condo?"

"Occasionally I will see them. I've been keeping a close eye on the news. Nothing in the papers about Fossett's murder. No news is good news, right?"

"Right. How's Jack doing?"

"Oh, the same. He questioned me about the move to Manford, but after he saw the house, he's a happy camper. We took a quick tour around town. They have a new shopping mall, even a Dick's Sporting Goods store. Jack wants to put an application to work there as soon as he can. Then, I drove by our old house. Boy, the scenery has changed so much since I remembered it. I'm sure as soon as we settle here, he'll be fine."

"Well. I tested a money transfer yesterday. And within five minutes, the money was sitting in my account in Ocotal. Awesome. Other than that, I'm getting used to being a touring fugitive. I'm just on my way back from the beach now and I think I might try some snorkeling. Looks like fun."

"I wish I was there. I miss you, already."

"Only time will tell, sweetheart. Is Jack around?"

"Would you believe he's on a date"

"You're kidding me. With a girl rather that talk to his Dad? Well, good for him. Maybe that young lady will take his mind off other bothering things."

"I believe her name is April."

There was some silence in their conversation, not knowing what more to say, Charles spoke, "Well, I'll let you go. I'll call you next week. Make sure Jack is with you. I want to talk to him. One more thing, the next time I call, it will be from the pay phone at the villa. I'm downtown in Ocotal right now. When I call, you can write down the number of that phone, in case you need to contact me in a hurry. The phone is right outside the restaurant door and I'll let the people inside know."

"All right. Please be careful and we miss you already. I love you. Goodbye." Who was Emily fooling? She had more fun with Sergio the past month than the last ten years with Charles.

"I love you too, honey. Goodbye."

***

With the investigation of William Fossett's murder at a standstill, both Konrad and Fritz were becoming frustrated. They didn't have a murder weapon, and no solid leads on who killed Fossett, but they had the body of Alice Oliver. With a little luck on their side, her death could be connected to Fossett's murder. They did have a set of a footprints at the scene of the crime, a. .38 caliber bullet slug found in Fossett's doorway frame, a spent shell casing, fingerprints of Dennis Reading at Fossett's house the night he was murdered, one arsenic pill from Oliver's mouth, four witnesses who had credible information, and two missing suspects. Other than that, everything was purely circumstantial and speculation. Even with all the experience under their belts, they still needed the pistol with matching fingerprints or the killer to turn him or herself in. Simple as that. Otherwise, there was a worthy chance this case could end up as a cold case file.

The officers sat at their desks in the precinct office discussing the whereabouts of Dennis Reading or Helen Kruger. They had leads, good ones and bad ones, ranging from seeing the pair in Mexico to back in Chicago. But the job of being a good detective was to be persistent and never leave a lead untouched. Being persistent usually paid off. Sooner or later, they were convinced that they would find the killer.

"Hey, Mike. Guess who left the country?" yelled a voice from across the office.

"Don't tell me, our disappearing duo, Reading and Kruger?"

The officer approached Konrad's desk and tossed a sheet of paper in front of him. He picked it up and read the news, then shook his head. He looked at Billy Fritz and broke the news to him.

"Fricken' Collier. He fled to Cozumel, Mexico. Now, why would he do that? He booked a flight with his credit card, leaving this past Sunday morning."

"I'm still not convinced he had anything to do with it." remarked Fritz.

"Never take anything for granted." Konrad sat, mulling over his next move.

"Billy, grab your coat. I think we need to pay the wife a visit. We need some answers."

The unmarked squad car pulled out of the parking lot on its way to 105 Cedar Street. What was behind the sudden departure of Collier? And why now? They had to find out.

When Fritz parked in front of the condo, they noticed a Chicagoland Real Estate "For Sale" sign planted near the main entrance.

"I know Jan," Billy said, "she sold my brother's house last month."

More interesting was another sign taped to the front door of the Collier condo, "For Sale." He's in Mexico, they're selling the condo.

"What's next, Billy?" Konrad said sarcastically.

Billy pushed the doorbell, moments later, Emily unlocked the door and opened it slightly.

"Mrs. Collier. How nice to see you."

She didn't say anything, expecting another wisecrack from Konrad.

"Your husband, is he home?"

"No."

"What a coincidence. We discovered that he left for Mexico early Sunday morning."

"Then why did you ask me if he was here when you knew that?"

"Why is he in Mexico?"

"He has a job interview there. I'm not sure when he'll be back."

"May I ask why your condo is up for sale?"

"None of your business, good day." Emily slammed the door.

Konrad turned to Fritz. "She didn't look very happy, did she? And I'm getting sick and tired of doors slamming in my face. I want a tag on her. I want to know what she's up to. Things aren't adding up right and I'm gonna find out why."

***

Emily's relationship with Sergio had stumbled a bit. The time it took organizing their plan, selling the condo, and traveling to Manford to buy a house, took away much of her precious time with him. Now, she was in position to make up for lost time. Jack was leaving with the Legion team on a baseball trip to southern Illinois for four days. The state tournament. Four days with Sergio would seem like a lifetime of being in his arms, feeling his touch, and reveling in his power to please her. She wanted to make up for the lost time, without hesitation, she dialed his number.

"You must be horny as hell."

"Just as horny as you are, sweetheart. My son left this morning for his baseball trip and I'm all alone for four days. Do you think you can keep this horny, undersexed, nymph of a woman satisfied?"

"Gee. Only four days?"

"We don't even have to get out of bed. How does that sound?"

"You're incredible. Let me take care of a few things and I'll head over there."

"You know where to find me, Lover boy."

"Okay."

Not a minute later, her phone rang. "That was fast. Are you on your way?"

"Excuse me, Emily, this is Jenna Findlay."

"Oh, yes, Jenna. I thought it was my son Jack calling me."

"I just wanted to let you know your closing is on the eighteenth, a Wednesday at eleven o'clock at my office. I know we discussed you'll be putting forty thousand down. Are you still planning on that?"

"Yes, of course. And as soon as I sell this property, I'll most likely pay off that mortgage. When Charles's parents died, with the money he received from the sale of his parent's house and a life insurance policy, we paid off the mortgage on this place."

"I see, very good. Well, I'll look forward to seeing you on the eighteenth."

"Sounds terrific, goodbye."

"Goodbye, Emily."

As soon as she ended her conversation with Jenna, her phone rang again.

For God sake, what now?

"Afternoon, Emily, this is Jan Sturtevant.

"Oh, Jan. I was just thinking about you."

"I have good news for you. I have three very interested prospects who would like to see your condo tomorrow. Are you comfortable with that?"

"Absolutely. In fact, I'll be in Manford all day tomorrow. The condo is all yours."

Emily lied about Manford. She'd be in Chicago, in bed all day, but in Sergio's bed.

"Terrific. Keep your fingers crossed. Hopefully one of them will put an offer on your place."

"They're crossed."

Chapter 34

Goodbye, Windy City

A solid break in the Fossett murder case couldn't have come at a better time for Detective Konrad. For weeks, it seemed every lead they received and checked out only led to a dead end. Mike was sitting at his desk, drinking a diet Coke and reading the Tribune, waiting for the lead that would break the case. Then, the break came, Konrad's phone began ringing.

"Detective Konrad. Really? I'll be right down."

He spilled what was left of his Coke in his haste to grab his sport coat.

"Billy, let's go. I think we caught a big break."

The phone call came from the FBI Crime Lab downtown. The two detectives bolted from the Third Precinct and headed for the lab.

"What did they tell you?" asked Billy.

"That pill bottle found near Oliver's bedside? It had a print on it and it wasn't Oliver's."

Konrad avoided the loop traffic, making good time to the crime lab, dashed into the building and headed directly downstairs. For security, he and Fritz produced their badges at the entrance of the lab and looked for Steve Denison, the lab technician.

"What do you have, Steve?"

"It took us longer than usual, but we got a solid thumb print. We ran it across our data base and it identified to a William Hill, alias Bill Winslow, alias Bill Wilson. His last known address is on North Rodale Street, a famous flophouse area. A pretty long rap sheet too, from petty theft to robbery, even assault with a deadly weapon. Released from Joliet four months ago."

"Print that out for me, Steve. I need to review it."

It was back to their squad car and on their way to 1155 N. Rodale, desperately hoping to find Mr. Hill, or whatever name he went by.

Konrad pulled the receiver from the police radio, "Squad three-four-three requesting backup, eleven hundred block, North Rodale Street. Possible murder suspect."

"Squad three-four-three, back up notified. En route to destination." responded the dispatcher.

"Roger, ten-four."

Konrad and Fritz remained in the squad car until their backups arrived. A few minutes later, three other cars rolled in. All the officers gathered near Konrad and Fritz, all wearing protective bullet proof vests.

"His name is William Hill, alias Bill Winslow or Bill Wilson. He could be carrying a weapon. I want him alive." Konrad passed around the rap sheet containing a picture of the suspect.

He pointed to each set of officers: "You two cover the rear entrance. You two patrol the lobby, and you two stay here. Check everyone coming or leaving the building. Let's go, Billy."

The detectives entered the flophouse and went directly to the front desk. Konrad and Fritz flashed their badges to the startled hotel clerk.

"You seen this guy lately?" Konrad shoved the rap sheet picture toward the shaking man.

"Yeah. That's Bill Wilson. He moved out a week ago."

"What room was he in? Is it vacant?" Konrad barked.

"Let me check. Aah, room 327, it's empty."

The shaken clerk handed the key to room 327 to Konrad. He grabbed the rap sheet and hurried to the elevator, followed by Fritz. On the third floor, they located room 327. Konrad withdrew his pistol and stood to the side of the door, letting Fritz knock. There was no answer, so Konrad inserted the key into the lock and opened the door. They entered the room with their pistols drawn, but it was useless, the room was vacant. Nothing in the room but a twin bed, no sheets, a small wooden table with two chairs and one pole lamp. Nothing else and no evidence to collect.

"Maybe we can send over CSI. They may be able to lift some prints. Who knows, maybe the prints could match the one found on the pill bottle." said Fritz.

"Yeah, it wouldn't hurt. I'll let them know when we get back to the office."

Both detectives left the building and drove back to the precinct. On the way there, Fritz asked Konrad, "You know, that old man that lives next door to Oliver. Maybe it would be worth our while to interview him again. Let's show him this picture, it's possible he saw him the day she was murdered. Covington is a couple of miles from here. What do you think?"

"What do we have to loose. Let's go for it."

They drove back to headquarters and looked for the missing person report regarding Alice Oliver.

"Got it. Xavier Pennington, 117 E. Sheridan."

A short time later, they parked their squad car along the curb in front of 117 Sheridan and walked to Mr. Pennington's front door. They knocked, knocked again. You could hear the latch unlock and the door slowly opened.

"Mr. Pennington, I'm talking to?"

"Yes.

"My name is detective Mike Konrad, my partner Billy Fritz." they showed Mr. Pennington their badges and he nodded his head, recognizing they were police officers.

"We're here to ask you a few questions regarding the death of Ms. Oliver, your neighbor."

"It's a shame, you know. She was such a sweet lady, helped me whenever I needed help. I'm going to miss her."

"I understand. Do you remember anything peculiar the day she was murdered. Did you see anything or hear anything?"

Pennington stood silent, rubbing his chin. "I do remember that day. I went out to get my mail, around 10:30 or so. There was this old pick-up truck parked in front of Alice's mail box, rusted out in places. Then this man was running from her house, in a hurry, I guess. As soon as I went to get my mail, I heard the truck start up and when he took off, he almost ran me over."

"Could you see the driver?"

"Well, yeah. He was tall, had a beard and curly hair, but it happened so fast, I was more concerned of not getting run over by him."

Konrad pulled the paper with the possible killer's picture and showed it to Mr. Pennington. He stared at the picture for several moments, then, "Boy, it sure looks like him. He doesn't have a beard in this picture. Again, it happened so fast and I was scared."

"Okay. Here's my card. If you can remember anything, please give me a call." they retreated to the squad and just about to leave when…

"Ohhh. There was one thing I remember that was, sort of, odd. It was his license plate. It was all letters and no numbers. It said "Hillbilly. I think it was spelled, H-L-L-B-L-L-Y, something close to that."

"That's great news. Thank you, so much." Fritz wrote the info in his notebook and looked at Konrad. "William Hill. I think we got our man, Hillbilly."

***

It was back to headquarters and Fritz began the search correlating William Hill. The first look directed him to Department of Motor Vehicles. He punched the letters H-L-L-B-L-L-Y and, sure enough, that plate was registered to William Hill. On January 5th, he purchased the plate, 2001 Chevrolet Silverado, gray, and registered it under the address of 98755 W. 15th Place. When Fritz wrote the information down, he phoned dispatch and asked them to send a squad to that address and look for that truck. All they could do now was wait and locate the truck. The next morning, Fritz received a phone call from dispatch.

"Ohh, great. Okay, thanks. I'll let Mike know." Billy swung his chair around facing his partner. "That address Hill put down on his vehicle registration. Well, no such place, a bogus address. "

"Shit. That figures. Well, put out a BOLO for that truck. That's the only chance we have left. I'm hoping he's still in Chicago."

*****

Today was Emily's closing in Manford. Her grandfather clock struck nine chimes, letting her know she'd better be on her way for the eleven o'clock appointment. She grabbed her purse, her keys and cell phone, then checked her purse to make sure she had the certified check for $40,000.

She realized that once the closing was final and the keys to her new house were in her hand, selling the condo in Chicago would not be a big issue anymore. The previous week, her and Jack had started boxing some of the smaller items. They filled boxes after boxes of smaller items, like pictures, knick-knacks, books, movies and clothes, mostly things they could handle instead of the movers. Her and Jack had the entire weekend to pack as much smaller items because on Monday, Capable Movers were scheduled to move all the furniture and boxes to her new house in Manford. After the movers moved everything out of the condo, she contracted A-1 Maintenance to clean the vacant unit. It would all be in Jan's hands then, a clean, vacant property to sell to prospective buyers.

The closing went as well as expected. She had her keys and Jenna Findlay had her commission. Since she was in Manford with an hour or so to kill, she wanted to see her house again. She unlocked the door, walked inside and visualized in her mind how all her furniture would sit, even down to the last picture hanging on the wall. She noticed a small bouquet of flowers sitting on the kitchen counter. The card read, "Congratulations. I know you'll love living in Manford." The card was signed by Jenna.

Aww, that was so sweet. She considered the idea of inviting her over for dinner one night, but unpacking, some painting and repairing her relationship with Sergio, would come first. Taking a final look around, it was time for Emily to head back to Chicago. She locked the door and said goodbye, but by the end of the next week, Emily and Jack would be calling Manford their new home.

***

When Monday arrived, Jack and Emily were back in Manford directing the movers where to put her furniture, piece by piece. Jack was hard at work painting his bedroom, setting up his man cave and forgetting about Chicago. By the end of the week, they had settled into their new home, all the furnishings were in place the way Emily had pictured them, still, Emily studied the each room, moving a piece here and there, until she was completely satisfied.

Jack was elated with his new sanctuary. He had complete control of the second story and the feeling of living on his own. He had his TV, his computer, his own bathroom, and the privacy he wanted, and away from Emily. He was excited and Chicago.. totally forgotten.

"Are you getting hungry? Why don't we take a ride into town and check out the mall. What do you say to that?"

"Awesome. Can I stop off at Dick's Sporting Goods and fill out an application? How cool it would be to work there, wouldn't it?"

The Cadillac cruised in the direction of the new mall. During their ride, their discussion was about their new house and how excited Jack was about his awesome man-cave. As they neared the entrance of the mall, you'd have to be blind not to miss it. Jenna was absolutely right, the mall had everything a shopper could ask for. Emily dropped Jack off in front of Dick's Sporting Goods, then looked for a parking space near the building. When Jack finished and before Emily had time to find a parking spot, he came running toward the car.

"Wow. That didn't take long."

"I can fill out an application over the Internet."

"Gosh. They make everything so easy nowadays, especially over the Internet. How long will it be before we're able to do anything using just our computers."

***

They left the mall parking lot and looked for a restaurant, ruling out any fast food chains. They wanted a place to sit and enjoy their lunch and talk. They were on Main Street heading west, when they passed the Save More Automall.

"Emily, look at that red Jeep. Is that awesome, or what?"

Jack's dream car was perched on the steel rack directly in front of the car dealer's lot. A bright red Jeep Wrangler, sporting a tan canvas cover.

"Holy cow. I could see myself driving that beauty. Once I get my job at Dick's, maybe we could stop back here and look at that Jeep. You think so?"

Emily said nothing, but in the back of her mind, she resolved to the fact she would buy her son that red Jeep. After all, his birthday was approaching soon, and Jack did need transportation getting back and forth to school, maybe to work. Ever since Charles left, she saw Jack becoming more distant to her, keeping to himself, and her relationship with Sergio didn't help matters either. Besides, she could afford to buy it, she was a millionaire.

The song, "Who Could It Be Now?" echoed from her cell, alerting Emily she had an incoming call.

"Hello. Oh, yes, Jan. What's up?" Emily began smiling, looking at Jack, "Terrific. Yes, absolutely I'll accept their offer. Okay. Thank you so much for the good news. I'll talk to you soon." Emily closed her cell and looked at Jack.

"I just sold the condo."

Chapter 35

A Bite In The Ass

Dan boarded a local bus that would take him to his new important job, working for UniCell Wireless. He'd been around long enough to know a legitimate business when he saw one, and what he saw was a front created by Helen to protect…what? He knew Helen all too well, so keeping quiet and saying nothing would ease his relationship with her. He sat, pondering how his life has drastically changed over the last few weeks, from traveling to Europe discussing financial business to take it on the lam, swiftly fleeing to California as a fugitive. He tussled over the thoughts, what if he stayed back in Chicago? Telling the detectives exactly what happened and even the plan he had with William and the seven million dollars. Ironically, it all boiled down to money. It was what kept Dan from telling the truth.

The bus stopped and Dan departed, walking a block south and then turned right to locate the building of "UniCell Wireless, Inc." He entered and saw a small office off to his left where Helen was sitting and waved to him to enter.

"Fine. You've made it. Sit down." Helen's commands were always short and to the fact. Very familiar to Dan and he knew all to well what was to be expected.

"What actually is "UniCell Wireless"?

"If you must know, we are a consulting firm that selects a variety of wireless programs for specific businesses."

"We? I don't see any other people here. I don't see anything here that resembles wireless products." It sounded sketchy, but he looked around her office for anything that resembled a business. There were no products in sight, no advertising signs, no papers on her desk, nothing but a simple, bare office. Although Helen did have her laptop sitting in front of her.

"This is just my office, Dan. Instead of driving into LA. every day, I have this place. It's close to home." She rose from her chair and walked toward the door. "Follow me. I'll show you your office." Dan followed her down the dark hallway to another small room, smaller than Helen's. In fact, it was more like a storeroom. There were no file cabinets, only a small office desk with a chair, a phone, and another laptop.

"This is it? C'mon, you're joking, right? No windows?"

"Well, its temporary. There's another room that I'm going to remodel. For the time being, you'll be using this room."

"What do I do?"

"You'll be taking orders, processing them, and ordering materials for each client. I just started this business, so it may be slow for the next month."

Dan didn't argue with her. For as long as he had known Helen, he'd understood how conniving, demanding, and manipulative a woman she was, but as he stood in front of her looking into her eyes, he believed her. She had her ways and Dan learned quickly not to cross her path. Whatever and whenever she said anything, just do it. Helen left, Dan sat down and waited for a call. And waited. He got up from the desk and wandered around the building. In the rear of the building, behind all the offices, a large warehouse was scattered with boxes and old furniture, but mostly junk. As he made his way back to the offices, Helen appeared in the hall and told him to come to her office.

***

"Collier's wife is named Emily, they were married, now divorced. He has a son named Jack. Supposedly, he moved to Mexico. Their condo is on the market and she bought a house in Manford, Illinois. Now, why did all of this happen?"

"You think I have all the answers? Beats me. Maybe she has a boyfriend. Maybe Charles never told her about the seven million. Maybe it was their plan all along?" Dan sat, lighting up a cigar.

Helen tapped a pencil on her desk, thinking. "I'm thinking the only way to get our hands on that money is we have to set a trap. Somehow, find something more important to Collier than the money. Possibly with his ex or his son."

"What do you mean "trap"? Kidnapping them? Whoa. This is getting really crazy. Anyway, how can we contact Collier, we don't have a clue where he's at."

"Well, damn it, think of something. You're the one who started this." Dan knew better to stand there and argue with her. He's seen this before. Helen was becoming agitated. It was time to take a walk.

***

Charles was still on the prowl, looking for his vanishing queen. Every day, like clockwork, he visited the Playa beach hoping to see her. If he did, she would not get away like before. This time he would offer her a beer and get to know her. As he sat on the hood of the Toyota, scanning the entire beach, sipping on his beer, he saw something that caught his attention. Off in the distance, toward the far south end of the beach, a man wearing shorts looking his way through binoculars. Charles studied the man. Was he being watched? Did someone find out where he was and start spying on him? Five minutes, ten minutes passed and the same person was still focused on him. Charles slid off the hood and began walking toward the stranger. The man saw Charles approaching, dropped the binoculars around his neck, and took off running. Charles began chasing him, but by the time he reached where the man was standing, he was nowhere in site.

Why did he take off running? Jesus. Was he was found? Someone knew where he was, already.

This extremely bothered Charles and he became agitated. He's been in Ocotal for only two weeks living like an average tourist, enjoying the simple life, relaxing, and now paranoia has taken center stage. Could it have been Reading? Was Charles jumping the gun? The person was to far away to be recognized. But if it was Reading, it certainly created fear and doubt in Charles's mind. He dropped his empty beer can in a nearby trash can and hastily walked back to the Toyota.

No. It couldn't be him. It's only been a couple of weeks since I got here. He couldn't have found out that quick. Could he?

He pulled out of the Playa parking lot, still keeping a close eye out for anyone resembling the likes of Reading. He entered the town of Ocotal, parked the Jeep and walked around. He stopped for lunch at a small cafe, then stopped at the grocery store to buy something for dinner, all the time keeping his eyes alert for Reading. Was his freedom in jeopardy now? All of a sudden, he couldn't take anything for granted. Yes, that could have been Reading or wait, what about Dugan? Now, Charles really began to panic. He had to switch gears and think of positive things rather than people of mystery. After all, Charles was living the "Life of Riley." Each day he spent in Guanacaste Providence was like living in a dream. The weather, the scenery, the freedom, the money. It all added up to his lifelong vacation.

As weeks passed, Charles returned the rented Toyota and purchased a used four-wheel drive Jeep. It was comparable to the Toyota in size and performance, but didn't have the open air qualities the rental had. He hasn't noticed anyone suspicious, like Reading or Dugan lately and shrugged off the thought of them finding him. Maybe it was just a tourist enjoying the ocean and saw a man running toward him, got scared and took off. But, it never left his mind, like a bad habit.

***

The sounds of the disagreeable howler monkeys and the rehearsals of toucans outside his bedroom window were present every morning, no morning different than the past. Those sounds made living in the resort extremely enjoyable. Neither the monkeys nor the birds had any sense of time, but every morning, give or take five minutes, they had Charles awake by 6 o'clock. It didn't bother him. The earlier he rose, the more time he had to enjoy his paradise. Each morning began with a fresh pot of coffee, then shuffling out to the deck, collapsing in the hammock, and looking at the Pacific Ocean. He just laid back with his mind at ease and wondered how to spend his day. On occasion he would drive back to the beach looking for his elusive jewel. Still, no reward. Although, his thoughts were now two-folded: her, and the man with the binoculars, it haunted Charles's mind, along with the menacing feeling of getting caught. But when you steal seven million dollars, someone will come looking for you, eventually. If ever he did get caught, he believed it must be like dying. No more celebrating birthdays, watching Super Bowls, or sipping on Margaritas with small colored umbrellas. It was isolation, loneliness, shame, boredom, all rolled into one 8' x 12' concrete cell.

Jesus Christ. Think of something else, man, he muttered.

He leaped from the hammock, spilling his coffee, and rushed to the kitchen sink to splash cold water on his face. It won't go away, buddy. For as long as you live, your thoughts will constantly echo in your mind with what you did. Was his conscience getting the best of him? It was getting that way. You never should've stole the money. You should've told the Kaiser people about the allocated tax money. You should've told Konrad about Fossett's plan to embezzle his clients. You should've never listened to Emily. You would still be back in Chicago working. You could fly back and explain everything, return the money. No harm, no foul, right?

***

Suddenly, the idyllic views from the kitchen window erased

those confusing thoughts from Charles's mind. They can't find me. I'm supposed to be in Mexico. How would they know where to look? Emily was the only one who knew. Was Emily behind all this? Wasn't it she who convinced Charles to hack the money? What about the quick divorce? What about leaving the country? All of it was her idea. Everything revolved around Emily. It made sense, but what was true? Here we go again, his conscience versus reality. He pounded his forehead on the kitchen cabinet. Then he stood silent with his head against the cabinet door, his mind at ease. It was just a bad thought. He had to find something to do to keep his sanity. What about snorkeling, playing a round of golf, or a drive to Santa Rosa? Yes, that was it. Santa Rosa National Park. That's where he'd go.

The park would be an ideal place to get his mind off his conscience. It was a place Charles visited before and lost the sense of time. He packed a small lunch, a cooler with water and beer, and his binoculars. The Park was approximately sixty miles from the villa, but the trip went quickly. The balmy warm weather, the scenery, and getting away from the agony of his thoughts kept his mind at ease.

At the park, he stopped at the Ranger station and explained his reasons for visiting. Just like before, he was tourist and a birdwatcher. The Ranger handed him several brochures about the park, and a pamphlet about La Casona. Suddenly, without warning, a swarm of insects attacked him and the ranger. The ranger ducked and waved his arms rapidly, trying to keep the insects away from them.

"Ouch!" One pest was on a mission to attack Charles's left arm. It happened so fast he didn't have a chance to retaliate against the assailing insect.

"What the fuck are these?" both were flinging their arms in the air repelling the attacking insects.

"Son of a bitch. That hurt. What are those things?" Charles feverishly scratched the bite asking the ranger.

"They must be a swarm of bot flies. Nasal bot flies, I think."

Charles rolled up the window as the ranger turned and started running for his life back to his shack. "Or they might be torsalos."

He stomped on the accelerator pedal, the Jeep squealed it's tires and fled the pesky insects. Charles followed the asphalt road leading through the park, noticing numerous roadside signs informing visitors the directions to certain points of interest. He wanted to visit the La Casona mansion. As he continued, more road signs appeared. Finally, the La Casona sign appeared, and he followed the arrows leading to the attraction.

The brochures that the ranger handed Charles reflected about the mansion's history. About how it was built more than a hundred years earlier, and why it was built in the middle of a jungle. There were so many intriguing questions about this mansion, Charles wanted to find out some of the answers. He approached the entrance and was greeted by a young girl about seventeen years old, displaying a very tanned complexion. She wore black wire-rimmed glasses, which made her appear scholarly. She explained that the mansion, once a military hideout, was a museum now, displaying artifacts about its history. Charles was in awe of the architecture, the paintings, and the exquisite imported granite tiles lining the floors throughout the mansion. Why was it built here? Who built it? What did it cost to build? Who lived there? All those questions were answered by his young guide. After the impressive tour was over, he climbed back into the Jeep to get more maps, noticing his left forearm. The bite had become reddened and started to swell.

He continually scratched the bite to ease the itching, but it persisted. On his way home, he would stop at a drug store and inquire about treating insects bites, buy whatever they recommended and, hopefully, the itching would stop. He focused his attention back to the pamphlet, where he noticed a paragraph and pictures about Witches Rock.

Hmm, sounds like a place to see.

He overlooked the map, calculating the route, where fifteen minutes later he saw the sign indicating the direction of the point of interest. Witches Rock stood alone in the Pacific Ocean, approximately a football field from Playa Naranjo beach. He exited the Jeep and walked toward the beach noticing many tourist taking pictures, swimming or just soaking up the sun. Since the day he first saw his dream girl, his eyes stayed focus on seeing her again. How ironic it would be if he saw his dream girl here. Fate works in mysterious ways, Charles. Among many tourists, there was a group of surfers battling the coastal waves, some were very good. It was pretty cool to witness the athletic ability of each surfer, manipulating that small board, some struggled to keep their balance and some struggled to stay dry.

***

A short distance from where he was standing, he spotted several benches along the sidewalk that ran parallel the entire beach. An excellent location for people to sit and view the beach and the ocean. He went back to his vehicle, retrieved his lunch and cooler, sat down on the bench, relaxing, taking in all the views. To his amazement, some of the female swimmers were topless.

All right! I gotta stop here more often.

He grabbed his binoculars and began a closer look of the tantalizing beach-goers. As he scanned the beach, it was noticeable to him that he was the only tourist with binoculars that centralized on the nude sunbathers. Noticing his guilt, he switched to watching the surfers. They would paddle out to a certain point and catch a wave, then repeat the same routine over and over. There were many surfers at the beach, maybe 10 to 15, but as he kept watching, one caught his eye. He focused on that lone surfer, paddling out past the wave, then hopping onto his board to contest the powerful waves. From one ride till the next, Charles never saw the surfer lose the battle with the massive waves. The surfer never fell. Amazing.

Charles looked at the bite on his forearm, it seemed to worsen and the itching got worse, too. He contemplated whether if he should see a doctor or stop at a drugstore to pick up some ointment. The times he drove through Ocotal, he did remember seeing a drug store, but he never saw a medical facility or a doctors office. On his way home, he'd drive into town, stop at the drug store and get some ointment to treat the irritable sore.

His lunch was over and Charles continued to watch the surfers. The unbeatable surfer Charles had his eye on finished his successful conquest and was headed his way. The beaches supplied portable showers for surfers or swimmers to wash off the salt water or just to cool off. A group of them, clinging to their boards, headed up the sidewalk in

***

Charles's direction, all of them stopping to wash off. What! Oddly, his favorite surfer turned out to be a girl. *No way, it can't be her. Or is it her?* He remained glued to the girl and when she removed the rubber suit, all that was left was her bright red skimpy bikini.

Yes! He was sure this was the same girl. She stood under the rushing water, rinsing her short blond hair and sexy, tanned body. Then Charles noticed the tattoo on her left ankle. It was a re-creation of the devil, a devil between two hearts. Charles remembered the saying, "a rose between two thorns," but why the devil between two hearts? Was it a reflection of her personality? Interesting, Charles thought. She began to dry herself, carefully wiping every inch of her tantalizing body. She picked up her wet suit and surf board then proceeded toward the parking lot. Charles was like a magnet. He hoped she didn't think he was stalking her, but in reality he was. He was infatuated with her looks, her sexiness, her mystery, even her surfing talents. Plain and simple, Charles was obsessed with this beauty. As she started up the engine, Charles tapped on her window. She looked, smiled and a short wave before the tires screeched against the pavement and dissolved the chance of talking to her. As the car started to disappear, Charles quickly focused his binoculars on her license plate. *"56W6767, 56W6767,"* he kept repeating to himself. It was a start. He could keep his eyes open for a black BMW when in town or just traveling around. How many of those cars were around this area? Or, the possibility of finding the owner via the Internet? There was nothing more to do at the beach and looking at the bite, by all means, he had to get to the drug store. He was a little depressed, but after the day's events, he couldn't complain. He knew something about her.

The Jeep coasted down the road toward the Villas, looking for the possibility of finding a drug store without driving to Ocotal. It didn't happen, not one to be found. He tossed the idea of driving to Ocotal, but it was getting dark, he was tired and hungry. Tomorrow, his first priority would go and get the ointment for his sore. Charles guided the Jeep up the escarpment, into the parking lot and locked it up. Once in the villa, he washed the bite with soap and water, squeezing the bite letting a trickle of blood and puss escape the sore. To him, it didn't look good. He wandered to the refrigerator, opened the door and removed the left-over meat loaf, grabbed a beer and sat on the sofa in the living room. The bright red bikini, he thought how great it would be to have her companionship, a lover, or just someone to talk with on lonely nights. His thoughts shifted about Emily and Jack, how he missed being with them and how lonely he's been since last seeing them. The only people he'd had conversations with were the workers at the Villa. They were very friendly, but they had their own families and only a few spoke English. Along with the loneliness brought fear to Charles, not to mention, paranoia. Where ever he went, the chance he'd be discovered, the chance of losing everything and the hardest of all, the chance of spending the rest of his life in prison.

Chapter 36

So Much For The Internet!

Several days had passed since Dan's first work day at his new job. He wondered about Helen and how she got started in California after her fallout with her brother. He screwed her so badly, she didn't have much to stand on when she moved out west. Now, she owned a new Mercedes, an office building, and had started her own business. Was this for real? He knew she was a shrewd and very clever woman, but to get where she was so fast was unimaginable to Dan. He tossed that around while lounging on his sofa watching TV. And what about his plan to seize or pilfer the seven million from Charles? Dan couldn't conceive an answer as to why he informed Helen about the money in the first place. Maybe he should've never let Helen in on his scheme after all. If that was to be, he would still be in Chicago and cooperating with the police, he was completely innocent and hadn't done anything wrong.

He had all the time in the world, he thought. After eating his microwave dinner, he sat watching a reality show on TV about contestants traveling around the world competing in peculiar and comical stunts for large sums of money. Dan laughed even though he thought the show was stupid. As he continued watching, the thought smacked him in the brain like a Nolan Ryan fastball.

Wait. This is it! This is how we can get our money! Thought after thought raced through his mind, calculating a plan to recover the elusive money. He grabbed a sheet of paper and began jotting down his thoughts. He had to tell Helen as soon as possible, but it was late and he'd have to wait till tomorrow at work. In his mind, it was brilliant. He couldn't wait till he got to work the next morning, and when he arrived, he raced to into Helen's office.

"I got it. This is so cool, it's so off the wall that it'll blow your mind." Dan held his head with both hands, dancing in circles, totally amazed with the thought of his plan.

Helen eased back in her chair. "Well, what is so cool that I need to know?"

"I was watching this reality show on TV last night that I know will get Charles's kid's attention. What if we set up a fictitious reality show. I mean, we can somehow locate his email address and send him emails about participating in this reality show. After a week or so, we tell him that he's been selected and has to come to California for an interview. Think about it. We could offer like a million dollars, a chance to travel around the world. Now, who wouldn't jump at that chance?"

"How would we know he's getting the emails?"

"You're people back in Chicago can figure that out. We can send an email once a week or every day. At first, just send a message about the show, tell a little about traveling, the winnings, that sort of stuff. We'll call it, umm... Extreme Realities. That will catch his full attention."

"Sounds crazy, but I like it. Christ, Dan. It's so weird that it just might work."

"Ohh, once we get his attention and he comes to California, we'll kidnap him and hold him for ransom."

"I know I'm desperate and I want that money. Let's try it. I'll call my contact in Chicago. He can get the kid's email address. Once we get that, you start emailing."

"When can you call Chicago?"

Helen found her cell and started the call.

"We've got a plan that might work, but I need Collier's kid's email address. Can you get that for me?" She stood listening. "The sooner the better."

Chapter

New Excitement In Jack's Life

It didn't take long for Emily and Jack to settle into their new residence. Living in a small town was an easy adjustment for each of them. But, if they had to compare differences, the traffic and the noise compared to peace and quiet, certainly the latter was the deciding factor. It was coming back home for Emily. She remembered the friendly people in Manford, something that eluded her in the big city. Here, her neighbors were always around when she needed them. They helped her plant flowers, or with odd jobs in and around the house. Jack tried to help too, but his interests were elsewhere, and he could forget ever becoming a carpenter. Then came Sergio. His presence at the Dearborn house was becoming an issue with Jack. He hated Sergio. All he did when he arrived was lounge around watching TV and ate everything in sight, sponging off Emily. She tried her best to smooth the edges regarding Sergio and Jack's relationship, but the harder she tried the more complicated it became. All she wanted were the nights she spent with her lover. The way he touched her, satisfied her, and in return her desire to please him. She longed for the weekdays to fly by, setting up those special weekend nights to fall asleep in his arms, and put all her thoughts about Charles behind her. As weekends passed, Emily sensed that the conflicts between the two caused Sergio to become evasive, less paying attention to her and more feuding with Jack. That caused her to be insecure about Sergio's commitment to her. The dissension grew and Emily realized how it affected her life with both of them. It was becoming a war zone.

Over the weekends, Jack avoided hanging around the house. He worked more at Dick's and spent his time off with Aaron, his best friend. During the week when Sergio was gone his relationship with his mother was rekindled, they talked and tried to spend time together. Emily would take him out to dinner at least one night a week, which Jack seemed to enjoy. She tried to explain to Jack about Sergio, but when his name surfaced, Jack always brought Charles into the equation. That abruptly ended all conversation about Sergio.

When he began working at Dick's, he met Aaron. They hit it off well, so well that the pair were inseparable, spending much of their free time playing games on the computer, hanging out with Terri, Aaron's girlfriend or having pizza at the Pizza Shack. When he received his first paycheck from Dick's, he purchased a new Motorola Droid Razor smart phone, almost every student owned a cell phone. If you didn't own a smart phone, you were uncool.

As Jack's birthday became days closer, Emily bought the red Jeep he dreamed of owning. Jack was ecstatic when Emily drove the car home and handed him the keys. He bolted from the house, jumping up and down, not believing what was happening.

"Mom, this is so cool. Wait till Aaron sees this. It'll blow his mind. Wow, mom. Thank you so much." It was an odd situation for Emily, hearing Jack call her mom. It was always, Emily. She hoped it would ease the tension between all of them, and let her get on with her life with Sergio. One thing for sure, Jack spent more time away from home, riding around, working and more important, away from Sergio. In the fall, he'd be attending his senior year at Columbia High School, Jack was steadily employed, earning money to buy personal items such as clothes, cologne, computer games, and more pizza, life was good. Aaron introduced Jack to a new web site that had all the kids at school buzzing. It was called "You Tube", a website he had to see. There were hundreds of videos, from freaky stunts to exotic sexual innuendos. It was wild. Jack spent a lot of time on his computer after school and would call Aaron when he found anything on You

Tube to share a laugh or joke. The Internet offered endless opportunities, plus it provided him with a personal email address, a gallery to collect his pictures from his smart phone, another way to connect to his friends without using his phone. So cool. He looked forward every day to opening his email box and reviewing what was sent to him. It was like getting real mail. He received an occasional email from Aaron and laugh about it's contents, and Dick's Sporting Goods would send frequent mailers about upcoming sales or earning reward points, but a lot of mail was junk, spam..

The summer was over before you could blink your eyes. Starting his senior year, Jack looked forward to attending the new high school, especially parking his new Jeep in the school parking lot. He would be cool.

On a particular Saturday morning, Jack opened his computer and read through his emails. This was odd, a curious email from Stardom Studios that attracted his full attention. *Stardom Studios?* At first he was hesitant, but his curiosity swayed him to open the link and if it was junk, he could always delete it. So, Jack opened the message from the mysterious sender.

"What would you do if you had a chance to win one million dollars?" The question was spelled out in bold, capital letters. "Are you ready for an exciting challenge in your life? A chance to travel, appear on a national TV show, meet new young people, explore exciting enchanted islands? Best of all. It's FREE. We are Stardom Studios, the producers of Extreme Realities, Incorporated, the new TV reality show that will air next fall on CNK. We are looking for individuals who are ready for that extreme challenge in their life. People who are outgoing, risk takers, daring, competitive, and above all, wanting that $1 million dollar first prize. It's as easy as 1-2-3. Just fill out the attached questionnaire and email it back to our studios. So, go ahead. What are you waiting for? You could be our first million dollar winner. It's your chance of a lifetime."

What! Jack slumped into his chair, staring at that email and contemplating what he should do. A chance at a winning a cool

$1 million? Delete it or save it? He thought the possibility it could come true. How cool it would be to win $1 million bucks and to travel, but best of all, getting his Dad back. It sounded and looked legit. Nah. Jack second guessed himself, it could never happen to me. Not with his luck. His mouse found the delete tab, one click and gone…Oh, well!

***

The next day, Sunday night and Jack returned home from work to find Sergio lying on the couch, eating something, and watching football. Emily, who didn't like football, was snuggled up against, him watching the game.

"How was work?"

Jack didn't reply, just made his way upstairs. He'd spend the rest of the night on his computer, laughing at You Tube videos and playing a terrorist game installed on his hard drive. The next day would be the beginning of another boring week of classes. Little did he know, he'd have a big surprise awaiting him at school.

Chapter 38

Paranoia...Then Sayonara

Charles didn't hear the screeching monkeys or the numerous birds that regularly got his day started. Instead, it was the sound of rain pounding on the villa roof. He struggled out of bed and walked to the rear sliding glass doors. It was raining so hard he could barely see the ocean. He stood watching the raindrops slapping the large leaves of the surrounding trees, wondering what his day will bring. How long would the rain last? Mother Nature was the boss today and if she wanted to cry, so be it.

The bite on his left forearm itched and the more he scratched, the more it irritated him. The tube of lotion he purchased at the drug store was almost empty and the results weren't in Charles's favor. In fact, the bite seemed it was getting worse. He walked back to his bedroom, got dressed, and returned to the kitchen. Still figuring out what his day might bring, he sat at the kitchen table sipping on his coffee, when suddenly, the rain stopped and the sun blazed through his kitchen windows. Amazing how the weather in the tropics could change so fast. He stepped onto the deck. The morning's air was so refreshing. The aromatic fragrance from the foliage after a rainfall was like cracking open a new can of Glade and spraying the air all around you. This was what Charles loved about Costa Rica. A different world from living in the Midwest. He drifted to the edge of the deck and looked toward the Villa's office, where he noticed a man leaning against the vending machine, smoking a cigarette and starring in his direction.

***

Here we go again…remembering prior incidents and strangers.

He stood frozen and focused for a moment, then went to the kitchen, grabbed his binoculars off the kitchen counter and zeroed in on the stranger. Was it someone he knew? It could only be Reading or Dugan, he thought, but it wasn't them. Charles's memory flashed back to the man at Playa beach. Could he be the same person? His brain was spinning fast, names kept popping up, all sorts of idiotic questions surfaced. Maybe you should've known better when you let that hacker Dugan hit the "Send" key that transferred the seven million to the Switzerland bank. Charles picked up the binoculars to get another look. But as he made contact, the subject was leaving and only his back side was visible. Charles made his way out of the villa, rushing down the awkward, slippery wooden path. Incredibly, without falling, he made it to the bottom to see the car disappearing down the wet asphalt road. Charles zoomed in on the vehicle. It was a small black…what? Get the license number, idiot! 56W…Shit. The car was gone.

He turned back up the path and headed to his villa. All the way, his brain was stuffing countless thoughts into his mind about getting caught and the people hunting him. Everything was becoming more bizarre. That black car. That license number, 56W. His beauty queen from the beach. What the hell was next? He was back in his villa and in front of his computer. If that was Dugan, he would be the only person capable of hacking the money. But, why would he be down here? He opened the web site of Clairden Leu, inserted his passwords, and the site opened. Whew! The money was still there. Relieved, Charles knew he couldn't trust Dugan anymore. In fact, who could he trust? Not even his loving wife, Emily. He sat, considering his next step. Thinking about Dugan, it wouldn't be safe leaving the money in a Switzerland bank, it had to be moved. Time was getting dangerous and moving it was his only option. As quickly as he could punch the computer keys, it was over and done with. His money was now with him in Costa Rica. Satisfied, he slouched in his chair. Dugan was a master at hacking and as Charles sat, pondering, it didn't make any difference where the money sat, Dugan would find it. Another crazy thought appeared to Charles. Was it possible that Emily and Dugan had a plan of their own. After all, wasn't it Emily who found Dugan? What else could happen? The more he thought about Emily, the more sense it made to him about her involvement with Dugan. He had his doubts in regards to the quickness of him getting to Costa Rica, even the unnecessary divorce. It's been over a month since they last spoke and Charles felt guilty about that, especially not talking to Jack. Maybe he should try calling them this Saturday and ask Emily some intriguing questions. Yes, I have to do that. Then reality dawned on him, Emily doesn't live in Chicago anymore, so how do I get a hold of her. I have no phone number?

He noticed the "Chicago Tribune" icon on the computer page, something he hasn't looked into for awhile about the news of Fossett's death. The page opened and Charles searched the paper for any articles regarding the matter. He read page after page and nothing appeared. Was it good news that the investigation came to a standstill? He didn't know, but it was something that he had to look into on a daily basis. He bookmarked the page, closed the computer down, then refilled his coffee cup.

***

To keep a low profile, Emily began working as a receptionist for Teeth-R-Us. Charles insisted that she find work and keep their involvement under the radar, not to cause any more suspicion from Konrad and his clan. One afternoon, Emily happened to be in the right place at the right time while she shopped for groceries. Eddie Barnett, who had a crush on her in high school, ran into her. They reminisced about their school days and how their lives changed after graduation, then asked her if she was ever looking for a job, she should stop in and see him. Ironically, she was hired the next week. Emily knew she had Eddie wrapped around her little finger. Her hours were very flexible and her salary was adequate, honestly, she didn't care if she made $10 an hour or $100. She was there to keep a low profile and the cops at bay.

***

As soon as Dan finished his coffee, he grabbed his jacket, turned off the TV, picked up his cigars and hurried out the door. He would walk to the corner of Truman and Deere, pay for the Chicago paper, and wait to board a bus to the office. He didn't know what Helen had planned for his day, but spending some time there was better than sitting in his apartment doing stupid crossword puzzles. He didn't see Helen's car. In fact, there was not one car in the parking lot.

UniCell Wireless. Right.

He knew once he entered the building that Helen was gone, so, what was he going to do that day? He took off his jacket, went to his office and lit up a Dutch Masters cigar. There were no notes from Helen regarding something for him to do, so Dan sat and opened his computer. For the past week, Dan has sent an email every other day to Charles's son, not having a clue whether he has received them or not, Dan kept sending the email. Once the computer opened to his home page, again there was no returned emails. Dan felt he was grasping for straws, having no idea how to get the money and no help from Helen. His only shot was to keep sending the email. As he was about to dump the cigar ashes into the ashtray, he noticed a stack of business cards sitting atop of a stack of papers on the corner of his desk...*Director of Talent Evaluation*. He chuckled. It had to be Helen and what was she up to? He began to laugh as Helen appeared at his doorway.

"I didn't hear you come in."

"How long have you been here? Did you check for any emails? Did you send out the email?"

"Yeah. I did. Nothing."

Dan set the cigar in the ashtray. "Nice cards. Whats up with these?"

There was a buzz from her cell phone alerted Helen she had an incoming text. She flipped open the cover and read the message, stood silent, and looked at Dan.

"Any news?" Dan pried.

"Nothing. Listen. We're running out of time. I think you better go back to Chicago and find Collier's ex, this Emily chic. Maybe these emails aren't getting to her son. So, I think this is what we should do. Whatever you do, find out where the money is and where Charles Collier is. Understand?"

"Me, back in Chicago! Are you crazy? Don't you think it's taking a huge risk for me to go back there? If I get caught, everything is down the toilet." Dan sat back in his chair, knowing full well Helen was dead serious.

"Jesus Christ. Wake up and smell the coffee, Dan. You think that woman will talk to me? You're the only one who knows what we need and can get it from her."

"I don't know, Helen. You've got people in Chicago. Let them do it."

"No. It has to be you."

Dan stood still, realizing Helen was fervid. Whenever Helen spoke, Dan listened. "When do you want me to go?"

"The sooner the better."

"Excuse me, Miss Helen. There are two gentlemen asking for you at the front door."

Tyrone had been the janitor for that building for as long as the Dodgers had been in LA. Well before Helen even thought of moving to California. He never missed a day of work, even worked on Sundays, until Helen forced him to take every weekend off and spend it with his family, if he had one. Helen never inquired about that.

"Okay, Tyrone. Tell them I'll be right there." Helen looked at Dan and she wasn't smiling.

Dan picked up Helen's cell phone and saw the text printed on the screen: *Colliers not in Mexico. Get to ex now!* The text was from MKonrad, CMPD. The same cop chasing him? Dan set the phone back on the desk and walked to the office door, out of sight but within range to see Helen. He now knew who her contact was back in Chicago.

"Helen Kruger?" asked the older of the two gentlemen.

"Yes. What can I do for you?"

"I'm Detective Durango, FBI, and this is my partner, Detective Sloan. We would like to ask you a few questions if you don't mind?"

"What is this in regard to?" Helen was getting nervous. She knew what they were there for, but prayed for an Oscar performance.

"It's about your brother, William Fossett. You know about his death?"

"Of course. I attended his funeral. I know he was murdered. Did they find the person who killed him?"

"That's why we want to talk to you." With many years of experience, his standard format was to let the person being questioned do all the talking. Let them tell the story. Detective Durango kept his questions short.

"Do you remember where you were the night of his murder?"

"Hold on a second. Are you insinuating that I murdered my own brother?"

Helen's act was getting good. It sure sounded convincing to Dan.

"We understand your relationship with your brother was troublesome. Back in ninety-seven, you filed a lawsuit against your brother. Can you tell us about that?"

"That was long ago, gentlemen. That issue is buried and in the past. We both moved on with our lives. Now, if you'll excuse me, I have more important issues to attend to."

"Miss Kruger, just one last question. We have proof that you were in Chicago the night your brother was murdered. So, if you don't come straight with us, we have the authority to bring you downtown for more questioning."

Helen stood, frozen and scared, "You'll have to talk to my lawyer."

Helen closed the door and stood, her head down, visibly

shaken as Dan approached her. They looked out the side window, watching the two detectives drive away.

"They'll be back, Helen."

"God damn it. We gotta move fast now. Our time is critical." Helen hustled to her office as Dan followed her.

"Looks like I'm leaving for Chicago tonight."

"It's the only move we have left. They're going to be watching me day and night. The only chance I have now is becoming invisible. Somehow escaping without them seeing me."

"You and me both. I'll go out the back door, through the alley, and walk home. I'll pack and get a taxi to LAX. The sooner I get to Collier's wife, the quicker we can get to my buddy Charles."

"I won't be able to contact you or you contact me. I'm sure they'll be tapping my cell. How can we stay in touch?"

"I know how. A Radio Shack isn't far from the apartment. I'll buy untraceable cell phones. I'll leave you a phone at my apartment and I'll jot down the number of my cell. I'll call you as soon as I get into Chicago."

"Good idea. We have to stay in contact. That's really important."

"You can hide out in my apartment. Stay there till I get what I need from Collier. Can't be more than a week or so. There's enough food. You won't have to go out at all. You have any cash here?"

"Yes." Helen opened her desk drawer and removed a steel lock box. She removed several bills and handed the money to Dan. "When you leave for the airport, leave your keys under the doormat. You better get going."

***

It took Dan about forty minutes to walk from the office to his apartment, ditching every cop car that drove by and avoiding busy streets. As soon as he arrived, he started packing some clothes, then remembered, they needed untraceable cell phones.

He glanced at his watch. He had plenty of time to buy the phones, finish packing and then leave for the airport.

He returned from Radio Shack with his pockets $150 lighter. He purchased two cell phones with untraceable numbers and each phone with a two hundred minute calling card. His luggage was packed. He took one last look around the apartment and left a note and the cell phone on the table for Helen. The doorbell rang. He glanced up, hesitated, then crept toward the front door. It was Helen. He wiped the beads of sweat from his brow and let her in.

"Perfect timing. I picked up a set of phones. Here's yours with your number and here's my number. To be on the safe side, don't store my number in your phone, just memorize it. Also, my computer is here. You can check for emails, hopefully Collier's kid will answer and keep sending an email every other day. Got that?"

"I was thinking on my way over here. While you're at the airport, purchase two tickets from Chicago to here, in case he sends back the email. Here's two thousand."

"Yeah, good idea. I better get going."

"Do I need a password to enter your computer?"

"I printed it on the side."

"I guess that's it. I'll take a bus until I get a couple miles from the airport, then grab a cab. That will keep the cops off my tail."

"The cops can do that? Oh, no. I took a cab from the studio to here."

"You what!" Dan stood astonished, thinking Helen was smarter than that. "They're watching you, every second. Jesus Christ. Now, they're probably watching this place. I gotta get out of here. If they come crawling around here, call me as soon as you can, okay?"

"Yeah. I'll think of something. I'm not going anywhere."

Dan sneaked out the door, but instead of taking Truman Avenue to the bus stop, he slipped through the alley behind the apartment. He kept walking until he saw a bus coming and flagged it down.

Hours later, the stewardess was taking Dan's order. A Jack Daniels with a lime twist.

Chapter

The Dating Game

Arriving late at school that morning, Jack hustled to his locker, collected his history text, slammed the locker door and darted to room 203. The halls were crowded, but Jack weaved in and out, just like Aaron running around end, avoiding would be tacklers on his scramble downfield. Hitting the brakes, Jack used the classroom door to break his slide, then entered his history class as the bell sounded. Cornelius Stewart was sitting on the edge of his desk, as always, his glasses in the same position they were in the day before, like they were glued to the tip of his nose. Mr. Stewart, students called him "Old Crony", shook his head at Jack as he passed.

Come on, I'm not late.

The old fart was such a dick about tardiness, he began the morning with another lecture about being punctual. "It's an excellent example of good character, and good character is the solid foundation toward your future. Be aggressive in all your endeavors; working hard equals a successful career." Okay. We've heard all that before.

"You look fantastic this morning."

"My, oh my. Aren't we Mr. Polite today."

Before Jack could open his text, Crony cleared his throat. "Clear everything off the top of your desks." He circled the classroom and handed each student a quiz.

Shit. Another pop quiz.

"You'll have the entire class time to finish the quiz. When you're finished, you will remain silent and begin reading the next chapter. Chapter Fourteen will be next week's discussion. You may begin now."

Jack, not at all ready for this, started reading the first question:

When did the Korean War begin, how long did it last and how did President Eisenhower end it?

Jack noticed the test was not multiple-choice. Meaning his probability of passing the quiz was less than fifty per cent. In other words, flunking it.

Dwight D. Eisenhower was our ____ president? Okay, I know this one. He was our 34th president.

If only Jack had paid attention to Crony's lectures and taken notes. Better yet, bonded with the group of students who did take notes and paid attention to the old fart's lectures. Jack finished the quiz just as the bell sounded, ending the class.

"Pencils down. Drop off your quizzes on my desk on your way out. Thank you."

Outside room 203, Jack dodged the crowd to catch up with April.

"That was a snap." April smirked.

"Yeah. A real snap."

They walked toward the locker area to exchange books for their next class. Jack remained silent, not sure what to talk about with April until she broke the silence.

"Your mother, Emily, seems to be a very nice lady."

"Don't let first impressions fool you, April."

"I'd like to meet her again and talk to her."

"And find out for yourself what she's really like?"

"That's not a nice way to talk about your mother, Jack."

He didn't respond, knowing that April was right.

When they reached their lockers, April selected her algebra book, closed her locker, and grabbed Jack's hand. Caught by surprise, he smiled as they began walking side-by-side to their algebra class.

"April, there's something I wanted to ask you."

"Anything."

"Well, I was…"

"Hey, dip-shit."

As Aaron slammed him in the back with his forearm, Jack's books fell from his arms, spilling notes and papers across the hallway floor.

"What the f…, Aaron? "

April helped Jack collect the scattered papers.

"Sorry, man. You're coming to the Culver game on Saturday, aren't you?"

"Hello Einstein, have I missed any of your games this year?"

"I guess not. I was just making sure. It's our last home game, which means all the seniors will play. We're gonna get our asses kicked."

"Yeah. I'll be there. Seven-thirty, as usual."

"You got it. I'll call you tonight."

Jack and April reached their algebra class, waiting for the bell to sound.

"Jack. I'm not doing anything Saturday night. Can I go with you to the game?"

Bang!! Fourth of July fireworks exploded in Jack's head. *Is she serious?* Adrenaline rushed through his entire body. *Pinch me, let me know if I heard that right.*

"Really?"

"Yes, really. It sounds like a lot of fun. This will be our first date."

"Oh, and about Aaron. I love to tease him…he's my best friend, you know. We have this standing bet on every football game. If he scores a touchdown, I pay for breakfast at Denny's, but if he doesn't, he pays. He's scored a touchdown in every game this year."

***

The sound of the Wrangler's engine startled Emily for the moment. Awaking from a well-deserved night's sleep, she lay in her bed trying to figure out what was happening. It was Saturday and she would be alone because Sergio was spending the weekend locked up for a minor probation violation. The clock on her night table flashed 7:40, so Jack should be on his way to work. Fantastic. Now what would she like to do on her day off? Spend money, of course. A big smile appeared, as she realized she had all day to spend on herself. Laboring to get out of bed and into the shower, she pushed the covers off her half- awake body and shuffled into the bathroom. She opened the shower door and dialed the faucets to the correct temperature. Satisfied, she stepped into her twilight zone. This was her time to pamper herself, the ten minutes to feel the rush of the hot water tantalizing every pore of her body. This was the time she dedicated to herself every morning, without a worry in the world. It was part of the new life of Emily Dearborn.

Chapter 40

It's Just A Small Dent

Main Street Mall had everything a woman shopper could dream of: Macy's, Carson Pirie Scott, JC Penney, Victoria's Secret, Bath Bath & Beyond, and several small, independent fashion stores eager to absorb Emily's money. She could spend hours looking at rack after rack of the latest fashions to fill her closet. Not that Emily needed more fashion in her wardrobe, but it was a simple fact that she had lots of money to spend.

She parked the Escalade and headed to Macy's Fall Sale—twenty to fifty per cent off selected stock the huge signs displayed in the store windows. Was this her lucky day or what? Three hours later, her arms full of bags and packages, Emily strained to get her car keys from her coat pocket. Continuing walking toward her car, she noticed a man standing near her car. *Who on earth could that be?*

"I…aah…seem to have had a small misfortune with your car." explained the Johnny-come-lately.

"You what!"

"Yeah, I was beginning to back out and leave when another car approached and passed, nearly hitting me. I wasn't paying much attention, still backing out, then I noticed your car in my rear view mirror. I hit my brakes as quickly as I could, but I was a bit too late in stopping."

Emily filled the back seat of her car with her purchases.

"Let me look." She found a small dent under the back bumper.

"All that I can see is a small crease near the bumper. Nothing major."

"Yes. I see that."

"I'm willing to pay for all the damages I caused. I don't think we need to inform the police about such a small dent. Do you agree?"

Emily nodded in agreement, but subconsciously thought she might get stiffed by this stranger.

"Here is my name and cell phone number. Once you get an estimate to repair the dent, please call me and I'll drop off a check immediately." He handed Emily a business card.

"How do I know this is really you?"

"Ohh," Dan handed her his driver's license. "Here, this will prove who I am."

She examined the license very closely. It was a California license, but everything on it seemed to be in order, even his picture. She handed the license back to him.

"Again. I'm very sorry for the mishap. I'm an honest man and I will pay for the damages. Please trust me. Just call that number when you get your estimate. I'll pay you then."

She looked over his business card and put it in her coat pocket. For some eerie reason, Emily believed she had seen him before. She was sure of that, but he was from California.

On her drive home, Emily removed her Blackberry phone from her purse and dialed Mesa's phone number off his business card. Was she being scammed? The number rang several times before his voicemail kicked in. "Dan here, but not here to answer your call. Kindly leave a short message and a phone number and I'll get back to you, ASAP."

Caught off guard, Emily couldn't find words to reply, closing her Blackberry.

Damn it, why didn't I say something? I'll call him again as soon as I get home.

Driving on Main Street she came upon Scott's Collision and Body Shop. It was as good a time as any to get an estimate. Besides, the sooner she got paid from the stranger, the better off she would feel. Scott's Collision and Body Shop had been in

Manford for ages, it seemed. She knew the brothers, Bill and Scott, from her high school days, but hadn't seen them since graduation. Scott greeted Emily inside the lobby of the shop, surprised after all these years to see her again. They talked about their high school days, living in Manford, and how their lives had changed.

"Wow. Lots of changes in my life since graduation. Marriage, kids, the business, local school board. What about you?"

"Same-old, same-old. Marriage, one kid, and a divorce."

"I hear you. Okay, enough about ancient history. What can I do for you today?"

"A couple of hours ago, some guy backed into my Escalade at the mall. Not serious damage, but there is a small dent near the rear bumper panel. He insisted on paying for it and without calling the police."

"Shame on you, Emily." Scott pointed to a small sign above the cash register referring to police involvement on ALL accidents.

"Emily, no matter how small the incident, always—and I mean always—get a police report. If you never met the person, how do you know he'll pay up? With a police report, everything on the report is valid and you have legal documentation. It could even affect your car insurance."

"Gosh. His card is my only proof of who he is. I hope I don't get burned on this."

***

Scott picked up his clipboard and estimate sheet as they headed toward the dented car. He inspected the damaged area, taking notes and jotting down information, while Emily rummaged through her purse looking for Mesa's business card.

"All right. Let's go inside and I'll punch up some numbers on the computer."

Scott soon pressed the last key, the printer snapped into action, and within seconds spit out one page for the estimate Emily needed.

"Looks like six hundred ninety-six dollars will do it."

"Oh! I never thought such a small dent would cost that much to fix."

"It's more labor than parts. We have to remove the back bumper and lower the rear panel in order to repair the dent."

"Okay, Scott. I'll call Mr. Mesa and break the news to him. As soon as I get paid, I'll call you to set up an appointment. Thank you, Scott."

***

At home, Emily took her packages inside and tossed the clothes on the bed, cramming the wrappers and boxes into an already filled trash container. When she went into the kitchen, she saw Mesa's business card lying on the floor. It must have fallen out of her coat pocket when she was carrying the packages to her bedroom. She read the card: Daniel R. Mesa, Director of Talent Evaluation, Stardom Studios, Pasadena, California. Now that was odd. What in the world would a movie executive be doing in a small town like Manford? Something felt strange to Emily, but accidents do happen. She set the card down on the kitchen table, removed a coffee cup from the cupboard, then heated her Keurig and popped in a K-cup of Green Mountain breakfast decaf. She needed something to settle her nerves. She sat down at the kitchen table with her Blackberry, picked up

Mesa's business card and dialed the number. It rang, once, twice, then…"Hello."

"Is this Dan Mesa?"

"Yes, who is this?"

"My name is Emily Dearborn. I'm the owner of the silver Escalade you backed into at the mall earlier this afternoon."

"Oh, yes." Dan's mind caught the flaw when she mentioned Emily Dearborn. He was positive this was actually Emily Collier. If she was hiding something, then he understood why she was using another name.

"I did get an estimate from the local body shop in Manford. The estimate came to six hundred ninety-six dollars to repair the damages."

"Very well. That was quick. I can write you a check or do you prefer cash, whichever you decide."

Emily reminded herself that Scott scolded her. She'd never met this stranger.

"I prefer cash, if that's okay with you."

"No problem. No, wait, there is one small detail."

Emily braced herself for the worst. Was he going to hang up, tell her to fuck off, and that she'd never find him, or what?

"How do I get the money to you?"

She had to think fast.

"Could I meet you somewhere?"

"Well, I'm not very familiar with this town. I just got here yesterday."

"I understand. How about if I meet you at Denny's on Main Street, say tomorrow around ten-thirty?"

"That sounds good to me. I know where it is. I'll have the cash ready for you by then. Goodbye."

"Goodbye."

***

The Saturday morning began with a scintillating sun shining through Jack's bedroom window. It was a perfect day to...to do what? Oh yeah, go to work, of course. Jack stretched, rubbed his eyes, and scratched his head. The same routine every morning. He crawled over to the computer desk and plopped down. Opening his home page, he clicked on the "mail" icon. He entered his password to find fourteen emails ready to read. Ten were spam, two were from Aaron, one from Dick's and the last one from Stardom Studios. Again! Jack hadn't given a second thought to answering the other emails from Stardom. And like before, he'd delete it along with the rest of the spam emails. It was time to take a shower and get ready for work because it was a special day for him. His first date with April. *Oh, shit.* He'd better call April and let her know what the plans were and what time he would pick her up after he got off work.

"Hello, Jack."

"Hi, April. Are you ready for tonight?"

"Of course. This handsome guy from school has asked me to go to the football game tonight."

"Wow. Some lucky guy."

"Yep. I'm really excited about it."

"Gee, he must be the captain of the football team."

"Oh, you're so funny. What time will you be here?"

"Well, I get off work at four. How about if I pick you up around five? I'll treat you to dinner at the Cowboy Steakhouse. How does that sound?"

"Oh, so cool. I love eating there."

"I'll see you at five. Bye."

"Bye."

Chapter 41

Friends With Good Ole #7

Dan closed his cell phone and flipped it on the bed, thinking he had to innovate a plan to get the vital information from Emily. He pondered his dilemma: could he deceive such a plan or trick, or was his trip to this small obscure town in Illinois all for naught?

He glanced at his Timex, it was 4:15, time to fill his hungry stomach. He wasn't familiar with the area so he decided to drive around for a suitable place to have dinner. When he arrived in Manford, finding the Super Inn was a snap. He saw their towering sign off the exit ramp of I-57 and like most hotel chains boarding Interstates, they were surrounded by an assortment of fast food chains. This stop had a McDonald's, a Pizza Hut partnering with a Taco Bell, and a Dairy Queen all within walking distance from his room. But his taste buds were longing for a medium rare, juicy, charcoal broiled rib-eye steak partnered with a few glasses of Old Number 7.

He turned his rented white Toyota Camry onto Main street and headed east of the freeway toward the town of Manford. He drove through the town until he came upon the massive shopping mall. Towering like miniature skyscrapers were the signs of Macy's, Target, Dick's Sporting Goods, and other smaller stores. If there came a time to get something he needed, he would come here. But he was looking for a good steakhouse. And there it was. He recognized the familiar sign of the Cowboy Steakhouse, a place he's eaten several times throughout his travels. A great place for a tasty, char broiled rib-eye steak, a loaded cheesed baked potato and a fresh salad.

He walked toward the entrance with his wallet in his hand, checking his funds and counted nine $100 bills still left in his expense account. He was all set for a good dinner and a few drinks, a much needed night off. The noise was loud, the music blaring, but the atmosphere was exciting. Dan found his way to the hostess, left his name, and adventured into the bar area, while stepping on scores of disposed peanut shells.

"Good evening. What can I get you tonight?" the young brunette inquired.

"I'll have a JD and Coke with a lime slice."

"Coming right up."

The taste of his drink brought a smack to his lips, he knew one JD was not going to be enough. No, no. Not tonight. Dan had money in his pocket and liquor on his mind. He thought he deserved it, and why not? With the hectic timetable he was under, he needed a break to get his mind off Helen, Emily Collier, and the elusive seven million dollars. He ordered another drink, then another, devouring them as if they were just plain Cokes.

A male voice spoke out above the noisy crowd, "Collier, party of two."

What! The name Collier instantly triggered the alarm in Dan's brain. He perked his ears and eyes, looking for that party called. There they were. It had to be the Jack Collier he'd been emailing. His eyes followed the pair walking toward the hostess desk. A tall male, short dark brown hair, athletic body, and wearing a high school Letterman's jacket. Although Dan didn't have a recent picture of the young man, his looks strongly resembled his father, Charles. It had to be Jack Collier. His companion was a very attractive girl with long, blonde hair, and a petite frame, wearing a low-cut blouse with revealing assets. An eye-popping specimen. Looked like Jack had hit the jackpot with this young cutie.

The hostess escorted Jack and April to a booth not far from the bar area of the Steakhouse and in a good spot for Dan to watch them. Once they were seated, Dan caught the attention of the hostess and waved her over to him.

"I'd like the booth directly behind that young couple you just seated, okay?" He stuffed a twenty dollar bill into her palm.

"Why, of course. No problem. Your name, sir?"

"Mesa."

"It'll be just a few minutes, Mr. Mesa. I'll have them clear the table."

"Thank you."

Within minutes, the twenty bucks paid off. Dan was shown to the booth directly behind the pair and had a clear broadcast of their entire conversation. His full attention was aimed toward them and not so much on his delicious rib-eye steak.

"I hope Aaron wins his game tonight." April exclaimed.

"I doubt it. Culver is undefeated this year. Besides, all the seniors will play tonight, meaning, the odds of them winning are slim to none."

"That's too bad. Who knows? Maybe Aaron can win the game by himself. You think so?"

"Well, Aaron's their best player. He could score a touchdown every time he touches the football. It wouldn't surprise me."

"Well, we'll see. You just never know."

"Absolutely. Our team's offense is better than average. Its been the defense that has lost the games this year, and last year, and the year before that."

"I'm excited. The game will be fun for me, win or lose." April admitted.

"Yep. And Aaron and I will be at Denny's for breakfast, as usual, on Sunday morning. Either he pays or I pay, most likely me."

Dan muttered to himself, *Sunday breakfast at Denny's, huh.* How did the old saying go...killing two birds with one stone, first the kid then Emily. Dan chuckled, swiped up his check off the table and left the steakhouse still laughing. Dan drove the Camry in the direction of the Super Inn. But, before going back to his room, he'd stop at the first liquor store to buy a pint of Jack Daniels and a liter of Coke. No limes. The night was still early, so back in his room, all he wanted to do was drink, watch TV, and seriously think about killing two birds. He placed his keys, his cell, and the refreshments on the desk under the massive mirror, looked it the mirror and the reflection said it all, hello to Mr. Greed. He'd need ice for his drinks so he searched the room and found a small blue plastic container in the bathroom, perfect to use as an ice bucket. Down the hall and next to the elevator, he located a room with an ice dispenser, two vending machines, and a machine to rent DVD movies. Dan examined the selection of movies to pick from, but nothing suited his interest, so back to his room he went. He filled his glass with whiskey, turned the TV on and with the remote in his hand, scanned the channels to find something interesting to watch. But most important, Jack Daniels would highlight his night. The first channel that appeared was ESPN broadcasting a local college football game. That would do. For all he cared, if the Muppets were on, he'd watch that.

He had all day tomorrow to create a game plan, a plot to set up Emily. He had to be cautious, smooth talk her, make her feel that he was a nice man and she could trust him. Ask questions, but don't create any suspicion. After all, Dan was in the movie industry, right? He thought out his plan carefully and decided to talk just about the accident. Maybe a few questions about living here and about her family. When Dan got the feeling that Emily was comfortable, at ease with him, he'd hand her the check. Yes, the payment would be made by check. He'd have to convince her that, since it was the weekend, the home office could not wire the cash to him in time. She'd buy it. And besides, before the rubber check bounced, Dan would be long gone. Dan swallowed what was left in the pint of JD. When he finished the last drink, off went ESPN, off went the lights, and good night to Dan.

Chapter 42

Bumping Into The Wrong Man

Jack pulled into Denny's parking lot with Aaron right behind him. He waited for Aaron to get out as both walked into Denny's restaurant.

"Let me see, I can't remember the last time I bought breakfast?" Aaron reminded Jack.

Jack punched Aaron in the left shoulder, saying, "You idiot. You never have. Besides, they handed you that game last night. Fumbling the ball on their own goal line."

"Hey. We won didn't we? All wins are good wins. Kind of nice to be on the winning side for a change."

Once inside, the waitress ushered them to a booth. "Coffee?"

"No thanks, orange juice for me." Aaron said.

"Ditto."

The waitress returned with their glasses of juice, ready to take their order. They both ordered their favorites, the same breakfast they order every Sunday morning.

When they finished their breakfast, Jack picked up the check while both put on their jackets and made their way to the cashier. As Jack reached into his pocket for his money, his eyes were studying the receipt. Bammm! A stranger and he collided, sending Jack in the direction of an occupied table. Jack stretched out his arm to catch the back of a chair, keeping him from landing on the table. Just as he looked up, the stranger was just standing there, like he was never hit. The man was kind enough to extended his hand to Jack and helped him gain his balance.

"Sorry. I wasn't looking where I was going." The stranger said nothing and walked away.

Jack glared at him. He looked at Aaron as if to say, "Where did this guy come from?"

"Okay. I'm fine. No problem."

Outside, Jack said, "It could've been ugly if I fell on that table."

"You would've had egg on your face, get it?" Aaron burst out laughing.

"Did you know that guy?"

"Nope. Never saw him before. It was just an accident. Hey, don't forget, tomorrow night the Bears and Packers on TV. You're still coming over, right?"

"Watching it on your TV? Absolutely, I won't miss that. Your Dad still going to let us drink beer?"

"Of course. He'll be drinking with us."

"Hey, we better get to work."

***

Dan located a booth next to the window looking out to the parking lot, still watching the two young lads laughing and getting into their cars. What he was looking for was Emily's silver Cadillac.

"I'll have a cup of decaf and an English muffin." Dan said.

He handed the menu to his waitress, gazing out the window. Another late Autumn day, plenty of sun and plenty of colors. All the trees surrounding Denny's validated everything said about the fall. The reds, oranges, yellows, and greens were in perfect harmony. How could anyone dispute this season as their favorite. That was why people from miles away visited the Midwest states that have the best fall foliage.

The waitress arrived with Dan's decaf along with his English muffin. While he ate, he thought more about his approach to broadsiding Emily. Get her to say something she didn't want to say, a slip-up, perhaps. Several cars entered and left the parking lot, but still no sign of the Escalade. He looked at his watch, it was not quite ten-thirty yet, but Dan was early. He sipped his hot decaf, then noticed the Escalade pulling into the parking lot. Dan couldn't help admiring her beauty. Her dazzling red hair, her ravishing body. Gee, could he be so ruthless as to con this lady out of seven million dollars? Money was the root of all evil and not having his hands on the money, Dan was evil. As soon as Emily entered the lobby, Dan stood and waved to her. She peered across the crowd of people, then acknowledged him.

"Good morning."

"Likewise."

When the waitress approached, Emily handed her the menu and said, "I'll just have a cup of coffee, please."

"Let me apologize again for the trouble I've put you through."

"There are far worse things going on in this world than a small dent. Within the next week or so, the dent will be fixed, and as they say, all's well that ends well, right?"

She reached into her purse for the estimate from Scott's Auto Repair and gave it to him.

"I never realized how such a small dent could cost so much to fix. Can you believe that?"

"Oh, I've seen worse." Dan examined the estimate, then stuck it in his front pocket.

"I, ahh, have one small problem. I phoned my boss last night, but because of the shortness of time, and today is Sunday, he can't get the cash to me in a reasonable time. I beg your forgiveness, but I can only pay you with this check." For some reason, Dan was caught off guard and totally messed up his strategy.

"Oh, boy. Mmmn…I hope I don't get stung by accepting this?"

"Please. I assure you everything is warranted. I would encourage you to call our office first thing Monday morning. They can confirm our banking reputation and even offer you the person in charge of our account."

"All right. I'm putting a lot of trust in you."

Dan smiled with his honest face, wrote the check out to Emily, if only she knew.

"So, this is Manford. How long have you been living here?"

Emily raised her arms and motioned as if to say, *You don't want to hear about my life.*

"It's such a small town, and my life is much like this town, very small. I grew up in Manford, went to college in Chicago, and met my husband in Chicago. We stayed in Chicago because of his job, and gave birth to our only child, Jack. Then came other problems. Soon after that, we got divorced. I moved back here with Jack, went to work, and found out that living in a small town is not always perfect."

"You have a son named Jack? I have a daughter named Jaclene. Does Jack still live with you?" Dan was such a liar, he couldn't help laughing inside.

"Yes. Jack is now eighteen and a senior at the local high school. He works part time for Dick's Sporting Goods at the mall."

"Really, now. What a coincidence. I was just in that store yesterday afternoon, looking for a warmer jacket, and a very nice young man helped me."

"Jack's a fine boy. My only hope is for him to continue his education and prepare himself for a great future."

"I wonder if he was the salesperson who helped me?"

"Very possible. He has a blooming personality, always wanting to help people."

"Does he ever see his father?" Was Dan pushing his luck?

"Oh, no. We have no idea where his father is. We haven't heard from him in quite awhile. We sure hope he's still safe, but he hasn't made any effort to contact myself or Jack. I don't know if he wants it that way or not. Our divorce was pretty normal because I wanted to remain friends. Just for the sake of Jack."

"That's so sad. It seems like many people share your same problems these days. I've always told my ex that if I ever win the lottery, I won't have any more problems. My dream is to move to Switzerland, buy a nice, warm, cozy cabin in the mountains and enjoy the rest of my life there. No more traveling for me, unless it was at my leisure. Just be with the right person to help spend my money. So, what would you do if you had a lot of money?" After letting that question out, Dan was straining his luck, he cringed waiting for her answer.

"Yes, don't I wish. I have dreamed about that too, but hasn't everyone? Occasionally, I'll buy a few lottery tickets, only when the pots are extremely high. How does that saying go? If I had any luck at all…"

"Maybe someday your dream will come true." Could Emily be telling him the truth about Charles and the money? Was is possible that Charles had Emily thinking he really doesn't have the money, but does? More important questions still need answers. Dan believed he was getting closer and Emily was loosening up. Should he ask her why she moved from Chicago and why her husband moved to Mexico?

"Gosh, look at the time. I have several errands to get done today, so I better be off."

Frantically, Dan needed another chance to meet Emily and get the answers he desperately needs.

"You know, I've had a very nice time talking to you. I'm going to be in Manford for a few days and this may sound pretty forward. Would you consider continuing our conversation over dinner?"

"Well, that does sounds nice. I've enjoyed the talk too. Unfortunately, tomorrow night is the only night I'm free."

"Sounds terrific. I'm free tomorrow night, too. Tomorrow night it is. I ate at the Cowboy Steakhouse last night. Had a wonderful meal. But, if you know of a better restaurant, I'm open for suggestions."

"I'll think about it." Emily hesitated, then jotted down her cell phone number on a napkin. "You can call me tomorrow and let's see what happens, okay?"

He walked side-by-side with her to her car, "You enjoy this fine Autumn day, Ms. Dearborn."

"You too. I'll talk to you soon."

So it's Dick's Sporting Goods, huh?

Dan knew the mall was just a short drive from Denny's. He decided to stop there on his way back to the hotel, see if Jack was working, and perhaps steal a few answers from Jack. Get him tip-off his Dad's whereabouts.

***

"Hello, may I help you find what you're looking for?" asked a young clerk wearing a green polo shirt with Dick's logo on the pocket.

"Jack Collier. Is he working today?"

"I believe he is. Look in the shoe department located at the rear of the store."

"Thank you."

Dan casually drifted in the direction of the shoe department. He stared at the rows of shoes: Nike, Reebok, Pumas, New Balance, Adidas all the while seeing Jack straightening the shoes on display racks.

"Excuse me?"

Jack turned to address the question and was surprised to see the stranger who nearly knocked him down at Denny's. He was sure of it.

"Can I help you?"

"I think so. I'm looking for an inexpensive jogging shoe, size ten and a half."

"Any particular brand you have in mind?"

"Not really."

"As you can see, we offer a wide variety of price ranges, anywhere from forty dollars up to one-hundred sixty dollars. Most brands carry both the expensive and the not-so-expensive shoe. It depends on what the customer is looking for. In saying that, I think Acids and Nike have the best low-cost running shoe." Jack pulled down a couple of display models.

"Amazingly light shoe. They look well-built too. Are those the only colors they come in?"

"Gosh, no. Let me go back to the stockroom and see if I can find shoes of each brand in different colors. Give me a few minutes." Minutes later, he returned with his arms full of boxes.

"Here, sit down and go through these. See what you think. Also, I found a pair of Reebok's that list for fifty dollars.

Dan sat on a small bench, and began the ordeal of trying on every shoe Jack brought out. To make conversation, he asked, "You like working here?"

"Oh, yeah. I've been here about four months now, ever since I moved to Manford."

"Funny, though. You look awfully familiar. Where else have I seen you?"

"Not to be rude, sir, but you were the person who bumped into me and my friend at Denny's this morning."

"Ahh, Jesus, that's right. Again, I apologize. I just wasn't paying attention to what I was doing."

"No foul, no harm, right?"

"I like these and the color is cool. I'll take the Nike's."

"Excellent choice. You'll like them."

Dan withdrew his wallet and presented Jack his business card.

"Say, listen. Here's my card. I work for a company from California called "Stardom Studios." You ever hear of it?"

"No, sir." Befuddled, did he just say Stardom Studios? The emails he's been deleting lately.

"We produce a reality show called "Extreme Reality". I'm in the area looking for young, energetic people to participate in the show. Perhaps you might be interested?"

"In California? Gee, I don't think so. I've never been out west."

"Well, keep that card. Someday, it may come in handy. You never know when you might be in California and looking for some challenging, exciting adventures. Just give me a call."

He put the Nike box under his arm and walked toward the checkout counter, but before he got there, he deposited the Nike box on an empty shelf.

Jack stared at the business card. Sure enough, it read Stardom Studios, the same company that sent him numerous emails, which all he deleted. Was this a coincidence? Puzzled, Jack read the information on the card. Dan Mesa, Director of Talent Evaluation, Stardom Studios, Pasadena, California. Was he right? Maybe this card would come in handy someday. Jack pocketed the business card.

Chapter 43

A Dinner For Love

Early on Monday morning, Dan woke up to the thunderous sound of children running outside his door. *Damn it. Can't a guy get a good night's sleep around here?* He reached over to the night stand to see what time it was. *I don't believe it, 7:10 in the fucking morning.* It was earlier than Dan had been getting up lately, but he was wide awake now. He rose, turned on the TV, scratched and wandered into the bathroom.

What am I going to do today?

He shuffled through the packets of coffee and found one containing decaf, unzipped the package and poured the contents into the automatic coffee dispenser. While his coffee brewed, he stepped out of his underwear and jumped into the shower, letting the hot water rush down his body. He knew he had to start putting pressure on Emily. There were only two answers he needed: where was the money, and where was Charles? If he could pry that out of her today or tomorrow, he could book his flight back to Los Angeles.

Done with his shower, Dan picked up the cup of fresh-brewed coffee and sat on the edge of his bed. His cell phone began ringing.

"Yeah?"

"I'm calling for an update. What have you found out?" It was Helen.

"Not much yet. When I got here Friday morning, the first thing I did was hunt down where she lives. I followed her to the mall on Friday. You'll love this. While she was shopping, I backed into her Caddy and dented the rear panel. She got an estimate for six hundred ninety-six bucks. I wrote her a rubber check, so I gotta get what I need in the next two days or else." He took a sip from his coffee cup.

"You still have the concoction I gave you?"

"Yeah. If I can't pry anything out of her without using it, I will use it. Okay, Helen. I'll think of something today. I'm taking her out for dinner tonight. Maybe I can get her drunk or something, but I'm not leaving here until I get what I want. She's hiding something, I can tell. She goes by the name of Emily Dearborn now."

Dan rose from the bed and stared at the reflection of his nude body in the mirror.

"Yeah, yeah. Everything okay out there? The FBI still lurking around?"

"Nothing here, been pretty quiet. I haven't left the apartment at all."

"Good, keep it that way. Keep your fingers crossed and with a lot of luck, I'll see you by the weekend."

Dan closed his cell with the thought of getting Emily drunk still on his mind. That's my chance. *Yeah, tonight I'm gonna get her drunk and let her tell all. She'll tell me anything I ask her.* Dan slapped his hands together, pumped up with his new plan.

The silver Escalade floated down Main Street as if Emily was driving on a road in the clouds. Such a smooth ride and so easy to handle. Buzz, buzz…The sound of her cell phone echoed from her purse.

"Hello."

"Emily, Dan Mesa here."

"Well, hello again. Don't tell me, you must be hungry?"

Laughing, he replied, "As a matter of fact, yes. That's why I'm calling you. What do you say to dinner at seven tonight?"

"I think that can be arranged. I'm never shy about having a good meal and sharing it with good company." Emily sure had a way with words when it came to romantic rendezvous.

"Excellent. I'll let you choose the restaurant."

"Hmm. I was thinking of Italian. We have one of the best Italian restaurants within one hundred miles of Chicago right here in Manford. It's called Simoni's."

"Okay, it's settled. Italian cuisine at seven tonight."

"Sounds great. I will meet you there around seven."

Emily instantly thought of Sergio. Could it happen, again, with another total stranger? *You're such a slut, Emily!*

"Oh, Dan. Do you need directions to where Simoni's is located?"

"I can find it."

"Great. See you there at seven."

***

Emily arrived at Simoni's just a few minutes before 7:00 and slowly pulled into the valet area in front of the main entrance. The valet, Jimmy, opened her door and watched her slide out from under the steering wheel, exposing enough skin that he thought he saw her red underwear.

Wow. "Good evening, Madam."

"Well, good evening to you too…Jimmy."

Inside, there was no Tony Simoni to greet her, only the maître d'. She spotted Dan sitting at the bar and went to join him. He rose, his hands reaching out to join hers, then Dan leaned forward and surprised Emily with a soft kiss to her cheek.

"That was very sweet of you."

"You look spectacular tonight. What do you have a taste for?"

The bartender made his way to serve them.

"Good evening, Emily. Nice to see you again."

Stan was a spitting image of the same bartender Jack Nicholson befriended in the movie "The Shining." An elderly, tall, skinny with a receding gray hairline and wearing a red plaid vest.

Emily was no stranger to the employees of Simoni's because, either alone or with Jack, she attended the restaurant at least once a week.

"Good evening, Stan. I have a taste for a vodka martini with two olives. And, Stan, I'll have Absolut vodka, please."

"Certainly. You, sir?"

"A Jack Daniels with coke and a lime twist."

They talked about politics, her job, the weather, but not in that order. Simple bullshit to Dan, but anything to keep the conversation going and keep her drinking martinis. They finished the first drink and ordered another.

"Did you get a chance to call our office regarding the check I gave you?"

"Oh, gosh no. I completely forgot, but I'm not really worried. I called Scott and tried to schedule an appointment. He told me they were really booked and it might take a couple of weeks to get the dent repaired." How Dan loved to hear that. A couple of weeks, awesome.

Carol, their waitress, interrupted their conversation to say their table was ready.

"I'll have Carol bring your drinks to your table, Emily," said Stan.

"Thank you, Stan."

They were seated in the back dining room, away from the busy tables of chattering customers. Dan liked that, because he could have a quiet conversation with Emily and discreetly begin prying into her recent past. Carol returned to their table with their drinks and two menus. It had been a while since Dan tasted authentic Italian food and with his hectic flee, the only Italian food he had was either Italian beef sandwiches or pizza.

"Everything looks delicious. What do you suggest?"

"Every selection you see, you can't go wrong. From the appetizers to dessert, it's fantastic. Does one stand out to you?"

Dan looked above his menu. "The Veal Parmesan sounds tempting."

"It is, believe me. I've had it before, you'll love it. I'm leaning toward the Crab and Shrimp Cannelloni. It's one of my favorites here."

It wasn't the dinner menu on Dan's mind, it was getting Emily to talk. Timing was important, but don't push her buttons. Be patient. His meal was everything Emily said. Delicious, and more than he could eat. He pushed his chair away from the table. "I haven't had a meal like that in a very long time. Even living in California, nothing can top this. I'm glad you picked this restaurant."

"That's why I come here so often."

Dan was such an easy target for very attractive women and sitting across the table from him was another bull's-eye. As Emily kept the conversation going, Dan's mind was traveling in the opposite direction. His only goal this night was getting Emily drunk and getting her to tell all, but if she did get drunk, could she wind up in Dan's bed that night? His eyes were frozen to her face. So alive and stunning, each stroke of makeup perfectly in place. His eyes ventured below her face to her plunging neckline and the exposure of her cleavage. She was an amazing woman to look at with a ton of assets, more than Helen would ever own. An unconscionable thought occurred to Dan, could he walk away with the grand prize? Well, the temptation was tantalizing, but if Emily confessed, he'd have enough money to embrace any woman he wanted. Money will buy anything, he thought.

"You know what? I have a taste for wine. Let's order a bottle." Emily announced.

At Emily's request, he ordered a bottle of Cabernet Sauvignon.

Moments later, the wine arrived, both glasses were filled, and Dan proposed a toast, "To Emily, hoping your future brings you millions."

They both burst out laughing, "I told you about my luck, Dan. It's all bad. But I'm curious. Tell me more about your job and the movie industry in California."

"I have a unique and interesting job. I work for Stardom Studios, which is a reality-based production company located in Pasadena. My job is to interview possible contestants and report back to my bosses. Too much traveling, though."

"But of all places, why are you here in Manford?"

"Good question. Actually, I'm not supposed to be here. We had some complications in Chicago with a particular contestant's contract. So, while I'm waiting for that to get resolved, I drove out of Chicago and found this place. It was purely by accident that I landed here. Right now, I'm waiting for a phone call from our legal people telling me to drive back to Chicago and get the contract signed. Once I have that, I'll fly back to LA."

"I'll bet those contracts can get pretty sticky, huh?"

"You must understand all reality shows need participants to launch the series. We're looking for certain individuals who meet our criteria. That is, outspoken, out of the ordinary, interesting backgrounds, peculiar, just plain different. In the television world, ratings are what the shows are all about. With high ratings come higher interests from the sponsors. Therefore, more money. People who watch reality shows love the drama, and seeing their favorites lose causes more drama. The show becomes more popular, more viewers, again more money. The more dramatic we make our shows, the better our chances for continuing the series." Dan amazed himself at how clever he was. After the story he told Emily, he actually thought he did work for Stardom Studios.

"I see, pretty interesting."

As Carol began clearing their table, she asked, "How was everything tonight?"

"Stuffed and delicious." replied Dan.

Dan emptied the wine bottle by refilling Emily's wine glass, noticing that she was nowhere near being intoxicated. She had four martinis, half a bottle of wine and sitting across from Dan, calm as ever. Was Dan's plan backfiring? Trying to pry the answers he needed by getting her drunk would cost him a small fortune. Now what? Should he use the concoction Helen gave him?

Minutes later, Carol reported back to their table and placed the check in front of Dan.

"Would you care for a nightcap, Emily?"

"I don't think so. I'm so full right now."

"Everything was fantastic. The food, the drinks, your company. What more could a man ask for?" Dan lied. What else could he say?

"I'm happy about that and thank you for inviting me."

"Purely my pleasure, Emily."

They walked to Emily's car. She opened her purse and fumbled to find her keys. Finally, she had them in her hand.

"Well. I suppose I won't see you again." Dan didn't want to say that, hoping Emily might suggest something else, and she did.

"Oh, you never know. It's a small world out there."

This time it was Emily who planted a kiss on Dan's lips. A kiss with meaning to it. Maybe an invitation?

"There happens to be a chilled bottle of wine sitting at my house. Just sitting there, waiting for the right man to explode the cork."

"Am I the right man?"

"Well…follow me home and find out for yourself."

How excited was Dan? If there was one area of his body that could talk, Emily was in for a real treat.

***

They entered the house from the side door of the kitchen, removed their coats, and Emily handed Dan the bottle of wine. That clever young lady, Dan thought. She had this planned from the beginning. What was she up to? The loud pop from the bottle of wine made Emily jump. It sounded like a shotgun going off, sure to wake up Jack. But she realized that Jack's Jeep was not in the driveway. Of course. It was Monday night and Jack was at Aaron's house watching the Bears game. Quickly, Emily glanced at the clock on the stove. It was only 8:30, which meant Jack wouldn't be home for a couple more hours. Awesome. Two free hours… It was pure addicting excitement, being sexually intimate with a perfect stranger, and Emily was very familiar with that scenario.

As Dan began to fill the wine glasses, Emily slipped out of her shoes and grabbed him by his tie. She led him through the living room and into her bedroom, but he didn't need her to lead him. He was eagerly awaiting what was in store for him. A lonely, horny woman getting laid, that's all. Emily lit a few candles near her bed, then tantalized Dan by slowly removing all her clothes, piece by piece until she was stark naked. The candles shed enough light, exposing the accentuate qualities of her body. That was what he had hoped for the minute he saw Emily at Denny's, to be a slave to her desires. He stripped off his clothing and embraced Emily's hot, inviting body. Their kisses became more passionate as his hands explored more of her body, slowly falling onto Emily's bed.

"Do it, Dan. Now."

After what seemed to be hours later, they lay still intertwined. Few words were spoken, but each knew they'd experienced an unforgettable night. Emily sneaked a look at the clock on her dresser. It was 10:50 pm. She was pushing her luck with Dan, both still naked and fondling each other. She had to get him out of the house before Jack's Jeep arrived, or there would be hell to pay for Emily.

"You better get going. My son will be home shortly and I need to avoid a million questions from him."

"I hear ya." He gathered his clothes, scattered on the carpet, and made his way to the bathroom.

"You were a beast in there, Dan. I must have reached a dozen times."

"It was the woman in you that brought out the man in me. You excited me to the point that I couldn't quit. It was amazing."

"Dan. You think we could meet again before you leave?"

"I could have you all year long. I can't get enough of you." They embraced and engaged in one last, passionate kiss.

"Call me, okay?"

Chapter 44

Anyone For Chinese Food?

Outside, the air was brisk and chilly, causing Jack to see his breath. The moon was full and the entire sky illuminated by a million floodlights. From Aaron's house, the drive to his house was approximately seven miles with lots of turns and stop signs, but once he reached South Street, it was a straight shot into his driveway. When he turned on South Street, his view caught two red lights backing out of his driveway. Where would Emily be going at this time of the night? Now closer, Jack saw the car was out of the driveway and heading toward him. The headlights temporarily blinded him, but he shielded his eyes from the bright lights. The vehicle was a small white two-door sedan, not the Escalade and definitely not Emily. It was a man behind the wheel. Who in the hell was that? With the driver's window open, Jack got a good view of the driver.

Now what's going on?

Jack parked his Jeep, walked to the back kitchen door and turned on the lights. The car nor the driver he didn't recognize thinking, maybe it was someone lost and turning around in their driveway. Anyway, he turned off all the lights and hustled upstairs. He sat at the end of his bed, undressing but still thinking about the man in the white car. He didn't recognize the car, but the face drew his attention. *Think Jack.* He tried to shut his eyes and fall asleep, but it was really bothering him. He knew that face. Was it at the football game, at the restaurant, at school, at work? Where? His eyes were heavy and he was about to fall asleep when the bulb flashed in his brain. He sat up in bed staring into the darkness. It was that person from the TV show. The same guy who bumped into him at Denny's. The guy from Stardom Studios. Now he remembered. What the hell was he doing here? And with Emily!

This was not a coincidence. This couldn't happen by fate. There was something to this and had he to find out what it was. The next morning, Jack finished his breakfast, ready to leave for school. He didn't think Emily would be up this early, and as expected, she was still in bed. If he didn't inquire and ask her now about last night, it would give her all day to develop a lame excuse. He crept into her bedroom to wake her up, but seeing her sound asleep, he decided to let the matter go. Besides, whatever she told him would be a lie anyway, so let her deal with it.

Jack snatched his books and keys from the table, but in his haste the keys fell from his grip and landed on the floor. There, in plain sight, was something he didn't want to see. Another business card from Mr. Mesa. He was here last night, alright and with Emily.

"Are you kidding me?" He picked up the card, tossed it on the kitchen table and left. Later that morning, Emily awoke on cloud nine. She danced into the kitchen and prepared a cup of coffee, then sat at the kitchen table. She noticed Dan Mesa's card laying on the table. Damn it. Did he leave this here last night? She thought to herself, or did it fall out of my jacket? Oh, shit. I bet Jack saw this card this morning. How am I going to explain this to him? Debating whether she should keep the card or dispose of it, she dwelled on her decision. If she threw it away, the possibility of another fantastic night with Dan would be in jeopardy. It was a no-brainier. She picked up the card and pulled her wallet from her purse, opened the wallet, but saw another card of Dan's. Where did the second card come from?

An unambitious Emily sat in her living room sipping on her second cup of coffee and watching the snow gravitate to her front lawn. She remembered when the weather was bad in Chicago, Charles would always remark, *If you want the weather to change in*

Chicago, just wait five minutes. Living in the windy city, how true that was. She snuggled on the couch, as sensual thoughts passed through her mind about her wild ravishing night with Dan. She wondered how Charles was doing in Costa Rica, and Jack with his new girlfriend at school. Since the past several months, Emily reflected upon the happenings in her life and how drastically her life has changed. All because of money, a lot of money. Her eyes were mesmerized by the tiny white snowflakes falling leisurely from the sky. She hadn't heard from Dan since Monday night and wondered how he liked seeing the snow falling, being from California. What if he received his important call? Has he left Manford? Should I call him? She sat, daydreaming and staring out the window. If I do call him, will he think all I want from him is sex? Her nights with Sergio were awesome, but just that one night with Dan made her forget about Sergio. His performance was mind blowing. She needed another night with him, but if he was gone, so were her hopes.

The beginning of the fall season brought the miraculous colors from the trees, cold weather, and also brought the holidays. Always an exciting time for the Collier family, starting with Thanksgiving, followed by Christmas and New Years. Emily loved to Christmas shop. She reminisced the times she and Charles shopped for Jack when he was young, buying clothes and toys and watched him on Christmas morning how excited he got. Oh, those memories, they were priceless. Times have changed for both her and Jack. The family had separated and with the holidays rapidly closing in, decisions had to be made. Should she cook an elaborate dinner for Thanksgiving only for them or she could always invite friends to share the turkey, such as April's family, their neighbors, the Kaplings, or even Sergio? Emily tossed the ideas around, but the more she thought about it, the more reasonable it became clear to her, it would be easier to take Jack out for Thanksgiving dinner.

From the holidays and into the New Year, Emily realized that coming of a new year meant tax time. Charles always took care of preparing and filing the family's taxes, but Charles was not around. This year it would be her responsibility, definitely something she was not familiar with at all. There was an alternative, contacting an outside accountant to file in her behalf was a valid option. What were the consequences if she did that? Emily would have to disclose the funds concealed in a Switzerland bank to the IRS. The more she thought about the predicament, the more she was convinced that nobody knew about the money. Who better to have those answers than Charles. She needed to contact him and have him tell her what she should do. She had to find out soon, but Charles was a thousand miles away. Filing her taxes was a serious problem, but so was hiding the seven million dollars. What if I don't file any taxes this year, let a year pass by. Then the IRS wouldn't know about the money.

She decided to log on to the Clairden Leu website to make sure the money was there and how much money. The Clairden Leu was the bank that Charles worked with during his entire career at Priority. He knew and trusted the people there and they worked well with other accounts that Charles opened for his clients. She moved to her desk, sat behind the computer, then opened the Clairden Leu website. She typed her password, hit the "enter" key and seconds later, the monitor displayed the bank statement. Instantly, her eyes were focused on the line producing the balance… $7,356,275.50. The account, and the problem, was all in her name, maybe that was a stupid move on her part, maybe they should've left everything in Charles's name. Emily didn't have a clue what to do. Her emotions were beginning to scare the hell out of her. With all the talk, the planning, the divorce, never did they realize filing taxes could cause a major problem. She remembered the phone number where Charles was staying. She closed the computer down and picked up her cell and about to dial that number, then became aware she could not use her cell phone. It was traceable. Whenever contact was needed, they had to use pay phones.

The chimes from the grandfather clock struck eleven and she

put away the problem of taxes for the time being. It was time to get ready for work. She took a quick shower, dressed, and left the house, putting the tax situation on the back burner. Only Dan was pictured in her mind. Since his arrival, Sergio was set aside, temporarily forgotten. She knew that Dan would be leaving soon, but she wanted one more night in bed with him, one more souvenir to store in her memory. She unlocked the car door, started the engine and backed out on to South Street. It's been two days since she last spoke to him. Did he get his call ordering him back to California? She wanted to call him, but she didn't want the rejection of knowing she would never see him again. If he was back in California, he was out of her life. She got up the nerve to flip open her cell and dialed Dan's number.

"Hello. Are you still alive?"

"Oh, yeah. I'm still here, catching up on some paperwork, making some phone calls, same old BS. Still waiting on that call."

"Well. I'm on my way to work and I'll be getting off at six. What if I bring some Chinese carryout to your room?"

"You sure have a way with food, don't you?"

"I try to do my best."

"I'll stop and get some vodka and limes."

"I can't wait. What is your room number?"

"I'm in 203, in the back of the motel."

"Fantastic. I'll see you about six thirty."

The time couldn't come fast enough for Emily. All afternoon, her mind was on Dan and her eyes were on the clock. It was his superhuman ability to endure, methodically pounding his body into hers. His knack of knowing the correct places on her body that begged him never to stop. She thought about all the men she'd had in her bed, but Dan was different. She couldn't put a finger on it, he just had the amazing ability to please her more than any other lovers.

Arriving at the Super Inn, she parked in the back, but had to enter the motel through the main lobby. All the outside doors were security protected, but once inside, she took the elevator to the second floor. Finding room 203 was easy and she tapped lightly on the door. Dan opened the door stark naked, and everything he owned was at full attention.

"Oh boy. My lucky day."

Emily dropped the Chinese food on the desk and fondled Dan's present.

"This will be way better than Chinese food."

She began to disrobe, still fondling him. He helped her remove her clothes, so that they were both naked and lying on the bed. The session was in full force, each knowing that by the time they were finished, the Chinese food would be ice cold.

Chapter 45

Loose Lips Will Sink...

The walls of room 203 were starting to cramp Dan's style. He'd been in this room for six days now, getting impatient and restless. His patience wasn't the only thing running out. So was his money. His plan was not panning out and taking longer than expected. Emily still hasn't confessed to the whereabouts of Charles, much less the money, and he was convinced Jack knew nothing about either. Emily was his only target. Something had to happen quickly because his scheduled flight back to LA. departed the next evening. If he could stop the sex for a night and concentrate on getting answers instead of getting satisfied, he might catch his flight on time. But, was his desires replacing his objectives? The pressure was on Dan. Tonight, Emily had to spill out everything to him, otherwise the chance of becoming a millionaire was fading fast.

He remembered the day he and Charles met. A new employee of Priority and, according to William, would be working under Charles, helping with accounts and setting up new contracts, the basic protocol. This was how William's scheme to get rich started. In order for the plan to work, he hired Dan, putting him under Charles's wing. Let Charles do all the work, especially the Kaiser account and when the time was right, he would pull the trigger. That account was Charles's life. It was his and his alone and he didn't want any of Dan's input. In fact, Charles would not let Dan see any of the outlines or contents of the account. It was always under lock and key and never out of the sight of Charles. William too, kept a very keen eye on the Kaiser account. This account was the key to closing his future, just transfer the money to an offshore account and escape to never-never land. Dan comprehended how time has changed his life and so did William's plan. If William was still alive, Dan would be buying a new house in Interlaken and not chasing answers in Illinois. But, right now, spending the entire week in Manford, he still wasn't sure if Emily had the money or even knew about it. Maybe that's why they divorced so quickly and why Charles quit work at Priority. Maybe Charles had a plan that was slicker than William's? Steal the money, hide it from Emily, get divorced, and then leave the country. As he studied his thoughts and further moves, it could be possible that he'd been barking up the wrong tree and the trip to Manford was all for naught. Furthermore, Charles was a very clever man.

Buzz... Buzz... He answered his cell.

"Do I still arouse you?"

"Just hearing your voice gets me that way. How are you doing today?"

"I'm doing just fine. Nothing to complain about. No one listens to my complaints, anyway."

"Really. You'd be the perfect wife, you know that?"

"I was, until a year ago."

"You'll have to tell me all about that. Wives seem to have great stories about their ex's."

"You want to meet again and have dinner tonight?"

"You must have been reading my mind. I was planning on calling you, but the attorneys called and I have to leave tomorrow for Chicago. I want to see you before I leave."

"Aww, that's not what I want to hear. I would love to see you tonight, for the entire night. Where should we go?"

"Let's try the Cowboy Steakhouse. I have a taste for a rib eye steak." He was getting a familiar feeling between his loins, and if he continued with those thoughts, a good chance he'd lose his appetite.

"I'll meet you there, say about seven?"

"Fine. I'll save you a seat at the bar."

Dan closed his cell and looked at his watch. A quick shower, dress, and fifty-five minutes later he'd be sitting at the Steakhouse bar. What was left of his brilliant scheme had withered. He was facing defeat in the eyes of Emily and was sure she knew nothing about the money. There was no use interrogating Emily, because he believed from what she was telling him, she knew nothing about the money, other than being a recent divorcee. They'd have a pleasant dinner, talk about nonsense and sexual innuendos, or the possibility of her visiting him in sunny California. One thing for sure, they'd end up back in room 203, screwing till they dropped. She would eventually leave, then he would leave. So long to Manford, good bye to being a millionaire and farewell to the house in Switzerland. Dan fought hard, but conceded that Charles played a better game, he came out the winner and beaten Dan to a pulp.

The bar at the Steakhouse was only half full, so Dan picked one empty stool and ordered his usual. When his drink appeared, so did an aluminum pail of salted peanuts.

Might as well join the crowd, so he reached into the pail, collected a handful of peanuts, started cracking them and tossing the empty shells to the floor.

"I'm here."

He swiveled his stool and saw Emily, dressed for the kill with her red hair pushed up, her earlobes saddled by a pair of diamond stud earrings, a light blue, satin blouse that barely covered her breasts, revealing she was not wearing a bra. Every breathing male sitting in the bar had their eyes popping out and so were Dan's.

"I swear. You get better looking every day."

"I'll have a Makers Manhattan, please."

They talked about Dan leaving the next day, which led to lingering kisses and another drink or two. When their table was ready, both grabbed their drinks and was escorted to a secluded table in the back of the dining room. The waitress brought another round of drinks when Dan surprisingly observed Emily's eyes starting to droop, and her words were beginning to slur, too. She was getting drunk? After six days, a stupid car accident, costly drinks and dinners, his luck was about to strike gold. Go ahead, Dan, start probing her with detailed questions. If she dodges, back off. What do you have to lose?

"When was the last time you saw your ex?"

"You mean Charles, my long lost husband?"

"Yes, if that's his name? The last time we talked, you mentioned your divorce, then both of you moved from Chicago. You're here and where is Charles?"

Emily took a long drag on her cigarette. "Oh, I think he left for South America, Mexico or was it South Africa? Hmm. No wait, I really think it was Costa Rica. Is there such a country? Anyway, he said the country was breathtaking and wanted me to join him."

Finally, if she would've ordered a Manhattan days before, he'd be on his way to Costa Rica by now.

"Before, it was Mexico. He wanted everyone to think he left for Mexico, his plane fare was to Mexico. It was a cover-up you see, now he's in Costa Rica."

Dan was all ears, even moving his chair closer to Emily so that he wouldn't miss a single word she said. Emily was reaching the point of absolutely being drunk. "Is he still there?"

"Umm, I don't know. I don't think so. I can't remember when we last talked. Its been a long time and even Sergio has forgotten about him."

Boy, she is smashed. Who is Sergio?

"How come Charles wanted to move to Costa Rica?"

"The money, sweetie." Emily's arms were waving and her voice was getting louder. Everyone around them could hear what she was saying.

"I think. I think that's why he quit working at...shit, I forgot where he worked. In Chicago, that I know. He was on a very important case about some lost money...or taxes, or some crazy thing like that. But, he told me it was millions. Then, I think his boss died. That was the final straw, he wanted the money."

Dan caught the attention of his waiter and ordered her another drink.

"So, Charles left for Costa Rica with millions of dollars in his pocket. Why didn't you go?"

Emily had difficulty keeping her cigarette lit, let alone finding the ashtray. Her elbow slid off the edge of the table spilling her drink, that didn't surprise Dan. Any question Dan asked, Emily responded as if she was in a trance, hypnotized, and under his control.

"It was our plan to get divorced, split up, then find a bank overseas. We laughed a lot, because it was so easy to do. No one knew about the money, except Charles and me. No one. Not even the people who owned it." Emily's laughter and boisterous actions were becoming a nuisance.

"The money is overseas? How were you able to do that?"

She finished another drink, looked around, and whispered, "That was the best part. Our TV broke, so the store sent this cable guy, a nerd, well…he was telling me all about his relative, maybe his brother-in-law, anyway, he went to prison for computer hacking." She giggled an annoying laugh. "A hacker! And the rest was history."

Sensing the feelings from the surrounding crowd, Dan needed to get what information was left and split before people start complaining to the management.

"Wow. How much money did you get?"

Emily sat in silence, reacting slowly to Dan's questions.

"Charles said it was close to forty-eight million, but after we used a hacker. In reality it was less than that, I think."

"Jesus. You're rich now. Did Charles take the money to Costa Rica?"

"Duh. He had it set up in Switzerfield, or some big city there. It all had to do with tax this or tax that. I don't know. Charles took care of everything."

Dan was ecstatic. He had all he needed. Where the money was, how much for certain and…who cared about Charles? His next move was to talk to Helen, create a way to get the money out of Switzerland, and into their hands.

There was one more question Dan had to ask. "What was the name of the bank in Switzerland?"

"Huh? Why do you need the name of the bank? Why do you want to know that for?"

He had pushed his luck too far, and as drunk as she was, she was creating a scene that Dan had to get away from.

"Excuse me, Emily. I need to use the men's room."

She never heard what he said. She sat, staring aimlessly into nothing, puffing on her unlit cigarette.

Dan reached into his pocket and tossed a crisp one-hundred dollar bill on the table, enough to pay for their dinner and to cover the tip. He left by the main entrance, and sped to the Super Inn. Funny, it took him only a day or so to get into Emily's pants, but it took him nearly seven days to get out of them. At his room, he gathered his already packed luggage, checked out, and bolted his way up the Interstate to Chicago. He couldn't get to O'Hare any faster, but on his way, he had to make one urgent phone call.

"It's over. I got everything and I'm on my way to O'Hare. Alcohol was not her best friend, at least it wasn't tonight. She was so drunk, she couldn't find her ass with both hands. Spilled everything out, sang like she was auditioning for My Fair Lady. I'm on my way to the airport. As soon as I get into LA., start thinking about getting me to Costa Rica, okay? We're rich, we're rich, you hear that? We're rich."

Chapter 46

Where Have All The Flowers Gone?

Emily was still waiting for Dan to return from the men's restroom. *Why was it taking him so long?* It was time for another smoke. Jesus, a new pack of cigarettes she bought before coming to the Steakhouse was almost empty.

I have to quit smoking, or quit drinking. She tried to light the cigarette, but her motions and arms were not cooperating with her. She had the match lit, but finding the end of the cigarette was nearly impossible. She had consumed so much alcohol that her eyes were barely open, she was getting very tired and controlling her body functions was bordering on ridiculous.

"Excuse me, Miss." Her waiter startled her. "Is there anything else I can get you?"

"What? Umm, did you see where my friend went?"

"I believe he left. I saw him exiting through the front door and I haven't noticed his return."

"He's gone? No. Look around some more. His name is, ahh…Fuck me! What's his name?"

Her cigarette had fallen from the ashtray, beginning to burn a hole in the white tablecloth. The waiter picked up the cigarette and extinguished it in an already full ashtray. He carefully removed Dan's one-hundred-dollar bill wedged between the salt and pepper shakers to settle their bill. Whatever was left over, if anything, would be his tip.

Emily was talking to herself, her words slurred as she tried to find her drink on the table. The waiter stepped back and signaled to the floor manager, Joe, to see how intoxicated Emily was. It took

Joe only a few seconds to realize he must get her out of there before something embarrassing happened.

"I'll go call the cops. They'll send a car out here and give her a ride home."

Ten minutes later, two uniformed officers helped Emily get to her feet. They asked her about her car and where she lived, but she was so intoxicated she had no idea where she was or who she was speaking to. Their only alternative was to let her spend the night at their house, sobering up.

***

The alarm went off in Jack's room, reminding him to get up and get ready for school. As he sat on the edge of the bed, yawning, he looked out the window that overlooked the driveway. Only his red Wrangler was parked in the driveway, the Escalade was gone. What's was Emily up to now? He finished breakfast and was about to leave the house, but to make sure, he would check and see if she was home. He walked through the living room to her bedroom, her door was wide open, the bed was made, but there was no sign of Emily. In all likelihood, she must be with Johnny-come-lately from Stardom Studios. He couldn't believe the reputation she was creating, spending nights with men she barely knew. Not long after her divorce, Sergio magically appeared, and now this joker. Jack's temper was starting to rile. He shook his head in disgust and hustled out to the Wrangler. He didn't want to be late for school on Emily's account.

***

"Hey, hey! Why am I in here?" Emily shouted through the black steel bars.

The sound of hard rubber soles walking on tiled floors got closer to her holding cell.

"Well. I sure hope you're in a better mood this morning."

"Why am I here?"

"You don't remember, do you? You were so intoxicated last night, the manager of the restaurant called and we had to bring you here. You were to drunk to drive and couldn't even remember where you live."

She stood still for a moment, trying to remember the night before. She rubbed her forehead, hoping to stop her head from pounding.

"Jesus. Can I get a cup of coffee, please?"

"Sure. This way." The officer unlocked the steel door and led her to the police break room where Emily sat at an empty table. Moments later, the officer placed a cup of coffee in front of her.

"Do you have any aspirin? My head is splitting."

"Sorry. We're not authorized to hand out any type of pills or medication. You want cream and sugar?"

"No. Just plain black coffee, thank you."

"Take your time. I'll check back with you in a few minutes, okay?"

Emily tried to remember events that got her here. Why did she drink so much? All she remembered was talking to Dan over dinner, then his remark about using the men's room. After that, she drew blanks.

"If you're ready, we'll give you a ride home. You do know where you live, don't you?"

Emily felt the thunder in her head, but produced a small smile and a chuckle. "Yes, I do remember. This is so embarrassing. I can't believe I did this. I'm not a person who drinks a lot. Honest."

"Yeah, that happens. The manager was pretty nice about it. Said your friend left money to take care of your dinner, then took off. Your vehicle is still parked at the restaurant. He said it was okay to leave it there, but you'll need to pick it up sometime today."

"Some friend, huh?"

Emily gave the patrolman her address, ten minutes later he

turned on South Street and dropped Emily off in front of her driveway.

"Well, I'm home. Thanks for the ride. I hope I don't ever see you again."

They both laughed and Emily let herself out of the squad car. Her eyes circled the surrounding neighbor's houses. She prayed that none of them witnessed the scene, being escorted to her house in a police squad car, talk about embarrassing. Finally inside, Emily collapsed in a chair at the kitchen table, exhausted. She thought about Dan, the night in jail, and her car. How was she going to get it? She couldn't ask Jack, at least not now. She'd be better off not telling him anything, especially where she spent the night. He would never forgive her. The only logical resolution was calling a taxi.

That god damn Dan. Why did he leave me there when I was so drunk? I'll call him. He owes me an explanation.

She searched for her cell phone, trying to remember where she had it last, and found it in her coat pocket. She dialed Dan's number.

"Hello, Emily."

"What the fuck happened last night? And where did you go? You just left me there like a piece of garbage." Emily was furious.

"I'm sorry, but I can explain everything," Dan lied again. He knew she would call, he knew how drunk she was and that she wouldn't remember anything. He could tell her the most bizarre story and she would believe him.

"At dinner last night, I got a call from my partner. You remember when I told you I had to use the men's bathroom? Well, it was a call I had to take. Anyway, it was extremely necessary that I got back to LA. immediately. I tried to tell you last night, but you were out of it. So, I had no choice. I had to leave."

"I'm so pissed off at you. Do you know where I spent the rest of the night? In the Manford jail. You fucking moron."

Wow, she is pissed, "I am sorry, Emily. Calm down. You must understand the urgency I was in."

"You told me there were contracts that needed to be signed by some people in Chicago. I don't think you saw those people at ten o'clock in the evening. Explain that!"

Oops, he did tell her that. Think fast, Dan. There was a lull before Dan replied, "Well, that's why my partner called me so late. He took care of the problem himself. Those contracts were signed and faxed back to him earlier that evening. Everything was in order and I didn't need to stop off in Chicago and meet them. All I had to do was catch the first flight back to LA."

"You better be telling me the truth."

"Trust me, Emily. If and when I see you again, I'll make it up to you, I promise."

She had to see Dan again. When they were together, she lived in a fantasy world and he had the Midas touch.

"Listen. I have to go. I have people waiting for me in my office. I'll try to call you later in the week. Goodbye."

Dead air. She closed her phone. Sat confused and wondered if she'd ever see him again, she could not hold back her tears.

Oh, my aching head. She eased over to her kitchen counter and hit the brew button on her Keurig. While her coffee brewed, she filled a glass of water and swallowed three Excedrin pills, hoping the pounding in her head would stop. *Thank God for these.* With a full cup of steaming coffee in her grasp, Emily headed for the living room and the soft, comfortable sofa. She just wanted to relax and let the Excedrin do it's job. Why can't I get him off my mind? I'm here and he's in California. How am I supposed to see him again? It wouldn't happen, she was convinced she'd never be intimate with Dan again. She thought about the brief time they spent together and how a small accident started everything. Was it purely by accident that Dan appeared in her life? Was she beginning to fall in love with him? Or, was it just his sex? Charles could never her make her feel the way Dan did. Neither could Sergio. But was it fair to compare Charles to Dan? She did love Charles, but did her love vacate him now?

Chapter 47

Quickly It Started...Quickly It Ended

Another week of classes ended at Columbia High. Jack removed the books from his locker he'll need for homework, grabbed his jacket, and waited for April to give her a ride home. She came around the corner of the hallway, showing off her signature smile and alluring beauty. Jack was a lucky guy and fate was definitely on his side. No more boring days for him, not with this girl. Out the front entrance, the couple held hands on the way to the student parking lot and hopped into the Jeep.

"What's your Dad got planned for tonight, April?"

"Who knows. I'm a senior already, but the two of them think I'm still in grade school. I wish they would let me grow up."

"It makes Saturday night all the better."

"True. What do you want to do Saturday night?"

Jack hesitated to answer, but he knew Emily and Sergio would be in Chicago Saturday night, leaving the house all to himself. There were times when their relationship was hot, but that's as far as it got, never leading to intimacy. But, Jack was anxious for it to happen and having the house for himself, all alone with her, this would be his opportunity to find out? How would he push her buttons, would she jump at the opportunity, or become offended by his advancements? She could drop him like a hot potato, and end their precarious relationship. For Jack, there was only one way to find out.

"You know what? Emily won't be home Saturday night. She's going to a party in Chicago with that moron, Sergio. So, we'll have the entire house to ourselves. We could rent a couple of movies and…"

April had a sexy gleam in her eye as she looked in Jack's direction. An all to familiar look reflecting back on April's past history. She knew perfectly well what Jack was insinuating, if he only had a clue about her past.

"Awesome. You and I together, a couple of scary movies. Ooh, that would be fun."

"Then that's what we'll do. The entire night to ourselves."

Jack pulled into April's driveway. He turned off the Jeep, put his arm around April and kissed her cheek. She responded, moving closer, she put her arms around his neck and eagerly planted a long, meaningful kiss to his lips. Her hand slid down across his jeans in the direction of his crotch, moving in smooth short strokes and rubbing that inviting area. Did she accidentally put her hand in the wrong place? Jack wasn't sure what to think. He sat silent, taking it all in.

April slipped from their embrace. "I can't wait till tomorrow. You'll find a scary movie, won't you?"

"One that will blow your pants off?"

"Oh, boy. Now that's a leading question. Call me tomorrow and let me know what time you're picking me up, okay?"

"Will do. Have fun tonight."

As usual, Jack stopped at McDonald's and picked up a couple of burgers, fries, and a large Coke for his ride home. No doubt, his dinner too. He noticed Emily's car and a new shiny black Corvette in their driveway. That asshole Sergio was in the house. He pulled the Jeep behind the Escalade and walked to the house. Inside, Sergio and Emily were hugging, playing their love game, not caring what Jack thought. It was sickening to watch them, even more sickening to Jack picturing her and asshole sharing a bed together. He slammed down his books on the kitchen counter and walked past the two fools.

"Can't you say hello?"

Jack said nothing, opened the fridge, pulled out another Coke and hustled upstairs as if he were the only person in the house.

"Okay, be that way."

He moved to his computer, flipped it on and sat sipping his Coke. When his home page appeared, he saw there were more emails in his mailbox. He typed in his password and glanced over the junk, debating what to open and what to delete.

Are you kidding me?

The same email from Stardom Studios appeared again. He opened the page and briefly read what it was about. This time, the email was different. It started by using his first name, Jack. None of the previous emails ever mentioned his name. How did they know my name? The email contained an application to fill out, and a small paragraph explaining the rules if he was selected to participate in the show. It also mentioned the chance of winning one million dollars. He sat there, looking at the screen, debating with himself on what to do. He decided to fill out the application, hoping it would put an end to the stupid emails sent to him. He couldn't be lucky enough to be selected, but maybe lucky enough to end those constant emails. He hit the "Send" icon, then deleted the email entirely.

"Jack, were going to get something to eat. Do you want to come with us?" Emily shouted from the bottom of the stairs.

"No."

"Suit yourself. We'll be back later."

Jack sat at his desk, looking out the window, watching them leave. Sergio was following Emily, but as they passed Jack's Wrangler, Sergio landed a juicy hocker on Jack's driver-side window. Seeing that, Jack sprinted toward the front window.

You fuckin' asshole! He hurried down the stairs and out the kitchen door, but it was too late. The Corvette was rapidly on the move up South Street.

I'll fix that bastard. When Jack got back to his room, he picked up his cell and called Aaron.

"Hey, what's going down?"

"That son-of-a-bitch, jerk-off idiot, Sergio just landed a big hocker on my car window."

"What!"

"We got to set this creep straight. Help me think of something that will really piss him off. Something to his baby, that shiny new Corvette he owns."

"Whoa. You're that mad at him?"

"Yeah. I hate him. You know, something that will make him stay away from Manford."

"Hey, listen, I gotta get going. Terri is waiting in the truck. I'll think of something and I'll call you later today, okay?"

"Okay. Sounds cool."

Jack was still looking out his window at the glob of mucus stuck to his window. He swiped a couple of paper towels and glass cleaner and cleaned the mess Sergio left. Now, he had to get ready to go to work. When Jack got off from his Saturday shift, he climbed into his Jeep, opened his cell and dialed April's number.

"We're going to watch a movie about the Sharks and the Jets," Jack explained.

"A football movie?"

"No. West Side Story. You mean you've never heard of West Side Story?"

"Nope. I'm afraid not. It must be an oldie."

"A little bit. It's a good movie, one that you'll like. I'm on my way home now, so I'll stop off at the video store and look for some scary movies."

"Cool. I'll watch anything."

"I'll order us a pizza and we can stop and get it after I pick you up. Around 6:30."

"I'll be ready, see you then."

Aaron once told Jack that if he wanted to watch a really scary movie, rent "Islands of the Ghosts." He said Terri never opened her eyes, that's how scary it was. So, Jack stopped off at the video store and rented both movies. By the time he reached home, only Emily's car was in the driveway. The Corvette was gone and the house was his for the entire night. Yes, the Corvette. He remembered to call Aaron and talk over how to piss off Sergio.

Piss him off so bad, he'd never show his face around here anymore.

"Did you give any thought to our farewell gift to Mr. Pinhead?"

"Well. Those tires on a Corvette are very expensive. So is the paint job. I'm was thinking of flattening a few tires and accidentally getting too close to his door with a screwdriver."

"Oh, man, awesome. That would really, really piss me off if it was my Vette. April is coming over tonight and I'm not sure what time Emily will be getting home, but as much noise as they make, I'll know when. Just keep your cell next to your bed and I'll call you as soon as they come in. Oh, bring a flashlight and signal me when you get here."

"Got ya. Did you get that movie I told you about?"

"Yep. And I'm on my way to pick up April now."

"Cool. Lots of nudity in it. That's why I think Terri had her eyes closed all night."

"I'll see you later." Jack closed his cell and placed it on the console between the seats.

His first stop was April's house and then the Pizza Shack—a large cheese, sausage, green pepper, onions, and pineapple, Jack's favorite. Then, the night Jack has been waiting all his life for will finally happen.

Eager to begin their promiscuous night together, Jack and April dashed up the stairs to Jack's bedroom. April carried the pizza while Jack grabbed two Cokes from the fridge and followed her. They sat on the couch in front of Jack's plasma and began devouring the delicious pizza. He remembered the dream about April he had weeks before: alone in his bedroom, the movies and then, the exhilaration. They began watching West Side Story, Jack explaining to April about the two rival gangs. The White gang, called the Jets, and the Latino gang, called the Sharks. It was a love story set in New York, about the leader of the Jets falling in love with the sister of the leader of the Sharks. Fights broke out, Tony got killed, end of love story. They sat together, enjoying the movie and when it was over, still half the pizza remained. Jack picked up the pizza to take it downstairs to the kitchen. "April, you want another Coke?"

"Okay. Can I use the bathroom up here?"

"Sure. I'll be right back."

***

Jack left and April powdered her nose and other parts. But when Jack returned, he stood in the middle of his room holding two Cokes looking for April. He looked over to the bathroom, the door was wide open and no sign of April.

"I'm over here, silly."

There, laying under the covers of his bed, April waved him to join her. He was caught off guard. His first reaction was that they still had another movie to watch, but he realized that was a stupid thought. Why waste time watching a movie when they both knew that having sex that night was automatic. He dimmed the lights while undressing, and joined April. They kissed and fondled each other, exploring their bodies and kept the small talk to a minimum. Suddenly, April moved her body on top of Jack, still kissing his lips, then his neck, then slowly maneuvering her way south. She was certainly not a novice like Jack was. All he kept thinking about was April's ingenious abilities and not about the pleasure he was experiencing. How did she ever learn to do that, and with who? The sensation accelerating through his loins became uncontrollable. He tried to hold it back, grunting and keeping his eyes shut, but it was no use, the volcano erupted. He opened his eyes to see how April reacted to his inexcusable mishap. As he watched, she kept to her business, never missing a beat. He was shocked. Knowing her for a very short time, and even less time to get her into his bed, his girlfriend was quite a surprise. A veteran at the age of eighteen, capable of handling any sexual pleasures as well as… his mother, Emily?

April finished her business and rolled over on her back and pulled Jack toward her.

"Your turn, lover. Give me all you got."

It was time for Jack to step up to the plate. Hit a home run just as April did. It would be his first time to have intercourse with a female. He mounted her with his legs inside her thighs, ready to enter her hot, awaiting body.

"Jack, you have condoms, don't you?"

"Huh? No, I, ahh."

"Get off, wait." She slipped out from under the covers and retrieved her purse. She removed a package of Trojans and handed them to him.

"We have to practice safe sex, Jack, right?"

"Of course."

He opened the package, applied the condom, and resumed his position on top of her. He was working up a sweat, trying to imitate the professionalism that she had. He listened to her moan, to her heavy breathing, and to her asking him to stop. But every time he stopped, she cursed him and told him to keep going, faster and harder. It seemed like an eternity to him, but the escapade eventually came to an end. Jack was totally exhausted and just rolled off April, who laid motionless, not saying a word.

"Where did you learn how to do that, Jack?" Jack froze. *Where did YOU learn how to do that?*

He wondered where that question came from. Of all people to ask that, April should know better. A blow job, condoms, several positions, what was next?

"All natural talent."

"You did this before, didn't you?"

Jack remained silent. What about her? Certainly, she had, and with whom? How many lovers had she had? To keep from getting into an argument, Jack kept quiet.

April crawled out from the covers and walked to the bathroom, not bothering to cover herself up. He watched her standing in the light, her breasts fully exposed and full of beauty. She washed off her private area…well, not very private anymore because it now belonged to Jack, anytime he wanted it. What kind of past led her to be so adequate, so knowledgeable, so bold, taking control of everything? It was amazing to him. When she returned to the bed, she sat on the edge and took something from her purse. He couldn't see, still overwhelmed by the entire ordeal, Jack just laid motionless, staring at the ceiling. Was she lighting up a cigarette? He didn't see any smoke nor did he smell the odor, but she was doing something. She took a long sniff, then tilted her head back, taking a deep breath.

"Are you catching a cold?" Jack heard her sniff, thinking she was blowing her nose.

"I'm reaching another orgasm."

He still didn't understand what she was talking about. He got closer, looked over her shoulder and saw a small, plastic bag. Its contents contained a small lump of white powder. He was stunned, shocked. He jumped from the bed, yelling at her.

"Jesus Christ. You gotta be kidding me. You're on dope?"

"Relax, Jack."

"No, I ain't gonna relax. Not that shit in my house. I can't believe you're on drugs. How long have you been doing that? Who got you hooked on it?"

She sat up and started to get dressed.

"Answer me, April. How long have you been taking drugs?"

"Just take me home, Jack." April snarled.

How he had fooled himself thinking she was the all-American girl living next door. His high hopes were shattered and gone. It was over just as fast as it started. After they got into the Jeep, neither said a single word between them the entire trip to April's house. As soon as he pulled into the driveway, she had the door open. She jumped out, slamming the door so hard that a small crack appeared in the glass.

"That's it! We're finished." Jack said as he burned rubber from the driveway.

***

Loud chatter and giggling from downstairs awoke Jack.

Obviously, they were home and clearly both had to much to drink. He remained in bed, waiting for the noise to stop, then he would call Aaron and begin their assault on Sergio's black beauty. He glanced at the clock radio—3:18 am. Jack remained awake, at 4:05, all was still and quiet throughout the house. He got out of bed, moved to the front window and saw the vehicle parked along the curb, conscious that Sergio was spending the night. He was confident both were fast asleep., so he picked up his cell and dialed Aaron's number. It rang and rang till Aaron's voice mail answered.

Wake up. Where is he? Jack waited five minutes and redialed the number. The same result.

Dammit. I'll do it myself. I'll fix that bastard.

He got dressed and slipped his hunting knife into his back pocket. Silently he descended the stairs and went out the kitchen door. The night was as dark as black paint, only the dim light from a streetlight on the opposite side of the cul-de-sac reflected off Sergio's car. Jack sliced the first expensive tire. Whoosh… He could hear the air escaping. He chuckled and moved on to the next tire. Whoosh… The car sank from the escaping air. Cautiously, he stood and searched the area around him, not a sole in sight. The air was still and the night even calmer. With the knife in his right hand, he gouged a long, deep scratch along the driver-side door. Without warning, bells and sirens bellowed through the still night. Jack had forgot about the security system built into Corvettes. It was so loud, so blaring that he got scared and began to run. He panicked and turned, but never saw the fire hydrant in front of him. He hit it hard and fell to the ground, injuring his knee. While laying on the ground and trying to get to his feet, he felt an agonizing blow to his rib section.

"You little fucker. That'll teach you to mess with my car." Sergio kept on kicking.

Jack tried to get away. He rolled over and struggled to get to his feet. Another shot, this time, a crushing blow to the side of his head. He staggered and stumbled another five or six feet until he hit the ground.

"I'll kill you. You're gonna pay for this." Sergio kicked the helpless body again. When Emily arrived, she grabbed Sergio around the waist, pulling him back.

"Sergio. What are you doing? You're gonna kill him." Emily bent down to help the wounded youngster. Then she saw his face.

"Jack!" She took off her robe to wipe the blood dripping from Jack's nose.

"That little son-of-a-bitch. Look what he did. He's gonna pay for this, you hear me?"

"Leave us alone! You didn't have to hit him so hard. You almost killed him."

"Serves him right. No one fucks with Sergio or my Vette."

She helped Jack limp into the house. She sat him at the kitchen table and wiped the stained blood from his face. The bleeding had stopped, but she noticed blood on his torn jeans near his knee. There appeared a small cut and a deep bruise.

"Do you want me to call for an ambulance?"

"No. I'm okay. Just my ribs hurt."

She helped him to the stairs and slowly into his bed.

"Take these aspirin. They'll relieve some of the pain. Now, try to get some sleep. We'll see how you're feeling in the morning. If you're still hurting, I'm going to take you to the hospital."

Jack said nothing. He closed his eyes, grimacing as his painful body sank into his bed.

***

When Emily awoke the next morning, her bed was empty. Sergio was gone. She never heard him leave, but she didn't care. For months, she sensed that their relationship was slipping away and the altercation with Jack inevitably sealed it.

The pain in Jack's side was still as sharp as when Sergio first kicked him. He thought his ribs were broken. He sat up in bed, rubbing the area, trying to get the pain to subside, but when he stood up, the pain lessened. He walked around his room and sure enough, the pain eased considerably. It wasn't a broken rib after all, just a deep bruise. He shuffled to his desk and opened the computer. Would there be another email from Stardom Studios? He hoped not. Unfortunately, there it was, yet another email.

The caption read, "Congratulations!"

What? The word congratulations caught Jack's full attention. He opened the email immediately and began reading: "Congratulations, Jack. We carefully read through your application and thought it was exactly what we are looking for. Enclosed is a voucher that you can download and print out. Two tickets on Sunset Airlines, redeemable whenever you're available to travel to our studios. I encourage you, the sooner you book your reservation, the better your odds of being selected on Extreme Realities. So, start your adventure now. Email us back with your reservation date and time. Again, good luck to you, and we hope to see you soon." Signed Dan Mesa, Director of Talent Evaluation.

Holy shit. It happened. Jack was so excited he immediately went to the Sunset Airlines website and began looking for the earliest flights to Los Angeles.

Luckily for him, the Thanksgiving vacation at school was only two weeks away. He'd have five days off from school and plenty of time to spend in LA. But, two tickets? Who would he take with him? Never mind, he'd decide that later. Right now, he'd book his flight.

Chapter 48

Two Tickets To Paradise

It was the start of a new month, November. Konrad and Fritz compiled a series of questions they wanted to ask Emily Collier, but Emily lived out of their jurisdiction. They had to obtain permission from Manford Sheriff Joe Cutter to interrogate her. At first, Cutter hesitated with the go-ahead, he wanted more substantial grounds about why, when, and how come. Cutter was an old fart, sticky in his ways, who should've retired years earlier. He loved the town of Manford and all the residents who stood behind him for nearly 33 years. He knew Emily when she was a young child, even babysat his kids, so it became a delicate situation for him. Should he contact Emily and let her know the detectives wanted to talk to her? He knew all about police work and formality prevailed. He'd stay out of their way and let the detectives handle their business.

His phone rang on his desk. "Mike Konrad."

"This is Joe Cutter, sheriff in Manford. Well, you big shots got your way. I got a call from the Illinois FBI concerning Emily Collier. You may come down and speak to her. We'll play your games."

"Excuse me, Sheriff Cutter, but this is not a game. There have been two homicides and two individuals who we are on the run. All we want to do is ask her a few questions. It won't take long, I assure you. In fact, you may sit in while we question her."

"Very well. Do you know what day you'll be arriving?"

"Tomorrow. The sooner the better. When we get there, we'll talk to you and fill you in with all the details regarding this investigation. Then you'll understand."

"All right. I'll see you then. Goodbye."

Fritz and Mike collected their materials and moved to a small conference room adjoining their offices. Here they would double-check their questions, review their strategy, and hope the trip to Manford would be opportunistic.

***

After Jack read the good news from Stardom Studios, he launched his printer into action. He downloaded the voucher from Sunset Airlines and printed out the tickets for the flight. All he had to do was figure out what day and what time he wanted to leave. He sat back and thought about it. What could go wrong? He would fly out there, proceed with the interview, and after it was finished, spend the following days looking at some college campuses. A piece of cake—and it was all free. He gingerly hopped to the table near his bed and entered Aaron's number.

"I thought you were going to call me last night?"

"I did, you stupid nerd. All I got was your voice mail."

"Really? I had it sitting next to my pillow. It never rang," Aaron replied. "What's up?"

"Because you never answered your phone, I got the shit kicked out of me."

Aaron started laughing. "No way. How'd that happen?"

"I flattened two of his tires and when I began gouging his front door, the sirens and alarms went off. Scared the crap out of me. When I started to run, I fell over the fire hydrant. I hit the ground hard and when I started to get up…Wham!! The asshole kicked me in the ribs. Hurt like hell. Then he kicked me behind my right ear."

"Holy crap. He caught you! How'd he get out there so fast?"

"I don't know. Thank God, Emily came out and stopped him or I might be lying in the hospital or a morgue right now."

"Hey, man. I'm sorry. You know I would've been there for ya."

"Yeah, its over. He went back to the city. Emily was really pissed off at him, so I hope he never comes back here again."

"Well, you fixed him. You got his baby."

"And by the way. You remember that reality show I mentioned to you awhile back, Extreme Realities? The one that kept sending me emails every week?"

"Yeah. I remember you mentioning that."

"Guess what. They want to interview me. Sent me a voucher for two tickets to fly out there. You wanna go with me?"

"Whoa. To LA.?"

"Yep. I'm thinking around the Thanksgiving break. We'll have most of the weekend to goof off. Maybe look at some college campuses. What do you think?"

"Awesome. But I better ask my parents first."

"Okay. Do that. Then let me know as soon as possible. I gotta book us a flight."

Jack ended the call and hobbled down the stairs to the kitchen. Emily was there, ready to take his breakfast order.

"How do you feel this morning?"

"Sore. Sorry I got you into this. But, that's what he gets for spitting on my Jeep."

"Jack, that was very wrong. Even if he spat on your car, damaging his car was revenge. Revenge is not the proper way to handle a situation like that."

Jack decided to say nothing. Maybe she was right. What he did was wrong, but Sergio was wrong and he started it.

"You want bacon and eggs?"

"Yeah, I'm starving. Mom, I might be going to California over the Thanksgiving break."

"For what?"

"For weeks, I've been getting emails from this studio company in LA. Some reality show and they're looking for contestants. So, I finally filled out an application a couple days back. Yesterday, they emailed me back wanting to interview me. Even sent two airline tickets."

"Jack. Hold on a minute. Why didn't you tell me about this sooner, these emails? What studio?"

"Stardom Studios. A couple of weeks ago, I accidentally ran into a guy at Denny's. Then, later that afternoon, this same guy came into Dick's and bought a pair of shoes. He gave me his business card, saying he was from Stardom Studios."

Emily was stunned. What was Dan up to now and why her son? Now, it started to make sense her, him showing up in Manford and that face, she remembered. Emily was trying to put two and two together, was Dan Mesa really Dennis Reading?

"Can I go?"

"Let me think about it, okay?"

"Did you know this guy from Stardom Studios? I found his card lying on the kitchen floor."

"No. Not anyone from California."

LIE !

"How did his card get into the house?"

She couldn't fool Jack. She should've told him about the accident in the Mall parking lot the day it happened. It was Dan Mesa who hit her. That's how the card got into the house. He gave her his card because of the accident.

"Oh, wait! He was the guy who hit my car at the mall. Yes, oh…what was his name? He gave me his business card. It must have fallen from my coat pocket." What an act she put on. *Was he buying it?*

Jack finished his breakfast, not believing a word Emily was telling him. She was full of lies because he was here in their house, sleeping with her.

Chapter

In His Own Prison

"Hey, Mike. Got some real good news for ya." A patrol cop walked into Mike's office, carrying papers, ready to hand them over. "You remember that BOLO you put out last week? The one regarding the Chevy Silverado with Hillbilly plates.?"

"Yeah, what's up?"

"They found it this morning, in of all places, Covington. And guess who was driving it?"

"No shit. William Hill?"

"You got it. They're on their way here right now."

Mike couldn't have heard better news. Another solid lead. He contacted Fritz and told him to meet him in the interrogation room where they could begin questioning the person that murdered Alice Oliver.

There he was, sitting alone, starring at the two way large window in the room. He was well aware of what was behind that window, he stuck out his tongue and saluted them with his middle finger. This was nothing new to Hill. It was called the "waiting game", sitting for hours, alone with your thoughts, knowing you're being watched from that creepy window. After two hours, Konrad and Fritz entered the interrogation room, Mike sat at the table while Fritz stood reading the Miranda rights to Hill, a quote he has heard often enough.

"You William Hill, or Winslow or Bill Wilson?"

"What the fuck! What do you want from me?" He sat, agitated, fidgeting in his chair, appearing very nervous to the two detectives.

"Relax. We just want to ask you a few questions, that's all."

"You ain't got nuttin' on me. I'm telling you, I didn't do nuttin'. I've been clean as a whistle ever since I left the big house."

"June tenth. You know where you were that morning?"

Konrad pushed three photos in front of his suspect. "Her name is Alice Oliver. You killed her. You probably would've gotten away with this except for one stupid mistake."

The first photo showed the body of Oliver lying on her bed, dead. The second photo revealed the brown pill container on the bedroom floor, the third picture, a close-up of Oliver's bruised neck.

"We got you dead to rights, Hill. Your prints are on the pill container, on the front door and, even on the suitcase. Remember the old man next door? Well, he remembers you, even your license plate. Hllblly. You're being arrested for the murder of Alice Oliver."

Hill just sat still, looking at the floor. He needed a lawyer and fast. He was going back to the big house.

"You wanna make a deal with us? You're looking at life in prison, no parole. Think about it."

Both detectives left the room and locked the door. Hour after hour slowly eased by, letting Hill tussle with his conscience. *This is the torture you get, sitting alone, meditating to yourself...either you start talking or they punish you with silence, contemplating your sanity.*

What kind of deal we're they looking for? Maybe second-degree murder and not first-degree, a chance for parole? If Hill accepted they're deal, it meant exposing Helen.

Did Hill understand the ramifications that would emerge once he accepted the deal. Hours later the door unlocked and the detectives entered.

"We got a lineup ready for you. We brought in the old man who lives next door to Oliver. When he was standing near his mailbox, he got a good look at you and your truck. Let's go."

After the lineup, Hill was brought back to the holding cell and booked for the murder of Oliver. He was read his Miranda Rights, which he has heard numerous times before, and traded his clothes for a bright orange jump suit.

***

The luxurious and tranquil villa had turned into a prison cell for Charles. His left arm has swelled to the size of a baseball bat from the bite that occurred a three weeks ago. He was petrified to leave, fearful that by chance he might encounter one of his stalkers. Was there only one? How many were looking for him? Every time he looked out his kitchen window, he saw someone staring back at him. He couldn't erase the haunting battle within his conscience that every second, every minute, hour of the day, the thought of getting caught, loosing his money and that scare the shit out of him. He was captive to his own paranoia. He had stopped eating, not because of hunger, but because he was trapped in a web of insecurity.

The insect bite on his arm was blistering, getting to the point that he needed a doctor's care. He never noticed a Doctor's office while he was in town and the nearest hospital was back in Liberia. He was caught between a rock and a hard place. He washed the sore every day, hoping it would get better, but it hadn't. Somehow, his infection coincided with his delirious mind. With all the surroundings upon him, being stalked, the money, not eating, all adding up to mass confusion. Simply, Charles could not comprehend what was happening in his life. He paced the floor of the villa day and night, pounding his head against the walls, peeking out the windows and looking for faces that were looking for him. He was alone and scared, with no one there to help him when he desperately needed it.

No doubt in his mind, they wanted the money. What if he should withdraw all his money from the bank? But, how? How much is seven million? One suitcase, two, three? He pounded the table. His frustrations were mounting and the pressure seemed to make the villa shrink. He got up and peeked through the window.

Incredible, now there were two people standing near the main office looking in the direction of his villa. He was trapped and he knew it. But he didn't know who they were.

Early the next morning, Charles looked out the kitchen window and to his surprise, there was no one standing at the main office. He had to get his money and the risk of leaving his villa was a risk he had to take. He dressed in long pants and shirt, wore a baseball cap pulled over his eyes, and dark sunglasses. His mission that morning, drive to the Ocotal Providence Bank and get his money. Cautiously, he walked down the path to his Jeep, and like a hawk, kept his eyes wide open, pinpointing strange incidents or suspicious individuals. Incredibly, when the Jeep breezed past the main office where his stalkers stood watch, he was surprised to see that no one was around. Hurriedly, he pressed down on the accelerator and raced past the office and out to the main highway. Arriving at the bank, he parked the Jeep in the rear parking lot of the bank and surveyed the area. Satisfied that no one was around, he got out of the Jeep and entered the bank. Five minutes after the opening of its doors, he approached the only teller behind the counter. Nervous, he removed his statement book from his back pocket and slid it toward her.

"I want to close out my account."

The teller looked at the computer screen in disbelief. She had never encountered a customer with a balance of million of dollars. "Well, I, ahh..Umm... Excuse me for a minute, I'll be right back."

Charles watched her move to a desk occupied by an elderly man and handed him the statement book. She whispered something, then both looked back to Charles. He removed his glasses, stood up, and approached Charles.

"Mr. Collier, I am the bank manager. Do you have any identification? A passport?" Charles handed it to the gentleman.

"Yes. Well, Mr. Collier. We don't have that large amount on hand at our bank."

"What do you mean. Where's my money?"

"It's not that simple. Yes, your statement proves you have that amount, but realistically, that is just a figure."

"I had that money transferred from Switzerland. Did it come by mail, or FedEx? It must be here. They told me they sent it." Making a statement like that proved how delusional Charles had become.

The banker stared at him. Was he serious? Any idiot would know that banks float their capital. All banks provide clients with credit statements verifying their investment, but smaller banks never have that large amount of money available instantly.

"Well. It would take us several days to…"

"Listen, I want it now. It's here, and I want it now!"

"You must understand how the banking system operates, Mr. Collier."

Charles's brain could not comprehend what the manager was trying to explain. He had spent more than sixteen years in the same capacity as the manager, but confusion dealt the cards. Unable to understand the ordeal, he was losing it and creating a scene in the bank lobby. To avoid any more disturbance, the manager clutched Charles's arm and escorted him to his office and closed the door.

"Please, Mr. Collier, we will get you your money. But it will take us a few days. You must understand that."

"Well, all right. I'll be back on Friday."

"Fine. We will call you as soon as it arrives."

"No, you can't. I don't have a phone."

"Very well. You come back here on Friday."

Charles rushed out the bank's doors and cautiously drove across the road to the drug store. The store was empty even the pharmacy was closed, so no chance of talking to a doctor about his infection. He wanted to get back to the villa as quickly as possible. If they were following him, they'd know Charles was gone and would invade the villa and ram shack it. He didn't have time to stop and see a doctor, nor did he know where a doctor was. What he needed was something to treat the infection on his arm. He found a bottle of antiseptic, paid for it, and left. When he approached the villa office, he saw the same small black car parked in front of the office. He slowed down as he passed, nobody was sitting in the car. The license number on the back of the car, 56W6767, the same license that belonged to that beautiful girl. What's going on? Out of nowhere, two men emerged and began walking toward Charles. He stomped on the gas, screeching the tires, speeding up the hill. He was positively sure his money was in extreme jeopardy, why else would they be here? He bolted from his Jeep into the villa, locking the door behind him. His heart pounding through his chest, he stood near the door, looking out the window to see if anyone was behind him, but saw nothing. The only thing he contemplated, was he safe in his own prison? He moved to the kitchen table and sat down. His fears were mounting in a wild rate of speed, fearing that his villa was under attack, Charles had no time to shop for food. He hadn't eaten anything for days because of his fear. Knowing he had to get food into his stomach, he got up to see what was in the small refrigerator. It was empty, except for a pint of milk. He took a swallow, then spit out the milk, it was sour. He had nothing to eat and nothing to drink, except water. The pain caused a loss of energy in Charles's body, weak, he struggled to the living room sofa and collapsed. He had to do something, but he couldn't comprehend how many days until Friday. He began scratching his arm. Where was the antiseptic he bought? It was where he left it, on the front seat of the Jeep. Charles couldn't hold back the tears.

***

Early on Thursday morning, Detective Konrad and Fritz met at the Third Precinct office to gather their materials. It was D-day for Emily. The two detectives were on their way to Manford to interrogate their target hoping Emily had some answers for them. As Konrad drove, Fritz entered Emily's address into the GPS directing them to the correct location. They parked the squad car along the curb of the cul-de-sac, dismounted the squad and approached Emily's house. Mike rang the doorbell and seconds later Emily Collier, or was it Emily Dearborn, came to the door. Their unexpected appearance caught her off guard.

"Good morning, Mrs. Collier, or is it Dearborn? Nice to see you again."

"What is it now? You're a long way from home, aren't you?" She debated whether to let the officers in, or tell them to see her lawyer. Obviously, they knew something. They knew Charles was gone and they knew her maiden name. So, why are they standing at her front door?

"We have a few questions that we need answers to. May we come in?"

If she let them in, she'd have to answer their questions. If she slammed the door, it would only get worse. They'd be back and not so friendly. Reluctantly, she gave in and let them enter the house.

"Would you care for a cup of coffee, officers?"

They took off their coats and sat at the kitchen table. "Yes, a hot cup of coffee sounds good right now."

Mike looked around, wishful of finding a clue, anything Emily left carelessly laying around. A slip-up by Emily, maybe a letter from Charles, or a post card, something that would make this trip worthwhile. She set a cup in front of each officer and stood, leaning against the kitchen counter, her arms folded across her chest.

"Well, what questions do you have for me?"

"When Charles left for Mexico, what company hired him?"

Jesus Christ. I should've never opened the front door. I'm screwed. What kind of answer could she pull from the rabbit's hat now?

"Gosh. He told me, but since our divorce, I think it was a company from New York."

"It was Cozumel, Mexico, correct?"

"Yes, I believe so."

They pounded away at her. Each of her lies compounded each previous lie. She watched as Detective Fritz wrote down every answer she gave. She knew that later on, her answers would come back to haunt her. What else could she do? Tell them exactly where Charles was?

"Did you know Dennis Reading? Helen Kruger? Alice Oliver?"

"Yes. I knew all of them, not personally, but through Charles. I never met Dennis Reading or Helen—whatever was her name. Alice was the secretary at Priority, and I would see and talk to her on occasion."

"Did Charles ever discuss with you about the relationship between William Fossett and Helen Kruger?"

"Charles had mentioned that the two of them were bitter enemies. She was the talk around the water coolers. He told me several times that she would storm into the office and race to William's office, screaming and throwing things at him. It was a good laugh among the employees."

"Did Charles ever mention the financial troubles that William had? That he extorted nearly seven million from Priority's clients?"

Her heart sank. She felt like fainting, or more like throwing up. They knew about the money and possibly, that was the reason Charles fled to Mexico. The detectives must know everything. For Emily, she was like a ship at sea, with all its sails up, helpless, not a breath of wind blowing, just sitting dead in the water.

"Umm. No. Charles left his work at the office. He never brought it home." This was her last lie.

They all became quiet. Fritz stared at the table. Then he noticed a card lying near the ashtray. When Emily picked up the empty cups and moved to the sink, he snatched up the card and looked at it briefly. He saw the name Dan Mesa, Director of Talent Evaluation, Stardom Studios, Pasadena, California. He also saw the phone number crossed out and another number written in pencil. He wrote the information on his pad and replaced the card.

"Mrs. Collier, you've been very cooperative. I thank you. I have one last question and we won't bother you anymore. The name, Sergio Canasta. Do you know him or ever heard that name before?"

Chapter 50

I'd Die For $7 Million Dollars

It was the week before Thanksgiving break and Jack had his flight booked, his appointments to visit USC, Stanford and UCLA all set up, but his bags were half-packed. He was still waiting to hear from Aaron and hoping his parents will allow him to fly to California with him. Jack was keeping his fingers crossed, because he dreaded going alone. The thought of Aaron's parents ruling out the trip and if that happened, Emily was not a last minute fill-in. He would devise some lame excuse to tell her because if she came, it was to see Mesa and not the colleges Jack had appointments to. His relationship with April had ended. They still remained classmates, but he didn't look her way or ever speak to her. If she wanted drugs in her life, she would have to find other druggies to hang around with. It was fun while it lasted, although after the separation, Aaron informed to him about seeing her with another guy the same night she lied about spending time with her parents in Chicago. Hanging around with Aaron, Terri and other friends was far better than having April seducing him into the drug scene. There would be no more lies, excuses, rejection, and no more sex.

On Wednesday, the last day before the break, Jack was standing beside his locker when Aaron approached him.

"Hey man, I'm sorry, but my parents are saying no. It's a family thing, you know, the holidays? I guess our entire families are gathering at my uncle's house for Thanksgiving dinner." His head was down, talking and not looking at Jack. He was sad and he knew he let his best friend down, but for Aaron, there was no way out of it.

"That's okay. Maybe we'll get another chance when we're in college. Maybe a football game. Who knows."

Aaron hugged Jack. "What time are you leaving on Friday?"

"The flight leaves at 10:15 in the morning. I'm hoping I can go alone. I don't want Emily going with me."

"Why not? You have two free tickets."

"Long story. I just prefer to be by myself."

"Well, I gotta get going. I'll see you when you get back, okay? Have fun and bring me back a USC T-shirt. I like those colors." He punched Jack in the chest, then hustled his way down the hall.

***

Spending the holiday without his Dad caused Jack to lose interest in many things, including his Thanksgiving appetite. Emily hadn't mentioned anything about this year's dinner—if they were eating alone at home or going to a friend's house. It wasn't a holiday to him, after all. He reflected on past Thanksgiving dinners, how Emily got up early, cooked and baked all morning long, for the three of them. He and Charles became couch potatoes, watching football on TV and feasting on turkey sandwiches when they were hungry, relaxing and bonding with his buddy. It will never be the same, Jack thought, not knowing where his Dad was or if he was still okay, he kept his hopes up. Within the past months, his world had turned upside down. But what if… if I win the million dollars on that reality show, my Dad could quit his job, move back here, and we could restart our lives. Yes. He became excited and even more determined to travel to California, determined to winning that grand prize. It would be a dream come true getting his Dad back home.

"Do you want me to drive you and Aaron to the airport?"

"No. We have it all planned out. I'm going to pick up Aaron around seven, go have breakfast and then drive to Midway."

The lie would stop Emily from going. If she didn't find out about Aaron not going, he'd be on his way.

"Before you know it, we'll be back home and back to school."

"I know. Seems like weekend trips just fly by. Are they meeting you at the airport?"

"Yep. I guess we go back to the studio for the interview. After that, Aaron and I are going to look at the college campuses. Our flight on Sunday leaves at 12:30, arriving at Midway around 5:30 in the afternoon."

"Honestly, I feel a whole lot better that Aaron is going with you."

"Gee, look at the time. I still have some packing to do. Should I wake you up in the morning before I leave?"

"You better, or I'll change the locks on the house and you won't be able to get back in."

"Night."

"Night, Jack."

***

The music blasted from the radio at his bedside. Time to get up and get going. For a few seconds, he wondered whether he was doing the right thing. Winning the million dollars and having his Dad back home, no doubt about it. With all that was happening to him lately—his break-up with April, the fight with Sergio, no communication from his Dad—this was a great time to get out of Manford. He was going to be the next million-dollar winner on Extreme Reality.

He scrambled out of bed, showered, and dressed. His bags were packed, including his duffle bag containing his camera, toiletries, notebook, and other small necessities. He took one last look around the room, making sure he had everything he needed and then went downstairs. The house was quiet and Emily was still sleeping. Quiet as he could be, he picked up his luggage and duffle bag, opened the back door and made his way to the Jeep. The trip from Manford to Midway was approximately an hour drive. He drove the Jeep into the over night parking lot, wrote down the location so he'd remember where he parked the Jeep and proceeded inside the terminal. He was two hours early before his scheduled flight would depart, but checking his bag, scrambling through security, he'd have enough time to stop for breakfast.

He boarded the plane, located his assigned seat and buckled himself in. He was thinking how cool it would be, selected to participate on the reality show, even to come out the winner. The flight went quickly. He had a small lunch, a couple of Cokes, and before he knew it, the plane landed. He gathered his baggage and followed everyone else off the plane to the lobby, where he noticed a man holding a printed sign reading "Collier". That was the man. How could he forget that face?

"Mr. Mesa?"

"Well, you made it. Excellent. I have a limo waiting. Follow me."

They dodged the rushing crowds of people until they reached the waiting limo. How fancy, Jack thought, first class accommodations. During the ride, Jack felt uneasy in the presence of Dan Mesa. How could he accept being in his presence of a man that was having relations with his mother? It was an eerie, an awkward position, but Jack remained silent, taking in the scenery of warm California through his limo window.

"So. This is your first trip to California?"

"Yes. Although I might come out next summer. I want to go to college here. Maybe USC or UCLA."

"Is that right. Studying what?"

"I'm interested in computer animation or computer graphics. My dream is to work in the movie industry."

"Well, this is definitely the place. When we get to the studio, you'll get a first-hand look how the industry works. Lots of people doing lots of jobs. How old are you, Jack?"

"I'm eighteen now, but I'll be nineteen in June."

"Let me explain a little about the show. We've sent out twenty-five interview appointments, fourteen males and eleven females.

Over the next four weeks, we'll conclude our search and only ten will be selected for the show. If you're selected, you'll have to sign a contract. Since you're only eighteen now, we'll need the signature of both your parents."

"Wow. My mother can sign, but my father is working in Mexico.".

"Ohh. Well, maybe we can work around that."

They talked until the limo stopped in front of Casa Truman Apts. "C'mon in for a second. I forgot your application on my desk. You can grab a Coke and we'll be off again."

Jack stepped out of the limo and walked behind Dan. Suddenly, the limo sped away.

"Mr. Mesa, the limo is leaving."

"That's okay. Andrae was low on gas. He's going to fill the tank and come right back."

***

He opened the door and they walked inside.

"Sit down, Jack." He removed a Coke from the fridge and poured it into a glass cup, "I'll go get your application."

Helen was waiting in the spare bedroom, watching what was going on. Dan entered and whispered to her.

"One minute and he'll be out like a light."

Minutes later, Jack dropped the Coke and his entire body went limp. They dragged him into the spare bedroom, sat him down and tied his hands and feet to the chair. Dan checked the knots, pulling in one direction then another. He was satisfied that even Houdini couldn't escape this ambush. He took a roll of duct tape from the paper bag and strapped the tape around Jack's mouth. "There. He's not going anywhere."

"You still have Emily's number on your phone, right?"

"I got it. We'll let him sit here overnight. Then I'll call her and break the news. She'll have no other choice. She'll have to contact Charles and tell him we've kidnapped his son. A simple ransom, they give us the money, we give them back their kid." Dan was rubbing his hands together like Satan himself.

***

Since the move to Costa Rica, time had been unlimited for Charles. There were no schedules, no appointments, no deadlines. Just endless time to experience anything Costa Rica offered to him. Whenever he woke up, he would hop into the Jeep and drive in any direction just to get lost, enjoy the scenery and points of interest. But not now. He lay in his bed in the dark villa with the pain in his stomach matching the pain in his left arm. A string of sweat beaded slowly down the temples of his painful face. A fever had developed and not an ounce of strength to fight it. He barely had enough strength to roll over and turn on the lamp on the night table. On the table was the bottle of antiseptic. He doused the infected swollen arm with the remaining fluid from the antiseptic bottle and began scratching the sore, but the more he scratched, the more it bled. He cursed, angry with himself for not seeing a doctor, much less listening to Emily's advice, taking the money, and leaving the country. There were always the "why" questions that Charles struggled to unravel. Why, why did it have to go on like this? Why did he go to the park that day he got bit?

When the bedroom became brighter, a new day had begun, but for Charles, now it was a struggle to stay alive. Even breathing was a struggle. All he could do was lie in bed, with nowhere to go and nothing to do. He lay motionless, his eyes scanning the room until he saw the Devil, in the form of two black backpacks sitting on the floor where he dropped them. Evil backpacks filled with eternal happiness, daring Charles confront them. The seven million, the useless seven million that he'd never get the chance to enjoy or even spend a penny of. Those black bags were his ticket to happiness, to how he would enjoy the rest of his life—rich and back with his son. He knew he was close to dying and it didn't matter what he thought, because his mind couldn't comprehend right from wrong. He thought about Jack. His only son that he loved so dearly. He shook his head and began to cry. He was realizing the truth about his monumental mistake to let greed replace the importance of his family.

Jack didn't deserve this. He reflected on times spent with him. Remembering the day he was born, his passion for baseball, and all the Harry Potter movies. Charles smiled. When he decided to take the money, he thought it was the best for his family and how their lives would change. They'd be one big happy family. It changed all right, instead, it was an 180 degree turn around. He was a recluse, hiding in obscurity and siding with the Devil. He took a gamble when bringing the Devil into his world and destroyed everything he worked so hard for. It was no use to him now. He had to find a way to get rid of the Devil.

With his last dying ounce of strength left in his body, he labored out of bed and wavered to his laptop on the kitchen table. He began to send an email to Jack.

> Son: I miss you so much. I've committed an awful crime and wish every day that it never happened. Costa Rica. Villa del Rico. Villa 16. Under the back deck. I hope you'll understand. I'm so sorry.
>
> Love, Dad.

He sent the email then erased it from the computer's memory. He was distraught, slamming the cover of the laptop, causing it to slide off the table and crashing to the floor. He sat silent, then rose and staggered through the kitchen to the sliding glass doors leading to the deck. Cautiously, he approached the railing, looked down and viewed the thick foliage growing beneath the deck. This was where he would kill the Devil. He strained to walk back to his bedroom and, one by one, he picked up each backpack and dropped it over the deck railing, watching each bag disappear into the stomach of the overflowing plants. It was over. No matter how much money Charles had, it was no use to him anymore. It all belonged to Jack now.

Drips of blood steadily oozed from the blistered sore on his arm. He was paralyzed, not coherent of the situation, watching his life drip to the deck floor. Each drop robbing away a minute of his life. He became dizzy. He turned and shuffled into the kitchen, his eyes blurred with fever, his hands grabbing anything for support. Suddenly, he clutched his chest. His body crashed to the kitchen floor, slamming his face hard into the ceramic tiles, his head bounced. His body laid motionless, no more birthdays, no more holiday celebrations, no more seeing his beloved son, Jack. The life of a millionaire, basking in the tropical sun, sucking down margaritas, that life was over. You don't bargain with the Devil, Charles.

***

Emily peered out her living room window, watching Sunday come to an end and impatiently waiting for a call from Jack. She was really mad at him. He had told her he would call as soon as they landed in LA. Three days later, she had not heard from him. Where did she go wrong? Why was her relationship with Jack so empty? Was it Charles's absence, or her promiscuity with Sergio, or Dan, or maybe everything combined?

Another glance at the Grandfather clock—7:30 pm. She kept her eyes glued to the end of her driveway, impatiently expecting the Jeep to arrive. Hour after hour the continuous chimes from the Grandfather clock told Emily something was wrong. She called his cell phone every hour, still drawing a blank. It was almost 10:00 pm., without a peep from Jack or Aaron. She couldn't wait any longer and made the call to Aaron's parents.

"Mr. Webber, this is Emily, Jack's mother. I'm sorry for calling you at this hour, but has Aaron got back from California yet?"

"Gosh, Emily. I thought you knew. Aaron never went with Jack. We were out of town over the Thanksgiving holiday."

"What? Aaron didn't go? Jack went by himself?"

"I guess. Aaron was with us all weekend. Is there something wrong?"

"The flight was scheduled to land in Chicago at 5:30. It's five hours later and I haven't heard from him. I've tried calling him numerous times, but he doesn't answer. I'm really getting worried."

"Did you call the airlines? Maybe their flight was delayed somehow."

"No, I haven't done that. I'll do that now. But, if you hear anything, please call me right away, okay?"

"I sure will. Goodnight."

When the airline representative answered, Emily asked, "How do I go about finding out which flight my son was on today?"

"I can help you. What is your son's name and where was he departing from?"

"Jack Collier, and he left from Los Angeles to Chicago."

"Thank you. One moment, please."

Emily tried to be patient, sipping her coffee and tapping her fingers on the counter.

"Thank you for waiting. From the information I'm seeing, Jack Collier was scheduled to board Sunset Airlines, flight 665 at 11:35 am. from LAX and arrive at Midway airport in Chicago at approximately 5:40 pm. According to the information, there was no Jack Collier on that flight. And, as I check more on Mr. Collier, I don't see any upcoming flights booking him. It's quite possible he missed his flight and boarded another airline."

"Are you sure?"

"Well, you might try to contact Midway and find out what airlines fly to LA. on Sunday."

"Well, I guess that's what I'll do. Thank you, so much."

No sooner had Emily set her phone down when it began to ring. Anticipating she would hear Jack's voice, she panicked when she heard a man's voice instead.

"Emily. This is Dan Mesa. You remember me?"

"Yes, Dan. Is Jack with you?"

"Your son is still here in Pasadena, but unfortunately, he's tied up right now."

"When is he coming home?"

"As soon as the seven million is in my hands."

"What in the world are you talking about, Dan?"

"Smarten up, lady. Did you really think your son was going to win a million bucks on some remote reality show? There is no Stardom Studios and no million-dollar jackpot.

You want him? Then fork over the money. Call your vacationing ex and make sure he understands the situation. No money, no more Jack." The call ended.

Emily collapsed in the kitchen chair, her uncontrollable tears streaming. Was this what she expected if their plan went haywire? The money was supposed to bring happiness, fun, excitement and all the good things. Instead, all it brought was trouble, disappointment, grief and pain.

Dan, whom she thought she loved, has kidnapped her son, holding him for ransom. The call sent Emily into a frenzy. Her brain was in fast forward and thinking that Charles must be notified on what was going on immediately. It seemed like eternity since they last talked, but the money was gone from the Swiss account and all Emily knew about Costa Rica was that Charles landed in Liberia, moved to a villa near the ocean, and when he called, most of the conversations involved Jack. From that point on, he could be anywhere in that country. She paced the living room floor, racking her brain and trying to remember anything Charles said about living in Costa Rica. She knew the villa wasn't far from Liberia, but there were numerous resorts near the ocean. She couldn't remember the name of the villa because nothing was written down. All at once she remembered that Charles gave her the number of a pay phone at the resort where he was staying. She ran to her computer desk looking for the number she wrote down. *Oh, where the hell did I put it? Jesus. Where is it?* She turned over the laptop and there it was, right where she put it. A small piece of paper taped to the bottom of the laptop. She ripped it off and dashed to her cell phone to call the number. She dialed the number, it rang and rang and rang, there was no answer. What time was it in Costa Rica? She didn't have a clue, but time was valuable. She waited a few minutes and dialed it again. Still no answer. For the next hour, she repeated the calls and never got through. Thinking of the time differential, it was possible that the resort office was closed. Her only alternative was waiting until morning to call. The next morning, Emily brewed a cup of coffee and made her way to the kitchen table. She dialed the number.

"Villa del Rico."

"I'm trying to locate my husband, Charles Collier."

"Oh, well, I'm just a caretaker here, but let me get the manager. Hold on."

"Why, yes. Mr. Collier has been here for several months."

"Yes, I know. But you see our son was involved in a car accident. I need to speak to him as quickly as possible."

"Oh, my gosh! I'll call Carlos and have him get Mr. Collier. Please hold."

"Thank you, but hurry."

Emily waited for some time. "I'm sorry, but Mr. Collier is not answering his door. In fact, I can't recall the last time I've seen him."

"Can't you open the door yourself and see if he's there? Maybe he was asleep."

"I'll tell you what, leave me your number and I'll call you as soon as Mr. Collier appears. Is that all right with you?"

"I suppose, but please hurry. This is a matter of life and death."

"I understand. I'll go with Carlos myself."

She pushed her cell away. She'd found him, but was not sure that Charles would want to talk to her. Why hadn't he been in contact with her, and with his son? What was Charles up to? She got up and poured another cup of coffee, pacing the kitchen floor, not taking her eyes off her cell phone.

C'mon, ring, damn it.

She could do nothing but wait for the phone to ring. Then it did.

"Hello."

"Emily. It's me again. Your long lost lover."

Emily said nothing. What could she say? That there never was any money? That Charles was actually in Mexico working for the Kaiser Foundation?

"Your time is running out. So is our patience. Did you contact Charles?"

"Listen. I do not know where Charles is. Costa Rica is a very big country, Dan. I haven't spoke to Charles in several weeks. You can ask Jack. In fact, the money isn't in Switzerland anymore, Charles took care of that. I can't help you. Let Jack go, you understand me?"

"This will be the last time I spell it out to you, bitch. If you ever want to see your son alive again, deliver the money. And stay away from the cops."

The phone went dead.

This could not be happening. Why, why, why?

Her cell phone rang again. She stared at it, then opened it.

"Mrs. Collier? Ricardo from Villa del Rico."

"Oh, yes. Did you find him?"

There was a pause before Ricardo responded. "I'm very sorry to inform you that we found Mr. Collier dead, lying on the kitchen floor. We have called for the police."

Chapter 51

Kidnapped…Did You Say Kidnapped

What the hell happened? Emily picked herself up off the kitchen floor, both hands clasped to her head, trying to recall what happened before she fainted. Her cell phone, still open, was lying on the floor under the table. Then she remembered the call from Villa del Rico and the news about Charles's death. What was she to do now? The body of her ex-husband lay thousands of miles away, seven million dollars lost in a foreign country, and if that was not enough, her son had been kidnapped in California. Frantic, she was at the end of her rope. She knew she needed help, but who was around to help her? Forget about calling Sergio? Call Dan and explain to him that Charles was dead in Costa Rica without leaving a clue to where the money was? What about Mike Konrad, the police officer investigating the death of William Fossett? She sat shaking her head, holding back the tears, thinking how big a hole she had to climb out of, desperately seeking help.

She picked up her cell again. The phone number from Villa del Rico remained printed on her screen. Emily wanted to know how and when it happened.

Ricardo answered the call and apologized to Emily about the tragedy.

"What happened to him? How…how…did he die?"

"I do not know. Perhaps the inspector would know."

"What now? Was he shot?"

"Mrs. Collier, I'd better let the police contact you so they can explain what needs to be done, okay? I wouldn't want to mislead you in any way. The police are on their way. I will have them call you shortly."

"Very well. I'll wait for their call."

What about the money, where was it now? The last time she knew was a week or so ago, when she opened the Swiss account, the money was there. As quickly as she could, Emily opened her computer and the Clairden Leu page. It was gone, the money is not in Switzerland anymore. What did Charles do now? He was the only person that had the answer, but now he's dead. Would the answer be dead, too?

Emily dropped her lifeless body on the sofa, disbelieving how a simple fete, obtaining the money has become a complicated, botched, mayhem, chaos problem all rolled into one. She needed a smoke. She reached across the side table for her purse, removed the pack of smokes and lit one up. She sat, contemplating what could happen next. Would Detective Konrad be knocking on her door, arresting her for stealing the money? Her cell began ringing, scaring the crap out of her, she answered the call.

"Mrs. Collier. I am Manuel Martinez, Chief Inspector of the Ocotal Police Agency."

"Yes, inspector. My husband, what on earth happened there?"

"Unfortunately, we'll have to wait for the coroner. The body has been dead for several days. Sooner or later, someone will have to make an appearance to identify the body and also collect his personal belongings. Can you do that?"

"I suppose. How soon do I have to do that?"

"Whenever you can. The body will remain at the morgue. We understand the circumstances. I will give you my number. Call me as soon as you know."

"Thank you."

***

Aaron was upstairs in his bedroom watching Sunday Night Football when he yawned and rubbed his eyes. It was a bit after nine pm. and he hadn't heard from Jack yet. His scheduled flight landed that afternoon, but it's after nine and still he hasn't heard from his pal. Maybe Jack was home and pissed off at him for not going to LA, yeah, that's it. Aaron had second thoughts about calling Jack. If Jack was mad, maybe it would be better to talk to him at school on Monday, let him cool his jets. The football game came to an end and Aaron was ready to call the night. Like any other night, Aaron always checked his emails before retiring. Maybe Jack sent one and explained how his weekend was going and why he wasn't home yet. Once opening his mail box, there were three emails from Terri, but one very peculiar email that stood out. An email from Charles Collier. Now why would Jack's father send him an email? He opened the link and began reading.

> Jack: I miss you so much. I've committed an awful crime and wish every day that it never happened. Costa Rica…Villa del Rico…Villa 16…Under the back deck…I hope you'll understand. I'm so sorry.
>
> Love, Dad

What the hell is this? The email was meant for Jack, but how did he get it? *Wow.* He fell back into his chair, trying to believe what he just read. *An awful crime. Costa Rica.* Aaron closed down the computer, found his cell and dialed Jack's number. It rang and rang, then the voice mail kicked in.

"Yo, Jack. Call me as soon as you can. I got an email from your Dad. You better read it." It kind of scared Aaron. Was Charles in trouble in another country and did Emily know about this? Then came a soft knock on his bedroom door. It opened, Aaron's father stood, then asked, "Son, Jack's mother just called and told me Jack hasn't returned from California yet. She's worried. Have you heard from him today?"

"No. I just called him and left a voice mail. Gee Dad, something isn't right. I can feel it."

***

When Aaron pulled into the student parking lot on Monday morning, Jack's Jeep was nowhere in sight. Possibly, Jack was running late because of the busy weekend he had in California or maybe his flight was delayed and he got home late. No problem. He and Terri waited at his locker, if and when he showed up, Aaron desperately needed to tell him about the upsetting email he received from his Dad. The bell rang for classes to begin and Jack still hadn't appeared. So, Aaron and Terri headed to class.

"I'll wait till lunch time and call him. I have a funny feeling inside and I'm worried about him."

"He's fine, Aaron. Wouldn't it be cool if he got picked to be on the show. Wow! A chance of winning a cool million dollars. A kid from Manford on TV? How cool is that."

"Maybe that's why he's not home yet."

Morning classes ended and Aaron met Terri for lunch. After they picked out what they wanted to eat, Aaron dialed Jack's number. Again, all he got was Jack's voice mail.

"I think I'll stop by his house on the way home. His mom might know more about it."

"You know Jack better than all of us, Aaron. He likes to keep important stuff to himself. If he was home, I know he would've tried to call you."

Aaron's Ford pick-up truck rumbled down South Street, closing in on Jack's house. The closer he got, the more unnerved he became. Jack's Jeep was still gone. He rang the door bell and a minute later Emily appeared.

"He's not home yet?"

"Come in, Aaron." Emily sat down, covered her face with her hands and began to cry.

"Mrs. Collier, what's wrong? What's happened?" Instantly, Aaron remembered the email from Charles. The crime, Costa Rica.

"Aaron, you need to help me. You're the only person I can turn to."

Aaron sat across from Emily, holding her hands and looking into the eyes of a frightened woman.

"Something wrong? Tell me what happened?"

She took a deep breath and began to tell Aaron the entire story. How it all got started, the money, the death of two people, the move to Costa Rica, the kidnapping of Jack and, the worst part, Charles was dead. She convinced Aaron that Jack knew nothing about the money and why his father fled to Costa Rica. She sobbed, praying for help.

"That explains it, Emily. Listen, before I went to bed last night, I checked my emails on my computer. There was one from Charles but it was addressed to Jack. How it got to me, I don't know. He mentioned a crime, the Villa and something under the deck, and that Jack would know about it."

"The money." Suddenly, Emily stood up. "He must have known he was dying, then hid the money."

"Emily, you need to notify the police. Without them, we may never see Jack again. Listen to me. Please talk to them."

"I…I'm…not sure what I should do. Charles's body has to come back here. Jack…we need to get to Jack before something bad happens to him."

"Emily, Charles is dead, Jack isn't. You have to concentrate on him. Do you know where he is?"

"No. Somewhere near Los Angeles, I think."

"Call the police, please. We have to save him."

"Wait a minute. I think I still have the detective's card." Emily walked over to her desk, opened the top drawer and shuffled through the debris until she found it. She dialed the number from Konrad's card.

"Detective Konrad."

"Detective, this is Emily Collier. I need your help as soon as possible."

"What seems to be the problem?"

"Something bad has happened. I need to talk to you."

"Okay. Are you at home?"

"I'm in Manford, at home."

"I'll be there this afternoon. Don't go anywhere." Konrad was beginning to fit all the missing pieces left in his crime puzzle and getting closer to solving it.

It was all making sense to Aaron. Maybe the email from Charles wasn't a mistake after all.

"Emily, I'm going to ask my Dad if he can help you. You know he's a pilot. I'm sure he could fly you to Costa Rica and help you recover Charles's body, maybe finding the money."

"Ohh, Aaron. Would he? I'm willing to pay him, whatever he wants."

"First things first. Let me talk to him. I'll call you just as soon as I have an answer from him, okay?"

"Thank you, Aaron. You know how Jack would thank you."

Within the next few hours, Emily saw the squad car pulling into her driveway. The door bell rang.

"Good afternoon, Detectives. Come in and please sit down. Well, I don't know where to start. But, to make a very long story short, Charles is dead. I got a phone call this morning from Villa del Rico in Costa Rica, informing me they found him dead in his villa. They don't know how he died, the coroner will let me know. And…Dan Mesa, who I believe is Dennis Reading, has kidnapped my son Jack."

"You've talked to Reading?"

"Like I said, Detective, it's a very long story. The more I think about it, the more I'm convinced I was conned by him. You see, about three weeks ago, I was shopping at the mall and when I returned to my car, this man was standing alongside my car. It was just a small dent and he convinced me not to call the police. He gave me his card, Dan Mesa from Pasadena. I fell head and shoulders over it. We became intimate. Then, one night he got me drunk. I think I told him everything about the money Charles and I took from Priority. He split that night, never heard from him until a few days ago."

"So, you're positive that Reading and Mesa are the same person?"

"Has to be. You see, during that time, my son was receiving emails from a company in California. I believe it was called Stardom Studios. Jack mentioned something about a reality show and winning one million dollars. They sent him tickets to travel to California for an interview. How could I've been so stupid?"

"How did he contact you?"

"A phone call."

"On your cell?"

"Yes. That was the only number I gave him."

"May I see your cell phone?"

Konrad punched a couple of buttons.

"Six-two-six. Fritz, is that the area code for LA.?"

"Could be, I'll check it out." Fritz copied the number onto his note pad.

"We can cross-reference this number and find out where and when the call was made. Did you ever take a picture of Mesa?"

"No. But when he was staying in Manford, he was at the Super Inn. He stayed in room 203 or 302. You could check that out, possibly his picture is on security cameras."

"That we'll do. Well, I'll be in touch. If I need more from you, I'll let you know. Sorry to hear about your husband but thank you for this, it's a big help. Oh, you know what villa he stayed at?"

"It was the Villa del Rico, but I'm not sure of his villa number."

Konrad and Fritz left, on their way to the Super Inn. Once they got there, they presented their badges to the clerk. They informed him about Dan Mesa and their need for more information. The clerk gave them the surveillance disk, the customer register, and a copy of Mesa's driver's license. On their drive home, Fritz installed the disk on his laptop while Konrad dialed the FBI number in LA.

"Yeah, can I speak with agent Kennison?"

"Agent Kennison."

"This is Mike Konrad, Chicago PD. I spoke to you a while back regarding the investigation of Reading and Kruger."

"Okay, yeah, I remember."

"I've got a lead on a phone number. A tip from a source said she received a call from him yesterday. 626-555-8978. Also, Reading is going by the name of Dan Mesa. M-E-S-A. May be living in Pasadena. One more thing, a California driver's license in the name of Dan Mesa, M22743-021-0050021, DOB 7-10-1971."

"Got it. I'll check this out right now. I'll call you back just as soon as I have results."

Mike closed his cell and glanced over to Fritz's laptop. "Good looking guy. No wonder his wife was banging him. He's the same guy we've been looking for."

***

The sudden rap on the front door startled Helen. She peeked out to see Dan holding two grocery bags. She unbolted the door and followed him into the kitchen. He placed the groceries on the counter, took off his coat, and opened a beer. Then he opened the door to the spare bedroom where Jack was sitting, tied to a chair near the only window in the room. Jack was hidden in the corner, out of view from the window.

Dan removed the tape from his mouth. "You hungry?"

"Why are you doing this to me? Let me go. I swear I won't tell anyone, just let me go, please. I want to go home."

"Sorry. You hungry, thirsty?"

He said nothing. What was going on?

Dan brought in a tray with food and a Coke, placed it in front of Jack and untied his hands, but watched him carefully.

"I gotta go to the bathroom."

"Finish your food first. When you're done, then you can go."

When Jack finished his food, Dan untied him and led him to the bathroom, but he placed his foot between the door and the jamb, so Jack couldn't lock the door. Dan returned him to the bedroom chair, retied him, and taped his mouth.

It was quiet inside Dan's apartment. Helen sat by herself, smoking cigarettes one after another, thinking. Dan stood in the kitchen, downing can after can of beer, also thinking. He focused on occurrences outside the kitchen window—on the long, wide sidewalk that seemed endless, watching people coming from all directions, wondering if any of them knew he was a kidnapper. He looked at Helen, but she was in her own little world and in one of her frequent moods. Still starring out the window, Dan started to seriously doubt the predicament he was living.

What if I just stayed at Citizens Bank? What if I never met Fossett or Helen? What if I continued my relationship with Emily? Ohh, so many "what ifs", damn it. Why am I running, I'm innocent. A lot of ifs and a lot of second guessing, but now his chance of becoming rich was in jeopardy. Holding their son for ransom, Dan's only hope rested in the lap of Emily, because she would be the one to contact Charles and force him to give up the money. After all, wasn't Jack's life more important to Charles than the seven million?

Helen's cell began ringing. She looked at Dan, debating whether to answer.

She flipped open the phone, recognized the number, and listened as the caller spoke, "You got a pen handy?"

Helen snapped her fingers in Dan's direction, motioning that she needed a pen.

"Go ahead, I'm listening."

"Collier is dead. Costa Rica, Villa del Rico. The money is in that Villa somewhere. Under the floor, in the ceiling, behind the walls, just find it. She's gonna be there in a day or two. You gotta get there before she does." The caller hung up.

"Who was that, one of your Chicago connections? What do they want?"

"We have big troubles now. Collier is dead. You gotta get your ass to Costa Rica right now."

"Charles is dead. How are we going to get that money? What the hell is happening here?"

Helen ignored Dan and paced back and forth, still smoking a cigarette. The news about Charles instantly, put her brain in overdrive. Since Charles was dead, was the money with him? The only way to find out was getting Dan on the first flight to Liberia. She walked to the kitchen counter and began writing on a piece of paper, then handed it to Dan.

"Collier stayed in this Villa, Villa Del Rico near Liberia. The money must be there. Look everywhere. The floor, ceiling, all the walls, under his mattress. Don't come back till you find it, understood?"

"Look, I'm getting really scared. Why don't your people go to Liberia? Why do I always have to do the dirty work?" No sooner than getting the words out of his mouth, Helen handed him a wad of cash. It was no use, Dan was on his way to Costa Rica.

***

As soon as Aaron opened the front door, he could feel the warmth from the crackling fireplace and the smell of the burning oak filtering throughout the entire house. His father was sitting in his favorite Lazy Boy, reading the evening news and enjoying a hot cup of buttered rum. He peeked over his eyeglasses as Aaron entered.

"Dad. Jack's Mom is in some trouble and we need to help her, quickly."

Gene put the paper down. "Trouble? What kind of trouble?"

Aaron explained the situation just as Emily told him. Jack was being held captive in California, his father was dead in Costa Rica and a large sum of money was lost.

"I know it sounds crazy, but it happened. Dad, if I went with Jack, I would be kidnapped also. Think about it, Dad, we have to help her."

"What is it I can do that the police cannot do, Aaron?"

"You can fly Emily to Costa Rica. There's a lot of money hidden where Charles was staying. We could help her bring it back here without going through customs."

"Whoa! Back off son. That's breaking the law. I know how you feel, but please, think about this. Let the police handle it. Anyway, I don't have a plane. And this money, is it stolen money?"

"No. It belongs to Emily." Aaron didn't know anything about the money, only hoping his father would give in.

"Aaron, in the last two minutes, you've told me you want me to drop everything, fly a woman to Costa Rica, cross customs with a large sum of money, and do it right away. If I agreed…and I mean if…it would take considerable time to organize such a thing."

Aaron turned away from his father and stormed to his bedroom. Gene still sat there, amazed at what his son told him. He started to think of the possibility that he could help. He took a sip from the rum, fixed his glasses and returned to reading his paper.

Chapter 52

So They Meet Again

The next day, Konrad received a call from FBI agent Kennison.

"We got a positive on that phone number. Listed to a pay phone, 300 Truman Avenue in Pasadena. Sent a detail out there, found a row of three payphones located in front of a drug store. Also, negative on that driver' s license. Most likely a forgery. I've sent a unit to that address to stake out the situation. Question anyone that uses those phones."

"Good. I have a positive ID of Mesa from a security video from a hotel he stayed at. Just as soon as I get a copy of his photo from the lab, I'll fax it to you. In the meantime, if we hear more about him, I'll call you."

Later that afternoon, Konrad was sitting at his desk when a clerk dropped off the photo from the security video. Konrad studied it, then opened his drawer and removed the Fossett murder file. He leafed through the contents until he came across the photo he took from Fossett's office. To be completely sure, he compared them. Yep, we have our guy. The photos matched, Dennis Reading was Dan Mesa. Without a second to lose, Mike hurried to the fax machine, dialed in Kennison's number and sent the copy to him. Now, all Mike had to do was sit back and wait until the FBI caught Mesa. There was one thing Konrad needed to do before the FBI began their hunt for Mesa. Contact Helen and tell her to get out of California as soon as possible. Forget about the money.

***

Gene Webber struggled to finish reading his newspaper. What his son Aaron told him struck a touchy nerve in his spine. He wrestled back and forth with the idea of helping Jack and his mother. He knew he could do it, but what were the consequences if they got caught? He folded the paper and stared at the dancing flames in the fireplace. If he told Aaron no, it was none of their business and let the police handle it, then Aaron would be difficult to live with, knowing he had let his best friend down. If he conceded and agreed to help, what was so wrong about flying a grieving widow to Costa Rica to pick up the body of her deceased husband? He took off his glasses, set the newspaper on the night table, and went up to Aaron's bedroom.

"Okay. I give in, I'll help her."

Aaron jumped off his bed and ran to his father and hugged him.

"We're doing the right thing, Dad. I know Jack would do the same for me. I better call Emily right now."

"Hold on a second. Let me call Jerry and see if his jet is available."

About an hour later, Aaron heard good news from his Dad that the plane was available.

"I gotta call Emily now."

"Emily, my Dad's going to help you. His friend Jerry is letting my Dad borrow his jet. Right now he's planning the flight schedule for us to leave tomorrow. We'll be over in the morning and discuss the trip, okay?"

"Aaron, I can't thank you and your Dad enough. Thank you, thank you."

"I'll call you in the morning. Goodnight."

It was a long night for Gene. Once Jerry agreed to let him use his jet, setting up a flight plan was a tiresome task. The LearJet 35-A had a range capacity of approximately 2,000 miles, meaning they couldn't make it to Liberia non-stop. Somewhere in between they had to land and refuel. He studied the maps and calculated the distance from Illinois to Costa Rica. Corpus Christi, Texas, would be the ideal location to refuel. He had flown to that airport several times and was familiar with the area and the field crew.

The next morning, Aaron and Gene drove to Emily's house to discuss their itinerary. Gene explained to Emily the route he planned to take, the best time to leave, and the possible problems they might encounter when arriving in Costa Rica. Emily agreed to everything, then asked Gene, "How much money will we need?"

Gene rubbed his chin, hesitated for a moment, then answered, "Probably five or ten thousand. We'll be refueling twice, that may run a few thousand. If everything goes according to plan, and luck is on our side, we should be able to leave Liberia that same day."

"You mentioned problems. What sort of problems?" She refilled his cup and listened closely.

"Well. From here to Texas, I don't anticipate any problems. I have a flight plan. It's from Texas to Costa Rica that will be critical, because I don't have a flight plan to Costa Rica. I'll have to make an excuse to land at Oduber airport in Liberia. Tell them I need fuel. If they allow that, then we're home free."

"So, what time do we leave tonight?"

"Eleven pm. I would think. About three hours to Corpus Christi and then another three hours to Liberia, arriving there around seven in the morning. That will give us enough time to rent a vehicle, drive to the resort, and hopefully solve your problems."

"I can't wait till this is all over," Emily said.

"Well, Aaron let's go. I need to drive to Donnerville, where the jet is, check it out and submit my flight plan."

"Okay. I'll get the money, pack a small bag, and I'll be ready as soon as you get here."

"We'll be there around ten."

***

Agent Kennison pulled the photo from the fax machine and walked into his office.

"Judy, get agents Little and Pike in here."

She didn't respond, but walked to the adjoining room where both agents had their desks. "Boss wants both of you in his office, right now."

When they arrived, Kennison began barking out orders without looking at either detective. "Here's a copy of your mark. Goes by the name of Dan Mesa. Also, may have an accomplice named Helen Hughes, negative on a photo. Get whatever you need from the lab. We need a positive ID, may be living near the vicinity of the drug store. Check the buildings across the street, a place for the stake-out. Keep me posted on every move from that address. Get going." That was Kennison, very direct and straight to the point.

Both detectives made their way to the police crime lab. They signed out binoculars, one Cannon PowerShot camera with a telephoto lens and equipped with high-speed film, one tripod, an ultra-sound detector, and two Walkie-Talkies. They drove an unmarked squad car to the address given to them by Kennison. They dressed in casual attire, blue jeans and t-shirts, shorts and sandals, the average clothes an agent would wear so that their target wouldn't recognize them. They drove by the target address a couple of times, getting a good feel of the surrounding elements, then parked the unmarked car across the street.

Nonchalantly, the pair walked into the warehouse, cased the place out and encountered the owner. They showed him their badges and explained that a robbery might take place at the drug store across from the warehouse. The owner stepped out of their way, and let them continue their business. Immediately, Pike and Little set up the camera and their sound tracker, then sat back, waiting for the appearance of Mesa. Each agent took turns watching for the target, but as the day passed, there was no sign of Mesa.

***

Dan stuffed the money into his pocket, then cautiously peered out the front door. He didn't see anyone around and no one walking up the sidewalk. He left the apartment.

"I believe our subject is on the move." Little put down the binoculars, looked at the target photo and hurried to the door.

"You stay here and watch the building, I'll follow him." Detective Pike hurried out the door so he wouldn't lose sight of Mesa. He noticed his target about 300 feet away from him on the opposite side of the street, walking at a very fast pace, constantly looked over his shoulder. Pike crossed the street, keeping a safe distance until Mesa flagged down a taxi, jumped in the vehicle and sped away.

"Damn." His squad car was more than a block away, so Pike sprinted to the car and quickly as he could, pursued the fleeing cab. Automatically, he picked up the two-way radio in his squad car and pressed the button. "Squad 251, 10-80."

"Squad 251, 10-20." replied the dispatcher.

"Traveling west on Truman Avenue, in pursuit of subject."

"10-4."

Kennison always had his police call radio on when he was in his office. He heard the call from Officer Pike and picked up the receiver.

"Pike, Kennison here. You sure it's Mesa?"

"Positive on that, sir. He must be in a hurry. He ran out and found a cab. He's in the cab right now."

"Don't lose him."

"10-4."

Kennison closed his call with Pike, then picked up the Walkie-Talkie that Officer Little had.

"Little."

"Yes, Chief."

"Anything happening there?"

"Negative. Nothing moving. No sign of the woman."

"Keep me posted."

"10-4."

***

When the trio arrived at Jerry's hangar, Gene had the jet serviced and ready for take-off. The only thing left for him to do was submit his flight plan, go over a couple of safety issues with Jerry about handling the jet, and then take off. Satisfied that everything was set to go, Jerry closed the main hatch and Gene taxied the jet to the runway, pushed the throttles forward, and the roaring engines soon had the flight in the air. Emily sat next to Aaron and held his hand during take-off. She smiled as if to say, "Thank you, Aaron."

The jet was cruising around thirty-five thousand feet. Emily listened to Gene converse with ground control while Aaron paged through the latest issue of Sports Illustrated. But for Emily, it was a whirlwind of grief. What else could go wrong? If she found the money, the first thing she was going to do was call Dan and get her son back. To hell with the money.

The sun's rays poked through the small window near Emily's seat, waking her. "Are we there?"

"We are here. I've radioed the tower at Oduber, they've cleared our approach, so we should be on the ground in about fifteen minutes."

It was a sunny morning in Liberia when Emily watched the jet descending toward the runway. When the tires met the asphalt pavement, the loud screeching noise startled and awoke Aaron.

"We're in Costa Rica?"

Gene followed the ground crew and guided the jet to a nearby hangar, idled the engines, and ended his conversation with the control tower. When the main hatch opened,

Gene climbed out of the cockpit and waited for Aaron and Emily to leave the plane. Already, at seven o'clock in the morning, the temperature was a balmy eighty degrees.

"Awesome. No snow and cold weather, huh Emily?" Aaron stretched his body and took in every ray of sun it could absorb. Emily put her hand above her eyes to shade the bright sun, watching Gene talk with members of the ground crew, motioning toward the jet, shaking his head in agreement, and shaking their hands.

"Okay. They're going to let us use a small van to collect the body." Gene glanced at his watch, "What do you say we grab some breakfast and after that, contact the police department?"

"I'm all for that. Let's go."

They walked to the white Chevy van and dropped their bags in the back. The city of Liberia was wide awake, and they didn't have any trouble locating a restaurant less than a mile from the hangar.

After breakfast, Gene extracted a map from his pocket, studied it, and memorized the roads that would take them to Ocotal.

"According to the map, Ocotal is about thirty miles away. Right near the ocean. Everyone ready?"

Emily thought it was no wonder Charles wanted to come here. The drive from the airport covered a beautiful landscape of what Costa Rica offered. The color of the orchids that grew along the roadside, the palm trees, and the scent of the tropical foliage had all of them awestruck.

"There's Villa del Rico." Gene said. The sign stood among heavy vegetation that almost covered the sign. If you weren't paying attention, there was a good chance of missing the entrance. They drove past the entrance of the resort until Gene saw a huge red, white, and blue sign reading, "Entering the Providence of Ocotal." Gene drove the van slowly, all of them looking for the police agency, until Aaron located it. A small tan, one-story, adobe structure, sitting all by itself, like it was a social outcast.

Emily entered the agency first. "Is officer Martinez in?"

"Yes," replied an officer dressed all in black, including his holster, pistol, shoes, and the transmitter pinned to his shoulder. The only noticeable object that wasn't black was a pair of shiny, steel handcuffs. The officer escorted them to Officer Martinez's office.

He sat behind his desk, talking on the phone and reading from a sheet of paper. He looked above the paper, saw the three Americans, and stopped his conversation.

"Yes. What can I do for you?" He spoke in broken English.

"My name is Emily Collier. I've come to bring my husband back home."

"Yes, yes, yes. Of course, please sit down."

With his office having room for only two chairs, Aaron was left standing. Officer Martinez walked to his filing cabinet and removed a red file jacket.

"Ummm. So sorry for your loss. The coroner has concluded his autopsy. The cause of death was infectious insect bite. You see, it's rare, but this does happened here. Bot flies. Nasal bot flies. Some carry the rare disease." He handed the copy of the death certificate to Emily, pointing to the line where she must sign. She sat, dumbfounded. He died from an insect bite, really. The unbelievable stroke of fate–or bad luck—that had her sitting in a police department in Ocotal, Costa Rica.

"We are going to drive back to the villa and locate some of his personal belongings. It shouldn't take us that long."

"Fine. But I think we collected everything out of the villa. Go, check it. When you return, you can find the morgue only a block away. I will be here. If not, you have my number." Martinez handed her a card from his desk holder.

Fifteen minutes later, Emily was entering the office of the Villa del Rico, taking off her sunglasses, and approaching the woman at the reception desk.

"I'm the wife of Charles Collier, the gentleman who was found dead in your villa a few days ago."

"Ohh, we're so sorry. I believe the police agency confiscated all of your husband's belongings, but let me check with Carlos." She picked up a small cell phone and dialed his number, for a short conversation.

"The villa was thoroughly cleaned out."

"Well, it was villa sixteen, correct?"

She entered some data into her computer. "Yes, that is correct."

"Would it be possible for us to take one last look? We've come from very far away. So, while we're here, we just want to make sure we have everything."

The young woman paused, understanding their request, but she didn't know how to tell Emily the problem.

"I'm very sorry, but villa sixteen has been rented out. It would be against our privacy policy to allow you to enter the villa while it's occupied."

Emily turned to Gene. The look on her face showed her displeasure. How were they going to get in there?

"I see. Thank you. We will talk to Officer Martinez. Maybe he can help us."

As soon as Emily walked behind the van, she noticed a shingle mounted to a post. It provided the location of all the villas within the resort property. Villa sixteen was down to their right and up the steep hill.

"Let's see where this villa is. Maybe there's a way to get under the deck without disturbing the guests," Emily said when they were back in the van.

Gene started the engine and drove in the direction the shingle pointed. The van powered its way up the steep hill and when they spotted another sign—Villas Fifteen through Eighteen—he pulled into the lot. They climbed out of the van and walked up the narrow dirt path, dodging low tree limbs and numerous blossomed plants. They got close to the villa, close enough to look inside the windows, when a man appeared from around the back deck.

"What do you want?"

It couldn't be. No...Emily turned as fast as she could and hurried down the dirt path, Gene and Aaron closely behind her. When they reached the van, out of breath, she was in shock.

"That was Dan Mesa. He's the one who has Jack. He's the kidnapper."

"What do we do now?" Aaron asked.

Emily stood for a moment and then got into the van. "We have to get away from the villa. I don't want him to see me. Drive down to the office, let me think this out."

Gene drove the van in the direction of the Mai-Kai, turned off the engine, and stared at Emily.

"I don't think he recognized me. He doesn't know about our

van. Let's just sit here. Maybe he'll leave, then we can get back up there." Emily suggested.

"Okay. I have an idea. This guy doesn't know Aaron or myself. For all he knows, we're guests just like himself. We could walk around the villa and see if we can find a way to locate the bags. We could tell him we're renting villa eighteen. How would he know?"

"Good idea. I'll stay here."

When Dan watched the intruders slip and stumble their way down the tricky path, he knew for sure it was Emily. He began to laugh. He also knew they would be back. They didn't come all the way here just to pick up Charles's body and not search for the money. Let them come back. He'd have a surprise for them. He went back inside, pulled his revolver from the kitchen counter, checked the ammunition clip, and tucked the revolver in his belt. He opened the glass doors, walked to the deck and looked out over the ocean. He leaned over the railing, ready to spit, when…what is that? He strained his eyes to see something black, a couple of black items. He bent closer to the railing. Then he realized what he had discovered.

Well, that goddamn Charles. So, this is where he hid the money.

He walked around the deck, his eyes strained for any intruders, looking for an easy way to climb over the wood railing and access the area below. At the very end of the railing, near the front door, he saw a small opening. With the aid of a sharp knife, he cut a limb here and there, opening an avenue beneath the deck. He found two black backpacks filled with the money.

Awesome. Totally awesome. The smile on Dan's face reached from ear to ear. He grabbed a wad of money and kissed it. At last, it was all his. He moved each bag closer to the front opening, easing his head out from the small trees, looking for anyone who might be in the wrong place at the wrong time. It was clear. He raced around the corner of the villa, carrying the backpacks and darted into the kitchen. He had it all figured out. On his flight from LA., the wheels in his head were speeding out of control. If he found the money at the villa, why would he need Helen anymore? Screw her and the boy. It would be all his. He could see himself sitting in front of a fireplace, sipping on a JD and coke in his new home in Switzerland. He still had one small problem, Emily. He needed to get rid of her and her companions, so he had to set a trap for them. Such a devious mind he had. He picked up the two backpacks and walked to the back deck, looked around, and tossed each bag onto the roof of the villa. Then he would leave, making sure Emily saw him, park his car beyond the main office and return to the villa, wait for them to break in and then attack them. Yep, that would work. He closed the front door and set the bait, leaving it open for them to walk in. He drove the car down the narrow roadway, parked in front of the office, and went in. He wanted to be noticed by Emily. He wanted her to think he was leaving for the day and they could raid his villa. He reappeared in front of the office, stood for a few minutes, and then drove away. Within a couple hundred feet, an opening appeared where he parked the car. He dashed into the forest, circled around the back of the restaurant, across the tennis courts and up the hill toward his villa. Cautiously, Dan surveyed the surroundings. It was calm, nobody in sight, so he entered the villa. He checked his loaded pistol, walked back to the deck and hid behind a mass of bushes, waiting. His trap was set.

"There goes his car," said Aaron. Gene saw the dust and made his way back to the van. Emily was there, anxious to get back to the villa. They waited in the van in case Dan came back. Twenty minutes went by. They drove back to the small parking lot, got out and made their way back up the beaten path. Emily reached the villa first, walked around the deck, looked into the windows and saw no one. She tried the front door; it was open. She hesitated. Did he leave the door open on purpose? Time was their enemy, so Emily opened the door and all three went in. They searched the rooms, but found nothing that belonged to Charles. When she headed to the glass doors leading to the deck, she saw Dan standing close to the villa, holding a pistol.

Emily screamed, "Oh, no! How did you…"

"Get inside."

They backed up until they were against the kitchen wall, their arms raised.

"I have the money, Emily. Too bad, you're a day late and seven million dollars short."

He took a chair from the kitchen table and waved to Emily to sit down. He tied her up, then tied Gene in another chair. He stood and began to back up, awkwardly he stumbled on Emily's chair and fell backward. Aaron seized the opportunity to tackle him, as if he were a defensive back zeroing in on the opponents' running back. He hit Dan so hard that the pistol flew across the kitchen floor and onto the deck. Aaron had his arm around Dan's neck, squeezing it as hard as he could, stopping the blood flow to his brain. A tap out as they call it in the UFC. Temporarily unconscious.

Aaron untied his father and helped him tie up Dan. They pulled the rope as tight as they could—not once, but twice.

Dazed and senseless, Dan's eyes opened. Emily held the gun. "Where's the money, Dan?"

"Up your ass. It's not here. I never found it."

"Then why did you tie us up?"

Aaron remembered the email from Charles, mentioning something was under the deck.

"Emily, it said under the deck. The money was under the deck. Dad, help me look."

They walked to the back deck and leaned against the railing, looking for any signs of bags or suitcases, anything out of the normal laying under the deck. Nothing appeared. Aaron leaned against the railing, about to say something to Emily, when a howler monkey sitting on the roof screeched. Startled, Aaron looked up. He didn't see the monkey, but he saw black straps from a backpack. He retrieved a broom from the kitchen, looped it through a strap and pulled. One backpack slammed down on the deck. Gene ran to pick it up, then watched Aaron climbed on top of the railing and collected the second bag.

Dan knew he was finished. He didn't murder Fossett, but when the cops find him, he might as well have done it.

"By the way, how did you find out about Charles being here?" Emily asked. "Last chance, Dan. Anything you want to tell me before we leave you for the cops?"

Gene stood next to her, holding a roll of duct tape.

Dan looked at the tape and then to Emily eyes. Still he kept quiet. Gene began to stretch the tape around Dan's face when Dan blurted. "You want to know who told me? You didn't know that he and Helen were married before, did you? She dumped me and married him. Then she found out about Hasid being murdered. If Charles hadn't found out about the seven million, he would've been next in line. It was KO....."

Abruptly, Dan clammed up.

Emily wondered what he meant, but they needed to get going. She motioned to Gene to finish taping Dan's mouth.

They drove to the Police Agency, where Officer Martinez took them to the morgue. Holding back tears, Emily identified Charles's remains then Gene and Aaron helped load the casket into the van. Emily rolled down her window as Officer Martinez approached the van, "The Los Angeles FBI are looking for the man in villa sixteen. You may want to check out that villa right now. There may be a reward."

The only thing left on her mind was getting Jack home safely. They boarded their jet, the casket loaded with the seven million dollars hidden beneath Charles's body, and flew back to Illinois.

Chapter 53

Save The Last Dance For Me

They say all's well that ends well. It was the morning after the frantic trip to Costa Rica, Emily sat in her living room, a cup of coffee in her hand, wondering whether the death of Charles or having all the money, would she do it all over again? Did it really end well? Her sole consolation was that even though Charles was gone, she still had the money and one big hidden secret. It cost two people their lives, plus three more will most likely end their lives in prison. She asked herself, was the money the evildoer, and she was the victim, that anyone would do anything for a price. All she had to do was look in the mirror, because right or wrong, she did it.

Buzz…buzz.

"Hello."

"Mrs. Collier. This is Agent Kennison from the LA. FBI."

"Yes. I've heard good things about your work, but haven't congratulated you yet."

"Well, thank you. My reason for calling you is that I wanted to update you concerning our case here. Dennis Reading, alias Dan Mesa, is being extradited from Costa Rica to our facility as we speak. Helen Kruger unfortunately escaped, but we have an APB out for her arrest. Your son, Jack has been rescued, he's safe and not harmed. Jack will be on a flight back to Chicago this afternoon."

"Oh, my Lord. I've been worried sick about him."

"He's doing great. He may be hungry, but our SWAT team did a fantastic job controlling the situation."

"What's going to happen to Mesa?"

"Mr. Reading has been charged with kidnapping and extortion and illegal possession of a firearm. When they arrested him in Costa Rica, they also confiscated a pistol in his possession. We'll send the pistol to our lab for ballistics, possibly the same weapon that killed William Fossett. As far as Helen Kruger, when we find her, she'll be charged with kidnapping, possible that she murdered her brother. We'll learn more when we interrogate Reading. Once we locate her, they'll both be locked up for quite awhile, that I know."

"What a nightmare. I am just lost here, wondering what's next for Jack and me."

"Well, both of you are safe now. You take care and enjoy your time with your son, okay?"

"That we will. And, if we are ever in LA., we owe you a spectacular dinner."

Kennison laughed, then said goodbye.

A huge weight was lifted from Emily's shoulders when hearing Agent Kennison tell her that both Kruger and Reading were responsible for Fossett's murder. Emily couldn't have done this without the help of Aaron and his father. She owed them dearly. She stared at the two bags on the living room floor, walked over to one bag and opened it. She counted out one hundred thousand dollars to give Aaron's father and another twenty-five thousand for Jerry, the owner of the jet. But, what about Aaron? Who knew Aaron better than anyone, Jack would take care of Aaron.

The morning and the entire afternoon seemed to drag by, almost like the hours stopped, waiting impatiently for Jack's Jeep to pull into the driveway. Another cup of coffee, another cigarette, another hour passed, still no red Jeep. And finally, here comes Jack. The Jeep stopped so fast, like it hit a brick wall. Jack flew out the door and raced to the house, embracing his mother as she stood in the open door, crying.

"I can't believe it's over, Mom. Did they find Dad?"

She looked into Jack's eyes, how was she going to get the words out, the words that will haunt Jack for the rest of his life. "Sit down."

"All that has happened within the past year, I wish I could turn the clock back and start over. Never, never did I ever see this coming." Emily's eyes were swollen from all the tears and grief swallowed her face. "Your father is dead."

Jack pushed her away. "No, no…that can't be. Tell me it's not true, Mom."

She was silent. What could she say?

Charles and Jack were so close. It was a pity that greed had taken away a person he loved so much.

"You need to know what happened." She began telling Jack the truth of the circumstances that led to his father's death. An hour later, he understood what had taken place over the past six months. He was better, knowing the truth, but bitter from being held in the dark. The night was getting late and Jack's eyes grew heavy, he was totally exhausted and wanted to go to sleep. They hugged again, said goodnight and retired for the night.

The next morning, Jack was back to the same routine, invading the refrigerator and having the same breakfast. That woke up Emily. She strolled into the kitchen, preparing the coffee maker for a much-needed cup of coffee.

"I want to go over to Aaron's house and thank him and his father. If it wasn't for them, your father would still be in Costa Rica and how would we get him home? I owe them a lot, Jack." She sipped her coffee waiting for him to say something. Jack sat motionless. "I have money set aside for Gene and Jerry. What should we give Aaron?" she asked.

Jack just sat, spooning his cereal and drinking his orange juice, thinking.

"Jack, I understand how difficult it is for you. Me too. Without their help, we would not be sitting here right now and you might be dead."

"Well, Aaron will leaving for college in the fall. How much money did you say you have in those bags?"

Emily knew what was coming next. Jack wanted something very, very special for his best friend.

"Why don't we make Mr. Annelli an offer for his business?"

"The Pizza Shack?"

"Every time we go there, Aaron was always telling us how cool it would be to own the Shack. Why don't we buy it for him?"

"We have the money. Yes, if that's what you want to do for Aaron, dammit, that's what we'll do."

He reached for his mother's hand. "Mom, I love you."

***

There were many changes in the upcoming years for Jack and Emily Collier and others involved in the plot to steal the seven million dollars. Dennis Reading, alias Dan Mesa, was found guilty of kidnapping and extortion, and sentenced to twenty-six years in prison. Forensic tests from the pistol confiscated from Dan did not prove to be the weapon that had killed William Fossett. Bill Hill, alias Billy Wilson, was guilty as charged in the murder of Alice Oliver, returned to prison serving life with no chance of parole. As far as Detective Mike Konrad, as the investigation grew into Fossett's murder, Konrad was added to the long list of corrupt cops from Chicago and sentenced to a four-year prison term for obstructing justice and withholding admissible evidence.

Helen Kruger still remained on the run.

After the loss of his father, Jack's relationship with Emily became much stronger. After graduating from Columbia High School, he and Emily spent several weeks vacationing in California, visiting college campuses, taking in the sights, and the best part—looking to purchase a house near the colleges.

The summer months gave him time to decide what college had the best program suited his goals. He chose the University of Southern California because USC had a long list of successful people, including many Oscar winners, who graduated from its programs and Jack wanted to be on that list. USC would be the start of his dream to become part of the movie industry and someday, own his own animation studio.

Emily decided to sell the house in Manford, or maybe put it to better use. They found the perfect house in Culver City, a two-story, four-bedroom with three baths, an entertainment theater, a large in-ground pool, and a spacious four-car garage that accommodated living quarters above the garage. If Aaron and Terri planned to visit, they would have a private place to stay for as long as they wanted.

After high school graduation, Aaron was anxious to get back on the football field and fulfill his dream of someday playing in the NFL for the Chicago Bears. His athletic ability paid off earning a full scholarship to University of Miami, Ohio. However, Terri's father became ill, and medical bills piled up that forced her to forego attending college and care of her family. She remained in Manford to undertake the farming business while Aaron attended college. They loved each other dearly, the temporary separation was hard to take for Terri, but in the long run, they'd soon be married and starting a family.

The future of the three friends was imperative, meaning miles would separate their friendship, but promised to keep in contact with each other. This didn't destroy the bond that had for each other, it strengthen it. When ever Jack had spare time, he would return to Manford and enjoy his times with the pair. Especially the Friday night tradition, eating pizza at the Pizza Shack. They danced and laughed, but was so remarkable to Jack was that every time they met for pizza, Aaron always commented how cool it would be to own the Pizza Shack. Well, little did he know about the secret Mr. Annelli and Jack shared. As their lives moved forward, the bond always remained a top priority. It was in July, Aaron's sophomore year at Miami that Jack received an invitation that he's been waiting for years. Aaron and Terri announced they were getting married in August.

The wedding was an historic day for all four of them. Of course, Jack was Aaron's best man. At the reception that night, Jack congratulated the newlyweds, a brief speech that ended with Jack presenting Aaron with two sets of keys. The first set, being the new owner of the Pizza Shack. Aaron sat stunned, but Terri was elated, kissing Aaron and Jack, and jumping up and down. Then came the second set of keys. Those keys opened the door to their new home, the house on South Street was given, free and with title, as a special gift to Aaron and Terri on their wedding night. All that attended the reception stood and cheered the trio. They hugged and kissed and a tear or two fit the occasion, all were bonded for life.

Playing football at Miami of Ohio, Aaron got a good taste of the winning tradition—playing on a winning team with a chance to play in the Fiesta Bowl. He was halfway to his dream, a shot at playing in the NFL. Unfortunately, in October of his junior year his dream disappeared. While running around end, he sustained a brutal tackle that severely tore one of the main ligaments, the ACL, on his right knee. He missed his entire senior year of football and never was drafted by any NFL team, but his family and his wife offered the support he needed. He graduated college with a degree in mathematics, got a job teaching math back in Manford at his Alma mater, Columbia High School. Life was good to Aaron and Terri. They sold the farm after her parents passed away and concentrated making pizzas instead of making babies. There was a change at the Pizza Shack. No longer would it be called the Pizza Shack, and in honor of his best friend, Aaron changed the name to Pizza Jack.

On a sunny warm May day in Culver City, Jack sat on the back porch in deep thoughts, reminiscing about his father's death. Maybe Charles did make some wrong choices in his life, but Jack knew it was all for the family. He thought he could win a million dollars on a reality show and provide a newer life for his parents, get his college degree and start a business. A business where his father would be working for him. Jack smiled. But, if it wasn't for Charles, where would Jack be sitting now? Certainly, not in Culver City, California.

During the last two years at USC, he worked hard as an apprentice at Camelot Productions, Inc. He gained immeasurable knowledge about making movies from well- known producers, directors, actors and actresses. Ever since he could remember, his dream was working in the movie industry, making movies. He and Emily had long talks about his future, her convincing Jack to start his dream, the sooner the better, she pounded into him, the exact words his Dad would've said to him. Finally, that day came. Jack invited Aaron and Terri to come to California and help celebrate his graduation.

Jack was always full of surprises and had another surprise up his sleeve and couldn't wait to show Aaron and Terri.

When the commencement ended and with Jack's diploma in hand, they left and drove to his favorite restaurant for dinner. With the most important people in his life with him, Jack and Emily cherished the time, especially reminiscing about high school, Denny's on Sunday mornings, Pizza Jacks, even laughed about Sergio's corvette. Wow, how they laughed and joked. The four of them left the restaurant and walked to the parking lot where Jack had parked his SUV. Just about to unlock the doors, Jack made an announcement.

"Now, Aaron and Terri. I have one more surprise I want you to see."

"Another surprise? Jack, you're full of surprises, aren't you? What now?"

"Patience, please. I'm going to show you." About a mile from Jack's destination, he turned and said to Aaron and Terri, "Okay, close your eyes. Don't open them until I tell you, okay?"

"Can you give us a hint about this?" asked Aaron.

The SUV came to a stop, Jack opened the doors to help Aaron and Terri get out. He positioned them so that when they opened their eyes, it was right in front of them.

"Keep your eyes closed, okay?"

He led both of them several feet down the sidewalk until they were standing in front of his surprise.

"Now open your eyes."

"Ahh. I don't believe it." Aaron said. "This is incredible. I remember you talking about this."

They looked up, staring at a huge, colorful neon sign mounted on a two-story brick warehouse. *Stardom Studios.*

"C'mon in. I want to show you around."

They began walking toward the front entrance when Emily noticed three people approaching her. Her heart jumped out of her chest when she recognized as they got closer, it was Detective Konrad. The unexpected appearance of Detective Konrad only meant one thing… *TROUBLE.*

"Well, well, well. Beautiful day in California, huh, Emily?" Konrad approached her, a toothpick separating his lips and the contentious smirk on his face. "Four fucking years locked up in that miserable prison. Every day that passed, I knew once I got out I would find you. Now, here I am."

Emily was frozen, rather a better word, in complete shock. How did this happen?

Konrad took one step closer, poking Emily in the chest with his right hand index finger. "Four years of thinking, four years wondering what you were doing with my money. That's what prison life gives you, time. But, fortunately, I had company. His name was Sergio Canasta."

Emily's head popped up, staring into Konrad's eyes. She was so in love with Sergio that she confided many things to Sergio. What could she do? Run and get Jack, shoot and kill Konrad. What would that solve?

"He's quite a talker, that Sergio. Spilled out everything I wanted to know, especially your sexual relationship with Fossett. Everyone, including myself thought it was Reading from the start. Well, well, well. You got some serious thinking to do, lady. I had a hunch that it was you. I could've turned you in long ago, but I needed to know where the money was. Now, I have all the answers. Have a nice day, Emily. I'll be in touch." All three were laughing as they slowly walked away.

"You've got it all wrong. I didn't kill William. I had no reason to kill him."

Emily watched them fade into the horizon, until she finally realized who the second man was. It was Dugan. For sure everything was flushed down the toilet. Her life, the money, whatever she had left.

Did she ever think this nightmare would ever go away? Having all that money, living thousands of miles from Manford, and experiencing a day like today. Now, her remaining life has returned to Hell, never able to escape those horrible memories.

Since the day Charles told her about the money, it had taken the foremost place in her life. The result was that she had encouraged and aided her husband in criminal behavior that led to his death. She had schemed to get the money for herself. She had risked the life of her son with her blind and selfish sexual involvement with his kidnapper. All for seven million dollars that belonged to who? Money now claimed by other schemers who undoubtedly planned to take it from her. Had her obsession to claim the now dead money been worth it? That thought would be with Emily Collier for the remaining days of her life. The haunting faces of Konrad, Helen, Dugan, and even the loving eyes of her late husband Charles.

"Charles, help, help me. Where are you when I need you the most. Come home, please. Please." She fell to her knees, weeping.

* * * * *

Note from the Author

Congratulations. You did it! You finished the story and I'm hoping you enjoyed it as much as I enjoyed writing it. Also, I would appreciate any feedback you may offer, either positive or negative, whatever the case, it would be very helpful to me. I do plan on writing another story in the future, so the feedback from my readers will benefit how I write a better story. You can find my website at: rkazbook.com. There you will find a page where you can post a comment and send to me.

Again, thank you so much for purchasing the book and hopefully, passing it on to other friends.

Ohh, before I forget, one more challenge. I have put together a short quiz, so let's see how well you do.

Turn page >>

The Quiz

1. On the day Charles scheduled his meeting with Ron Dugan, where did they meet and how would Dugan recognize Charles?
2. Being a small college in Chicago, Depaul's basketball team made it to the Final Four of the NCAA tournament. What team did they loose to?
3. Dennis Reading (alias Dan Mesa) always had an appetite for a good drink and a relaxing cigar. What was his favorite drink and what kind of cigars did he buy?
4. It was no secret, the life of William Fossett floated up and down but his partnership with Samuel Hasid put life back into William's ride. What was the name of the building they moved their business into downtown in the Loop?
5. The Pizza Shack was the place Jack, Aaron and Terri hung out. The only pizza they ordered was an extra large cheese, sausage, green pepper and what else?
6. When Dennis panicked and vamoosed out of Chicago, he changed his name, destroyed his phone and credit card and ditched the Escape. What town was he in when he bought the Chevy Impala?
7. Not long after Charles arrived in Costa Rica, he fell in love. A blond surfer literally swept him off his feet. There was one characteristic that immediately caught his eye. A tattoo. What was the design of that tattoo?

8. Finally, Detective Konrad is in prison, so you have replaced him and in charge of the investigation. With all the clues and evidence at your disposal, who are you going to arrest for the murder of William Fossett?

You can check your answers at my web site, rkazbook.com.

About the Author

While growing up in a small town in Northern Illinois, I spent my childhood as any normal young boy, riding bikes, fishing, building forts or playing organized sports. As I grew older, those sports became more competitive and demanding. I played football, basketball and baseball all four years in high school and received my share of rewards. As to this day, I still have my scrapbook reflecting those accomplishments during the 1960s and 70s. My dream was someday playing baseball in the Major Leagues. Unfortunately, my father, who had connections in the baseball world, passed away while I was still in high school and so did my dream.

My career began throwing mail instead of baseballs. I worked for the Post Office delivering mail out of the McHenry office and retired in 2009, after 30 years of service. While working out of that office, I met my wife, Jan. In 1985, we married and we were amazingly blessed with two outstanding daughters, Jenna and Kellye. We were extremely proud parents growing with our children, getting involved with their schooling and interests, gymnastics, softball, horse riding lessons, not to mention numerous pets. Such remembered precious times.

Once I retired from the Post Office, I had so much free time, what was I going to do? My golf game got enjoyable, but I was still antsy. I was just sitting around the house looking for something to do. Then, a dare from my wife, what about writing a book? A book!! Who, among my family, old classmates and friends would have ever thought that I could be an author. But I did it. You see, during my life, we've all heard the old saying, "Everyone has a hidden talent." It's finding that talent within yourself and pursuing it that makes you feel you've accomplished that talent. I know I've done that.

Now, I live with my wife in Manteno. Illinois. The girls are grown up now, married and have their own careers to fulfill. In our spare time (plenty of that), we enjoy going out to dinner with the kids, working in the yard or even, even being patient with my wife's golf game. A simple life? Maybe. Possibly another book? Who knows, that could happen.

While still working on publishing my book, I was diagnosed with esophageal cancer in April of 2018. It was devastating news to me and to my loved ones, but you have to accept it and fight back. The big "C" is familiar within our family. My grandmother and grandfather both died from leukemia, my youngest sister died of breast cancer, my niece passed with the same cancer I'm fighting and my brother-in-law left us with colon cancer. Having seen these people suffer, pain, agony, the mental suffering, now I understand what they went through and I feel for them. So, together with my family, we've decided to donate a percentage of my profits to the Danny Thomas Research Center for children. Someday, we will conquer this dreadful disease.

At this time, let me thank you for purchasing my book and hope you enjoyed the story. If you did, I would appreciate passing it on to your friends and any feedback, either positive or negative, is welcomed. You can post your comments at rkazbooks.com. Thank you, again.